A CAST OF STARS

A Cast of Stars

ALLAN PRIOR

A WILLIAM ABRAHAMS BOOK

HOLT, RINEHART AND WINSTON NEW YORK

First published in the United States in 1983 by
Holt, Rinehart and Winston, 383 Madison Avenue,
New York, New York 10017.
Originally published in England in somewhat different form
under the title Theatre.
Library of Congress Cataloging in Publication Data
Prior, Allan, 1922–
A cast of stars.
Originally published as: Theatre. 1981.
I. Title.   *823'.914*   *82-1029*
PR6066.R57T5 1982   *AACR2*
ISBN: 0-03-061943-2

First American Edition

Designer: Lucy Castelluccio
Printed in the United States of America
1 3 5 7 9 10 8 6 4 2

ISBN 0-03-061943-2

A CAST OF STARS

1

JILL Viner popped a contraceptive pill, and she smiled.

Her reflection in the mirror of the toilet compartment on the 747 smiled back. Dark hair, glossy and springy (by Larry of Vidal Sassoon's) steel-blue eyes from her shiksa grandmother, firm breasts needing no bra, and good teeth, courtesy of Dr. Kantry. All her own but straight and even. Hundreds of pounds and some pain, but worth every penny. Jill peeled off her tweed suit and slipped off her St. Laurent shirt. It was looking tired from nine hours of flying.

Why, Jill Viner thought, did I pop that pill? I'm not seeing anybody except the actor. And her relationship with the actor was to be—had to be—that of employer and employee. Any other way would be fatal. She knew that, Joe Dancy had taught her that. "Keep your distance. Keep cool. Never overpraise. Hardly ever praise at all. And never mix with the men." Joe had pointed his cigar at her, his fat comic's face serious for once. "The cast, however

1

famous, you don't mix with them. You're like the cowboy who may have to eat his horse. Capiche?"

"Certainly I capiche," she had replied frostily, sitting in Joe's cabinlike office overlooking Shaftesbury Avenue.

He had looked pained. "You don't say 'Certainly I capiche.' And another thing, remember. Always keep something back. Always. Something. Capiche?"

Joe had been a good teacher, and she had been a good pupil during the four years she had been his personal assistant. The most enjoyable part of her work had consisted of listening to him tell stories of how he'd started out in the thirties, with Henry Jacobs, how, when he decided to go on his own, he'd provided himself with a handwritten copy of Henry's client list. That was one of Joe's lessons she'd been careful to remember, and she had followed it virtually to the letter two months ago, when she was getting ready to leave and set herself up as Jill Viner Productions. The only difference was that the list of clients she'd taken with her had been Xeroxed, not handwritten. Would Joe hold it against her? Not bloody likely—that was how one played the game, capiche? Jill could almost hear the note of grudging approval in his smile.

She smiled, and sprayed Calèche over her neck, smooth and unlined yet, not bad for thirty-two, and pulled her latest buy, an extravagance from Zandra Rhodes, over her head. The flight would be in Los Angeles in fifteen minutes and she would be talking to the actor at the Beverly Hills an hour after that. There would normally be time to change at the hotel, but the actor's agent was meeting her at the airport and the agent was—almost—more important than the actor himself. She smiled sexily at herself in the mirror. Manny will like this dress, she thought. It's a bit obvious, but Manny will like that. He may not even notice that I'm smart as well. She shook her head. Manny would notice. Manny was pretty smart himself or he wouldn't be at the airport in person to meet her. "These days," Manny had rasped over the transatlantic telephone, "I have six young guys in dark suits to meet clients at the airport." Jill had said, "I'm only in L.A. the one night, Manny. I fly back to New York Friday. I have to see Maggie. It would be nice if you could come along and make it easy for me."

The silence on the line had been almost tangible.

"Maggie?" Manny's voice was like an electric saw now. "You're seeing Maggie in New York City Friday?"

"With my director, Josh Williams."

"She's in, she's interested, she's definite, what?"

"Not definite, Manny. I have to be sure she's right. I am asking her to play the queen of England, after all. And she is American, after all."

There was an even longer pause.

"You wouldn't think," Manny said—and his voice had ceased to rasp; it was almost normally rude—"you wouldn't think to send me a copy of the script, so I could give it to Austin, would you?"

"I would, Manny, but this is so important a play I can't let it out of my hands. You know how many sharks there are in this business."

"Most of them I know by their first name," said Manny, always pleased to take a doubtful view of human nature. "You mean, you want him to read it while you're here, the one night, make a decision in one night?"

"I have to know Thursday, yes."

"You got somebody else interested?"

"I haven't offered the part of the president to anyone else."

"But somebody else is interested, they're pushing you, right?"

"Manny, Austin will love it." He's biting, Jill thought.

"I hope not, if I speak for my bank. A play in the West End of London isn't a movie, moneywise, Jill."

He had called her Jill. That, from Manny Hiberson, was respect. "Doll," "baby," "wassername"—that was more Manny. Jill had spoken to him often, from Joe Dancy's office. He had never

3

known her name in those days. She said, "The deal will be very favorable for Austin. And you'll be able to do even better with his next movie."

"Since Austin won the Oscar," Manny had concluded, and his voice was filled with wonder at the behavior of actors, "all he wants to do is go artistic."

"This property is artistic, but popular," Jill said. "Do I see you Thursday?"

"The little worried guy in thick shades sitting in the big shiny white Rolls, that's me. I'll take you over to the Beverly Hills and do the intro." Manny's voice was almost velvet now. "I introduced a lotta people in my time, Jill, but this one I'm curious about. See ya."

Jill Viner had sat in her brand-new office in Shaftesbury Avenue (two months' lease only) and let the emotion flood through her: excitement. Pure, silent, screaming excitement. She had hooked Manny Hiberson's interest. She was on her way.

Jill touched her dark hair and smiled at the mirror.

Always keep something back.

Why, she wondered, did I take that bloody pill?

MANNY Hiberson was sitting in the back of his white Rolls in a white suit, a panama, and dark glasses, looking like a small alert bird of an endangered species, which in a way he was. Manny was one of the last of the old-time agents and had actually sat in Louis B. Mayer's office and talked right back to him.

"I won't tell you what he said after I talked right back to him." Manny glanced sideways at Jill as the Rolls tooled along. "But I think he might have listened to you. L.B liked a pretty face."

"You've got a lot of pretty faces in this town." Jill smiled. "I'm here on business."

"You're all business, from what Joe Dancy tells me."

Jill sat absolutely still. The cool air conditioning fanned her face. The scenery seemed to be moving, not the car. She would buy

4

herself a Rolls one day, and sit in it and make remarks to Manny like the one he had just made to her. Meanwhile, she smiled.

"You talked to Joe?"

"Truth to tell, I couldn't remember you. No offense. I was only in the office the once."

Jill still smiled. "And it was two years ago. We did talk, though. But I was just Joe's assistant."

"Joe and me go back a long way."

"The author offered the play to Joe. He refused it."

Manny's eyebrows lifted. "Joe didn't tell me he refused it."

"If it makes a million, who wants to be known as the producer who refused it?"

Manny laughed, the rasping sound that was almost mechanical. "Joe was always a percentage-player. That's why he'll never be rich-rich. But he'll never be poor-poor neither. Why didn't he want to do it?"

"Because it's dangerous."

It was Manny's turn to be still. "Why so?"

"It has the queen in it, it has the president in it. A lot of things."

"Like what else, for instance?"

The Rolls purred on, into the magic land.

"Like the critics. In London, they may not like it. They may think it's unpatriotic. Or too patriotic. Either way."

"And is it a good risk?"

"I think so or I wouldn't be doing it."

The fabulous houses and gardens along the soft avenues unfolded and took them in, and Jill felt, suddenly, perfectly at home. I will get a Rolls, she thought, if it makes a person feel like this.

Manny was chewing on her last statement, looking for grit. "You want to do this play just because it's dangerous?"

"I want to do it," Jill said calmly, "because, as the English say, it will put bums on seats."

"Bums on seats?"

"Bottoms on seats."

"Asses on seats."

"The English say 'arses.' "

"It's two different languages already."

The Rolls purred on. The soft evening light, after the cloud of London, was spectacular.

"Then why Maggie for the queen?" Manny was still again. "English she ain't, correct?"

"She's very Boston, she's very regal, she's very ice queen."

Manny nodded. "True. Her ass, or is it arse, would freeze hell over any time of the day or night."

"That is the sort of quality the part needs. And when we transfer to Broadway I won't have problems with American Equity."

Manny sighed in pure pleasure at the duplicity. "That I like. Except, I don't know about money."

Jill rolled down the window and took in a deep breath of the heady California air. It tasted vaguely of smog, smog and something else. Success? She closed the window. "Manny, your actor is not a ballsy leading man. You know it and I know it. Your actor got a great human part as the widowed guy in his last movie and everybody wept buckets when Maggie died, and now he's hot again and every producer in town wants him in a western."

"You must be listening to my calls in the office."

"He's a wonderful actor but before *The Last Good-bye* you couldn't sell him as a marquee name to any one of them. It isn't going to be any different for him once he does a bad western. In *The Queen of Finland* he'd be terrific."

Manny took a Turkish cigarette from a silver case, and lit it, with a gold Cartier lighter and an air of practiced gloom.

"Even the title is Maggie's."

"We can't call it *The President*, Manny. Even for you."

"I've known producers who would, like *that*." Manny snapped his fingers. "To get a piece of Austin."

"This week."

"Sure, this week. This is the only week we got, right?"

The Rolls slid into the drive of the Beverly Hills Hotel. Manny slumped in his seat. "How come you didn't stay at the Bel Air?"

"I like the Hills."

"You stayed here before?"

"Two years ago."

With Jimmy, she thought, before it was all over, and he went off with the rich, beautiful blonde from Santa Barbara. Maybe, she thought bitterly, it was the best thing that ever happened to me. It got me off my arse—sorry—ass.

"You stayed here with Joe?"

"Yes. And a friend."

"Ah. Did we meet? I can't remember."

"No, we didn't meet."

We didn't meet anybody that time, she thought. This time it will be different.

The chauffeur brought the Rolls to a halt outside the hotel entrance, and the bell captain came for her bags. He nodded to Manny affably, one old Californian from the Bronx to another. "Howya today, Mr. Hiberson?"

Manny got stiffly out of the Rolls. "I been younger, Harry."

"Me too, Mr. Hiberson, but not wiser."

"Wise is fine but I'd take younger."

"Me too, but what we gonna do about it, Mr. Hiberson?"

"I don't know about you, Harry, but I'm going to have a drink with this young lady. Will you tell them at the desk she's arrived, and take the bags in? . . . Oh, and let Austin know we're here."

"Sure thing, Mr. Hiberson. Nice to see you, Miss Viner. Have a nice visit."

Jill whispered, "How does he know my name?"

"Because it's his business to know it." Manny took her arm.

7

"How many of Joe Dancy's list of backers did you take away with you when you left?"

They walked into the hotel.

"The whole list. Didn't he tell you?"

"Didn't need to."

"Manny, I can see I will have to watch you in these negotiations."

"Lady, I been watched by the best."

JILL Viner sipped her margarita and looked around the Polo Lounge. There was nothing to see, since the place was almost black-dark.

"Seen anybody?" Manny fiddled impatiently with the bulky manuscript on his knees. His long, mottled fingers caressed the embossed and very expensive morocco cover. It was emblazoned with the Roman Q that was to be a feature of all publicity for the play.

"Frank Sinatra?"

"Francis in, is he? I didn't see him."

"Nor did I. Just testing."

Manny drew on his Turkish cigarette. "Joe tells me you used to be an actress."

"That was six years ago."

"Why you give it up?"

"Kim Novak called it a meat market. If I'm going to be in the market, I'm going to be the buyer, not the meat."

Manny inclined his head to the sentiment. "Me, I'm the meat middleman and I don't even like it."

"Nonsense, or you wouldn't be doing it."

Manny smiled through the white spiral of smoke. "What else would I do? Stay home? I got this house in the Valley and a wife hates the business. You know that? Hates the business. Always has. I dunno why I married her. You Jewish?"

"My father. My mother wasn't."

"Married out? That takes something I never had. You know, my wife won't have Hollywood people in the house? I got that big house out there and she don't want my friends in it. Crazy woman."

"How long have you been married to her, Manny?"

"Who's counting, except her?"

Something in the remark reminded Jill of her father. He had never said anything sad like that about her mother, but she supposed there had been moments. People said people didn't care, but it wasn't true. Her mother had brought nothing to the marriage except her blue-eyed good looks and a ready laugh and a sense of recklessness. No money at all. Hilda Viner didn't care. She laughed at poverty; she dared it to touch her, and she died young. Jill had been only ten years old. She felt pain whenever she thought of her mother, even now.

"Your father, what's he doing?" Manny was asking.

"A cashier. A sort of—"

"I know what a cashier is." Manny smiled. "I been one once before they canned me. You gotta be honest to be a cashier. In a store, is it?"

"In a cinema chain. Head office. He worked there thirty-eight years. Retired three years ago."

"On his own?" Manny seemed truly interested. "No other children?"

"Only me. I go and see him as often as I can."

"What's his name?"

"Isaac Viner."

"How old is he?"

"He's . . . let me see . . . sixty-nine now." Jill was shocked. "I didn't realize how old he was."

9

"I beat him by two years," Manny said. He stood up and took her arm, with a gentleness she did not expect of him.

"Come on, lady, let's go meet your actor."

AUSTIN Ames did not stand up when they entered his bungalow in the grounds of the hotel. He waved a sun-darkened, braceleted wrist toward them, in greeting, but remained firmly seated on his couch in the large cool room. A glass of milk and a dish of muesli stood on the table in front of him. A faint aroma of pot hung in the air.

"Hi, doll. Come in, sit down. Manny, give er . . ."

"Jill Viner."

"Give the lady a drink, why don't you?"

Austin Ames was shorter than Jill expected, which was why, she decided, he had not stood up. His height in *Spotlight* was given as five-nine. More like five-six, Jill thought, without his lifts. It didn't matter. The president didn't have to be a giant. Better if he wasn't. Both Carter and Nixon had been below average height. Small was beautiful, as far as Austin was concerned. Dark and intense, in denim from Calvin Klein and a gold amulet from Tiffany's, Austin was famous the world over. As an actor, not as a person—which is what a movie actor is—he was *liked*. There were rumors his closer associates liked him less. Rows, script troubles, walkouts—those were the stories.

"Well now." Austin smiled the celebrated sympathetic smile. "You're the lady who has the part of a lifetime for me?"

"I think you'll find it interesting." Jill was glad she had worn the Zandra Rhodes, a swirl of color that showed her off. Austin might be small-boned and feminine-looking but his glance flickering over her told her that whatever he was, he wasn't queer. "As soon as I read it, I remembered you'd been in London looking at plays and I—"

"I was in London looking at plays to bring to Broadway." His gaze went to a pile of scripts stacked on a side table. Jill knew they had been stacked there so she could see them. It told her that Austin was taking the meeting seriously. "I was hoping to find a play that would interest me enough to do it." Austin shook his head to Manny's offer of a drink. "You must think a lot of this play to bring it here for me to read. Tell me about it."

Manny said, quickly, "You were drinking a margarita, Jill. I hope I got it right for you."

Jill took the salted, frosted glass and let a little of her calf show. "I can tell you the history of the play, certainly—"

"No. Not that. The story. Tell me the story."

"You'll have to read the play for that."

"Lady, I have twenty scripts on the table here in front of me. Manny knows that; he's sent them to me. All I'm asking is, what's the story?"

Jill let the silence last a long time.

Manny broke it. "I think it's kinda different with a stage play, Austin."

Austin held up the braceleted hand. "Manny, please, I was a Broadway actor—when I worked!—for twelve whole years. I know there's a difference between a screenplay and a stage play, Manny. In a screenplay the writer is trying to please the producer. In a stage play the writer is trying to please himself. Both can get it right. Both can get it wrong. What I need is a script that is trying to please the actor."

Me, Jill thought. Me, Me, Me. Actor, meaning Me—not Actors, meaning the whole cast. Ah well. If there was anything she knew about, it was the psychology of the actor. She had lived with Jimmy for three years, after all, and Jimmy had been an actor right down to his socks.

"I think this play will please the audience, and they are the ones who matter in the end." Jill let a little thigh show. She had nothing on under the dress but a pair of panties, and she knew Austin knew that and was interested in the fact. The thing was not to let it get out of hand.

"The play is called *The Queen of Finland*."

"No such person, is there?"

"The queen in the play is the queen of England."

"Is this play historical, costume?"

"It's set in 1990."

"Why the queen of Finland if she's the queen of England?"

"Have you ever heard of Finlandization?"

"Sure. It's what the Soviets have been doing in Finland. Taking it over. No war, or like that. Just . . . infiltration, the taking over of the institutions of government, one by one. Until they have everything, without having to fight for it. And so on. Is that what the play's about?"

Jill sipped her drink. The actor could think. No wonder there were script problems. "It's about a lot of things, but yes, basically it's about what will happen—quite possibly—in Europe, in England, in ten, fifteen, or twenty years' time. Unless the United States and the European nations—together—care enough to prevent it happening."

Manny juggled another Turkish cigarette into his mouth.

"It's a political play, a propaganda play?" asked Austin.

"It's more than that. I think it's a masterpiece. I think it's as important as *Darkness at Noon*, maybe more so, because it's before the event, not after it."

Manny inhaled. "Political plays, they bother people."

"That's why Vercek wrote it."

Manny looked interested. "What do you know about him?"

"He's a Jew. And a dissident. He lived in Finland awhile. That's about all."

Manny brooded a moment. "You really think this is a masterpiece?"

"I've read a dozen plays each week for four years, as assistant to Joe Dancy. I walked out of a good job with Joe, carrying this play. Josh Williams, my director, thinks it's the best play to come out of Russia since Chekhov. He broke his contract at the National Theatre in London to do it. We both believe in it that much."

Manny said, "This writer . . ."

"Vercek."

"He's represented? He has an agent?"

"He doesn't have an agent."

Manny inhaled his cigarette and glanced at his watch. "He'll never get rich."

Jill smiled. "Who's to know, when we come to Broadway, maybe he'll need a helping hand. This play has big potential—"

Austin interrupted. "You're thinking Broadway already?"

Manny raised a manicured and liver-spotted hand in blessing. "Listen, she's talking to Maggie in New York City tomorrow."

"Tomorrow? You're going east tomorrow?"

"The morning flight out," Manny said in admiration. "I tellya, Austin, we got ourselves a little mover here."

The actor barely nodded. His eyes were on Jill's face now and not on her legs. He's beginning to look at me, she thought. That has to be an improvement. He said, "The queen is, who?"

"Maggie's the queen," Manny interrupted, sounding like her father, when he explained to his friends what a very important job she had. "Okay, she's American, but she's a Boston ice queen. No accent. And no Equity troubles on Broadway."

"Maggie's taken the part?"

"I'm talking to her tomorrow, and I'm talking to you today."

"She's seen the play?" Austin's voice was cold.

Jill smiled. If I smile once more today it'll stay on my face forever, she thought.

"Nobody's seen the play. Except one person."

"And who's that?"

"I have to make like a producer," Jill said. "I'm sworn to secrecy on that one point, in case the person concerned doesn't want to go on with it."

Austin asked, "Is it an actor? Is it for the part of the president?"

"I promise I'll tell you the moment I can."

"Then it is the part of the president?"

Manny looked at his watch again. "Austin, the lady has said she'll tell you when she can. That's fair, right? You might not want to do the play. . . ."

Austin beamed his famous smile at Jill. "Manny doesn't want me to do any play, especially in London. Manny wants me to stay here in the California sunshine and do one of these shitty westerns."

Manny sighed. "You know that ain't true, Austin. But I'm not gonna argue with you. I'm gonna go home and have my supper and watch TV." He put on the panama. "There was a time I left this hotel this time of day I was going off to sleep with Joan Crawford." He grinned. "Times change, like the man said."

Austin laughed. "Manny, you never slept with Joan Crawford in your life."

"How would you know?" asked Manny. "You wasn't even born." He shook hands with Jill. "Get some sleep sometime. That jet lag can be very nasty."

Impulsively, Jill stood and kissed him on the cheek.

"That's better than balling Joan Crawford," said Manny. "Especially at my age. At my age a large brandy is better. You don't have to take your clothes off for it."

Austin waved from his sofa. "Manny, you're a fake. You and Joan Crawford. Never."

Manny's words came faint from the soft night, the aroma of freshly watered crabgrass and smog drifting in the door as he left. "Now Crawford, there was a classy broad."

Austin shook his head, in amusement. "I love that old guy. I treat him bad and he ignores it. I feel about ten years old with him sometimes. But he doesn't want me to go to London with this or any other play. He wants me to stay here and consolidate my movie career."

Jill sat down. She said, carefully, "The money would be bigger if you stayed." It was always better, with actors, to be truthful up to a point. Then they couldn't blame you later. Joe Dancy had taught her that. She went on. "But a success on Shaftesbury Avenue? There's nothing quite like it."

"Shaftesbury Avenue," said the actor, nostalgically. "That's a real place. Not a goddam orange grove with smog."

Shaftesbury Avenue has its drawbacks, too, Jill thought. She did not voice them aloud.

"You are the one to judge what's best for you. Nobody else— agent, manager, wife, analyst, lover, girlfriend, boyfriend, masseuse, hairdresser, astrologer—none of them can decide your future for you."

"Hey, I like that list. How did you know I listen to all those guys before I make up my mind?" The actor looked doubtfully at the large morocco folder with the Q on it. "You want me to read this, call you tomorrow morning before flight time? You're staying in the hotel, right?"

"No, I want you to read it now."

"Now? Right now?"

"I did bring it six thousand miles." She opened her eyes wide at him.

Austin sipped his milk without enthusiasm. "You really expect a definite decision tonight?"

"You may say no. I don't think you will. But if you do, I can proceed with that knowledge."

"You still don't want to tell me who else has read it?"

"I have to play fair. It's on offer to you. You say yes and make my day; we sort out a deal with Manny and we're in business."

"It takes Manny a long time to sort out deals."

"Not this time. I've worked out what I can pay. The top people will all get the same money. Some cash down, most on box-office receipts."

"Promises, promises."

"That's how it has to be with a stage play. It's risk money for everybody, including my backers."

"Who are your backers?" Austin asked idly.

"Too many to list. You know what financing a play is like."

"The money is there, I take it?"

"All we need," Jill lied, smiling.

"I did a play on Broadway three years ago. I had hell on wheels with rewrites out of town, hassles with everybody in sight, and the critics—all two of them—hated it. It closed in a week. I said never again."

"That would be the comedy, *True Star*?"

Austin laughed. "You have a good memory. I'm trying to forget what it was called."

"Shaftesbury Avenue isn't Broadway. We won't go into rehearsals and start to rewrite. That's the American way of death. The play we'll do is in your hands now."

Austin looked horrified. "You mean this script is the Word of God?"

"You'll think so, when you've read it."

"I never knew a play yet didn't need the actors' thoughts."

"I'm only a producer. I've bought that play. It's the one we're going to do."

Austin frowned at that statement. Jill thought, He will be trouble with the script, but I need him. "Of course, every actor has different ideas about a part. Especially a part like the president."

"In the story, what's the president's role?"

He's still trying to avoid reading the bloody thing, Jill thought.

"The president—and the other characters—are all present at a meeting with the queen to decide if England gives in or doesn't."

"Gives in to what?"

"To the latest, and probably the final, act of Finlandization.

The one that puts the Sceptered Isle finally into the Soviet sphere of influence."

"And that is?"

"Look." Jill stood up. "I'm bushed. Read the play. It'll take you an hour, maybe not that long. If you like it, call me in my room."

Austin actually got up. He is small, she thought; he's a bantam cock. "Don't go," he said. "Have something sent over. You haven't eaten, have you?" She shook her head. "I know—steak, salad, a bottle of Mondavi Cabernet! I have to eat. It should be milk and muesli—I have this slight digestive problem—but what the hell!" He lifted the telephone and ordered, then sat down again, and after a slight hesitation rolled a joint and offered it to her.

"No, thanks. If I do, I'll really go to sleep."

"I'm only having one quick drag. Producers make me nervous."

Jill laughed. Austin was nice when he decided to be. Actors always were. She liked actors. Living with one was something else. "I'm not a real producer yet," she said. "This is my very first play. I expect Manny told you."

"Oh, sure." Austin inhaled and closed his eyes. "I don't know how you did it. I mean, got to me at all."

"Simple. I rang Manny and he told you."

"Yes, but your first play?"

"I pulled strings." I really did, Jill thought, or I wouldn't be here at all. I pulled so many strings I'm an unpaid member of the puppet master's club.

"You said you walked out on your boss? Why was that?" The actor didn't seem shocked. In London, everybody had been shocked. The English dislike change or anything that smacks of disloyalty, and her leaving could be made to look like both.

"He didn't want to do the play and I did."

"How did it come in?"

17

"The director brought it—in his own fair hand. It had been to the National and they didn't want to do it either."

"Seems a lot of people don't want to do this masterpiece."

"They'll be sorry."

"What did you do before you worked for Joe Dancy?"

Jill finished her margarita with a large swallow. The selling was getting harder, and she hadn't even started yet. "I was an actress. I went to see Joe Dancy about a part in a silly comedy. He didn't want me, he wanted a sexy milkmaid. He also wanted a secretary. As it happens, my father had insisted I do a year short-hand-typing before I went to drama school. He's that kind of father. Joe Dancy offered me the secretary's job and I took it. I became his personal assistant two years later. Four years of that, and here I am."

"Having learned a few things?"

"Yes, I hope so. Joe's good."

Suddenly Austin seemed to like her more, and she knew what had done it. She had been an actress. That made her one of the magic people, like himself. She knew about rejection, triumph, hate, and sweat-fear, and had, in her time, cursed directors and producers and moneymen.

"I like the dress. You wear it on the flight?"

"Old actress's trick. Changed just before we got in."

He laughed, relaxing. "It would be nice to act with real talent again, work on something worth doing again. I didn't start out to be a movie actor. I don't think movie acting has much to do with anything. If the camera likes you, you're there. In my case, the camera likes me a little but I never know how much. Okay, I'm a name, I got the Oscar, that was great. It's what I do with it that matters. But I love the stage. I feel good there. I played in seventeen successive flops off-Broadway, mostly just a spit-and-a-cough. That has to be a record, right?" Austin drew on the joint. He liked his memories too much, Jill thought, to be a great big star. She liked him for that.

The food arrived, and Jill was hungrier than she'd expected. As they ate, Austin regaled her with a list of the jobs he had done in New York City while he waited for somebody to offer him Hamlet at Lincoln Center. "Washing dishes, I did a lot of that. I polished cars. I took dogs for walks in Central Park. Once or twice I slept with ladies quite a little older than myself. Only when I was very pushed, frankly."

"Good training for the president." Jill chewed on her steak. It was very good. So was the wine. "If you want that job, you have to do a lot of things you didn't start out to do."

Austin swallowed his last mouthful of steak. "Singh is going to kill me. He says no red meat and he *knows* when I break down and do it. He's Indian and he's psychic, I swear to God."

"You mean Buddha?"

"I've never gone that far. Singh's good. Very stern. You stick to what he says or—out."

"Carter jogs and diets. Reagan rides. I don't think Nixon did anything. I can't imagine him on a health diet."

"That Nixon, what a foreign-policy man. Jeez! You remember, he said talking to Brezhnev was no different from talking to Jimmy Hoffa? The president in the play, is he Nixon?"

"If he was Nixon it would be a different play. But maybe a little." Jill felt her eyes beginning to close. It's the jet lag, she thought. That, and all the smiling. "You'll see when you read it."

"Yeah, I suppose." Austin stood up, the morocco folder in his hand. "You mind if I go in the bedroom and read it?"

Jill's eyes flashed wide open. "I don't mind if you read it on the loo. . . . I mean, in the can."

He grinned. "I kinda gathered that. You stay there. Don't go away." He went off into another room. After a moment the soft hum of sitar music filtered through the bedroom door.

Jill closed her eyes, then opened them again with an effort. She took the top script from the pile lying on the small table and opened it. It was called *Massacre at Moonrise* and was scripted by Hal

Schnelling and Herb Brian from an idea by John Walters and Jack Hamburger. It opened with a massacre of Indians at moonrise, and Austin, if he accepted the role, would kill a great many of the Indians, personally. Jill put the script back on the pile.

Her eyelids dropped and she thought, My legendary stamina is giving out on me. Jill had always played with boys as a child; she didn't care for girlish games; she had grown up to like men's company better. In Finchley, north London, the men were the winners, or anyway to hear them tell it. She had been able to run and swim with any boy her age; in fact she had run them into the ground. Until puberty, that is; until her breasts had started. Her father had always treated her as an equal, as a boy, especially after her mother died. She supposed the conditioning had paid off; she thought like a man in a lot of ways. Jimmy had hated that. She hadn't too many of the feminine weaknesses. She never cried, and she wasn't jealous, of anybody or anything. Jimmy hadn't known whether he liked that or not. He couldn't have liked it, because in the end he had gone off with the blonde.

Jill's head fell back against the large, soft cushions of the modish bamboo chair, and she slept.

"HI, producer lady!"

Jill wakened, in a slight sweat. The sitar music still hummed from under the door. She felt disorientated for a moment—jet lag, of course. She glanced at her watch. Eight-thirty. She had slept for a whole hour.

"Yes, what . . . Have you read the play?" She tried to keep the eagerness out of her voice.

"Come on in and I'll tell you."

Still half alseep, she crossed to the door and opened it.

Austin lay on the large bed, the script in his hand. The room was dark but not so dark she couldn't see that Austin was naked and that he had an erection. For a man of his size it was a very good average. She stayed in the doorway.

"Come in, Jill." The famous voice was soft.

"No, thanks. I see you liked the play."

"It's a good play. It's probably a great play. I might do it."

"Is that yes? Or is it no?"

"I have to cogitate a little." His eyes flitted down. "You ever see anything like that before?"

Jill said, "I had two like it for breakfast this morning. You want to do the play?"

"I dunno." Austin was laughing so much his erection was beginning to subside. Actors, she thought. "It depends who else is in it, doll, that's the question."

Always keep something back . . . however.

"Sir Harry is a strong possibility for the prime minister."

The erection had gone completely. "He's the other person who's read the play?"

"You know I can't say that."

"Okay. Okay. He's a terrible old scene-stealer, isn't he?"

"Yes, he is, but your part's a lot bigger. If you'll forgive me."

The actor laughed loudly and pulled on his shorts. "It wouldn't have been much good anyway. My shrink tells me I'm so guilty I can't make it with anybody except my wife. And I've been divorced from her for six months. That's why I'm in this place, holed up on my own." He slapped the script. "All right, if we can do a deal, I'm probably in." He reached for his jeans. "You fancy a couple of hours on the town?"

"I fancy a nice cool bed." Jill picked up the script. "I'll talk to Manny. We'll be seeing each other."

"Hey, you really going now?"

"I have to. I'm dead."

"You're a helluva saleslady, you know that?"

"No, but if it's true, it's a help. There's a bit of selling to do yet."

"Let me know if Maggie's in. Ring me, okay?" Austin pulled on a T-shirt. "That could affect my final decision."

"Promise. 'Night."

" 'Night."

At the door Jill turned. "That not true about your wife, is it?"

He shook his head. "No. Sometimes wish it was."

They both laughed, and then she was walking on the soft crabgrass toward the hotel, which loomed like a Foreign-Legion fort left over from *The Desert Song*.

Number one fish hooked. Or as good as hooked.

It was too much to hope for, and it had all but happened. The thrill of success went through her, as pure, in its way, as any orgasm.

I didn't take the pill for *him*, she thought.

Then who?

She would be seeing Josh tomorrow in New York.

Surely not Josh?

That would be very, very foolish.

That would be insane. In the soft moonlight, Jill Viner, vaguely troubled, made her way through the trees and into the hotel.

IN her bedroom, waves of tiredness flooded over Jill. She took off her clothes and debated having a shower, but she was too tired. She climbed into bed nude, and the scent of perfume reminded her that Jimmy had always insisted she shouldn't bathe before she went to bed at night. I don't want to smell soap, I want to smell woman. Poor Jimmy. He was always looking for something stronger, different. The blonde girl had been inevitable, but still it had hurt. Sex with Jimmy had been good; he had been an inventive lover. But somehow she had always felt him watching her, and that had made her uncomfortable. Still, she had tried; she had simply been too much for him, sex apart. As she had been too much for her previous boyfriends, one a student at the Central School like herself, the other a film accountant. Both had been quite successful young men, but she had been too ready to tell them how to run their lives and their careers, and they had both resented it and they had both left her. All her men left her, it seemed. She was too bright, too energetic, in the end too successful in an entirely different way from Jimmy's brand of success. He had started to live with her when she was an actress. She hadn't been very successful, so it hadn't mattered. He had found her success as Joe Dancy's personal assistant too much to take. What would he think of her now?

Jill smiled tiredly at the thought. Probably suggest I give him a part in *Queen*.

She still missed him, the presence of him, at night, at going-to-bed time. She hated to be alone at that time. Once she was asleep it didn't matter. She was growing used to it.

Josh? That was nonsense.

The pill had simply been a talisman, she decided. Something to pretend she wasn't alone in this town.

Comforted, if not convinced, she sighed, and sleep came like a hammer blow.

AUSTIN Ames stirred in Carmen Fernandez's plump young arms. He opened his eyes. The first streak of dawn filtered through the thin curtains at the window of the shack. The air reeked of the chili they had eaten hours before, mixed with a trace of the pot they had smoked, and of the milky scent of Carmen's baby, sleeping soundly at the far end of the place. Austin wondered if the pot affected the child and hoped that it didn't. If it did, there was nothing he could do about it. If he wasn't with Carmen somebody else would be, and pot would be smoked because Carmen would not screw without smoking pot first. He supposed she had to feel that the dope gave

23

her an excuse at confession. The crucifix hung on the wall, but its power was diluted. Girls like Carmen drifted to dope, and prostitution, although she hotly denied prostitution. "I only take because you insist and the baby is hungry." She always said the same words and she always tossed her long black hair the same way. She was sixteen years old. Austin had been seeing her, one night a week, for three months. She did not always remember his name, but her greeting was never less than warm, and she was prepared, once they had smoked and eaten, to do any and all of the things that Austin had never been able to do with his wife, Minna, who had been a Wasp and a puritan and had always demanded immediate payments for sex, in the way of gifts of jewels and furs. Carmen, at least, was what she was and only took the going rate. She had no idea who Austin was. He always took the precaution of wearing the same pair of dirty jeans and the same soiled shirt. Her curiosity about his expensive car the first time he came to see her had warned him. "Shit, whose is *that*, for Chrissake!" Now, he left the Jensen at an all-night garage and took a cab. Cab drivers looked askance at the address, but he bribed them heavily. He usually called on Carmen without appointment, on impulse, taking care to pick up supper on his way in. Grass and a bottle of wine he always carried in the car, and he brought them along too. He normally left fifteen dollars. More would seem eccentric.

Austin usually went to see Carmen when he was troubled.

Last night had been one of those nights.

He had stopped in and had a drink at Ma Maison and talked to one or two people he knew, but the troubled feeling would not leave him. He had made a great big decision, to leave this tinsel town, this company town of Hollywood, and show the world he had not forgotten how to act. This he had done on one reading of a play by an unknown writer, to be put on in London (if it ever was put on; it was dangerous enough to get itself banned!) by a woman producer he had never heard of, directed by somebody he had never met, who might hate him on sight. Sitting in Ma Maison, talking to

a young starlet of surpassing beauty (who had nonetheless improved it by a face-tuck she didn't need), Austin had felt the icy
sweat of fear. Almost but not quite as bad as the feeling he'd had
when his name was called out and he'd stood up to accept the
Oscar. With this very same starlet at his side, so the millions could
see he wasn't queer. Which he wasn't. He had tried it once and it
had been interesting, but it wasn't for him. Now the starlet put her
hand on his crotch under the table and asked, "Wanta go to my
place, have fun, lover?"

Austin knew that her idea of fun was to screw quickly without orgasm and talk at great length and in ass-numbing detail
about her nonexistent career. In many ways she resembled Minna.
Christ, he was a glutton for punishment, as Singh was forever
telling him. Austin had got to his feet, still feeling the icy sweat
clinging to his back, and muttered, "Got to ring Manny, be back."
But she had known he wouldn't, and he hadn't.

The next call had been to Carmen Fernandez.

Of course, he had to ring Manny sometime, but what was he
going to tell him?

It was always possible to back out. Jill Viner didn't leave until
the morning flight. Ample time for Manny to ring her and tell her
it was no go. Austin would shirk that job. After all, what was
Manny for? He took ten percent of everything, right off the top,
and what did he do? Well, he could ring the snooty English number
and tell her it was no go. Austin Ames was not going to risk his ass.
He was going to play safe, do the sensible fucking thing, for
Chrissake, once in his stupid life. He had done a lot, a whole lot of
stupid things. He had married Minna when everybody had warned
him against it. That had been stupid. He had tried to do it the
standard way, get higher lifts on his shoes, and pump iron (he still
did it when he remembered) between takes. Trying to be an all-
American guy, a movie star, a toughie. At five-six, for God's sake?
All that had been stupid. Of course he had done some non-stupid
things, a few. He had signed for *Good-bye* when nobody wanted

him except the director, and everybody including Minna had said *that* was stupid, but it had been the smartest thing he had ever done. He was hot now, he could do anything in this town. Anything, anyway, until the next movie flopped.

Carmen stirred and snored suddenly. A waft of hot garlic fanned his face. That Carmen. He smiled at the thick-lipped sensual, good-natured little face. Carmen lived the way she did and slept like a child. She came from a softer, easier culture. Not for her the study and the family pressure. His father had been a book-keeper, in Brooklyn of all places, something Austin kept very secret. Austin had tried to emulate him, failed, and gone to acting school on his mother's savings. They had died together in an automobile accident, firmly believing him to be a failure. Their insurance money had set him up; he had stopped taking any old job in off-Broadway productions. Word got out he was loaded. He wasn't; the money was small, but word got out he was loaded, he didn't need jobs. So the jobs began to come. Good jobs, nice parts. Finally, a big support in a play that went into the Brooks Atkinson and ran. From there the call to Hollywood, by a director he knew from the old days who had struck it lucky on the Coast, and wanted somebody who wasn't Hollywood. Then *The Last Good-bye* with Maggie, and the Oscar. Austin felt the prickly sweat break out all over him once again. What was he thinking about? The self-same director was offering him a movie, for Chrissake! All right, it was only a western, and the script needed the kinks ironed out of it, but what was he even thinking about, contemplating the Jill Viner offer?

Her tits. He had to admit it, they looked good.

Her eyes. Steel blue, he always fell for that. His mother Rachel's eyes had been blue. The Viner girl had stirred him, no doubt of it. Otherwise he would not have taken off his jeans for her. He was doing that more rarely these days, since he had won the Oscar. Minna had said it was childish and exhibitionist and had refused to cooperate. His groin stirred.

Carmen woke, got up with her eyes still closed, and walked to the john, in the half-light. There was a loud splashing sound, and Austin relaxed. No pretense here. No will-she-won't-she. When she came back into the room he pushed the sheet back and Carmen looked at him. "Ah macho," she said sleepily and put her soft, full lips to him. Austin lay under her skilled caress until he could stand the sweet pain no more, and pulled Carmen onto him. She rode him silently and sleepily in the soft light and cried her own pleasure with his. Then she kissed him and lay down again contentedly and put her arms around him and went back to sleep.

Austin dozed for an hour, making his decision, and then he looked at his watch and slipped quietly out of bed. He left twenty dollars on the wooden box at the side of the baby's cot. He would not be back, not for a long time anyway.

MANNY was waiting in the airport lounge to see Jill Viner aboard the morning flight. He was dressed in a white suit and panama hat identical to the ones he had worn the day before, and he was on his fourth Turkish cigarette of the day.

He greeted her with a smile of wry defeat.

"Good morning, young lady. I don't know what you did for Austin last night but he rang me at seven o'clock this morning when I was telling my wife for the thousandth time I hate her orange juice—she makes it herself, from her own oranges, would you believe?—and it's terrible. At this moment, Austin rings and tells me he's going into the play. So what did you do to him?"

"Oh my God. Hooray, Manny, hooray!"

Jill Viner's face was a study in delight. Manny could not remember when he had seen such pleasure on a woman's face. He wondered if a man could make her look like that, and he realized a man had: himself. He also realized that was why he had come down to the airport at this time of the morning, something he hadn't done in years. Who had he waved good-bye to that time? Was it Lana or Ava or Judy? He could not remember. All he knew was that it hadn't been as much fun as this.

"Oh, my God," Jill Viner was saying. "You know how to surprise a girl, Manny."

"So?" asked Manny again, fearing the possible truth, hoping it wasn't so. "What did you do to him?"

A smile played around Jill Viner's full mouth. "Nothing he wanted. Maybe that's why."

"Sure. Now he'll live in hopes and I'll have to come to London to see the play and pull him off you."

"If you're not there for the first night, all bets are off."

If I was only twenty years younger, Manny thought. Well, all right, thirty. Thirty-five, if you insist. He put an envelope in her hand. "That's a letter; we can base the contract on that. The terms are yours. If he's crazy enough to turn down a million dollars, then I'm not going to quibble about percentages. Maybe I should but . . ." He suddenly pointed his cigarette at Jill. "You ain't got the money yet and there's many a slip, am I right?"

"Nobody," said Jill Viner stoutly, "ever has the money for a stage play until two weeks before you open. It's a rule of the game."

"When I talked to Joe Dancy, which I did after you called me saying you were speaking from his office—"

"Which, technically, I was," Jill Viner said sweetly.

"You stab him in the back and even use his telephone to do it!" Manny was smiling. "He told me to be kind to you, you could be right about the play." Manny saw tears in Jill Viner's eyes. "Hey, I was only fooling about the stab in the back. If you're gonna be a top producer you'll have to take a lot more than that!"

Jill Viner wiped her eyes. "Now my mascara's run."

"Not a bit," said Manny. It had, of course.

"It was Joe Dancy saying be nice to me."

"Look, I'm being very nice to you; it's me you should be

crying for! I gave up a lot of commission for you. I gave you my best client."

"No you didn't, Manny." She blinked her eyes. "It was his decision."

"All right, I gave you access. I was a fool. But I gave you access. Deny that."

"I don't deny it. You're sweet." She kissed him.

"I haven't been called sweet since Lana Turner at a party in Malibu in the fifties. I'm not sweet."

"You are. You really are and I love you."

"Nobody's said *that* since 1942," said Manny. "And you have to run for that plane. Give my regards to Maggie, she's a lovely person, and phone me if you run into backer trouble. I can sometimes find willing angels. Anyway, God knows, it's got to be a good play. Austin Ames knows nothing about film scripts, women, sex, or money, but about plays Austin Ames knows."

"Good-bye," Jill Viner called, and grabbed her briefcase and ran.

Manny watched her go. He went up onto the observation platform and saw her 747 take off into the smoggy blue above Los Angeles. He felt good. He had just lost a lot of money and yet he felt good. Why was that? The client could do well, if the play prospered, and make even more money? Perhaps. That would not be for a couple of years at least, if it ever happened. By that time he would be seventy-three. So what did he feel so good about?

Manny's driver opened the door of the white Rolls standing outside the airport's main reception area against all parking regulations. Manny sat in the back and lit another Turkish cigarette with the gold cigarette lighter in the Rolls.

It felt good to be doing something that was right, and please a lot of people—especially Jill Viner, for whom he had a very warm regard. He could not have explained why, and he could explain most things. Youth maybe? Maybe. He didn't know and he wasn't about to try to work it out.

Maybe, he thought, it was just because he didn't give a shit.

He sighed. Yes. That was it. He was seventy-one years old. It was a wonderful morning. He hadn't been out at the airport this early in years. And he didn't give a shit.

"The office, Ben," Manny Hiberson told his driver. "It's at the same address as yesterday."

IN the 747, Jill Viner looked down at Los Angeles through the pale haze of smog. It was an enchanted land, and everything had gone wonderfully, beyond her dreams. All that *wasn't* right about her life was in the emotional area. And what good would come of stirring that up, in her present situation? None at all. Men were no use to her. What they all said they wanted—even when they probably didn't—was a pipe-and-slippers woman, and she wasn't that; it simply wasn't in her. She wanted a partner, not a king. Jimmy had actually called her a queen, in the last terrible scene before he left. Was it possible that was what she was, a sort of queen, like the queen of Finland? Jill tucked the morocco-bound folder, with the Roman Q on it, under her arm and smiled. Josh would laugh at that. Josh always laughed at her jokes.

The 747 climbed, and they were above the clouds.

Jill Viner closed her eyes and, jet-lagged, light-headed, and deeply happy, she slept.

JOSH Williams sat in the Edwardian Room of the Plaza, stared out at Fifth Avenue, and wondered what the hell he was doing there.

Putting his career on the line, he reminded himself grimly, was what he was doing there. Forty-six years of age, a time when most stage directors were beginning to look at the renewal clauses in their contracts, if they were lucky enough to have contracts (and he had been!). And here he was, behaving like a stagestruck boy of twenty, his whole future—all that he had left, anyway—riding on the ninety-four sheets of typing bound in morocco leather, lying on the table in front of him.

Integrity. That had been the word Sir Tom had spoken, high in his office over London's South Bank. The youthful Sir Tom's voice had held a certain surprise, as if *integrity* were a word he had never expected to use to Josh Williams. "I must say, Josh, I do admire your integrity. I must say, I really do." Josh had said nothing to that, since there was nothing anybody could say, as it was simply a polite way of calling a man a bloody fool. Which Sir Tom plainly thought he was, but was far too well-mannered to say so.

"I just think it's a good play and it should be done, Tom."

"Oh, I agree." Sir Tom had made a career of agreeing with people, then asking them innocent but devastating questions. "I do agree. The only question is, by whom?"

Josh had known what the answer would be, but he had hoped. Now he felt the hope drain out of his boots.

"Obviously not us, as I think you must have realized by now." Sir Tom sat down behind his large desk, and by that action gave Josh no option but to sit down as well, thus taking the confrontation out of the situation, a thing Sir Tom was skilled at, one of the many things he was skilled at—none of them, Josh thought, much to do with putting on a play like *Queen*.

Josh said, "I don't see why not, Tom. If this isn't a play about England, what the hell is it? And if this isn't a National Theatre expressly designed to put on plays about England, then what the hell is it?"

"Yes, I do agree. I see your point of view, believe me." Sir Tom sighed, much, Josh thought, as he must have sighed when the stagehands went on strike and closed the theatre down, costing the British taxpayer thousands of pounds. "I think it's a very interesting play indeed, remarkable really, since the author's a Russian."

"Vercek's a Jewish dissident, Tom. Not too well known. He wrote a few plays years ago, translated into German, Czech, and so on. None anything like *The Queen of Finland*." Josh looked past Sir Tom at the Thames, glittering below them in the late spring sunshine. It must be the season for impulsive action, he thought. It's the only explanation for the integrity.

Sir Tom mused. "His English is good. Astonishingly so."

"A lot of Russians learn it." Josh thought: I am one of the best stage directors in London. Everybody knows that. If I have no control over the plays I do, I might as well be the worst. He waited.

"The thing is . . ." Sir Tom was reluctantly coming to the point. "The thing is, Josh, I really can't see how we can do a play here with H.M. Queen starring in it, which is more or less what it amounts to, yes?"

"Yes, it does."

Sir Tom tapped his empty pipe against his teeth. "It has to be the queen of England. I mean, it has to be *our* queen. I mean it couldn't . . . ?"

Josh knew what was coming but he waited.

"What if . . . it's just an idea, but what if . . ." Sir Tom got to his feet. The warm Celtic face beamed. The hands described arcs. He radiated enthusiastic goodwill. It was now that he was at his most dangerous, as directors, actors, and even the bolshie stagehands had discovered. Josh braced himself for it.

". . . what if we don't *call* her the queen of England? What if we don't *say* any of it is actually *real*? Is it *absolutely* necessary that we call the Americans Americans and the Russians Russians?" Sir Tom beamed again. "It's an allegorical play in many ways, yes? It has some of the feeling of fable, don't you think? Our audience—our audience here—would fill in the blanks, they'd know what we were really talking about. Had you . . ." Sir Tom beamed even stronger. No wonder the stagehands—Cockneys led by Marxists, a combination to frighten Hitler—had given in for five pence an hour less than their asking price. "Had you thought of that solution, Josh?"

"I'd thought of it," Josh answered slowly, "but the most important thing *The Queen of Finland* has going for it is that it's *about* something. It's about what's happening in Finland now and might be happening here in two, three, five, ten years. If we put it in never-never land all we're doing is saying, Don't worry, it's all right, it can't happen here. We'd be copping out."

"Copping out?" Sir Tom stood up. The beam had gone. Now he was merely sad. "I could hover around and say I'll see. But honestly, I don't think I could change anybody's mind."

Josh blinked. "You've talked to the board?"

"Unofficially. Just a word. They're worried. It's H.M. Queen. In a play. Here. It comes down to that."

"I see." Josh did see. Sir Tom had cut off any possible flanking move. He probably hadn't done it deliberately, he had probably done it without thinking. "So it's no, a flat thanks-but-no-thanks?"

"Unless you'd like to talk to the author. See if he can be persuaded?"

"I wouldn't ask him."

"No. I do see that. There's a tiny last point, Josh."

"And that is?"

"The play was sent in to us, to the National, and therefore perhaps we should write, that is our literary department should write, to the author and explain our point of view, and suggest he come in and talk?" Sir Tom smiled to take the sting out. "He may be willing to go along with suggestions, who knows?"

"*The Queen of Finland* was sent directly to me. God knows why." Josh smiled implacably back. "I brought it in to you. If you don't want it, then, that's fine, but you'd have to get the Beefeaters from the Tower of London to wrest it out of my fair hands, Tom."

"Ah yes. Of course, I do see that." Sir Tom nodded. "It isn't, as it were, offered to us officially?"

"No, it isn't." Josh hefted the bulky, badly typed manuscript with the red smears across the last pages—what were they? he supposed red ink—from Sir Tom's desk, and placed it firmly in his briefcase and locked the case with the key. "There won't be a record anywhere, if it is a great success, that you didn't want to know about it."

"Oh, but I do hope it is a success, old boy." Sir Tom crossed to his cabinet and took out his whiskey decanter. He poured them both two fingers and added water to his own. "Josh, I'll talk to the office and arrange a termination-of-contract payment. It won't be much but it might help. Cheers."

"Cheers." Josh downed his drink in one swallow. "That's very good of you, Tom." It was. There was nothing in his contract that said anything about a termination payment.

Sir Tom leaned back against the ledge of his picture window (a favorite with photographers from the *Observer*) and actually filled and lit his pipe, a thing he did only under great emotional stress. None showed on his face.

"It's been how long now, Josh?"

"Six years next month."

"A long time for a director to stay here. You've done some damn good work for us, you know. There should be some kind of presentation or something."

"Please no. I might be coming back sometime, remember?"

"Of course. Of course you might. No, well. We'll leave that." Sir Tom sighed, denied the opportunity of making a speech. It would have been a good one, Josh knew. His speeches always were. And he would have meant it. He always did. Sir Tom blew out a cloud of Balkan Sobranie and said, a tinge of longing in his voice, "If only it hadn't been such a political play, with real people in it, and H.M. Queen . . . I'd have said yes. The H.M. Queen thing dishes it for us. We *are* the National, after all."

"Rule Britannia," said Josh, and left, carrying the briefcase with his future in it. Behind him he could hear Sir Tom calling the contracts manager.

JOSH glanced at his watch. Another hour to kill. Jill Viner had vetoed his suggestion that he meet her at Kennedy. Just as easy to take a cab in and meet at the Plaza, she had said, on the telephone, glowing from her meeting with Austin Ames. He smiled as he recalled her voice, vibrant with triumph. "He's in, all being well and no changes of mind. Josh, I really think we have him."

"Did you sign a contract with his agent?" Josh had asked. Hiring actors over more years than he cared to count had made him a pessimist. "The only time you can count on an actor is when he's in the rehearsal hall, drunk or sober, and complaining about his lines."

Jill had laughed at that. "You're a bucket of cold water as usual, Josh, but you're right, of course. I've spoken to Manny Hiberson and he's drawn up a contract based on the figures I gave him."

"Probably never expected it to happen. Did you talk a start-date?"

"I said August, possibly September. I had to say something."

"Better to have said a movable feast."

"I know, but out here they like definite dates, even if they cancel them. It isn't England; nobody believes in anything, including anybody's word, until it happens." Jill's voice took on an edge. "Aren't you knocked out at the idea of working with Austin?"

"Of course I am," Josh said. "You've done wonders, Jill, I can't really take it in. Ignore my skepticism. It's stupid of me, you've been absolutely bloody marvelous. Really. I mean it."

So he did. No doubt of it. She was marvelous. He had never met anybody remotely like her. All that animal energy. All that power and push. Yet she wasn't butch or lez or anything like that. She was womanly and attractive, to just about anybody. Including, Josh supposed, himself. He remembered the glowing, healthy skin and great-looking breasts, and he repressed the thought at once. Theirs was a business partnership and it must not become anything else. Anything else simply would not work. A producer and a director had enough problems to sort out, without complications of that sort. Anyway, Jill Viner wasn't interested in men at the moment. She had told him so at their very first serious meeting. "I'm off men." She had smiled across the teapot, at the Dorchester. "Just had a long, long story end. I don't want anymore for a while, thank you very much. Do you take milk before or after?"

It had been a straightforward hands-off, not interested.

Josh at the time had been glad to hear it. He did not want

complications either. He wanted what Jill Viner wanted. A great big roaring success in the West End of London.

Now, calling him from California, she seemed to have, against all the odds, taken the first important hurdle, and to be pleased with his reaction. Perhaps too pleased? Her voice had sounded warm and gentle, like that of a woman who had just made love. Except that she hadn't made love, he didn't suppose. She had landed the actor, hook, line, and sinker.

"Of course I'm delighted," he had repeated. "The idea of working with Austin Ames. Great. Terrific. Marvelous. Hooray."

Jill Viner laughed, a deep, throaty, slightly disturbing laugh. "Don't overdo it, Josh. I'll see you. Put your best suit on for Miss Maggie. 'Bye."

Once she had rung off Josh had felt unaccountably lonely, sitting in his tenth-floor room in the Plaza. He didn't care for the feeling. Loneliness was something he had grown used to since Alison had died. It had been hard at first but he quite liked it now. He had even become a reasonable cook, of very plain food. The pain of loss had passed away and now he could only remember her face with an effort. It was three years, after all. Time was the great healer. Trite but true. He had not felt he wanted to marry again. Becky, their daughter, was twenty, and married herself, to a scientist working in nuclear physics. He supposed grandchildren were the next thing on the list. Well, he was forty-six after all, although he did not feel it, any more than he had felt it the morning he went around saying his good-byes at the National.

Everybody had been astonished. Like Sir Tom, they thought Josh was a bloody fool, and like Sir Tom, they had been far too polite to say so. Even the sceneshifters and props men had looked surprised. "Thought you was like a fixture here, Josh, old mate. Place won't seem the same wivvout you, son."

Sitting in the actors' Green Room, glass in hand, Josh had relaxed and made light of it all. "Time for a change before death and arthritis set in, and besides I haven't worked in the West End for seven years."

"You'll find it changed," Bill Astle, a fellow director, had said. "It isn't this place, you know. It's box office all the way."

"I don't object to that," Josh had protested. "If a play's good, people will come to see it."

"Yes." Bill looked into his beer. "If it's a sex comedy with two or three television names in it. Is your play that?"

"How do you know I have a play at all?"

"Would you be leaving if you hadn't? Anyway, Tom told me. I think he expected you to back down."

"Don't tell the actors I have a play, for God's sake." Josh indicated a group of contract players who, at that moment, came pouring into the Green Room, having just broken from rehearsals in another part of the building. On learning Josh was going, and buying a round of drinks to celebrate the fact, they had crowded over and sat in a vast circle around him, dumping their tattered scripts and bulging handbags and scuffed briefcases and old sweaters and scarves and woolly hats, and cried out in drama and dismay, "Old Josh, not going, not leaving us; we don't believe it, not old Josh; where in God's name are you going, Stratford or the Shakespeare?"

"Neither," Josh had answered.

"It's the Belgrade. I heard they—"

"No. I'm not going anywhere, loves. Well, not anywhere definite. Not yet."

Bill rescued him, neatly, as Bill always could. "Don't ask him too many questions. He can't answer them yet."

"All under wraps, eh?" The actors shook their heads. "Probably Hollywood, eh, Josh?" one of them asked, and the others all laughed, loud and long. The idea of Josh and Hollywood amused them, and Josh could see why. Nothing in his record pointed to it. Like most hardworking contract players the actors had a dream of riches and stardom and an image of themselves huge up on the screen, all of it buried lingeringly somewhere far below their thousands of hours of Shakespeare and Ibsen and Strindberg and O'Neill. "Anyway, bloody good luck, Josh, whatever it is, and so say all of us."

I love them all, Josh thought; they're such children, such wonderful, naïve, talented children, and they really do sound as if they will miss me. He blew his nose to explain the tinge of moisture tickling his eyes and said, "It isn't a bloody funeral, you know, and I'll be shouting at you all again, I expect, somewhere or other, before the end of the world arrives."

"I'll bet," said one of the actors pensively, "old Josh has a play stuck under his belt."

"If I had, there wouldn't be a part in it for any of you lazy buggers!" declared Josh. "You are all fat and milk-fed, the whole lot of you. You don't know what a decent day's work is!"

Bill had grinned and the actors had looked sheepish. They knew, in a way, it was true. The National was a subsidized theatre—or rather three theatres—and it cost five million pounds a year (ten million dollars at the going rate) to run. Nothing like that amount came back in box-office returns, but it *was* one of the great theatres of the world. Actors, like everybody else who worked there, were paid by the state, the only difference being that they had no security of tenure (unlike the backstage people, Josh thought wryly, who were there for life and with a pension to carry home at the end of it) other than their length of contract, usually months rather than years, but usually renewed. On the few years of security they often married and started families and bought houses and cars. A job as a supporting player at the National was a plum in a British actor's life, a chance to do good work, the best, to be decently paid for doing it, to be free of the actors' penny-pinching and sometimes penniless existence: sharing a room in Earl's Court, hanging high hopes on the odd television job at the BBC in some awful costume serial, or a spit-and-a-cough in a twelve-week provincial tour of a dated Agatha Christie thriller. That, or possibly the dole, as everybody still called Social Security. Actors, sometimes eminent actors, drew it weekly at one of the two offices in London the Department of Social Security had finally delegated for the purpose, so that actors need not stand in line and be recognized by people who had seen them on television the night before and thought they were millionaires.

Directors never signed on the dole.

There was no law to say they shouldn't, but they never did.

Josh felt a sudden cold fear, sitting in the Green Room, the actors' laughter booming around him. People said, "Well, I can always go on the dole," but they didn't mean it; it was just something everybody said. "We all live in the welfare state, we all pay our insurance every week, we're bloody entitled, aren't we?"

It was very nearly death for a well-known actor to be seen drawing the dole.

For a director it would be suicide.

Anyway, he had four thousand pounds, saved over the years. It ought to have been more, it ought to have been a hell of a lot more, but he supposed that there had been no real reason to save. Until *Queen*.

Bill was saying, "If you go into the West End Commercial theatre, Josh, you won't get a nice Green Room like this or nice dressing rooms for your actors or a nice subsidized canteen or any bloody thing at all. You'll be back to basics, old son."

"I know," Josh said, "it'll be a wrench to leave the old Führerbunker." Which was what the actors called the massive concrete complex of the National, looming Germanically over the South Bank. With its terraces, bars, restaurants, vast scenery-bay and costume departments, it was indeed a wondrous sight. Tourists came in their hundreds every night, the sense of occasion heightened (and the resemblance to the Führerbunker, too) by the first-night tradition of firing off a monsoon gun, which heart-stopped every Thames gull and most of the population who remembered the Blitz.

The National was a bastion; it rode the Thames with the certainty of Drake and his sea dogs. What was he thinking about, leaving it all? Josh could not, at that moment, have said the words, "Yes, I'm going, I'm leaving, I really am." But the next moment Bill was putting another drink in his hand, a large one, and his hand moved to take the glass, and in doing so touched the briefcase containing the manuscript of *The Queen of Finland*, and he said, in a loud, clear voice, "I'll miss you a lot, you drunken buggers!" and they all laughed louder than ever, and one or two had tears in their eyes. Especially the little Welsh actress, Maeve, who had slept with him a few times and had wanted to move in and look after him, but who had understood when he said no. But who had moved on to Bill, who was, as ever, between wives. Bill had said yes to her, but Josh knew that—God knows why!—Maeve had been sorry he, Josh, hadn't.

"We'll all miss you, darling, you old bastard," Maeve said, raising her glass.

They bought him a going-away present and gave it to him the next day when he went in to clear out his desk. It was an original bound copy of *Mr. Bolfry*, just about his favorite play, probably because he had seen it as a young man, unforgettably well done by the Ulster Group Company, with Harry Goldblatt as Mr. Bolfry and Bob McCandless as the Reverend MacCrimmon. It must have been Maeve's idea, because she had done the presentation speech, and very nicely, too. Maeve would go a long way in the business. Josh had simply said thanks and fled.

On Waterloo Bridge he had stopped, looked back at the old Führerbunker, gloomy under a lowering English sky, and a lump had come into his throat. Then he had flagged a taxi and taken the script to lunch at the Savoy with Joe Dancy.

It had all promised so well, that lunch.

Joe Dancy had seemed very enthusiastic, Sir Tom refusing the play just an added spice. Joe had said that he would be very pleased to do it, if it was everything Josh had said it was at their previous meeting.

Then there had been silence.

Then there had been the letter.

No call. People didn't telephone news like that. The letter said no. Joe liked the play, it was all Josh said it was, Joe thought the play was a good, probably important piece of drama but . . .

The play had the queen in it.

Josh had told Joe the play had the queen in it at lunch at the Savoy and at their previous meeting, but obviously Joe had not heard him, or had thought he was talking about some other queen, Queen Elizabeth or Mary Queen of Scots or somebody safely dead.

It had taken half a bottle of Scotch to kill the feeling of anger that Joe Dancy's letter had brought with it. That, and a long, numbing hour wondering why the hell he had walked out of the National without actually having a production lined up.

Josh spoke aloud, to himself.

"I left because I was fed up with doing some damn pretentious load of artistic crap, pretending it was serious and had a relevance for today. I'm up to here with Marxism and sociology pretending to be art, and playwrights searching searching searching for something to be shocked and shocking about. I left because it was time to leave."

He drank more Scotch.

It didn't help.

Then the telephone rang and a voice he half recognized said, "This is Jill Viner from Joe Dancy's office. You haven't done anything with that play, have you?"

"No." His heart leaped. "Is Joe interested, after all?"

"No. *I* am. Don't go out, I'll be there in half an hour."

That was how Jill Viner had entered his life. Sitting in the

Edwardian Room in the Plaza Hotel, Josh Williams wondered, rather vaguely, how she would leave it. He could find no ready answer, save a feeling of pleasurable unease.

JILL sat in her cab, coming out of Kennedy, and felt the same sense of excitement (and something like fear) she always felt, driving into New York City. It was the sheer size, the harsh grandeur of it all. She hoped the eventual Broadway audience would understand *Queen*. Europe and its problems seemed a long way off, a world away. But she had made a good start. She had Austin, and Maggie was next. Jill began to make up her face with care, something she rarely did in the middle of the day unless it was very important. And it wasn't that. It was only Josh.

She snapped her makeup case shut and leaned back in the seat, feeling slightly troubled and yet expectant. Stop it, she told herself, but her heart began to beat a little faster, and nothing she thought about, not even *Queen*, could slow it down.

JOSH sat on in the Edwardian Room and felt slightly unreal and hung over. He had flown in from Heathrow the previous evening and had foolishly gone to a play on Broadway instead of going to bed. The play was all right, but when he took his seat it was already one in the morning by his body clock, and four in the morning by the time he had got to bed. After the play, he had walked Broadway for an hour, looking at the playbills and the theatre crowds, and very exciting it had been. Josh had not been in New York for almost eight years. His last visit, like this one, had been strictly professional. Josh rarely did anything or went anywhere that wasn't somehow connected with his work. Alison had always been at him about it. She had been in New York with him that time. They had gone to shows and eaten at the Four Seasons and at "21". Alison had been cheerful and uncomplaining as ever, her asthma

43

under control at that time. But Josh remembered he had been watchful, as usual, for the signs. He had driven her to the hospital in his pajamas six or seven times by then, and he had known that one time he would get her there too late. As in fact he had. He remembered her poor dear face, and tears pricked his eyes. Alison had been a good sort. Getting too bloody emotional by far, he told himself. Absolutely no point in it. Cut out the self-pity, concentrate on the job in hand.

Jill Viner and her bloody play. The woman would not be denied.

Josh remembered his first sight of her, from the window of his flat in Glebe Place, off the King's Road, as she paid off the taxi and turned her face up to the window. He had stepped back quickly. There was something direct and dangerous in that gaze, something that brooked no opposition. Jill Viner, standing in the busy little street on a Saturday morning, looked somehow different from the other strollers. The King's Road that morning was full of long-haired young men pushing prams and absurdly young mums pointedly not hanging on their arms (Alison's hand had always been in his before they took two paces), and Jill didn't belong to that scene. She looked much more Brompton Road—fashionable and moneyed, possibly; a young matron even, in her St. Laurent suit and Gucci shoes, on her way to Harrods. An unfashionably full figure (Josh had always hated beanpoles) and a confident, almost embattled air was the first impression Josh had, and the one he was never to lose.

Jill had looked around his room and accepted a sherry. She hadn't accepted his invitation to sit down, but stood on the hearthrug, glass in hand, rather as a man-friend might, and fixed him with that frank stare.

"Nice place. Have you lived here long?"

"Fifteen years. We came here when we left our first flat in Notting Hill. Myself and Alison, my wife, and of course, Becky, our daughter." He indicated the silver-framed studio portrait of

Alison that stood on her father's old mahogany sideboard, which had always been far too large for the room, and which he had always intended to get rid of, and never had. "Bought it on mortgage five years ago. The rents had begun to go crazy."

He wondered why he had mentioned Alison. He normally never did, especially with strangers, and even more especially with women.

"Your wife looks very nice," Jill Viner said.

"Well, she's gone actually." Josh always found it hard to say "dead."

"You've split up?" Her voice was pointedly neutral.

"No, I mean, she died. Three years ago. Asthma. She suffered from it a lot. It was a kind of release, as they said at the hospital, and I'm sure they were right."

"Oh, I'm so sorry, I should have known but I didn't."

Jill put her sherry down abruptly, and to his surprise he saw that her eyes were moist. He remembered thinking later how very spontaneously sentimental she was, and how much he liked her for it, but at the time his reaction had been any Englishman's to a woman's emotion: pure horror.

"Nothing to apologize for. She wasn't in the business so why should you have known? She was just a wife; most people didn't know her, hardly at all. She wasn't one for parties. Here, let me top you up." He had poured the Bristol Cream and she had murmured, "Thank you, but all the same . . ." And he had said firmly, "Really, it was all such a long time ago." He spread his hands and this time she sat down, and so did he. "I'm afraid, as you can see, I'm in a bit of a rut these days. My daughter married young, and she's living up in Scotland, so I sort of pig along." Josh wondered why he had said that. He was perfectly happy pigging along. He didn't want to do anything else. So he said, in a brisker tone, "Both here, and of course at the National. I've been at both addresses rather a long time."

"I like your flat and you don't seem to be pigging it at all; it looks very neat to me." Jill's gaze took in the rows of books and the good but worn carpet, and the Breuer chairs, which needed re-caning but were originals. Alison had bought them cheap in the Caledonian Market. She had been good at that kind of thing—patient, pleasant, and supportive. Josh had never been able to understand what Alison saw in him. Once, he had asked her. "Nice wavy hair, blue eyes, lovely skin, good teeth, and a sense of humor. Oh. And I thought"—Alison had held his hand suddenly—"my attacks won't scare him." Somehow, that had sounded the most important thing, and he had not minded. But they had scared him. They had scared him a lot.

Jill Viner was, he reflected, a very different kind of woman altogether. Extrovert. Ambitious. Self-reliant. A partner rather than a wife. Well, that was what she was. She had made the terms plain from the outset, leaning forward in her chair that sunny spring Saturday morning in Glebe Place.

"I read the play, and I think it should be done."

Josh had smiled at her determined tone. "I agree fervently. But how can you help? If Joe Dancy isn't interested, I don't see . . ."

The reply astonished him.

"I'm going to produce it myself."

"Do you have any backing or anything?" Josh had felt a sense of unreality. "I thought you were Joe's assistant."

"I am. Or rather, by Monday I will have been."

"Why, what happens on Monday?"

"On Monday I resign. Always provided you come in with me, as a partner."

Josh felt disappointed, but why did he have any right to be? "I haven't any money to invest," he said. "It's not a director's business to invest in his plays."

The girl looked slightly downcast and then said briskly, "Granville-Barker did it. I have two thousand pounds and I'm going to use it as risk money to get people interested. If I don't, then all bets are off and we both start looking for jobs. By the way, you shouldn't have given up your job at the National. Why did you do it? Joe Dancy wasn't sure of the play, was he?"

Josh stared uneasily and crossed his denimed legs. He was dressed in the King's Road Saturday drill, jeans and sweater and Adidas. His hair was too long, not too well cut, and he wished he was not wearing the gold signet ring Maeve had given him as an end-of-affair present. It made him feel a bit of a ponce in Jill's eyes, he supposed. So he said, rather harshly, "I guess I felt I needed a change." He got to his feet and took her glass. "Let me get you another sherry." As he poured it from the Waterford decanter that had belonged to his mother—one of the few things she had left him, since actresses don't pick up a lot of baggage—Josh said, "I have four thousand myself. It's all I do have. I could put it in, if we had a real prospect. But I don't see how we have."

Why on earth, he asked himself, did I say *that?*

The girl was spreading a sheet of paper, covered with names and figures, upon the small coffee table.

"What's this?" Josh helped himself to a Scotch. He normally never drank at lunchtime. This seemed a good time to break the rule. "The plans of the fort, or what?"

As soon as he had spoken the words he had realized that was exactly what the names were. Jill Viner's deep laugh told him so. "A comprehensive list of Joe Dancy's backers. The money they have put in previous productions of Joe's. Along with their credit rating and any personal notes, along of course with their addresses and telephone numbers." Her blue eyes glowed mischievously at him, and he noticed they had a speck of gold in them. She wasn't beautiful, like Alison, but she was . . . he searched for the words and when it came it surprised him. . . . She was healthy, vital. "My dear young lady, that is robbery with violence. It could even be actionable in law."

"Nonsense! Joe would be disappointed in me if I did anything else. Don't forget this is only a list of backers. It doesn't mean any of them will back *Queen*. Not yet." She smiled. "Now I have to be sure you're in. You and Vercek."

"Ah yes. Vercek. Of course."

"He's essential. I take it you have him tied up, letter contract, something like that?"

"No. I haven't even met him."

Jill Viner's eyes opened wide in disbelief. "You haven't even met him?"

She made it sound as if he were a total lunatic.

"Not much point in meeting him, is there, unless I can make him an offer."

Jill seemed to be having trouble with her voice. Well, it was nice to see her composure dented a bit.

"You do have his address and telephone number, I suppose?" she asked, eventually.

"Yes, I do. I did once try to telephone him but the number is that of a café. All you can do is leave a message. It seems he looks in now and then, to see if anybody wants him."

"And the address on the script? I suppose there is one?"

"Well. It's a sort of a poste restante place actually."

"A delivery drop?"

"Yes. A sort of newsagent's shop, I should think. It's somewhere down the North End Road."

"Would you mind if I had yet another sherry?"

"Not at all," said Josh stiffly and poured himself another whiskey at the same time. When he turned round from the sideboard she was laughing.

"What's the joke? May I share it?"

"One thing's obvious to me, that's all. You're a hell of a good director but I'll be the business partner, all right?"

"I didn't know we'd agreed to a partnership yet," said Josh coolly.

"Oh, we have. Unless you've tried some other management with *The Queen of Finland* and they've said yes."

48

"No, I haven't done that."

"Let's hope Vercek hasn't."

Josh found that he had suddenly gone very cold. "I must say I never thought of that."

"Why don't you ring that number you have for him and see what happens?"

Josh took out his book. He found the number and dialed. After a very long time a foreign voice—to Josh's skilled ear, Greek—answered.

" 'Allo, Kristos' Caff."

"I want to talk to Boris Vercek. Is he about, please?"

"Vercek? Who wants him?"

"I'm a friend. My name's Williams."

"Villums? I didden know Boris had any frien' Villums. He never said any frien' Villums might call."

"Is he there at all?"

"No. Vercek not here at all. Ring back some other time, you maybe get him then, hokay, gotta go now, got customer, 'bye."

"Can I leave a message?"

"No good if I don't know your name. And he no said Villums."

"Now look here! He wouldn't—"

A dial tone.

Jill Viner was looking irritated.

"Wasn't he there?"

"No. I talked to some unhelpful Greek. It seems he'll only take calls from friends and I'm not one of them."

"Did he say who he was?"

"It could be in the book, I suppose."

It was. Kristos's Café, 197B North End Road.

"There we are!" Her eyes were on him, daring him to pour more cold water, he supposed. "We can go down there now...."

"He isn't there now."

"That's only what Kristos said."

"If it was Kristos."

"It was Kristos." Jill Viner stood up. "Let's grab a taxi."

"I have my old Volks outside."

"Well, we aren't getting anywhere standing here, are we?"

As they were climbing into the Volkswagen—a traveling slum of old playscripts and jerseys and plastic shopping bags—she touched his arm.

"It was so nice of you to throw your four thousand into the ring. Really."

Josh started to say something indefinite and contradictory, just to muddy the waters a bit, when she added, "Of course I ought to have known you were a generous person. The way you directed *Time and the Conways*. Very sympathetic. Marvelous production. That's when I first noted your name. I've been a fan ever since."

So Josh said nothing, of course. What could he say? It was the best offer yet. It was the only offer.

He swung the Volkswagen out into the stream of traffic and tried to work out the best route to the North End Road.

HOW scruffy some parts of London look now, he thought. In some way it reflected the decline of the nation itself. How very different the city was from the late fifties, when he first came to live in Chelsea, just married and full of hope, living on ten pounds a week from a job as assistant stage manager at the Royal Court, or on some out-of-town tour. He had done every job thrown at him. ASM, props, holding the book—the lot; and for no money, just enough to live on. But there had been hope, the fifties were full of hope. Good theatre, everywhere you looked. Osborne, Wesker, Shaffer, Orton, Bolt. The great actors, Larry's *Othello* and Archie Rice, Plowright's Beatie Bryant in *Roots*. Wolfit's *Lear*, and his *Tamburlaine* at the Vic, Richardson in *Flowering Cherry*. The Court, every first night an event even when it mostly wasn't. God, those had been the days. Not that we are short of talent today. We aren't. We have the actors—McKellen, Finney, Scofield.

We have the writers too, but the new ones are off a conveyor belt, young middle-class Public School boys writing about the working class, mostly from a Trotskyite point of view. Romantic nonsense, really. England needs plays about her place in the world now, not plays about the thirties written by people who weren't even alive then. The nostalgia of empire is all very well, but the reality is the black plastic bags of refuse outside the box-offices and along the Soho streets, and the strikers picketing the hospitals, and the threat of nuclear war. It had taken Vercek to write that play. The eighties had started badly for Britain, and London should have looked depressed, but of course it didn't. London never did. Like Rome, it was eternal. Even the pedestrian precinct at Leicester Square, which was designed for the populace and had attracted only the drunks and addicts, still had a charm. Even Chelsea, over-publicized and groaning under the Saturday traffic, was still attractive in the warm sun. People loitered in their parkas and sweatshirts, the girls not too different from the boys at fifty paces, the long hair a badge of youth for both sexes, walking idly as people did everywhere in the cities of the West, sure that tomorrow would be no different from today. Again, it had taken Vercek to say that tomorrow could be different, and not for the better.

The Volkswagen nudged its way through the market, and everywhere young men and women shopped together, a development new to the Englishman, who twenty years ago would not have been found dead in a shop or store. Jill Viner said as much. "My father never went into a shop with my mother in his life. She made all the unimportant decisions in our house. Where we lived, what we ate, how much we spent and on what, and he made the important ones. What we should do with Red China, should we join the Common Market?"

Josh laughed, and thought how very nice it was, simply to

drive through the city with a lovely woman. For Jill was lovely, if not as obviously a sex symbol as Maeve. He stirred uncomfortably at the memory. Maeve had been the only girl (there had been a few one-night stands) he had thought of taking on, after Alison died. What had decided him against it, in the end, had been Maeve's sexual attitudes. She had held the initiative in sex, and she had been very inventive. They had taken each other in the backs of cars and over chairs, with and without clothes, in costume and out of it (Maeve was an actress to her toes), and in the end it had all just simply become too exhausting. Not physically—that had been something he could cope with, although sometimes with difficulty. Maeve's previous partners had been like herself, innovative and experimental, and his own experience with Alison had been none of that. It had been more affectionate than sensual, more emotional than sexual. Maeve was for taking sex without love, the way the middle-aged used to take it when he was a boy. Skeptically. As if it did not really matter, as if it were just part of a relationship and not central to it. Josh was forty-six and he could not take it as lightly as that. He moved uncomfortably in his seat. Jill Viner had started these thoughts, and he did not care for them. He was all right as he was. He had no need of a woman. Not, anyway, for the immediate future.

Jill pointed toward a dingy block on the left side of the North End Road. "Here we are!"

Kristos' Caff was exactly what it sounded like: small, steamy, and greasy-looking. It was empty apart from a gray-haired man sitting at a corner table, and two black youths in Chelsea scarves, drinking coffee and arguing football in Cockney accents.

Kristos looked exactly as he sounded: small and hairy and mildy surprised to see somebody like Jill Viner in his establishment. She didn't look the North End Road. Josh, on the other hand, wore the drab, blue-based uniform of the young, although he had a sneaking fancy he was too old for it.

"Two coffees, please," Josh said, as they seated themselves at a table. It was lunchtime but he didn't feel he wanted to eat at Kristos' Caff.

"Two coffees, nothink to eat?" was Kristos's reply as his wife (a stout feminine version of Kristos himself) attended the hissing urn. To serve people he did not know was plainly beneath Kristos's dignity.

"No, thank you," said Josh. "I don't think so."

"I got special lunch today, I got moussaka, my wife made herself, very good," said Kristos implacably.

"Perhaps, er, later." Josh smiled at the wife but she did not smile back. She had a very distinct mustache. Josh said, "I rang you earlier. My name is Williams. I'm looking for Vercek."

Kristos looked at him unblinkingly, but he was very still.

"You say you frien' of his, yes?"

"Well. I've never met him but—"

"You never met him but you say you are frien' of his?" Kristos's voice was low and disbelieving. "How is that, you are frien' but you never meet?"

Josh was beginning to get annoyed. "Look. I have business with him and I'd be very much obliged if you can tell me where he lives."

"I dunno where he lives."

Josh was sure Kristos was lying but he could not understand why.

"Will he be in here today, do you think?"

"Maybe. Maybe he just phone."

"If you have a number for him I'd be grateful."

"I have no number. He rings in. I just tol' you."

"Then you can't help?"

Kristos shrugged a Greek shrug. He didn't bother to reply but turned away, almost contemptuously. The wife of Kristos handed Josh the two cups of coffee, which turned out to be surprisingly good, and Josh carried them across to the table. Jill looked at him questioningly.

53

"I heard all that. I think they know where he is."

"Maybe they do but they aren't telling."

"Why should they be so secretive?"

"No idea. It's all so damn mysterious I'm beginning to wonder if he exists."

"Somebody wrote that play. He has to exist. How do you know he's a Jew?" Jill asked, suddenly.

"He said so in his letter to me. It's just a card really. The play came to the National addressed to me." Josh fumbled in a large manila envelope. "Here, read it yourself."

Jill took the card. The message was written in beautiful Italic script and concluded, "I like your work and I think you will like my play," and it was signed Boris Vercek.

Jill said, smiling, "Not even a question mark. He's sure of himself."

"Of course he is." Josh put the letter back in the envelope. "Anybody who can write a play like *The Queen of Finland* is entitled to be." He looked up to see Kristos's face looming over him. Kristos's eyes were on the envelope containing the playscript. "You want to see Vercek about some business, eh?" he asked. "About some special business?"

Jill smiled at Kristos with that eye-widening stare Josh was beginning to be wary of. Kristos ran a hand over his black hair.

"We have to talk to him about his play," said Jill. "You see?"

"Ah. His play?" Kristos straightened his tie. His gaze was frankly admiring. "You should have said this." The rebuke was for Josh who, wisely, said nothing. "Look, I tell you." Kristos was consulting his watch, a huge glittering machine on his simian wrist. "Maybe he come in pretty soon. You stay, have a glass retsina. I send over, on the 'ouse."

Jill smiled at Kristos and Kristos smiled back.

Josh said, "Please, we will pay. . . ."

Kristos regarded him coldly. "It is on the 'ouse." He smiled at Jill. "The lady like retsina, no?"

"Thank you," Jill said.

The wife of Kristos banged the cash register unnecessarily.

The atmosphere in the café changed. Kristos switched on the jukebox with a flourish. The wife of Kristos brought not two glasses of retsina, but a carafe. Several customers came in and ate plates of the moussaka, which seemed very good indeed. Josh began to feel quite hungry.

"I must say you can be quite shameless," he told Jill.

"I know, but it works." She sipped the retsina. "He's right. I do like booze, a bit too much really. I have to be careful or I put weight on."

I was right, Josh thought, an absolute extrovert. But not a bully, or anyway not yet, or anyway if she is she does it very cleverly. He asked, "Why did you stop acting?"

"How do you know I was ever an actress?" She looked surprised.

"I've been looking at actors since I got my first job in the old Swansea Rep at seventeen years of age."

She laughed, delighted. Kristos looked up at her laugh, and he looked delighted. Jill said, "I liked it but there's no dignity in it unless you're a great talent. And I wasn't. So I quit."

"If you could quit, you were right to."

"A man I knew very well told me one day that I'd never be a good actress, never mind a great one. I was too much myself, he said." Josh thought that he could well believe that, but he did not reply. She said, "My friend, and he was a good actor himself—"

"Would I know him?" Josh asked automatically.

"Jimmy Bolton."

"Worked with him years ago. Lovely actor." So Jimmy had been her boyfriend. "Helluva good character man. Jimmy has it all before him." What Josh meant was that Jimmy Bolton had failed, if only just, at being a juvenile. Nowadays his looks were beginning to go and he had to prove himself all over again, as a middle-aged character actor.

55

Jill poured herself another glass of retsina. "Jimmy Bolton wants to be a great star and he's forty-two and he's never going to be a great star. He's going to be a very good character actor the day he grows up."

"You didn't tell him that?"

"I did."

"Oh, God."

"I know. Now he's living with that blonde girl . . . American and rich . . . she adores him." She laughed, ruefully. "Well, he told me I was only a businesswoman, that I ought to be running a boutique or something and I didn't walk out on *him*, did I?"

"What you're saying is you took his advice but he didn't take yours?"

"When I got the job with Joe Dancy I realized that Jimmy Bolton was right. I am a sort of organizer. I am a sort of businesswoman. The business I know is acting, plays, *show* business. I saved my two thousand pounds in my years with Joe Dancy and here I am."

"Before that?" Josh asked. "Before, what?"

"Oh, the usual. Girls' school. The Central School. Then acting. Then this."

"Any other actors in the family?"

"I had an uncle, a stand-up comic, years ago. Harry Viner. He called himself the King of Kosher Comedy. Comedy with a K. My grandfather ran a music hall. That's all. You?"

"My mother was an actress, a rather good one. My father was a solid kind of actor. They ran a rep, went broke, never made any money but they lived in a better time, for actors. B.T. Before Television. My old man played a lot of Shakespeare. So did my mother. They had a crack at the best and the worst. They were pros. I suppose it was inevitable I got into the business at some level."

"I don't think"—Jill's eyes were shining and the gold fleck in them was very distinct—"that you have the slightest idea of how good you really are."

"Nonsense," said Josh. "But I do want to do this play."

The man with iron-gray hair suddenly got up from the corner, and sat down at the table. He wore a leather bomber jacket and baggy blue trousers. "Please don't be surprised. I am Vercek."

Josh said, incredulously, "You've been here all the time?"

"Yes. Of course."

"But why on earth—?"

"My apologies. It was necessary." Vercek raised a hand. Josh saw with surprise that two fingers were missing. "Kristos. Can we have for three please?"

"But of course, Boris. Coming at once, my frien'."

Kristos beamed. He called to his wife in Greek and crossed to them, carrying a new carafe of retsina. "I bring drink." He made room and sat down at the table, pouring retsina into everybody's glass. "You like Vercek's play, no? It is very fine play, you think?"

Jill said, "We both think it is a marvelous play. Don't we, Josh?"

"We want to talk to Vercek about it. I'm not sure if we have time to stay to lunch."

Kristos looked offended, murderous even. "The moussaka is the best in London—"

Jill interrupted, laying a hand on Kristos's hairy forearm. "We will be delighted, Kristos. Thank you."

Kristos beamed at her again; the wife of Kristos slammed the cash register unnecessarily again, and Kristos rose with a sigh. "I fix the food, hokay, excuse me, please."

Josh turned to Vercek, who was lighting a half-smoked cigarette. His maimed hand was brown with nicotine stains. His eyes were an electric blue, and he rarely blinked them. He looked to be about forty-five, but he could have been older. The stance of the man, Josh thought, using his director's knowledge of posture: he's watchful, he's wary, he's very scared of something.

"This play," he asked. "It is yours? You did write it?"

Vercek nodded. "Yes. I wrote it, Mr. Williams." He turned suddenly to Jill. "May I ask—"

Josh said quickly, "I'm sorry. This is Jill Viner. She's my associate."

"Oh yes. I see. You too work at the National Theatre, no?"

Jill shook her head. "No, I'm an independent producer. I want to put your play on in the West End."

Vercek looked puzzled. "But I sent this play to Mr. Williams, at the National Theatre."

"I've left the National. Both Jill—Miss Viner—and myself think your play is very good indeed and—"

"You have left the National?" Vercek asked. "Why?"

Good God, he's paranoid, Josh thought.

"I like your play and the National doesn't."

Vercek drew on his cigarette. "They don't like it, why is this?"

"They don't like the idea of H.M.Queen in a play."

"H.M. Queen? I'm sorry?"

"We sometimes call her that, H.M. Queen. Like that."

Vercek shook his head at the English way of doing anything. "For this reason they say no? I don't think so. I think there are other reasons maybe."

"If there are," Josh said, patiently, "they didn't tell them to me."

"Ah, but they wouldn't, would they?"

"Who wouldn't?"

"The apparatchiks. The politicians. The people who run it."

"They may be apparatchiks—well, one or two of them—but they aren't politicians, anything but."

The maimed hand drummed the table. The voice was low but insistent.

"Oh, yes. I think so. This is a political play. That is why they don't want it. If it was about a Tory prime minister, and the Tory

58

prime minister was portrayed as a lecher and an unworthy and corrupt person, I think maybe they would not worry so much, yes?"

"Yes," said Josh. "I mean no. I mean you're probably right. There's a liberal establishment, certainly; it's gone left-wing over the years, I grant you. But it isn't political in the correct sense of the word *political—*"

"Oh yes, it is." Vercek's electric blue eyes stared. The voice was lower still. "Everything is political, Mr. Williams. My play is about this, surely. My play is saying that in the process of Finlandization nothing is too small, nothing. No trivial works committee. No trade-union branch, however small. Nobody in the media, from a malcontent in the cutting room to a dissatisfied top producer. Nobody in the arts. Nobody in the public eye at any level. Nobody, of course, in the government or the opposition. Or in business or industry at any level." The blue eyes blinked. "Thousands of their brightest people are engaged in this task, thousands. Sometimes they are natives of the selected Finland. Sometimes they are not. Then there are the hosts of others, the supporters, the sympathizers. These people are rarely party members. They are very often middle-class young people in revolt against their parents or simply against life, which they think can be safe and perfect once they are in control. These people simply assist the seduction process because they know no better; they are softheaded, well-meaning tools." He sighed. "It is all part of a grand design. My dear friends, do you think the theatre is not included in this grand design? The theatre that puts on plays many thousands of people will see, not as many as teleyision or the cinema maybe, but people who are influential persons, opinion makers, people who can assist, at whatever remove, in the process of Finlandization? Of slowly taking over not only a nation's institutions but her attitudes? Of slowly, by propaganda at every level, making that nation unready to defend itself? Making sure that nation will fall like a ripe plum because it does not believe any longer in itself or its institutions? Or anyway, not enough to defend them, in words or deeds. So that when the final offer comes, after many trade pacts and two-way industrial deals, however small, when the question is, Finlandization or war, what do they say? What do *you* say, Mr. Williams?"

The maimed hand tapped the manila envelope containing *The Queen of Finland.*

"You say, Please come in, we don't want trouble. Please be our friends. You say please, Mr. Williams."

The maimed hand went rat-tat-tat. The slightly accented voice was almost inaudible. "I have seen it happen. I have written the play so that it will not happen here."

There was a long silence at the table.

Jill broke it.

"We both love the play, Mr. Vercek. We believe in it. That's why we want to put it on. We want to buy an option on it for two hundred pounds for six months."

"Two hundred pounds? All right. The money does not matter." Vercek lit a new cigarette from the end of the old one. "How soon will it be on? When can people see it?"

"Probably in September. That's what we are aiming for—"

Josh cut in. "It's only fair to say we might not get it off the ground."

Vercek's eyes turned to him. "Why would that be? Are there people who will stop it?"

"No. I'm sure there aren't. Why should anybody want to stop it? Of course, some critics and others may not like the queen being portrayed on stage, even if it is in the future."

Vercek made an impatient gesture with the hand. "You like it and you want to do it?"

"Yes. We both do."

"You will let me know when?"

"Of course," Jill said, looking quickly at Josh. "Look, we have to have something on paper."

Vercek stiffened. "On paper, why? Why on paper?"

"A business agreement; a letter setting out terms, royalties, that sort of thing." She smiled, but the charm did not seem to register with Vercek. "It's usual, Mr. Vercek."

"Send the letter here then, and I will sign it."

"Do you want to use an agent? It might be wise from your own point of view."

"No, I understand enough. I was once in the theatre in my own country."

"I had heard of your work but never read any," Josh said. "Some of the scenes, they have such knowledge."

"The theatre in England is not a serious place," said Vercek. "It is a social occasion, for people to dress up and look at one another's clothes and flirt. But it is all I have in these sad days."

"We must meet again soon," Josh said. "I have a lot of things I'd like to discuss." He added, not knowing quite why, "The original manuscript is marked in red ink—"

"Not ink," said Vercek, in a low voice only Josh could hear. "Blood." Josh stared at him. "I carried it out, many hours, many miles."

At that moment Kristos arrived, with the moussaka. The wife of Kristos busied herself laying the table, but desisted when Vercek stood up, abruptly. He bowed to them all and said stiffly, "I apologize, I must go. I have an appointment. We will meet soon, I know, good-bye." He looked from Jill to Josh and back again, with his electric blue eyes, and said softly, "My friends."

Then he crossed to the door and was gone into the noisy Saturday street.

"What did he say?" Jill asked, low.

Josh shook his head.

It was Kristos who answered.

"Vercek is a very strange one. But a good man, a very good man. He likes you. I can see this. I have known him long time now and I know. Enjoy your moussaka, best in London, I promise."

As they ate, Jill said to Josh, "Do you think it had anything to do with his hand? I mean, eating with us and so on?"

"I don't know," Josh said. "He had two fingers missing on the other hand as well." Jill stared at him, and Josh had one of those feelings of unease that only came to him once every ten years, as on the night Alison died (he had felt it would happen that night, somehow he had known) and the night they came into his bedroom at school and told him about his mother. "I hope," he said, "we're doing the right thing by him. He seems pretty paranoid. He could be a lot of trouble."

"This moussaka looks very good," Jill said. "I suggest we eat it."

They did, and it was.

But they didn't talk much during the meal.

SITTING in the Edwardian Room, Josh Williams looked up to see Jill Viner standing in front of him. She didn't look as if she had flown seven thousand miles in one day and then three thousand the next, with some very important negotiating crammed in between.

She looked healthy and vital and rather radiant.

Jill kissed him on the cheek and said, "Hello, Josh darling, do they serve booze in here? I need a large drink." She sat down and took his hand in hers. Her eyes shone. "Josh, my love, I do really and truly believe we are on the way!"

Josh had a foolish impulse to kiss her on those full lips. He resisted the impulse, sternly. None of that.

He could not help wondering what her reaction would have been if he had.

MAGGIE met them at the door of her apartment on West Tenth Street.

It was a pleasant, unpretentious place in perfect taste, full of Colonial furniture and pieces from the time of the republic's innocence. It was puritan and spare and polished, and it gave off an air of elegance and tradition. In that, it was, Jill thought, exactly like Maggie herself. Vassar and the Yale School of Drama and stage productions off and then on Broadway, each one a step up from the last and not a single one of them anything less than a star vehicle. Maggie was a star from the start. The wonderful bone structure (she would be a beauty until she was sixty) the ash-blonde hair, the pale, ever-so-slightly-almond-shaped eyes, trim, slim figure, long hands and neck: all this made her a thoroughbred, a woman fit to be a queen.

She was so right that Jill almost stopped breathing.

Maggie even had a maid, and the tea was excellent. "English

people always complain about our tea." Maggie smiled, and it was the most royal smile in the world. It was superior but only because Maggie was superior, there was kindness in it. "So I got a real teapot at Harrods the last time I was in London and I learned how to make it properly. Warm the pot, a spoonful for every person and one extra, boiling water and a woollen cozy over the pot, and let it stand for four minutes." She smiled again. "This is Earl Grey. I hope Ellie has got it right; we rehearsed it this morning!" The smile was very sure, Jill thought; the tea will be marvelous: and of course it was. They ate some scones with it, and Maggie complained gently that it was impossible to obtain English cakes and bread in Manhattan. Marie Antoinette, Jill thought, remembering the bleak ghettos of the city. Let them eat cake. She smiled in pure joy and then saw Josh's warning look and straightened her face.

They talked about the play Josh had seen the night before and about Josh's production of *Time and the Conways* that Maggie had seen at the National. The maid cleared the teacups away, and Maggie smoothed her pale gray dress and said, "It's a wonderful play, *The Queen*. I like it very much."

"It's a great part for somebody." Josh knew how to talk to his actors, Jill thought, so easy and relaxed, no pressure. "It's the title role, and in a good theatre it could have a long run. Or anyway long enough to make a little money for the backers." Josh lit one of his cigars, asking permission with a lifted eyebrow. "It's a long role, and not easy. It's never easy to play royalty. It's so difficult to be human size. Unless, of course, like Mary Queen of Scots you're executed. Then there's a condemned cell scene and a scaffold scene. Sorry we can't offer you one of those."

Maggie raised her large limpid eyes. "It's still a tragedy, I think. This lady, once ruling over a great empire, reduced to meeting with peasants, peasants who have her in their power. That's tragic."

"Of course she has a choice," Josh mused. "The American

president is offering her assistance. He's even prepared to go to war for her. Perhaps."

Maggie shook her lovely head. "She knows her people don't want war over anything. Even the threat of war. All they want is peace and quiet. At any price. For herself, this woman would fight, she would die, she is the last of a long proud line. Wonderful part." Maggie hesitated. "I don't know if I can take it."

Jill and Josh stared at her, stunned.

Josh was the first to recover. "Is there something about the part that worries you?"

Maggie looked at her long slender hands. There were no rings. "In that connection, I do have a worry, yes."

"What is it?" Josh asked, his voice genuinely sympathetic.

"The queen, playing a real queen. That worries me."

"It's ten years in the future," said Josh. "I don't think the audiences or the critics are going to make contemporary references—"

"Yes, but it *is* the queen, isn't it?"

There was a moment's silence. Josh said, "Yes. Of course. That's the great selling point of the play. Of course, we'll be asking you to take the blonde hair down a little and to look—well—older. But we don't ask for realism. We don't want a portrait. Nobody expects you to offer any kind of mimicry."

Jill said, "*The Queen of Finland* is a fictional situation. If we said it was anything else, I expect we would be carted off to the Tower!"

They all laughed, and then Maggie looked serious and inspected her hands again. Josh asked, "Did you have any other worries?"

She shook her head. "About the play, no. Of course, all kinds of problems are bound to crop up, as they do in any production. No. It's . . . not the play that worries me."

Jill and Josh looked at each other, perplexed. The muted

sounds of traffic percolated into the room. They waited, and as they waited a sudden knocking came from the ceiling above their heads. The effect on Maggie was dramatic. She stood up, held her hands in front of her, very tightly, to stop them from trembling, and said, "I have a friend upstairs. He's very ill. Would you excuse me a moment?"

Josh said, "Of course. Please go to him. We can wait. No hurry at all. Is there anything we can do?"

Maggie smiled quickly. "No, I don't think so. Just excuse me for a moment, will you?" She left the room and in the silence Josh half whispered, "Does any of this mean anything to you?"

"Nothing." Jill had looked up Maggie's file in the *Daily Mail* morgue in Fleet Street, courtesy of a friend. It had been a roll call of luck and riches. Well born, talented, beautiful, winner of Emmys and Oscars, a catalogue of success, achieved without, apparently, sweat or strain.

From upstairs came the mumble of voices, Maggie's low and soft, and another, a man's, high and, it seemed to Jill, possibly strident. They could not easily distinguish the words. Josh moved around the room, inspecting the objets d'art. Plainly, he did not think it proper to listen to other people's conversations even when they were of commercial or artistic interest to him. In that, Jill thought, he was very English. She tried unashamedly to listen, but Josh mumbled about the pieces in the room (a Colonial chess set, a long clay pipe, a Confederate cap-badge) and so made it impossible for her to hear anything.

After a few minutes, Maggie came downstairs again. She seemed even paler than before, and she had a look of icy determination on her face. "I'm so sorry. Philip isn't at all well. I don't think I should be away from him for too long."

Josh put down one of the chessmen. "No, of course not. We quite understand."

Like hell we do, Jill thought. We haven't come nine thousand miles to leave with a maybe. "Maggie, why don't you tell us exactly what the problem is? Then we can face it, and see if we can solve it. Together." Maggie looked at her, surprised, but said nothing in reply. Jill pressed on. "You've said you want to do this part, and we all know it would be wonderful for you, and you for it. So, please, tell us the problem—"

Jill got no further, for the door of the room was flung open and an apparition stood there: a very thin, middle-aged man, with a blue wool dressing gown thrown over his pajamas. The pallor of desperate illness waxed his features, and his eyes were deep and dull in their sockets. He had been handsome, Jill thought; he had been a big man, but now his bones shone through his skin. Poor man. Poor, poor man. We talk downstairs while you lie above, looking like this. She said, in a low voice, "Maggie, I'm sorry, we'll go." She stood.

"Indeed you will not." The man's voice was deep and strong. He moved to the nearest chair and sat down. He took deep breaths, slowly, and they all stood and watched him, especially Maggie, whose eyes never left his face. Poor man, poor Maggie, Jill thought.

"I didn't come downstairs, first time in two months, to find I don't have an audience."

Maggie crossed the room and stood behind him, her long hands on his shoulders. "This is Philip. As you see, he's ill. He shouldn't be downstairs. Philip, I think you should—"

Philip said, "Shut up, Maggie." He leaned forward with a great effort, and said slowly, "She liked the play. I've told her to do it."

"I can't do it, darling." Maggie looked away. "It opens in London in—whenever. . . ."

"We were hoping September," said Jill.

"September. There's no possibility. I have to be here with you. You know that."

"If I'm here in September." Philip's tone was dispassionate. "There's no guarantee of that, is there? It's four months away."

"Philip, please don't talk like that, darling." Maggie looked ready to cry. So much for the ice queen, Jill thought. She's not cold or even cool; she's on fire.

"Maggie darling, would you get my pills? They're on the side table."

Maggie was out of the room like somebody possessed.

Philip smiled tiredly. "You see? It's no use to her, all this. Now, I want her to do this play. I want her to get away from me. I'm going to die anyway, and I don't want her here when I do. She's a very lovely girl and I don't want her to go through all that. She's nursed me for four months as it is."

"The problem?" Josh asked.

"Cancer, of course." Philip indicated a decanter on the sideboard. "About a finger of brandy would help. If you would?"

Josh poured it very quickly and handed it to Philip. He sipped it gratefully. "First I've tasted for six months. They take you right off it. Gets in the way of the medication." He grimaced, whether in pain or at the taste of the alcohol they could not tell. "I plan to go out on about half a pint of this stuff one day, but don't tell Maggie I said so."

Maggie came back downstairs at that moment, with a bottle of pills and a glass of water, on a tray. That's regal, Jill thought, she even found time for a tray. Maggie said, "Darling, I don't think alcohol is a very good idea, do you?"

"Yes, I think it's a helluva good idea." Philip crossed one leg over the other, exposing a painfully thin shank. "I should do it more often. Look, Maggie, I don't have a lot of breath, so I'm not going to waste any. This is a hell of a part, in a hell of a play, and I'm not having you turn it down for any reason on God's earth and that includes me."

Tears were in Maggie's lovely eyes now, and she was shaking, ever so slightly, from head to foot. Jill crossed to her, and put her arms round Maggie's shoulders. Josh said, "I think we can talk to Maggie about this another day, when it'll be easier for everybody."

What day, for Jesus' sake, Jill almost screamed. We fly back tomorrow, and we have to go back with an answer, a yes answer, or we have no play! We're back to leafing through *Spotlight* and ringing agents who don't know us, enquiring about the availability of actresses who would be absolutely wrong for the queen. The queen is sitting right here in this room with tears in her eyes. We are not leaving until she says no in a very loud voice, a scream at least. Jill said, "Maggie, Philip seems very impressed with the play. . . ."

Philip said, "I am. So impressed I even drew a set." He tugged a sheaf of papers from the pocket of his dressing gown. "I used to be a stage designer. Gave it up and went into movies. I was a fool. I did a lot of stupid things. You see that, in the end. Anyway, it impressed me enough to take a pencil and sketch out a design." He pushed the drawings at Josh. "There you are, no charge. I think you should go for a futuristic look, because it is the future. You'll need a dais, as the author says. . . ." Philip coughed, and fought for breath for a moment, waving the hovering Maggie away. ". . . And I think the queen should wear a tiara throughout, a full crown would be too much. I've done another little sketch there, on the other piece of paper. . . . I think you've no option but to use backdrops—windows or anything would be wrong. . . . I'm sure Buckingham Palace is full of heavy paintings and tapestry and all that but it would look fustian and wrong. . . . Anyway, that's what I think. . . ."

He fell silent and sipped his brandy, looking at Josh. There were two bright spots of color on his waxen cheeks now, and his eyes had a little flickering life in them. Josh took the papers gingerly, and looked at them for a long minute. They were well and skillfully done; Jill took that much in with a quick glance. She willed Josh to answer the way she would have answered, but she was beginning to know him well enough to realize that he was extremely stubborn and extremely truthful in a profession where neither quality was generally thought to be of use. Josh looked up, finally. "These are very good."

Jill closed her eyes in pure relief.

Maggie smiled warily and sat down.

Philip tried a gallant smile. "Only reason I came down, to hear you say that. Give our guests a drink, Maggie, and I'll have another very small brandy."

"Do you think you should, darling?"

"Well, of course I think I should or I wouldn't ask for it, now would I?" But he was smiling to take the sting out of his words, and Maggie took his glass and poured a little brandy into it. Philip sipped it, and talked technicalities with Josh, who seemed genuinely interested in what he had to say. They talked about eyelines and materials and the possibility of a moving dais. "Easy to pack; one set really, but you re-dress it when you change the scene to 10 Downing Street, or the White House or the Kremlin," Philip explained. "All that, of course, before the big second act when you're stuck with the queen in the throne room for the rest of the play. . . ."

And Josh said, "Of course I'll hand these notes on to whoever we get to design. I think they're damn good, I really do."

As they continued to talk Maggie gave Jill a martini and Josh a Scotch and had nothing herself. She had eaten no scones either. Her figure was as it was because she looked after it, or more probably, because she had no need of the reassurances others needed: food, alcohol, affection.

No. Not affection. Yet, did she need affection? She needed to give it, that was obvious. Was it possible that Maggie had received affection in plenty, all her life, a surfeit of it, because of her looks, her mind, her talent, and now she needed it no longer? Certainly she was unlike any other actress Jill had met. She was modest, Jill thought, because she did not need to be anything else and never had.

"I'm sorry," Jill whispered. "Is Philip going to be all right being up so long?"

"I don't know," Maggie answered. "But he's happy. I haven't seen him look like this for a long time."

"Have you been together long?"

"Four years."

70

"I was with a man four years. We split up." Jill wondered why she said that.

"Oh how awful." Maggie shook her head. "I didn't know how much I loved and needed Philip until he fell ill. I just feel I have to stay with him."

"Of course." Jill nodded. She knows that isn't what Philip wants. Why does she have to deny him? Then she felt bad for thinking that, and looked pointedly at her watch. "Look, I think we should go. We have things to do and we've stayed too long."

There was a silence. Philip broke it. "You'll be talking to the William Morris Agency then, and fixing the contract?"

Josh looked at Maggie. "Nothing would give me greater pleasure, but . . ."

Maggie said, quietly, "Philip, if you think I'm going to leave you alone in this place while I go away across the Atlantic to work, you don't know me. . . ."

Philip held up his hand, wearily. "I do know you, Maggie. I know you want to do this play more than anything in the world. Which is why I'm saying what I'm saying. You go to London and do it. I'll be here when you come back. And I'll have lots of friends in, and I have a nurse, you know, and I honestly don't want you around me, darling, not at the end. Now will you please say yes to these nice people and let me go upstairs, where I can lie down with an easy conscience about the whole thing?"

Maggie wailed, "Oh, darling, I can't, I can't, I can't!"

The total disintegration of the woman shocked them all.

"Of course you can't. We understand," said Josh.

Jill cried, "No, Philip, it's no good. Look at her!"

Philip interrupted. "It is good; it's the only good thing that'll happen to her this year! She has to have something to hold on to when I go, and this play is it, I know it is." He took a deep and terrible breath and stood up. "Miss Viner and Mr. Williams, Maggie's answer is yes. Talk to her agents, do a deal. She'll see you in London on the first day of rehearsals." He extended his hand and

Josh shook it. Jill kissed him, on the cheek. He smiled tiredly and said, "That was nice. Good-bye. It was good to meet you. If you use the design give me a tiny credit. I'd like to be attached to the project, however humbly." At the door he nodded, and closed it. They could hear him walking very slowly up the stairs.

Tears were streaming down Maggie's cheeks now. She slumped in the chair and stared at nothing.

Josh put his hand on her shoulder. "We'll understand if you don't want to do it."

Jill kissed Maggie's unresponsive cheek. "Maggie, you have to do it. You can't go against the man's wish, can you?" As she said this, Jill felt Josh's thoughtful eye upon her. He was very clever. He was letting her do the hard-selling; he was preserving his own goodwill with the actress. He would probably be working with her in the future and he wanted no awkward memories. Jill said, "You don't have any choice, do you, Maggie?"

After a very long silence, Maggie said in a whisper, "No, you're right, I don't."

They let themselves out very quietly, as if in the presence of death, which, Jill thought, of course they were. In the taxi back to the Plaza, Josh did not talk to her once. When she looked at him, there was a solitary tear running down his cheek. She wanted to kiss him very much at that moment, but she didn't. She wondered how he would have reacted if she had.

From her suite, she telephoned Maggie's agent at the William Morris office. He was glad to hear she was ready to work again, but surprised that she wanted to do a play. The agency had been tempting her now and again with plum parts in movies but not too hard because they knew her delicate personal circumstances. They would talk to her and be back to Jill. They took note of the terms offered—five percent of the box office plus a thousand dollars a week, run-of-the-play contract terminable by either side after six months' option both ways for a Broadway transfer—and awaited a formal offer by letter. They noted Jill would fly back to London the following morning and they could contact her in her Shaftesbury Avenue office from noon onward. The agent looking after Maggie at the Morris office was impressed by Jill. When he heard Austin Ames was all but finalized and that Manny Hiberson had accepted the same terms, he laughed and said, "Miss Viner, that's a play I wouldn't mind a piece of myself."

But he knew, and she knew, that with a stage play nothing was final until the final curtain on the first night, and not even then. Still, it wasn't every day an unknown London producer, and a woman at that, did a deal her way with Manny Hiberson.

Jill put the telephone down and turned to Josh. He was sitting looking out the window, over the city. Josh was a thinker, a man who felt emotion for people. His job taught him to wear other people's shoes, and feel their feelings, and the meeting with Maggie and Philip had obviously affected him. For herself, Jill had learned only to consider other people's feelings inasmuch as they influenced events. In business—and producing a stage play was business—sentiment could be a crippler. Joe Dancy was a sentimental man and she had seen him give parts to the wrong actors—or actresses, usually actresses—because of it, excusing it all by saying, "It's not an important part. Anybody can do it."

Every part was important. Every actor was important. Everything mattered, and it was nonsense to pretend it didn't. Jill had the uneasy feeling that the reason she had to keep telling herself that was because under it all she was a very sentimental person. She would never have considered being an actress herself if she hadn't been.

"Hey!" she called. "They're surprised about Maggie taking the part."

"I'd be surprised if they weren't surprised. I'm astonished."

"Are you, are you really?"

"Of course I am. Do you know what the odds are against getting those two? So long you couldn't put them on paper."

"You'll be able to work with her?"

73

"I've worked with the best at the National. Joan, Vanessa, Irene, Peggy. If I could handle them, I can handle her. Anyway, we liked each other, and that's all that matters. We have to like each other, in an animal way, or it's all cerebral and it goes cold. I'm not worried about Maggie. The person I am worried about is Austin Ames."

"Why?"

"He's a method actor; he's done the Actors' Studio bit. He's the kind of actor who needs a reason for everything; it's the full Freudian treatment for every text. Or so I hear. We don't do a lot of that at the National. I suppose it's Larry's influence hanging on from his time there. Larry thinks an actor should put on the frock and say the lines. That's the English way. We're too reserved to tear ourselves to pieces off the stage, although we don't mind doing it on, Larry more than anybody. Look at his Moor. Incredible. His Richard Three. Absolutely strip-off stuff. But the discussion bit isn't us, isn't me. I'm not used to it, and I must say I'm a bit worried about Austin Ames, yes."

"Have you seen his movie, the Oscar winner, *The Last Good-bye?*"

Josh shook his head. Theatre people never went to the movies. Jill riffled through the pages of *The New York Times*. "We can see it just across the street."

"We ought to be seeing some stage stuff really."

"No, we shouldn't. What can you learn there?"

"I suppose you're right." Josh seemed hesitant. She could not think why. "All right then. Let's go, we can eat later."

JILL found *Good-bye* a tear-jerker done with immense style and brio. Maggie as the wife who dies, and Austin as the man left alone, were the whole thing. It was a cheap movie, done with two famous stage actors, about a wife dying, and it had swept the United States. Twenty million gross, all very simply and beautifully acted, movie-size, the gestures small, the emotions held in. Jill thought, sitting in the darkness of the theatre, Those two are going to be just great when they can let themselves go in *Queen*. A thrill of delight went through her, and she reached out, before she knew it, and touched Josh's hand. He turned to her, and she saw that there were tears in his eyes.

"Sorry," Josh said harshly. "This is why I wasn't keen." He blew his nose. "I knew the story. I'd read the reviews; I thought this might happen. I'm a bloody fool, sorry."

No, she thought, you're not the bloody fool, I am.

He still loves Alison, or anyway the memory of her. Well, of course he would. He's that kind of man. Jill felt a pang of what she could only identify as jealousy, and concentrated on the image of Austin and Maggie on the screen. Maggie was closing her eyes for the last time. She looked very beautiful. She would probably look something like that, Jill thought, when she actually did die. Her rightness for *Queen* was an incredible piece of good luck. Now only British Actors' Equity had to be convinced she was essential for the role. It was the hurdle Jill would have to take sooner or later, but she resolved later, when the casting was complete and had, overall, a British look to it.

The lights went up on Austin Ames walking away from the funeral, and they left the movie theatre to find the lights on in the city and the streets alive with theatregoers and traffic. They walked, and talked. Josh said, "It was a very good movie. Most movies are good. They can hardly be anything else, all those new images hitting the eye every few seconds. The only thing that stops movies wiping everybody else off the board—the stage particu-larly—is the fact that ninety-nine percent of their stories are crass and the whole industry's chasing the box office. It has to, no option. But that movie was uncommercial; it was about death. It could have been a stage play, it was so well written. As Jerome Kern used to say, there's a lot of money in being uncommercial." He added, "I'm glad I saw it. It'll help me with them both."

They walked back to the hotel.

"I don't want to eat dinner," she said. "I think I'll have a snack in my room. Join me?"

Josh hesitated, then smiled. "A club sandwich and a beer and eight hours' sleep. That sounds like heaven."

The club sandwiches were succulent and the Heineken was ice-cold. They ate with appetite, and with a sense of celebration. Josh visibly relaxed, and lit one of his cigars. Jill was recognizing that as a sure sign of contentment in him. Obviously, he was trying to cut down. Just as obviously, he was only half succeeding. He looked good in his lightweight gray Daks suit and cream shirt—very English, and much more in character than he did in denim, she thought. Anybody over forty in denim looked as if they were playing a part. The part of somebody younger than they really were. It was like combing your hair forward, which Josh, having a good forehead, had the good sense not to do; it deceived nobody. He's lived a lot of his life, she thought. He knows things I don't know yet; he's more cautious, but he's still brave enough to throw up his job at the National because he believes in *Queen*. There was steel somewhere; there had to be.

"Who are we going to cast"—Josh blew out a cloud of smoke—"as the prime minister?"

"I told Austin Sir Harry," Jill said coolly.

"You did *what?*"

That made him sit up and take notice, Jill thought.

"I told Austin Sir Harry. I didn't say he was sure."

"Thank God for that. We'll never get him."

"Why do you say that?"

Josh took a deep breath. "Because he's always booked up months ahead. And because he only does leads and the prime minister isn't a lead. It's a good supporting part, very flashy, and he'd be wonderful, I agree, but no chance."

"Never mind that. Tell me why you think he's right," Jill asked. "He's a great name to have on the marquee, one of the biggest English names. He'd bring his own following, which is considerable; he always does. How old is he?"

"Nobody knows, not even himself!" Josh laughed. "The greatest Shylock of our time. Possibly of all time. The best Malvolio. Probably the best Iago in living memory, a wonderful poetic Shakespearian." Josh pondered. "In *The Queen of Finland* the prime minister's a high Tory, one of the few left by that time, and he'd be marvelous. I can almost hear him. But it isn't a lead and he always plays leads."

"I enquired around, before I left London," Jill said. "The old boy isn't sure he wants to do the big ones anymore. He's in need of money, as always, and at this very moment he's in the heart of the Sahara Desert, in an Arab epic, playing an English consul, the script written by the producer, who happens to be an Italian. After that, *Queen* would seem like an oasis in the Sahara, wouldn't it?"

"Yes, I know he has a high life-style; he has a big house somewhere in Dorset. But I can't see what we can offer him."

"We can offer him what we offer Maggie and Austin. Same deal."

Josh shook his head. "That's a lot of money gone already and you still have the Russian to cast."

"Who," she asked, "do you think for the Russian?"

"He has to be a bear, he has to be a puritan, a professional, a realist, and yet he has sincerely to believe in two things. Power first; then, second, that *his* system is better than the one out there." Josh got to his feet and looked out at the blaze of New York. "It's not an unplayable part but there's no sympathy in it, because the author has come to hate everything the Russian stands for, and only a great character actor could get near it, and nobody I can think of *would* do it, because it's unsympathetic and all actors, I mean *all* actors, hate unsympathetic parts. . . ." Josh shook his head. "There's nobody obvious. We'll find somebody of course, and spend most of rehearsal telling him not to worry about the audience hating him."

"You'd settle for that?" Jill was disappointed.

77

"I'm not settling for anything, love. I just happen to have cast plays, some of them quite important ones, a few times before." Josh was being defensive and superior. The tone was to remind her that she was only the producer, only a girl who ten minutes ago answered the telephone in Joe Dancy's office. Jill was nettled but she said nothing. Josh went on. "There are a lot of actors who could *play* it, as they say. We might find a good central European emigré actor although they're in short supply and getting older these days. I don't know, there'll be somebody."

"It's a very important part," Jill said, flatly. "The Russian has all the cards. Finlandization has worked, he's in charge of events, it's his moment of triumph. He doesn't come in until the play's half over, but after that it's his play almost as much as it's the queen's." Jill allowed her voice to turn cool. "And you think there'll be somebody?"

Josh laughed outright. "Don't be so bloody intense, Jill." At least he wasn't calling her "love" anymore. "You've just landed Maggie and Austin, although how you're going to get British Equity to agree to Maggie, I don't know."

"They'll agree if we have Sir Harry as the prime minister."

"It would help, certainly, but I don't know if it'll be enough."

"Look, this nonsense of American Equity and British Equity at each other's throats has to stop sometime. If a play like *Queen* is put on on Shaftesbury Avenue *and* Broadway, I can't see how either of the actors' associations—British or American—can object!"

"They will, just the same. They'll take a lot of convincing, Jill."

Josh's tone was mild. She was too vehement, Jill knew. It scared most men off her. It had scared Jimmy off her, and Jimmy wasn't easily scared. Moderate it a bit, she told herself, don't scare this man. There's really no need for that. All this is is a business relationship; keep it cool.

Josh was saying, "Anyway, if you have any bright ideas for the Russian, tell me, I'd love to hear them."

Jill remembered Joe Dancy. Always keep something back.

Even from your director? Even from Josh?

Even from him.

"Let me surprise you." She smiled, and stood up. "I'm bushed. And it's midnight."

Josh was on his feet in an instant. "Good Lord yes. Here I am, chattering on, and you've done the round trip." He picked up his morocco-bound copy of *Queen*, which never seemed to be out of his hand. "I'll let myself drift off, reading the Russian part again."

"Don't," Jill said. "Get your rest. You're going to need it."

It was quite dark in the room now and Jill felt him come toward her, and she welcomed it and closed her eyes and thought, You fool, always hold something back and you do this, you let the bloody biology take over, it's nonsense . . . and then his lips brushed her cheek quite softly, and he said, very quietly, " 'Night, Jill darling. Sleep tight. See you in the morning, love," and he was gone quickly out of the room.

Jill stood in the darkening gloom quite a long time, wondering at herself. Then she switched on the light and went into the bathroom. She ran the bath and took off her clothes and looked at her breasts and legs in the mirror and thought, Am I that unattractive? And laughed at herself for the thought. Then she searched in her bag for aspirin—she had a sudden feeling of tension—and her fingers touched the packet of contraceptive pills.

Jill laughed. What a fool she was.

In the next room, Josh heard the laugh. He thought, What a bloody fool I am.

MAGGIE sat at his bedside and looked up at Philip in astonishment.

"You *did* that, you got all the film clips together without my knowing anything about it?"

"It wasn't difficult." Philip shifted around in the bed. "I sent

79

Marge over to Jack Lewis at CBS. He clipped it all together for me, for old times' sake." Marge was the night nurse.

Maggie knew he was in pain, but it wasn't time for his pills. Not for another hour. She would have suggested he take them now but she knew he hated them. They made him feel dopey, and he usually fell into a drugged sleep soon after he had swallowed them. Ah dear God, Maggie thought, what have I done to deserve this? How am I going to live without him? What will I do when he's gone?

"Come on, put the cassette in the machine, woman, and let's see what Jack Lewis was able to find."

Maggie took the cassette and fitted it into the recorder, but she didn't switch it on yet. Is it because, until I met Philip, I had everything too easy? Am I paying for that now, she wondered. Am I about to embark on another success, *The Queen of Finland*, made easy for me by Philip? Will it be another triumph for Maggie Stride, bought at the price of a man's loneliness in his last hours? Of course, the doctors said he might not last that long. September was still some months away. But if she could keep him alive until Christmas, surely that would be something. Surely that would expiate her previous golden fortune, her unceasing tempting of the fates.

"Are you going to play the thing or not?" Philip's voice was edgy. He was in great pain now, she knew.

"Why not have a pill, darling? I know it's a little early, but—"

"It's an hour early, Maggie. Exactly one hour early."

"Oh, my darling dearest." She sat on the bed and took his head in her hands. He stiffened. He did not like her to get emotional; it didn't help him. Yet his pain tore at her. She willed herself to feel it with him, to halve it, but she knew it was a fancy, a stupid actress's fancy. The crab was tearing at his lungs, not hers. Christ, what could she do, what? "Why not break the rule for once, darling? Have the pill now and we'll watch the clips together. It can't be very long, can it? There can't be a whole lot of material on file."

Philip hesitated, grimaced, and reached over and took a pill from the box. "Jack Lewis says he has hours and hours of material, going back years. They kept it all. You know how the American public is about royalty. So he's spliced a representative group of stuff together and put it on tape for us. He says it runs the whole tape, an hour exactly." Philip swallowed the pill and took a sip of water. "Put it on, Maggie. I don't want to fall asleep while it's running, do I?"

"No, of course not, darling." She switched on the machine. "I've been thinking since we saw those people. I really shouldn't do this. Leave you. I shouldn't do anything until—"

"Until I'm dead?"

Maggie was shocked. They never used the word. They pretended, like two children playing house, that nothing could touch them, but of course it could. It could and it would.

"You know that wasn't what I meant."

"Maggie, you know my feelings. You've said yes, and you're not going back on it because I'm not going to let you go back on it. Now watch the nice film clips Jack Lewis labored on, at CBS's expense, to put together for you."

Philip propped his pillows behind him, refusing her move to do it for him. The pain was ebbing a little, she knew. The pills were very strong; they acted quickly. There was nothing faster or heavier, the doctors had said, unemotionally, this side of almost total unconsciousness, which, in the end, would have to come, naturally.

Philip reproved her. "Watch the lady. You're going to be *her*, after all."

"Well, not exactly her, am I? I mean, it's a performance. It won't be an absolute copy; I couldn't do that." She saw he was grinning. It was his old grin, from before, just there on his face for a moment. Tears came to her eyes, and she turned her head away from him toward the first picture, that of the queen at trooping the color, and she almost missed the absolutely correct seat of the queen as she rode sidesaddle (surely nobody else in the world rode side-saddle any longer?) surveying her Brigade of Guards in full array, the standards of the empire blazoned with battle honors from Inkerman and Waterloo and the Somme and Alamein, a thousand years of history, and the severe little lady riding sidesaddle embody-ing it all, inheritor and queen of it all.

Maggie caught her breath. There was something in that stance—a fortitude, a stoicism—that caught her imagination. What was it *like*, actually to sit there, on the specially tried and well-trained thoroughbred, and represent all that honor and battle-blood and imperialism, all that *history?* How was the severe little lady able to do it? What was the training needed to make her sit absolutely motionless for minutes on end, while the bands blared and the sergeant majors yelled and the guardsmen stamped their boots and wheeled and turned, perfectly in step, their bearskins heavy on their heads, their stiff pipe-clayed belts gleaming white against the red tunics? What was the training *like?* How did you ever survive it and remain, at some level, an ordinary human being?

The scene on the television screen changed, and there were pictures, in black-and-white now, of the queen as a child, with her sister and her parents in the garden of a house, which looked like an ordinary house to Maggie (who had been brought up in a large house herself), and the queen didn't look unhappy, or under any strain other than the strain put upon any middle-class child who must learn to behave properly and show respect to elders and not interrupt and think about other people before herself. All the things, in fact, that Maggie herself had been taught in the large house, with the large garden in Stonington.

Maggie began to watch the film clips with a very real sympathy.

"She didn't know she was going to be queen at this point. She didn't really know for another couple of years," Philip said. He tapped a book at his pillow. He had obviously been reading it during the night, while the night nurse was on duty and Maggie slept. "It was a surprise to them all, the abdication of Edward, her father's brother. Her father became king and she knew she would be queen from about the age of ten or twelve."

"Most queens don't know it'll happen to them, I suppose," Maggie mused aloud. "They marry a king and that makes them queen."

"With her it was different," Philip said. "She was like Elizabeth the First or Victoria. Eventually, she knew it was going to happen."

Imagine knowing that, Maggie thought, imagine growing up knowing *that!* She moved forward on her seat, her sympathy now total with the little English girl in the white frock with a sash at the waist. Maggie had no brothers, and her father had wanted a son to go on in Wall Street after he had gone. It was nothing her father had ever said. He was a good man and very proud of Maggie.

The film clips had moved forward in time, to the war, and showed the queen in uniform, driving a jeep. She seemed very serious and practical and had plainly mastered the job of driving and perhaps maintaining the vehicle. So she wasn't just a paper princess. She had to do the ordinary things too, for she was the queen of democracy, not a Marie Antoinette or a Christina. It was a life, Maggie saw, not in essentials unlike her own: a period of training at good disciplined schools and academies of one sort or another, and then a lifetime of working in public, always on parade, as the queen was at trooping the color, always open to criticism and therefore always to be seen to be above criticism, every single action of every single hour of every day thought about and debated upon, the whole reinforced by a certainty of destiny.

Not unlike, Maggie thought, the certainty of a vocation.

Born to be an actress, the grown-ups had said of Maggie on the soft lawns of her childhood. Born to be a queen? It did not seem, as she sat there in the darkening sickroom, to be so very different.

"Wonderful poise," Philip said, softly. "I was wrong about the tiara. She should wear a crown all through the play. She's the queen. The queen should wear a crown to remind everybody who they are and who she is. Tell Josh that when you see him. Don't forget."

"No, darling, I won't." Maggie was watching the further film clips, a montage of the marriage. The wedding in Westminster Abbey came up, in black-and-white still, with the real color of the pageantry only hinted at, the princess absurdly young but not nervous, the prince a fine, commanding figure at her side. Here she felt a tug at her heart. Her own prince was stricken, and lay mortally ill.

The princess had lived with her prince, and her children, and she had done it gracefully, and not unlike Maggie's own mother, sweetly matriarchal in tweeds on lawns and in woods, and later, at hunt balls and the opening of parliament, and at the coronation itself, twenty-seven years ago. The queen, still young, sitting alone on the ancient throne, the Archbishop of Canterbury placing the crown on her head, so gently, the vast crowd in the abbey hushed. What did she feel at that moment, Maggie wondered. Was it anything like getting the Oscar? It couldn't be, surely. The comparison was ridiculous. And yet, and yet . . . Maggie was searching for anything in her own experience that might somehow connect with the part. Surely she had felt something deep at that moment, the moment she had known that the responsibility was now hers, she carried on her head the crown of Elizabeth, that there was no going back to being, even at one remove, an ordinary person again, that nothing beckoned save duty, duty, duty.

That all the training had been for this moment, and all the moments of triumph and crisis that were to follow, Maggie imagined, letting the fancy of the future take over from the reality of the past, culminating in the crisis meeting in act two of *The Queen of Finland*, where the power of parliament had all but gone, and nothing stood any longer between the denial of the glorious past and the acceptance of the brutal present.

What would this queen have done?

Followed the advice of her ministers, as the playwright suggested, and capitulated, giving way after a terrible clash of conscience and training? The one saying, You cannot give away what it has taken a thousand years to put in your hands, and the other saying, You have no choice, you are not an absolute monarch, you have to take the advice your ministers give you. They are the elected ones, you are not.

Would she do that, or would she say no?

Maggie found herself wondering, torn by the dilemma she knew the queen would have to portray on stage. The words were good, but she would have to flesh the words out with actions, habits under stress, small movements the audience would learn to recognize in the character. Already she had noticed the little twitch of the hand on the skirt hem; the unruly lock of hair that needed attention at the most awkward times; the queen's ability to stand absolutely still on all occasions—the most difficult thing to do, on or off a stage; the ability to smile and seem to mean it—*and* to mean it, she corrected herself. The end, yes, the end would need to be looked at again, to be discussed with the director. Josh seemed a flexible man. He might move toward her thought of perhaps the queen showing more fight—even more fight than the last scenes suggested. Of course the playwright would object, but playwrights always objected to suggested changes in their text, and they were not always right to do so. The end of *The Queen of Finland* was very black. It left no hope. Maggie wondered about that. She would have to read the play again and again before she said anything of this. The text would tell her. The answer would be in the text somewhere.

Maggie felt a thrill of genuine excitement. This was a great part. It was a Joan of Arc part. It was that good.

She turned to Philip. The room was now dark and she reached to switch on a light. Then she saw he was sleeping, so still he could be dead. Maggie moved quickly forward and found that he was breathing, very lightly, as he usually did in the first moments of drugged oblivion. Maggie pulled the covers gently over Philip's arms, and tiptoed out of the room, picking up, as she did so, the morocco-bound folder with the Q embossed on the front.

AUSTIN sat, in his Armani sweatshirt and his Calvin Klein jeans and blue-and-white Adidas, looking at Manny Hiberson in his white suit in Manny's office on Sunset Boulevard. Austin was annoyed because Manny was not annoyed that he had finally decided to elbow *Massacre at Moonrise*, even when the director had pleaded and offered to hold the movie back for him. "Look, Manny, I had this call from Bernie Moss and he said you had talked to him and told him I was saying no. Well, I *am* saying no, Manny."

Manny sighed and lit another Turkish cigarette. "That's what I told him, Austin. I said, Austin is saying no. He's going to London to do a play."

"You didn't have to tell him that." Austin shook his head. "He said I was a shmuck. *Massacre at Moonrise* is a ten-million-dollar budget and it's all mine and everything, and he was crying on the telephone, Manny, and saying the movie won't go if I'm not in it. What the fuck am I thinking about leaving this town when I'm so hot and his movie is dead unless I do it!"

Manny surveyed his cigarette. "It probably is."

"Ah, Jesus, that makes me feel a whole lot better. I mean, he's an old friend."

"In this business, there ain't no such animal." Manny looked through his smoke at Austin. "Look, you want to change your mind, so change it."

"You'd like me to, wouldn't you? You'd like the commission on *Massacre at Moonrise*. Go on, admit it!"

"Sure. I'd like the commission on *Massacre at Moonrise*. Who wouldn't? But the decision is yours, Austin, and you've already made it."

"Yes, I have, and I'm not about to change it."

"That's what I'm saying, Austin."

"No you're not. You're saying I should do *Massacre at Moonrise* and make a million bucks and stop being a sucker. Everybody in town will be saying that, once they hear I'm going to England to do this play. They'll think I'm crazy if I don't do *Massacre at Moonrise*."

"Sure they will," agreed Manny. "But that don't mean you'll be wrong." His secretary appeared around the door, but Manny waved her away. Austin was a good client and Austin was worried. Who wouldn't be worried? Was he doing the right thing? Who knew? Manny said, "Sometimes it doesn't do any harm to be crazy in this town. I've known it to help."

"You're just saying that, Manny."

"Okay, I'm just saying that. What else should I say?"

"Say I'm doing the right thing going to London!"

"Okay, you're doing the right thing going to London. Am I just saying that? *Sure* I'm just saying that. But, Austin . . ."

"Yeah?"

"You want to do this play, right?"

"Right."

"You're all fired up about it, right?"

"Right."

"If you stay on at the Beverly Hills the telephone is going to keep ringing from Bernie and his producer and the head of the studio and then they're all gonna come round for drinks and maybe dinner and they're gonna bring broads and maybe the contract— sure they're gonna bring the contract—and at about three in the morning in Scandia or someplace, you're gonna sign." Manny sighed. "And I'm gonna be there holding your hand while you do it, Austin."

He lit another Turkish cigarette. "Bernie and everybody are gonna be sore at me, whatever happens. As of now, they think it's money, that you're not serious about London. Okay, maybe you've got an offer but you're holding out for more, and I have to tell ya I think they'll pay more, Austin. Today, in this town, they'll pay more. Next time, who knows?"

There was a long silence. Austin brooded unhappily. Traffic noises filtered into the room from Sunset. The light bounced off Manny's white walls. Helps to keep me awake, he explained to visitors. Why Austin should want to leave the sun for London's rain and fog he didn't know. He hated even going to New York City these days. As a boy he'd never felt the cold, even in the depth of the snows. Now, he shuddered at the thought. But his blood was thin. Shit, he was old, he needed California. Austin was young, he didn't; probably didn't notice if it was raining. He said, calmly, "Austin. My advice, you want to do this play, and even if you have signed, it's only a letter contract, I could get you out of it. But my advice is, you want to do it, get your ass out of this town today."

Austin sat up at that. "You think so?"

"Sure of it. You stay, you'll sign for *Massacre at Moonrise*. You want that?"

"Jesus, no!"

"Then out of town. Pack a bag. Scoot."

Austin stood up, slowly, all five-six of him. What the hell, he'd never make it Redford-big in movies, Manny thought. Lovely actor, wonderful voice, nice brown eyes, lovely smile, electric little fella, but no screen presence, still more the stage actor, not butch enough, not for the average lead. *Good-bye* was one in a million. Not sexy enough, neither. Which was a laugh. The guy had slept with more broads than Errol Flynn. Stage, that was where he belonged. That girl was right. Jill Viner was right. "Where would you go?" he asked Austin.

"I'll ring you when I get there." Austin didn't shake hands, the new, top young actors didn't do it now, it belonged to an older America, they thought it square. Even after a big deal they didn't do it. The executives did, they gladhanded you, but the actors? They looked sheepish and stared at their funky boots and mumbled. Manny liked a handshake. He'd shaken hands with the worst and the best and it had meant something then. Hadn't it? Sure it had. It had meant "no hard feelings." Now, he wondered, did people have feelings at all anymore? So there was Austin, waving that fucking Indian Hi sign from the door.

"And thanks, Manny. I love ya. You didn't want the commission after all. I owe you, Manny."

"Sure, sure, you owe me, you make a great big hit in London. Then I can sell you for twice the price." It probably wasn't true. Austin Ames might be cold potatoes by then. "Have a good trip, wherever you're going. Good luck, Austin."

Austin made another little wave and was gone.

The sunlight in this fucking place is getting too strong, Manny thought. I'll have it changed from white to dark blue, for Chrissake. He puffed on his cigarette and wondered if he had steered Austin the way he had because of the girl, Jill Viner. Well, why not? He was an old man and she was a young girl. He was entitled.

And anyway, Austin wanted it. It was the right decision for him, right?

He wondered idly where Austin would go. If he did go.

AUSTIN booked into the Sheraton in Washington, carrying only a grip, under the name of Jones, and did his famous disguise number of dark lightweight suit, striped tie, and rimless glasses. It did not deceive the receptionist at the Sheraton. "Mr. Ames, very nice to see you. If there's anything I can do at all, just let me know."

Austin looked around the crowded lobby. "How many people have you seen today? I mean looked at?"

The receptionist was surprised. "I don't know, sir. Maybe a hundred, two hundred."

"How long did it take you to recognize me?"

"Oh, I knew you at once, sir. It's the eyes, I think. I saw *The Last Good-bye.* My wife and I loved you in that. She cried a lot."

Those goddam huge close-ups, Austin thought. Everybody

knows me and I don't know two dozen people. I'll have to wear shades. Austin hated shades. He felt his actor's art should be able to save him from recognition without resorting to shades.

The receptionist was asking a question, the one they all asked. "When can we hope to see you in something new, sir? What's your next movie to be?"

Austin found a smile. "Not sure yet. Oh, by the way, I'm not here."

"Naturally, sir. But, well, I think you'll have a problem keeping it quiet. The taxi driver probably knew you. The price of fame, sir."

"Yes. Sure. Well, do your best."

"Rely on it, sir. Your next one will have to be good to beat *The Last Good-bye*. I've changed your suite, sir. I think you'll like what we have."

"Thank you," said Austin. Shit, he thought.

It was indeed a splendid suite, but it was not what Austin had come to Washington about. He had come to Washington to contact, very quietly, his old friend Hank Hughes. He took off his shoes and his coat and put on his shades and rang Hank Hughes at his office.

Hank was incredulous. "You're here in Washington now? Where?"

"I'm at the Sheraton, Hank. Listen, I'm trying to keep this cool. I don't want the press or anybody around me. And I want to talk to you privately."

"You stay at the Sheraton! At any hotel you'll get press. Can you tell me what you want me to do, Austin? Hell, what are old actors for?" Hank Hughes had lasted three months at the Actors' Studio before the Boss told him to go into government like his father and his grandfather before him. Hank was a sensible man and he had taken sensible advice, kindly given. But he loved the theatre—this Austin knew—down to his socks.

"I can tell you, Hank, but it's going to surprise you."

"Well, surprise me, for Pete's sake."

Austin surprised him.

THE president was stockier and tougher-looking than his news-paper pictures, or even his television appearances, suggested. In his pictures, on the television, one factor was eliminated, and Austin Ames, looking at the smiling man in front of him, looking deep into his eyes, taking in, *breathing in*, the aura of the man, knew what it was. Power. Naked power. He'd seen it, felt it before, surround-ing heads of movie studios. They had been circled by acolytes, as maybe the president was, but they were only making movies, for God's sake. This man had the welfare of his country, and of the world, in his hands every minute of the day. How did he cope with it? How did he sleep nights, if he slept at all? How did he know what to say to the Russians or the Chinese or, even more, the dread media? Know *exactly* what to say, when, how to say it? The president had to be an actor, sure. He had to present himself to the country through media looking for the tiniest slip, media destruc-tive and capricious, if Hank Hughes was to be believed. "The media think they can make and unmake presidents, and sometimes I not only think—I know—they can. Open government? Shit!"

Hank Hughes had sounded bitter. "It's a big enough job to run this country without having to report to the nation every time you go to the can. Which all the presidents since Johnson have had to do, and look what's happened to them all! The media've harmed them, embarrassed them, upset them, in at least one case helped destroy the man. And you come to me, Austin, and you say, Can I meet the president? I want to put him in a *play*. Jesus, you guys are crazy. Why should I help you? All you'll do is something that makes news, and it'll be *wrong*, too. That man has the toughest job in the world, and in the end, the way our Constitution works, the final decision is all his." Hank Hughes had debated. "I'll do it, Austin, because I trust you. You're a helluva fine actor. And, shit, the play might as well be real, if you can get it real—and if anybody can, you can. Would a garden party do you? It'll only be for a minute or two, y'know? There's one the day after tomorrow."

Here was the garden party and here was the president.

And here was Austin Ames, drinking him in, breathing him in, looking, looking, looking, as he had been looking since the president hurried, smiling, surrounded by his aides and the secret-service bodyguards, onto the White House lawn. Slowy hurried. That was it. The pressure of the office was so great, so unremitting, that the man who held it had to move slowly, cautiously, in public at least. Everybody was watching him—most people almost obsessively as Austin Ames was watching him now—as the president took his hand in a gentle grip (how many handshakes a day was it, 110 on average?) and said, "Nice to see you here today, Mr. Ames. Hank Hughes told me you were in town and I thought, I must see what he looks like in the flesh. I have to tell you my wife has run *The Last Good-bye* three times. I saw it the first time and I must admit I had to blow my nose a few times. Congratulations on the Oscar and on a fine performance."

"Thank you, Mister President," said Austin wonderingly. It was done so easily, so naturally. All genuine. The president *had* seen the movie. He spoke about it for a couple of minutes, and Austin listened and smiled and watched and thought: It's a sacrifice, the office is a sacrifice, you have to give everything to it. You shouldn't be able to relax and chat on a lawn, but this man can. It's power, sure. That's a cliché. He's an actor, sure. He has to be to reach his people. All great politicians have to be actors, like all great lawyers and probably all great public men since civilization began. But this man was calm and easy and seemingly unworried and natural, and yet the eyes, the eyes were very, very tired. Just for a moment it showed—not when he was talking to people, but when he wasn't talking to them, between introductions, between the smiles. I have it, Austin decided. I think I have it.

The president was moving on, but he found time to ask the inevitable question. "What's the next one to be, Mr. Ames?"

"Not sure yet, sir."

"It'll have to be good to beat *The Last Good-bye*. Good luck with it."

"Thank you, sir."

And Austin found himself with a trickle of moisture in his eyes. Shit, he thought, noticing the president's trick of smiling and looking dead straight at the person he was talking to, and not looking away or behaving in any way as if he were the center of things, yet being the center of things all the time.

"That help at all?" Hank Hughes was at his side.

"Help? It saved it."

"Huh?"

"The play. I can do it. I know I can do it."

Hank Hughes shook his head. "If it's a success I'll tell the prez why you wanted to see him. And if it's not"—Hank grinned—"then I'll still tell him."

JILL stood in the middle of her suite at the Ritz and checked to make sure everything was just right. The drinks were plentiful and were to be served from the bar by George, for whom she had specifically asked. Four waitresses would circulate with the drinks and canapés, quite substantial ones. She knew many of her angels would be going on to a West End theatre and wouldn't eat until curtain-down, if then. They were all theatre buffs, her angels (or rather Joe Dancy's angels), or they wouldn't *be* angels, as Josh had remarked.

Josh was wearing his good gray suit. Was it the only one he had? He hadn't had his hair cut either, but she didn't suppose her angels would mind that. Joe Dancy's angels, at the parties she had organized for him, had never minded people looking arty. The angels were there because they were stagestruck. There was no other possible explanation for them, as Josh had again said. So few ever made any money out of their investments. Of course, there was always the one chance in seven you might. And then you were on the way to making a very large profit. All you had to do, if you were an angel, was to sort out the winners from the losers.

Gamblers, wonderful gamblers, thank God, Jill thought, every last one of them.

"Drinks, food, brochures . . . Where are the *brochures*, Josh?"

Josh looked up from his chair. He was actually reading *Queen* again, while she stood in the middle of the room in a complete state of panic. "Josh, put that script down and tell me if this place looks all right."

"It *is* the *Ritz*." Josh smiled. "It will be marvelous. It ought to be. It's taking most of our money."

"Hush!" Jill looked around, but George and the waitresses did not seem to be listening. They were going about their duties, professionally, with the aplomb of the servants of a great hotel. "I know it's costing us the earth but how else can I get to all these people fast? I can't go through Joe Dancy's long performance, write personal letters to everybody, then telephone them a week later, and have lunch with them a month after that, can I?"

"It's the traditional way with the smaller investor, isn't it?" Josh accepted a glass of champagne from George. There was a twinkle in George's eyes. He was a veteran of this kind of occasion. Jill took a glass, too.

"Yes, of course, it's the traditional way, Josh, but it takes months and we haven't got that many. We must get in a West End theatre by the end of September, at the latest, or we'll be lost in the winter rush. That way, we can be a fixture in the West End and doing good business by Christmas. I can just see us, playing to full houses over the New Year, ten thousand pounds a week coming in at the box office."

"That way," said Josh drily, "some of the angels might even get their money back."

"I don't intend," declared Jill, "that anybody should lose money on *Queen*. Nobody."

"The way you're dishing out percentages to Maggie and Austin Ames I don't know how much is going to be left for us."

"We'll be all right, if it runs."

"It'll run," said Josh, lighting one of the long havana cigars from the box she had given him, on impulse. She was tired of watching him smoke the mild Dutch ones. He seemed to puff both with equal pleasure. One thing about Josh. He was no snob, no elitist. Except where his work was concerned.

"The flowers! George, the flowers!"

George waved, and as if he had used a magic wand the waitresses came in smiling, with large bowls of gladioli and roses, white and red. "All fresh an hour ago, madam. I kept them in the cool until this moment. They will look very good, I think."

"George, thank you. I'm so jumpy. I'm never like this usually, am I?"

"When you were with Mr. Dancy that time, I think yes." George smiled and deftly refilled their glasses from his bottle of Möet. "I think you need one more glass, madam."

"Thank you, George, this will do me fine. And congratulations on the suite. It looks absolutely splendid."

"Thank you, madam."

George returned to supervise the food and his waitresses, and Jill asked, "How do I look?"

She was wearing a black-and-silver-striped dress, new, at a cost of two hundred pounds she did not, strictly speaking, have, and she knew how she looked.

"Sexy. Very sexy."

"Well, don't sound so surprised!"

"Sorry. I haven't really noticed, I suppose."

For God's sake, Jill thought, I only bought it to see your face when I told you how much it cost.

"How much," Josh asked idly, "did it cost?"

Anybody would think she was married to the man.

"I've had it for ages," she lied, without a tremor.

96

"Looks jolly nice anyway," replied Josh with approval and a little warmth in his tone now that it was not a debt on their joint exchequer. What was left of it.

Which was two thousand pounds.

Eight hundred pounds was due on the office rent at the end of the month, two weeks away.

And Josh thought the party was a risk. "Nobody invites angels to parties at the Ritz and gives them champagne and caviar. Nobody pays their first-class train fares from places like Leeds and Manchester."

"Nobody except a real impresario," she had told him. The ones like Barnum, and like Cochran, who used to get his money from the City of London, sitting in Dickensian offices in Mincing Lane, talking about showgirls to the money barons of the old City firms—all that was gone. The City firms were all run by accountants with rimless spectacles who disapproved of showgirls during working hours. An impresario now had to be a hardy creature, a man or woman for all seasons. She remembered Herbert Wilcox's statement, "When I was broke I always moved into Claridges." And Jack Hylton's "Spend the clients' money! They love it! It's as if they're doing it themselves!"

Well, she wasn't spending the clients' money. Not yet. Until now, all they had spent had been their own.

"The brochures, Josh!"

"There they are, once again, on the table in front of you."

So they were, half hidden by the large bowls of flowers.

"You'll fix the film, won't you Josh?"

Josh looked at his watch. "The operator will be bringing it round in fifteen minutes."

"The screen?"

"The screen is already here." He held up his hand. "There it is, behind the curtain. All we need is no angels to turn up."

"They'll be here." Jill laughed. "One thing I learned about angels, working for Joe Dancy, is that they can't resist champagne.

Especially if it's free. Do you know, I had to get free theatre tickets for the Criterion for the Misses Dobbs from Leeds, to get them to come here at all?"

"How much was that? No, don't tell me!"

"I got them twofers, using my out-of-date Equity card."

"That's good news."

"The bad news is they were still five pounds each."

"The Misses Dobbs had better invest."

"They invested in every show Joe Dancy ever put on. Never less than five thousand pounds." She glanced at her closely written list of angels' names and previous investments, clipped inside the gold-crested brochure with the large crown and the Q on the front of it. "They're typical small investors. We can't get the show going without some of their money." Jill sat and sipped her champagne without tasting it. "Of course, the big money has to come from Prince Ahmed and Jerry Glass."

"*Who?*"

She had forgotten: always keep something back. But Josh was her partner, wasn't he?

"Joe Dancy's two aces in the hole. The people he never even told me about."

"Will they both be here tonight?"

"I've sent them both invites but they didn't reply."

"Which means they won't."

"No, it means if it can be fitted in with gambling in Ahmed's case and work in Jerry's case."

"When you say Jerry, you do mean Lord Glass, the tycoon?"

"Of course I do."

"Why on earth should that old boy invest in stage plays? He's a millionaire a few times over."

"Because he started as a performer and he loves the theatre. Television's bread and butter to him. The stage is cake."

"And Ahmed?"

"Suite at this hotel, which is partly why I chose it. He has all the petro-dollars in the world. Some of which we stand in dire need of."

"That," said Josh, "is true. How did you find out they were investing in Joe Dancy's shows if Joe didn't want you to find out?"

"Joe had these two clients on his books, always referred to as Mr. Smith and Mr. Jones. Joe had no imagination, which is why, as Manny Hiberson says, he'll never get rich, or poor either. He used to telephone these people secretly, but sooner or later they'd call him back, and after a while I realized they were his big moneymen. Without them he was sunk. The little people, the two and three hundred, up to two or three or even five thousand people, like the Misses Dobbs, they only provided about a third of Joe's investment. The rest came from Mr. Smith and Mr. Jones."

"And from Joe Dancy himself?"

Jill looked shocked. "An impresario investing his own money in his own show?"

"We've invested our money." Josh looked pensive.

"Because we have to start somehow. But Joe Dancy never, ever invests his own money. He puts his name on the masthead, sure, 'Joe Dancy Presents,' but the money is all his angels'. Nobody else's. And Joe Dancy Productions takes forty percent of the gross, for just finding the play, finding the theatre, finding the actors, and putting the play on."

"That reminds me," Josh said, "we haven't sorted ourselves out yet. Do *we* take forty percent of the gross?"

"No. We waive our management fee, but it won't be the usual deal most managements make. We'll be fair with these people, because it's the only way to get them to invest. They don't know me. The offer to waive our management fee will impress them, I can tell you. I don't think it's ever been done before."

"What do we live on," Josh asked, "when we've refused the management fee?"

"We take wages. Enough to live on. A hundred pounds a week each. Plus genuine expenses."

Josh shook his head. "I can see we'll never get rich."

"Oh yes, we will," said Jill Viner. "What we won't get is poor, like Joe Dancy."

"Joe Dancy isn't poor!" Josh protested.

"Compared to us he will be," Jill promised, rising to her feet to greet the first guests of the evening, the Misses Dobbs from Leeds, who were early and flustered.

"Good evening, ladies," said Jill. "Welcome to our little get-together. This is Josh Williams, our director. And this is George, who will now give you a glass of champagne."

NEITHER Prince Ahmed nor Lord Glass turned up at the party. Which was possibly just as well, since there was very little they would have had to say to each other. Jerry Glass was a millionaire who had made his money since British television began, and Ahmed had had his since the Arabs had quadrupled oil prices to the West. At least Ahmed was in London spending his money. As for Lord Glass, he rarely left the City, and was reported to be a closer man with a dollar, in his own words, than his father, who had been a cross-legged tailor in the East End. Except where the theatre was concerned. There, Lord Glass was a gambler. He isn't here, Jill thought, but I'll find him—in his office probably. Tracing Prince Ahmed had been easy. She had made a discreet call through George the barman and discovered that Prince Ahmed was indeed at the tables, playing for his usual very high stakes in the Ritz casino, at that very moment.

So the two big backers were not present in the smoky, noisy room, but everybody else was. Jill floated around talking to them all in turn, referring quickly to the little list, pinned inside her *Queen* brochure, before she approached each new group. Name, and usual sum invested—those were the two items to memorize. First, the Misses Dobbs, in sensible provincial evening dresses, who would be leaving early and who were sipping champagne rather daringly, being Methodists—and Yorkshire-woollen Methodists at that—for six generations and more. The Misses Dobbs had money, but the word to use with the Misses Dobbs was not *gamble* but *invest*. The Chapel had strong views on gambling, whereas investment was prudent and proper.

"A splendid investment for you, I think, Miss Agatha," said Jill. "Something with royalty in it is sure to draw the town."

"Royalty?" said Agatha Dobbs. "Really? I'd no idea. Who?"

"The queen."

"The queen? Really?" Miss Agatha looked at Miss Emily. "Well, that *is* something quite new."

"Is it allowed?" asked Miss Emily sharply.

Miss Emily was sharper than she looked.

"We don't say it's the queen. Well, not exactly. It's in the future."

"Oh, it's not that dreadful science fiction, is it?"

Josh intervened, charmingly. "I once did a science-fiction play, not at the National." He was following Jill around, talking art quietly after she had talked money tentatively. The two ladies gazed at him raptly. "Since then I have always said, I have seen the future and it's a lot of rubbish."

"Just what we think. We do so hate the sci-fi, is it?—when they are on the television."

Jill handed them an investment form. "If you're interested, we can accommodate your investment."

"Oh, I don't know. We normally deal direct with dear Mr. Dancy, you know."

"I thought you'd be interested in this one, you see."

"Well, we are, of course, and it's ever so nice of you to invite us to your party and to get us tickets for the Criterion, but—"

Jill moved on, saying, "I'll be talking a little more later."

"I hope we'll be in time for the second house."

As she left them to join the next group, Jill heard Josh's reassuring voice behind her. "We're hoping to get some very good actors in *Queen*, and Miss Agatha Dobbs's excited, "Oh, really, who?" and Miss Emily's, "Have you thought of Mr. Harrison? It's about time we saw him in the West End again."

Josh said, "That's a very interesting thought, Miss Emily. Did I give you a brochure?"

The boy's learning, she thought. He's having to. He isn't hanging his hat on a contract at the National anymore.

Colonel Chase-Gordon, from Wiltshire, was her next client. The colonel was in a blazer and regimental tie and he was to the point. "Good evening, madam. May I introduce my wife. Hmm, now look here, I see the play's called *The Queen of Finland*, yes, I've had a quick look at your brochure thing and I hope it isn't goin' to be a take-off of royalty because if it is, I tell you straightforwardly, madam, I shan't invest."

The colonel's top investment to date—with Joe Dancy—was two hundred and fifty pounds.

Two hundred and fifty pounds was two hundred and fifty pounds. Jill smiled.

"Colonel, it's far from being that. I think it's a most important and timely play. If it's saying anything on those lines, it's to the effect that the West had better look after itself or it'll go down, as Greece and Rome did."

The colonel gulped his champagne.

"If that is indeed what it's saying, dear lady, then I might very well invest in it."

All two hundred and fifty pounds, Jill thought. Never mind.

"Here's your investment form, colonel, in case you feel like having a flutter with us. Did you get your corsage, Mrs. Chase-Gordon?"

"Yes, I did, and I must say it's a very charming party, Miss Viner. We are enjoying ourselves very much."

"I'm so glad. I know you'll excuse me if I move on?"

"Of course, so nice to meet you."

Leaving them, she heard the colonel mutter, "Damn attractive gel, don't know how she got our address, I only bet with Joe Dancy as a rule, but this thing sounds promisin', I must say."

Jill greeted (after a quick glance at her list) a certain Jack Millard, a wholesale grocer from the north of England. Mr. Millard was without Mrs. Millard, and very much with a young actress, a thin ash-blonde Jill recognized from *Spotlight* and the odd television play. Jack Millard's last investment in a Joe Dancy production had been on the order of ten thousand pounds, with a reserve of five thousand more, which he had also invested. He had lost the lot, yet here he was again. Jack Millard was a man to take seriously.

"Good evening, Mr. Millard, how nice to see you. Miss Woods."

The little ash-blonde actress looked startled. "Have we met?"

"We were in a commercial together once, about milk."

"Good God, was that you?" The girl looked delighted. "What happened?"

"I gave up acting and got into business."

"Well, good for you, darling. It's a dog's life sometimes. Well, isn't that terrific, Jack?"

Jack Millard was looking at his brochure and showing signs of restiveness. "I think you're in the right game, Miss Viner." His eye on her was mildly lecherous. "Business. Not that acting lark. You do all right no matter what happens. I lost fifteen thousand on my last investment with Joe Dancy. So did a lot of other people. Joe didn't lose anything. In fact, he had a management fee of about fifteen thou himself."

"I think it was twelve and a half," Jill said. "Although I shouldn't be talking about Mr. Dancy's business. And he had an office to run and all the other expenses."

"I know all that, love," said Jack Millard wearily. "But my point is he couldn't lose money. He was getting his management fee off the top no matter what happened to the play. And the play lost money, the angels' money. And, speaking as an angel, I'm unhappy about that."

"Jack, darling," said Pat. "The theatre's a risky business but you're always investing in it." She winked at Jill on Jack Millard's blind side. "I can't think why."

"To lean on this young lady to give you a part, if I put ten thousand in it." He was still looking at the brochure, but he seemed to be serious. "She's a good little actress, Pat here."

"Oh, Jack, please, this is so embarrassing," interrupted the girl. "Don't talk shit, please, Jack."

"I know she is," answered Jill smoothly, touching the actress's bony young arm in reassurance. "We have one big part for a young actress. We have no ideas for it, but I'm sure Josh Williams will think about Pat if her agent puts her forward."

"Think about her," said Jack Millard. "That's bugger-all use, love. Will you guarantee he'll audition her?"

"Jack, I'm going to the ladies'. Jill, take no bloody notice of the man. I don't know why I ever go out with him, I don't really." And Pat broke away, her pale face flushing.

"Now you've gone and done it." Jill liked the girl for speaking out. "She's upset."

"Just the same, will your Mr. Williams see her if I come in?"

"If you come in for ten thousand pounds, I'll guarantee it. What I can't guarantee is she'll get the job. That's up to him."

Jack Millard drew on his cigar. "Does she have a chance? Don't bullshit me, just tell me."

"Yes, she does." Jill reflected. She did. "It's the part of a young princess. It's small but it's a dream part, and yes, Pat's a good pro with lots of experience and I think she would have a chance."

"All right, that'll do, love." Jack Millard smiled wickedly. "But that's only if I put my ten grand in. I haven't decided yet, have I?"

"Of course not." Jill started to move on. "But please don't say anything to Pat or to my director, Josh Williams, about it. Leave it to me to see she has an audition. I can do that much."

"Like I say, I'm not in yet. You've no track record, have you, as an impresario?"

"It might change your mind if I told you that we are taking no management fee on this production."

"I'd only believe that if my own auditors saw the books!"

"They can, anytime."

"Jill, you can come and work for me. You tell a lovely sales story, it's like music."

"All true, Mr. Millard. Excuse me, won't you, I must circulate."

"I'll excuse you, love. And I'll have some more champagne." Jack Millard took a glass from a passing tray. "I might as well get something out of being an angel. It's cost me a packet, up to now."

"Twenty-five grand over the last four years. You haven't had a winner since *Soft Song*."

Jack Millard looked astonished. "You've done your homework. On second thought don't come and work for me unless you marry me. I want to keep my business a bit longer!"

Jill made her further rounds of the angels. They were a motley crowd and astonished and (she hoped) delighted to have a chance to meet other angels. Joe Dancy had always cannily kept the angels apart, arranging their meetings with lesser actors and star players singly, and never in groups in case the angels got together and decided to leave him. The angels always wanted to meet the actors, if they were ladies, and the actresses, if they were gentlemen. It was all part of the service, Joe Dancy had told her. "It's why they invest. They want to sniff the perfume and the greasepaint and the sweat. They're stagestruck. They might be tough as nails in private life but as angels they're putty. They don't really care how much it's going to cost them. Hundreds of them—hundreds—all different, and all the same. Mad as hatters, the lot of them, dear."

They didn't look it, in the suite at the Ritz. They looked what they were, small businessmen and -women: the man in steel-rim glasses had a newsagent's shop in Kentish Town; the fat lady in a fur coat was a Laundromat owner's widow from Southall. There were one or two retired army people (like the colonel), and gentlewomen (like the Misses Dobbs) and butchers and bakers. There was a baker anyway, making wheat-germ bread in Hampstead and doing well enough out of it to be at the party.

Jill thought, they don't look mad. Anything but. They look ordinary. Moneyed, yes, but not Ritz moneyed, which was why she had chosen the Ritz. Not champagne-and-caviar moneyed, which was why she had served champagne and caviar, but moneyed enough to give her almost half of the hundred thousand pounds she needed to put *Queen* into the West End.

Jill looked over at Josh at the far end of the room.

He nodded, and tapped the shoulder of the small man in glasses at his side. This was the camera operator. Jill signaled, "Ready," and Josh, calmly and, she thought, without any evident nerves at all (and she admired that; *she* was terrified), rapped with a glass on a table for silence, and then said, in an easy voice, "Ladies and gentlemen, my name is Josh Williams and I will be directing *The Queen of Finland*. I'm going to ask you to fill your glasses if you need to, because we are going to show you a very short extract from a recent movie that many of you will no doubt have seen. In a moment, I'm going to ask George to lower the lights. You needn't bother to sit or anything. It takes three minutes and fifty seconds exactly. Thank you."

There was a buzz of expectation. People in the mass always react with delight to any small surprise, thought Jill. I must remember that. They like to see you trying. I must remember that, too. The room darkened and the faces of Maggie and Austin came softly onto the screen at the end of the room. Again, there was a buzz, and the people strained for a better view of the famous death scene that had brought Josh Williams near to tears in the movie house in New York City. When the lights went up again, one or two people were dabbing at their eyes.

A very sentimental crowd, angels.

Jill stood on a small dais at the end of the suite.

"Ladies and gentlemen, you've seen Austin Ames and Maggie Stride in that famous movie. They won an Oscar each for that performance, as most of you know." Jill Viner took a deep breath and spoke with total confidence. "They have both agreed to appear in leading roles in *The Queen of Finland*."

At that moment, by arrangement, Tom Tully appeared in the doorway. He had under his arm fifty copies of the final edition of that evening's *Standard*.

WITH Tom was Jill's new secretary, Molly Budd, middle-aged, unflappable, and a treasure. Jill had won her away from Tennent's with a promise of an American trip with *Queen* when it went to Broadway. Secretaries did not get such goodies at a grand, established firm such as Tennent's, or anywhere else for that matter. There was not much in the theatrical world Molly Budd, in her sensible tweeds and glasses, did not know, and few people she could not reach, with her very private diary of telephone numbers of actors, actresses, designers, makeup girls, and costume ladies. Molly was costing only a hundred pounds a week and a steal at the money, but she had said yes to Jill's promise of twice as much the moment *Queen* showed a profit. So Molly had every reason for wanting the play to succeed. She took the *Standards* from under Tom Tully's arm and began to hand them around the room, one to each guest.

Tom's reply to Jill's questioning gaze was an ebullient thumbs-up. Everything about Tom was ebullient. Over two hundred pounds of well-tailored, well-shod flesh—that was Tom; patent-black hair parted in the middle, ex-RAF wartime pilot, ex–sports writer, ex-columnist, now the best (or so he said) theatre press agent on Shaftesbury Avenue. Tom had professed himself astonished at Jill Viner's suggestion that he should work on results.

Sitting debonairly in the bar of the Piccadilly Hotel, he had told Jill the facts of life, in a weary, professional voice.

"Look, dear, I'm an old hand at this game. I'm an old press agent and what you're asking me to do is, strictly speaking, unethical. Not that I have anything against being unethical." The large man had downed his massive gin and tonic with the air of somebody who drank a dozen a day, which he did and showed not a sign of the fact. "We used to have a saying when I was in the Royal Air Force. 'There are old pilots and bold pilots but there are no old, bold pilots.' You can cancel 'pilot' and substitute 'press-agent.' You're asking me to be bold, to pancake without a parachute. I don't need to be bold. I have a good little agency and a good name. Why should I risk it?"

"I'm not asking you exactly to risk it," Jill had said, knowing she was doing exactly that, but also knowing that no matter what he said, Tom Tully was an old, bold pilot and would go on being one until the day he pancaked without a parachute, to quote the phrase he was using in his altogether too vehement refusal of her offer.

"Look, dear lady, I'd be on my arse if either of the gents got stroppy—which, believe me, they could. You know what a theatrical press agent does. He keeps the newspaper columnists sweet. The minute he loses their trust he's finished." Tom Tully nodded as he said that, as if to convince himself that he had never violated a columnist's trust, which was, as everybody in Fleet Street knew, far, far from being the perfect truth.

"I know." Jill Viner had leaned forward prettily, and Tom Tully had seen the top of her splendid breasts and had automatically straightened his RAF tie. "I know," Jill repeated, "what most press agents do. They write out a mimeographed handout giving the names, addresses, and ages—yes, believe me, I've seen *ages*—of all the cast, with a list of everything they've ever appeared in, all taken from stage reference books. They always include the actor's biggest and latest flop, the one he's trying very hard to pretend he was never in. When they've done that they post the stuff out to every West End feature writer on every newspaper and then they go to lunch, secure in the knowledge they're working well."

Jill leaned back and the view ceased.

Tom Tully grinned a raffish grin and stopped fingering his tie. "Despite the scenery—and it's lovely—I heard most of that, and most of it's true, Jill." Now he was calling her Jill; he was beginning to think she might know what she was about. God, did it have to be knocked into their thick heads with a mallet? The answer was, yes, it did. "I think there's a lot in what you say. That is what most press agents do, or anyway the lousy ones. The good ones do a lot more and I'm one of the good ones. I arrange interviews, and although I push the cast at all columnists, I make sure every big columnist gets a bite—a special bite, all his own—at the people in the play. In this case, *Queen*."

He lit yet another Player's and drank most of another large gin and tonic. "I never use handouts. I do everything personally. Personal letter. Personal telephone calls. Personal lunches. I have a secretary to take notes and answer the phone. What I offer is a personal service but"—his brown eyes twinkled—"I need a play to service. I need to know who's in it; which West End theatre it is going into, and when; where it is rehearsing; when it is touring. Can you answer me any of those questions?"

"I've already told you Maggie and Austin are starring."

Tom Tully consulted his Cartier watch. "So you did. I can get that in tonight's *Standard* if you want it."

"I can do that myself," Jill said. "My secretary could do that. I want to hold that story back. I want you to get the other story in tomorrow's *Standard* diary, in the last edition only."

"Timing isn't the problem, truth is."

"What you'd be telling them would be a rumor, an unsubstantiated rumor. What's wrong with that?"

"The word in the trade is *plant*, Jill. And you've been in the business long enough to know that a press agent—or anybody—

doesn't plant stories that are come-ons. This is a come-on. And I never print come-ons. It's not worth it. In the long run, people get wise. Or whatever."

"That," said Jill combatively, "is crap, Tom. What about that story last year about the Coward revival? That was the biggest come-on of the year."

Tom Tully finished his gin and tonic with a pleased air. "Oh, you heard about that?"

"Everybody on Shaftesbury Avenue heard about it. You conned the whole press that time. And all you were selling was a Coward revival."

"You have to do something," said Tom Tully, "with a bloody revival. They're corpses, to start with. They take selling, believe me."

"I do believe you, but *Queen* isn't a corpse. It's a real, live play about something that matters. You've read it?"

Tom fumbled on the seat next to him and passed the morocco-bound folder back to her. "Kept me awake till two o'clock. Not many plays do that. Truth to tell, I don't read some of them." Tom Tully winked. "Not all through. Couldn't. The political ones especially. Anybody would think it was still the depression. I got my first job in the depression, copyboy on the old *News Chronicle* at a pound a week. They don't know they're born, these subsidized theatre people." Tom Tully sighed. "I have been known to promote subsidized plays just the same. Damn all else, sometimes."

"*Queen*'s a good play. You like it. It isn't subsidized. I can't pay you any money up front."

Tom Tully looked wryly into his glass. "That's a novel approach. I haven't heard it for years."

"Look, I know your usual rates. What I'll do, I'll double them once *Queen* is in profit. Can I say fairer than that?"

Tom Tully sighed again. "You can say a lot fairer. Who pays for my phone calls, my lunches, my photographs, my time, in the interim period?"

"We'll pay you expenses."

"Very nice of you, I'm sure."

"And if we pull it off, and I don't see why we shouldn't, you'll get twice your usual fee."

"I must be mad," said Tom Tully pensively, "to be thinking about it. It could cost me my best contacts in Fleet Street, if it goes wrong. And it could so easily go wrong. And we won't know for a week whether it has gone wrong or not, and that's a long time to wait." He finished his new and last gin and tonic with a flourish. "As I say, I would be insane to consider it." He put out his Player's. "Why did you come to me?"

"Because"—Jill smiled—"you're an old, bold pilot."

Tom Tully threw her an old-fashioned RAF salute.

NOW, in the suite of the Ritz, he was doing exactly the same salute, the fingers shaking ever so slightly at his temple. He was grinning. Tom Tully was enjoying this. He was enjoying it very much. He came across to Jill and put a copy of the *Standard* in her hand. "The diary's on page six." He lit a Player's with his old RAF lighter. "You'll have to buy me a gold lighter from Dunhill with a Q on it if this ploy works."

"Done." Jill turned to page four. It was there.

It was indeed.

She devoured every word of it.

"Tom Tully," she declared, eyes shining, "you're not only an old, bold pilot, you're a bloody pathfinder!"

"Pathfinder Leader actually," said Tom modestly.

Jill kissed him enthusiastically. He blotted her lipstick with his impeccable white handkerchief. "You might be biting me when the old boy's agents get on to you."

"I'll meet that when it happens, Tom."

"It'll happen. Rest assured."

The buzz in the room was even louder than the one that had

greeted the movie clip of Maggie and Austin. All the angels were turning to the pages marked by Molly Budd, the best secretary, Jill thought, in London. She was the only one who knew the facts. Except herself and Tom Tully.

Even Josh did not know the facts.

She had not told him. She wasn't sure why, except that directors had their own reputations to consider, and they were more difficult than press agents when it came to convincing them that sailing near the wind could be a fair tactic. Josh might have agreed but Jill hadn't been sure that he would, and so, reluctantly, she had said nothing, and would say nothing now.

Always keep something back.

Josh was at her side, incredulous. "Is this true?" He waved his *Standard.*

"It's just an item in the diary, Josh. It doesn't have to be true."

"Then it isn't true?"

"It isn't quite true yet, but it easily could be, Josh."

"Meaning it isn't true at all?"

"I didn't say that. And please don't speak so loudly. Just smile and say nothing. Please. I'll explain everything later."

"Have you sent copies of the play to the sirs?" His voice was cold.

Jill turned her eyes on him, opening them very wide. "Of course I have."

"Well, that's something, I suppose. What did they say?"

Jill held up her hand. "Not now, leave it until later." Again, she used her eyes. Somewhat to her annoyance, the trick did not work. Josh gazed steadily at her, and then said, "Jill, I don't believe a word of it. You and I are going to have to talk. I think you've been a bloody fool."

Jill suddenly felt weak at the knees. Nobody talked to her like that. Not her father, even. Not Joe Dancy, even. Not even the arrogant young sods in television studios who thought actors were shit. "All I'm doing is getting *Queen* off the ground, the best way I know how, which as a producer, impresario—call me either—is *my* job, not yours. You are the artistic person here and I'm the common saleslady. So let me get on with my business and just introduce me to the nice angels, there's a darling."

For a long moment she thought he would not do it.

His eyes stared into hers, and her knees felt weaker.

"Please, Josh."

Oh God, she thought, he won't do it. He's going to walk out. For Josh had moved away, toward the door. He turned and looked at her. Then he rapped with an empty glass on a table and, taking a deep breath, said quietly, "Ladies and gentlemen, I think Miss Jill Viner would like to say a few words."

There was applause—led by Tom Tully—for Jill, and she smiled at them all. Her knees shook. You used to be an actress, so be one. This is the big money day. It all happens now, in the next half-hour, or it doesn't happen at all. Act, for God's sake. Then she heard her own voice, level and calm and, thank the Lord, confident.

"Ladies and gentlemen, you already know that Maggie Stride and Austin Ames are booked for the play. As you also know, they are both American artists. We must have a British connection to make the play even more attractive to our audiences on Shaftesbury Avenue. I'm sure you've all read the item in the *Standard* diary." She smiled winningly at them all. "It mentions the names of Sir Harry and Sir Piers. It says—and we don't exactly know how the rumor came about—but it *says* that *both* these great actors have been approached to appear in *Queen*. At this precise moment, since nothing contractual has been yet signed, I cannot say more than the item does, which is simply that both of these actors, our greatest Shakespearians—one our greatest Shylock, the other our greatest Lear—have not appeared together since they played in *Othello*, one as the Moor, and the other as Iago, thirty-two years ago. We are hoping, ladies and gentlemen, to end that long break with *Queen*! With one playing the prime minister and the other playing the

Russian. I leave you to fit each one to his part yourselves. You would not be true theatre buffs if you could not. . . ."

The room was alive, the buzz loud and insistent.

Jill thought: It's now. This moment. She held up her hand for silence, and got it.

"I cannot say more than that, not on that particular matter. But all of you will have read the brochure and from that you will know what kind of play *Queen* is. I believe it to be the most important political work since *Darkness at Noon*. Political plays are rare. Good ones are rarer. I wish I could say the play was written by an English writer. I can't do that, but I think, and our very talented director Josh Williams thinks, and so does everybody who has read *Queen*, that it is a very fine and timely play indeed. But such a play needs great casting, and that, I believe you will agree, we have tonight. . . ."

There was some handclapping, again led by Tom Tully.

Jill let the silence hang, after the clapping had stopped. "I only want to make one more point. I am not taking a management fee. Nor is Mr. Williams. We are taking a very small salary until *Queen* is in profit. Then, and only then, will *we* be in profit." She smiled. "You're in with the same chance we are until then."

The buzz went up, as people turned to one another, and Jack Millard's voice could be heard saying to Colonel Chase-Gordon, "I think she means it."

The colonel's barracks-square voice seemed to speak for a lot of people. "Well, I can tell you, sir, I'm in, I must say!"

Jill held up her hand. "You all have subscription forms. If you wish to invest, please do. There is no limit, under or over a thousand pounds." She smiled again. "But I'm hoping for a good effort from everybody. At least twice what they last invested with Joe Dancy. You lost that. With *Queen* you'll get it back."

They all laughed, ruefully.

On impulse she added, "I'll have to have your decisions tonight, ladies and gentlemen, I'm afraid. I have a lot of people interested besides yourselves, but I wanted to give you first chance, because I know you are theatre lovers who deserve to be on to a good thing. I should add this. . . ." Jill kept her voice low. "There are no certainties in play investment. In that it's rather like horse racing. But I believe *Queen* to be a hot favorite."

Jill sat down to the biggest buzz of the evening.

"Bloody marvelous, old girl," Tom Tully whispered in her ear.

Molly Budd smiled at her as she gave out the pens with a Q on them that Jill had ordered from Parker's the week before.

Josh Williams was looking at her through new, and very angry eyes.

The angels were writing industriously, warmed by one another's enthusiasm as they did so. Jill closed her eyes. She felt drained and yet happy, as she had felt at the Beverly Hills Hotel after Austin had said yes, maybe. Why was she working so hard, her father had asked her wryly the last time they talked. What did she get out of it?

The feeling of triumph, the sweet sweet wine of victory. This.

"I CAN'T believe it. Jesus, what chutzpa!"

Tom Tully sat, a very large glass of gin and tonic in his hand, in the wreck of the Ritz suite. The dirty glasses and dishes were being cleared away by George and his team (all heavily tipped), cigar smoke still hung in the air, and even the flowers were beginning to wilt. It was ten o'clock. The last angels, Colonel Chase-Gordon and his lady and Jack Millard and the little actress, Pat Woods, were off to dine excitedly together in the Ritz restaurant, an unusual foursome even for angels. Now, Jill and Josh and Tom Tully sat and watched Molly, as she added up the final total. At last she looked up at them sternly through her gold-rimmed glasses.

"Fifty-four thousand, five hundred and fifty pounds," she announced calmly, as if it were not enough.

The telephone rang and George answered it. "Miss Jill? For you."

Jill crossed to the telephone, calling, "Say it again, Molly, it sounds like music!" Into the telephone she said, "Jill Viner. Who is this?"

It was Sir Harry's agent. Jill listened, said twenty words, promised to talk again, and rang off. She returned to the others, bursting to speak, but didn't.

Always hold something back.

"This," said Tom Tully, "is a miracle. Now all we need is another one. The two sirs both saying yes. Then we're really in business."

Jill wished Tom had said something else, anything else. She tried to cut in but Josh beat her to it, saying to Tom, "So we have absolutely no reaction from Sir Harry or Sir Piers? None at all?"

Tom Tully regarded him mildly. "You're in the office, dear boy. You should know, if anybody should."

"No." Josh's implacable eye was on Jill Viner. "I don't know."

"There's no problem, old son." Tom Tully was talking to reassure Josh. "Sir Piers is filming in Cannes. One of his money-making expeditions, some awful horror thing. Old Harry's at his house in the country." He sighed. "Dear old stick. The boys cost him a packet, I hear."

"He has a telephone," said Josh. "Somebody will tell him. Where did you send the script?"

"To his agent, naturally." Jill was decisive. She had to be. Josh should know better than to talk in public like this, or even before Tom Tully and Molly. It wasn't done.

"Was my name mentioned?" Josh was asking, ominously.

"Of course it was. You've worked with Sir Harry, and Sir Piers is bound to know your name."

There was a long silence.

Josh said, "Don't send anything out with my name on it again unless I sign the letter, Jill. I mean that. This piece in the *Standard* could backfire."

"True," said Tom Tully.

"It won't," Jill declared, hoping she was right.

"It was planted there to raise cash, I see that," said Josh.

"That's very nice of you, to see that." Jill couldn't resist it.

"But it was a stupid idea. I don't know whether it was Tom's or yours, but it was still a stupid idea."

"Well, thanks," said Tom urbanely.

"It was my idea. All mine." Jill was getting angry now.

"Don't you see that if either Harry or Piers goes to the press and denies ever having seen the thing, it's all been for nothing? And they'll do that tomorrow."

"Probably the day after, takes time." This from Tom Tully.

"All right. You sold the angels on Maggie and Austin and Sir Piers and Sir Harry. When they discover from their newspapers Sir Piers and Sir Harry are out, they may think Maggie and Austin could be out, too. And stop their checks."

"It's a risk, certainly." Tom Tully tried to pour oil on the very troubled waters.

"Yes, and one we had to take." Jill bristled. "Sorry you don't like it."

"No, I don't like it." Josh stood up. "My name was in that paper tonight." He picked up a *Standard* and read aloud, " 'Josh Williams, who has left the National Theatre to direct *The Queen of Finland*, says that Sir Harry was his first choice and he has high hopes that he will accept. He also said he was considering Sir Piers for the other role and had every hope of an acceptance there, too.' "

"What, dear boy, is wrong with that, pray?" asked Tom Tully. "Rather nicely put, I thought. Nice and ambiguous."

"Ambiguous, be buggered! I never said any such thing to anybody!"

117

"You did say that you wanted Sir Harry for the prime minister," protested Jill.

"Of course I did. He'd be marvelous. But he hasn't even read the play and here am I talking about Sir Harry being perfect! And considering Sir Piers! Nobody *considers* Sir Piers! He's done everything, everything! What sort of an idiot do I look to everybody in the business when I say I'm *considering* Sir Piers! I'll tell you, a bloody idiot is what I look!" Josh Williams took a deep breath. "I think I have said enough. If you'll excuse me?"

He stalked out of the suite.

"Ah, dear me, the laddie's upset." Tom Tully shrugged. "Sorry I spoke."

Jill jumped to her feet and followed Josh out. He was halfway along the corridor when she called, gently, "Josh, please wait!"

Josh stopped and turned round. His face was grim.

Jill walked to him, not too quickly.

"I did it for *Queen*. I did what I thought was right."

"I have a good reputation as a director but I can lose that overnight if either of these eminent actors says he has never heard of me or the play. Not only was it a stupid thing to do but it could sink the whole play. If your angels pull out. It's a risk you shouldn't have taken."

Tears were in Jill's eyes, but she refused to cry. She had never cried. Her father had brought her up like a boy and boys didn't cry, so she didn't cry, never never never. "I'm very sorry you think that. I think you're wrong. We had to take the risk."

He looked at her steadily. "In short, you make all the decisions, is that it?"

"That's why I'm called a producer, Josh."

"You should have talked to me first."

"All right. Oh, Josh, please. Maybe I should have. I'm sorry."

She turned and walked back toward the suite, waiting for him to call her, say anything, but he did not. At the door she turned and looked down the corridor; he was gone from sight. Ah, to hell with him. Why was she so upset? He just wasn't her kind of person. It was a business arrangement, and this was a business matter—no more, no less. She walked back into the suite, thinking she could have told him that Sir Harry's agent had telephoned, that Sir Harry might be interested if the money was right, that Sir Harry had been very amused by the director making him his perfect choice and Sir Piers only an actor "to be considered." Jill, of course, knew (said Sir Harry's agent) that the two old actors hated the sight of each other, always had, since that wonderful *Othello* many years before? Jill had said she knew. The point was, the money would be good. If Sir Harry wanted the part they could accommodate him, financially.

"Wouldn't it be nice if we could get them both?" she'd asked Sir Harry's agent. The agent had laughed. "A miracle, dear."

Perhaps. And perhaps not.

Now why hadn't she told Josh *that?*

Always keep something back?

Well, yes, but there was more, if she was to be honest. She had wanted him to respond on a personal level when she said please. He hadn't. Why had she tried? She didn't know. Jill rarely used sex as a weapon, being fairly sure it rarely worked. A hint of it, as a joke, a gag, a livener maybe, but sex—or did she mean love as far as Josh Williams was concerned? Surely not.

No. It was: always keep something back. That was it.

"Catch him?" Tom Tully asked sympathetically.

"He got away."

"Took his script with him though, didn't he?" Molly was a veteran of many backstage battles.

"So he did," Jill agreed, feeling a little better.

It was only to last until the telephone rang again and Josh Williams spoke to her from the foyer saying he'd been thinking about it and had decided to pull out of *Queen*. She could keep the four thousand pounds as an investment, but he was out. Sorry. Good-bye. Just like that. Jill put the telephone down, feeling very sick.

119

"Anything wrong?" asked Tom Tully. Molly knew better than to ask.

"Nothing," said Jill hollowly, "I can't handle."

To hell with Josh Williams and everything about him, she told herself. I have other things to think about tonight, and other things to do.

Tom Tully saluted that with a wave of his glass, and Molly looked sad and sorry. "Well, whatever else happened, we got fifty thousand pounds tonight, Jill."

"So we did," said Jill. "So we did."

LORD Glass—known to people who didn't even know him as Jerry—sat in his huge office in Glass House smoking one of his huge cigars. It was ten-thirty but he hadn't finished his day's business yet. He would be at his desk as usual tomorrow morning by eight o'clock prompt, saying good-morning to the cleaners by their first names. He had the reputation of being one of the best employers in the entertainment business, probably because he hated sacking people. Despite his hard-boiled appearance, Lord Glass was a softie. He loved a gamble and he loved to do a deal, almost any deal, any hour of the day or night. Which was why he had said, to Jill's call, "Sure, come up, let's talk now. Okay, why not now, when's better?"

Fifteen minutes later she was in Glass House at the top end of Oxford Street, sitting in a large leather chair with a drink in her hand. Lord Glass didn't drink, but he lit another havana with anticipation. "I saw the *Standard*. You're not telling me Sir Piers and Sir Harry are sure."

"Not sure. Good chances."

Lord Glass looked pleased. "You're flying a kite?"

"Between us, yes, I am."

Lord Glass looked even more pleased. "Will it go higher or come crashing down?" He didn't seem to need an answer. The very idea was enough to delight him. "I hear you have Maggie and Austin sewn up?"

Jill was genuinely surprised. "How . . . ?"

Lord Glass shook his head. "Manny Hiberson rang me. Just a courtesy call. He thought I might be interested in investing."

"Well, I don't know what to say, Lord Glass."

"Call me Jerry, everybody does—and listen. Manny and me are old friends from long ago, from the poor times. He knows I like a flutter in the theatre so if there's something nice moving, he tells me about it. If he knows. Of course, I lose money, usually. But who doesn't?"

"That was really nice of Manny."

"He liked you, he said so. He said you're a hustler." Lord Glass beamed approvingly. "And it pays to be pleasant to everybody, in this world. You never know who's working for you." He continued to beam. "So you've no more hustling to do, Manny's done it for you."

"I'll try to see you don't lose your investment this time. You saw my brochure? I sent it over by hand earlier."

"Read it with interest. Couldn't come to your party, meant to ring but I got busy." Lord Glass indicated his six telephones, in formidable array. "So, what you want to know is, am I interested in *Queen*?"

"Yes," said Jill a trifle breathlessly.

Lord Glass pondered. "What money do you need?" He answered the question himself. "A hundred thousand, the stars you're talking about, am I right?" She nodded. "You have how much?"

"Half. From my angels. Tonight, at the party."

"Not a bad night's work. Manny says Austin Ames and Maggie think it's a wonderful play and with them both I can't see it failing. But anything can fail. I like your brochure, but brochures don't put bums on seats. Do you have a theatre in mind?"

"Not yet." Jill decided on total honesty with Lord Glass.

Anything else would be detected at once, by a combination of wisdom and experience. "I need another fifty thousand. Then I'm in business."

"That doesn't seem out of this world. You have any other people to see besides me?"

"Yes, I have. One."

"Is he good for a large piece of the action?"

"I think so." Here, Jill knew she could not be honest. Prince Ahmed was a Saudi, but even a princely Saudi might not be a good idea to mention.

"Hmm. Good stars, half the money already, a director from the National. Looks good. Looks very good."

He smoked and beamed at her.

Jill sipped her whiskey, which she felt she needed, after that awful business with Josh Williams. "It seems I don't have a lot of selling to do. You're doing it for me."

Lord Glass beamed again. "Only because I like the sound of the thing."

"You can read the playscript if you want to. I have a copy with me."

He shook his head. "Listen, I've never read a stage play yet that I've invested in. I'm not a stage producer. I know TV and that's all I know. TV's big. You can modify your risks. There's no confrontation. The stage, it's a few hundred people in a big room and a few others trying to amuse them. It's terrifying. Terrifying. I know, I tried it once, a hundred years ago." Lord Glass had actually once been a stand-up comic. "Listen, did you ever have a relation Harry Viner, a comic on the music hall?"

"Yes, he was an uncle. A long time ago; I never saw him work."

"I remember him. Very funny. Didn't care if they laughed or not. All the chutzpa in the world." He smiled. "It's in the blood, no?"

Jill laughed. "He never got rich, I heard."

122

"Rich?" Lord Glass shook his head. "What's rich, except please yourself what work you do?" He puffed on his cigar. "Look, I have three calls booked, so I'll come to the crunch. I'll put twenty thousand pounds in *Queen*. The check's made out there on the desk."

Jill felt she was walking on water as he saw her to the door, a fatherly hand on her shoulder. "A joke Harry Viner used to tell: 'I'm sorry about the fire,' says Abie to Morrie. 'Hush nu,' says Morrie, 'that's tomorrow.'" He waved his famous havana. "Don't forget four tickets for the first night." He thought a moment. "Don't forget my cousin owns the Royal Theatre. I'll call him, get him to call you." He shook his head. "Sir Piers and Sir Harry? Good luck to you." He shrugged his shoulders. "And to me, also."

Jill sank, amazed, into a taxi in Oxford Street and told the driver, "The Ritz." Back to base. What a day! What a man Lord Glass was! Made up his mind before I ever got there. So, two down and one to go.

Ahmed.

PRINCE Ahmed, she reminded herself as she made herself up in the Ritz cloakroom. Made herself up very carefully. Prince Ahmed she had only met once, in Joe Dancy's office when, against Joe's rule of secrecy, he had come in to enquire about a very lovely actress in Joe's last musical, the one that had lost everybody money except Joe Dancy. Joe had given him the girl's telephone number, something Jill thought not proper. Joe had shrugged. "He likes the girls, it's why he invests. It saves him having to shop around for them, and anyway, actresses are more accommodating."

"Than what, call girls?" Jill had asked acidly.

"Look, she doesn't have to sleep with him or even have dinner with him, does she? Can I change the world? He's so rich it doesn't matter. If that turns her on, fine." Joe had blown out his cheeks. He didn't like to be thought improper. The legitimate theatre, unlike television or movies, was a very proper, almost a snobby business, in London. "Did you hear about the window cleaner who cleaned the Arab's window and the Arab said how much and the window cleaner said seven fifty, meaning seven pounds, fifty pence? The Arab gave him seven hundred and fifty pounds and said, 'Don't come back, it's too much!' "

Jill looked at herself in the mirror. Tired around the eyes, but who wouldn't be, after a day like this had been. And it wasn't over.

The plushly Edwardian Ritz Casino was busy, despite the hour, and Ahmed was easily recognizable, because he wore Arab headdress and a beautifully cut dark blue lounge suit from Gieves. He was playing blackjack, the fastest gambling game in the house, in a desultory way, and he looked bored, and very like Omar Sharif. Jill was not a member, but she had spoken earlier to the hotel manager and he had agreed that, if Prince Ahmed wished her to call and be signed in as his guest, he was sure the casino manager would have no objection. Nor did he. The casino manager was at Jill's side the moment she entered, taking in at a glance that she was a lady, wearing a suitable dress (thank God for the money she'd spent on it, and to hell with Josh Williams), and in no way one of the prince's lady friends. The hotel manager had plainly told him who she was and that she had rented a suite in the hotel for the evening's party. His manner was respectful. "Good evening, madam. I have been expecting you. If I may find you a table?" In a moment she was seated. "May I get you something to drink?"

"Thank you, no. I'm to see the prince."

"Yes, of course, madam. I will tell the prince at once."

As the casino manager leaned discreetly over the baize table and whispered in Ahmed's ear, a few heads turned, even more discreetly, in Jill Viner's direction. There are no secrets, personal or financial, in a casino. Absolutely none. The gamblers in this room all knew one another intimately. It was like a club. I wish a few of them were angels, Jill thought, instead of only one, and that one very dicey.

Prince Ahmed threw his three cards down stoically and rose, gesturing to his man, in flowing white robes, to tip the girl operating the blackjack game. Money, in chips or for real, was plainly nothing he ever touched. Or possibly even thought seriously about. He crossed the room—God, what a good-looking man!—and bent over and kissed her hand, in the French manner. "Good evening, Miss Viner. It was very kind of you to call by. I was getting very bored with myself, losing money." He sat down and crossed his elegant legs, and a pot of Turkish coffee appeared in front of him as if by magic. "Would you join me, or will it keep you awake tonight? I assure you it is very strong, the very best, much better for energy than alcohol." Oh Lord, she'd been drinking whiskey and he could smell it and found it offensive.

Jill said, "I'd love some, thank you." The coffee was very dark, so thick you could almost eat it, and the Turkish delight and nuts served with it were very necessary to relieve the strength of the liquid. Ahmed ate none of these things, but sipped water now and again.

"So." He smiled with devastating charm. "We meet for a second time."

"You remember me?" Jill was very pleased. "I wasn't sure you would."

"But of course. In Joe Dancy's office, as you said in your charming note, enclosed with the brochure." He inclined his head. "About which I must apologize. I have not found time to read it, until now."

Jill felt a blow. Yet, why? The brochure had been brought down here at eight o'clock and Ahmed had never moved away from the tables since then. What had she expected, that he would sit down and read it? In here? She smiled at the thought.

"You are amused?" His voice was very soft. "Why is that?"

"Oh, I somehow hoped you might have glanced at it."

"I'm so sorry. I apologize. I will read it at once. Is it long?"

"Only five pages. Take you about ten minutes, I'd say."

"Then I will read it, but not here. This is no place for business."

"Have you lost a lot of money?" Jill nodded toward the main action. They kept their voices low. Now, he frowned. "I'm not sure. Ali can tell me." Ali appeared at his elbow. Ahmed spoke in Arabic. Ali replied. Ali was very dark, almost black. Prince Ahmed was light-skinned, very nearly coffee-colored. "It seems we lost a trifle. Nothing serious."

"I'm sorry." Jill was very daring. "How much is 'nothing serious'?" Prince Ahmed frowned again. " 'Nothing serious' is ten thousand pounds."

Jill laughed, and a number of heads turned their way. Even the casino manager glanced in their direction. Ahmed rose to his feet. "I think we should discuss our business elsewhere, no?" And Ali drew back her chair and they were out of the timeless, underwater atmosphere of the casino, and whirring up in the Ritz lift, and then they were in Prince Ahmed's suite, at the rear of the hotel, overlooking Green Park.

"What a lovely room." It was: perfectly Western in all the essential furniture, but with Eastern rugs (probably priceless) and silk cushions and more low tables—gilt, wondrously inlaid. On the main low table stood what Jill took to be a hookah.

Ali bustled about and clapped his hands, and a houseboy no more than twelve years old, Jill supposed, and very beautiful, with huge dark eyes, brought the inevitable Turkish coffee, sweetmeats and dates and figs on dishes. "Please, do sit down and let me read your brochure." Jill sat, and Ahmed took the brochure with the Q on it, which Ali produced from beneath his spotless white robe. "I took a course in speedreading in English, you know? Very effective. Please time me, no? I am very quick."

Indeed he was. In three minutes by Jill's watch he laid down the brochure. He then closed his eyes for exactly thirty seconds. When he opened them again, they were very alert.

"I read the *Standard* piece. Do you have the sirs for certain?"

"Not for certain."

"I hear you have Maggie and Austin."

"Yes, we do." No secrets, it seemed, on Shaftesbury Avenue.

"What is your budget, a hundred thousand pounds?" She nodded.

"Do you have a theatre?"

She plunged. "We may get the Royal."

A pause. No more. A hesitation. No more.

"That is owned by Herbie Glass?" His voice was neutral.

"Yes, it is. But it's by no means certain."

A relaxation. Very slight. No more.

"You are asking for how much?"

"Whatever you have to invest."

"If I come in at all I will put in twenty thousand."

"That sum would be most welcome."

"I like to be the biggest single investor."

"I do have another investor at that figure." Jill felt she had to say it.

"May I ask who?"

"It would be improper to say. I'm sorry."

He nodded. "Very correct. It will, of course, if it is anybody, be Lord Glass?"

"I really shouldn't say, Prince Ahmed."

"Then it is Lord Glass. I see." His voice was grave. "That, I must say, troubles me."

That's the end of it. Jill stared into her tiny coffee cup. Muslim and Jew. Either way, it won't work. One of them will back out. And, if either does, that will leave me with twenty thousand more to find, in a hard, hard year for theatre investors. A sense of bitter despair came over her, for the first time that day. Even in the row with Josh she hadn't felt like this. Then there had at least been the hope she could change his view. What a fool she had been to expect to clinch it all as quickly as that. Joe Dancy would have taken six months to set up a production like *Queen*, and here she was, trying to do it in six weeks. Jill felt all the hope go out of her.

"Have you eaten supper?" Ahmed was asking. It was obviously his way of being polite, of brushing her off. Well, there was no need for that. She had given Lord Glass her word. He was in. She could not go back on that. Prince Ahmed was plainly out. There was no point in further discussion. She stood up, feeling very tired. "No, really, I mustn't. It's far too late. I'm keeping you."

He stood too, and placed his hand very gently on her arm. "All I'm having is a light snack. And I know these parties. They are so draining. You look tired. Eat a little." He clapped his hands smartly and Ali appeared round the door. "They are very good to me here. They prepare my dishes the way I like them. I asked Ali to order and I think they are here." Again, as if on cue, the waiters appeared, officered by Ali, with a splendid light supper of kebabs and rice and yoghurts. A bottle of Niersteiner was on ice, too. "For you. I do not expect Westerners to live as I do." Ali and the boy served them and then left, bowing, as they ate. Jill was hungry. The condemned girl ate a hearty supper, she thought. I'll have to send all the bloody money back. Oh, what the hell! She ate well but miserably, helped by Ahmed to the delicacies. And as she ate he talked, pleasantly, to lessen the blow of denial.

"Let me say what I think about the play. The idea of it, as put by the brochure. It seems to me a political play, and speaking as an Arab, and an officer of the government of my country, albeit only a member of the court, we have not yet imported democracy along with our Rolls-Royces and Cadillacs and refrigerators and football teams. As an officer of the court of an Arab country I have to be careful about such things. The play sounds to be political." He held up a beringed hand. "I know, I know, that is not how you would describe it, but plainly it is so. My feelings towards the superpowers are those of most Arabs. We fear them. Both of them. We fear the West. And the East. Why not? We have come from being nomads

128

in the desert, a brave and resourceful people, hard-living and hard-working and poor, to what? Oil-rich beyond dreams." He took the hookah and puffed. "We can give our people everything, make them soft, as your young men are soft in the West—oh, it's happening, dear Miss Viner—and when we do, what do we have? A people who can only gamble in casinos or run London delicatessens bought by their cousins from Italians at ten times the price they are worth!"

He passed the hookah to Jill and, perfectly naturally, she puffed on it. It was not unpleasant. After all it was only pot, which she had tried a few times, although she was not a regular user. Prince Ahmed was still talking. She felt rather light-headed. "The English laugh at us and they are right to do so. Yet they should understand us. They were once, not very long ago, a great warrior race, and now what are they? Soft and in peril, as we are. As the whole Arab world is. So the play says, the West can give us democracy and Cadillacs, which are better than the commissars and what they call democratic socialism. But the Arabs want neither. We are a people of the desert and our way of life used to suit us perfectly. The English loved and respected us. The Russians kept away from us at least. But now we have the oil and we are courted by both sides. And threatened by both sides." He sighed, deeply. "The oil was the worst thing that ever happened to the Arabs."

He took the hookah from her. She felt even more light-headed. She felt that she did not care what happened, to anybody or anything at all. She felt as if she were floating, floating, floating. The room was dark and Ahmed was darker.

To hell with Josh Williams, she thought. He doesn't care what I do. He wouldn't care if I went to bed with Ahmed. He wouldn't care at all. Would he? No. Of course he wouldn't. She closed her eyes.

Very softly Ahmed said, "Yes. The oil was the worst thing that ever happened to us. But all this must be very boring for you. We must talk business."

Jill opened her eyes: whatever else he was, plainly he was not

129

inclined to be sexy with her. It was just as well, she decided (possibly a little disappointed, was she?). The relationship between producer and angel had to be a businesslike one. So had the relationship between producer and director.

"I'm afraid I can't go back on the twenty thousand pounds I've taken from Lord Glass," she sighed.

"Naturally," Prince Ahmed said.

There was a long silence.

Jill felt slightly sick. Probably the hookah, she decided. "I'm sorry about that."

"No. No. Business, I understand."

The boy came in, gently enquiring.

"Yes, yes," said Prince Ahmed, "put the light on, Mohammed."

The boy switched on a small side lamp and waited in the shadows. Prince Ahmed pursed his lips.

"If I come in I have a condition."

"Yes?"

"I must have twenty-five thousand pounds. And you do not need to tell Lord Glass. I will not."

The boy let her out with a slight contemptuous smile.

IN the taxi leaving the Ritz Jill felt no desire to go home and sleep. The check in her hand for twenty-five thousand made everything possible. *Queen* was going to go on. It was a reality. It was going to happen. She hugged herself in an ecstasy of delight. She couldn't go home to her little Kensington flat and drink a cup of chocolate and go to bed. This was the culmination of everything she had worked for. It was a moment to share with somebody.

The taxi rolled sedately through the empty streets.

Jill leaned forward. "I've changed my mind. Glebe Place, please."

It took her almost five minutes to waken Josh Williams. When at last he answered, she called up through his intercom, "Josh, it's me. Come on, let me in!"

"Huh? It's four o'clock in the morning. What's wrong?"

"Big news. Open up."

Josh pressed the buzzer and the door opened. Jill walked in and up the first flight of stairs to Josh's apartment. He was standing in the doorway in an old woollen dressing gown, his thick gray hair in a tangle and a bleary look on his face. He didn't seem pleased to see her, but she was past caring.

"Josh, darling, I've got the money! I've got the bloody money, darling!"

"Don't shout, you'll wake everybody up. The other people around here get up at seven." As she stood staring at him, conscious she was swaying a little, he took her arm and half pushed her into the apartment. "Come in and sit down. What's the matter with you, are you pissed or what?"

Jill sat on the sofa and smiled, a little foolishly. "No, I don't think so. Maybe a bit. But I have every right to be. Josh! *I've got the money!*"

"Yes, all right, don't shout, just sit there a moment and I'll make some coffee." He padded into the kitchen, and she heard him run water and put the kettle on.

"Don't want coffee," she called. "I had coffee with Prince Ahmed." Nearly had sex with him, too, she thought dreamily, except he didn't want to. Would have, too, to get this play on. Or at least I think I would. Or was it because I hate you, Josh Williams? Or because I like you? Or because, God help me, I think I might even love you?

"No coffee," she called again. "I'll have a drink."

"You'll have coffee." He came back into the room. "It's sobering-up time."

"I'm not drunk. I did have a puff of his hookah, though."

Josh laughed. "You did what?"

131

"He had a hookah and I had a puff."

"No wonder you're high. That stuff's potent."

She waved her hand. Somehow she had fumbled a cigarette into it. She couldn't remember how. "Quite harmless. Anyway, he's in for twenty-five."

Josh simply said "Good," and looked at her gravely.

"And Lord Glass is in for twenty."

Josh said "Good" again. He didn't give her a light for her cigarette. He seemed to find her sudden appearance something of a nuisance. She tried to get to her feet.

"Know when I'm not wanted. We'll talk in the morning. Silly idea, coming to see you at this time. I'd forgotten you were an old, old man who needed his sleep. Just thought . . ." The words seemed to be coming out with difficulty. "Just thought you would be interested to know we were in business, right? Obviously a mistake." Jill somehow got to her feet. Her legs seemed rubbery all of a sudden. "I won't wait, I'll get a taxi. I saw a few cruising around."

Josh pushed her gently on the shoulder. He was smiling a little. That was an improvement anyway. "Just sit down before you fall down. Black coffee coming up."

"Told you. Don't want coffee."

But she sat down and sulked. All right. He didn't care, about her or *Queen*. Or if he did he had a damn strange way of showing it. To hell with him. She'd been right. He wasn't her kind.

"Coffee. Drink it all."

"Shove it. Don't want bloody coffee."

"What's the matter *now*?"

It was the accent on the *now* that was too much.

"What's the matter *now* is that I have just revived your career and given you a new chance after you walked out of the National without thinking what you were doing! 'What's the matter now?' instead of 'Thanks, Jill, that was great,' which it was, which it bloody well *was!*"

Josh just looked at her in silence and held the cup of black coffee in front of her. She swept it to the floor, and a stain spread over the ancient but splendid carpet. He just looked at it, and at her. Then he went into the kitchen and got a cloth and a bowl of warm water and came back and knelt down and blotted the stain away.

"Never mind the bloody carpet." Jill was still having difficulty with her words. "You can buy six like it when *Queen*'s a success!"

"I rather happen to like this one."

"You rather happen to like anything, anything at all, don't you? Except me? You don't happen to like me at all, do you, not one tiny little bloody bit?"

There. She had said it.

He blotted the last of the coffee stain dry and took the pieces of the broken cup back into the kitchen. He came back with another cup of black coffee in his hand (at least he wasn't asking her to drink it; that too was an improvement) and sat opposite her in a leather chair, at a wary distance.

"Jill, darling," he said quietly, "what's all this about?"

"If you don't know, you're blind."

She closed her eyes. The shame of her. The chutzpa. Never mind. What the hell. It was the truth.

"I'm glad we got the money. Sorry if I seemed put out. I was asleep."

He was evading the point. He was refusing to accept what she had said. He was English to the core; he was pretending she was drunk and didn't mean a word of it. The man was insufferable.

"Josh. Why I'm here is because I want to go to bed with you."

A long silence. Then, "Oh, is it? I thought it was because you'd set *Queen* up."

She laughed. "Well, that too."

He was looking at her very gravely from his armchair.

"It's not a very good idea, love. We're working on the same production. It gets out, the actors get to know, the production staff get to know. It makes for complications."

"Of course it makes for complications. Loving somebody always does make for complications!"

Jesus Christ, she must be mad! It was the booze. And the hashish. And the success. Or all three. Yes. It was all three. But there. She had said it. There was no taking it back. I love him, she thought. I must love him. I've never done anything even remotely like this before. I must. She stood up. "Where's the bedroom?"

He pointed. "Through there."

"Right." She walked unsteadily into the room, and there indeed was the bed. The sheets were crumpled, and around the bed lay pages of handwritten notes and a pair of glasses and the remains of a nightcap, Scotch by the scent of it. Slowly and deliberately Jill Viner took off her black-silver dress, and all the rest—of which there was very little—and climbed into Josh's bed quite naked.

"Josh," she called softly, and closed her eyes.

WHEN she woke up it was nine o'clock in the morning and the breakfast-time traffic was moving along Glebe Place. The curtains were still drawn and there was no sign of Josh.

"Oh, Christ," said Jill and got up unsteadily and staggered into the bathroom, which adjoined the bedroom. She groped blindly for Alka-Seltzers in the cupboard, found them, stirred them into a tooth glass and drank them down. Her head felt muzzy and her mouth dry and her legs heavy. She trudged back toward the bed. As she did so Josh Williams came in with a large cup of coffee. He did not particularly look at her nakedness but he did not look away either. She got under the blankets but did not cover up her breasts. Let him look. See what he's missing. His own fault. Sod him if he wants to live with a memory. Anyway, everybody who had ever seen them had thought her breasts wonderful and said so the first minute they saw them. Josh Williams didn't say anything except, "You can have this coffee if you promise not to throw it at me."

She laughed and took it. Her head was clearing. She sipped the coffee and felt better. He lit a cigarette and offered it to her. He was still wearing his dressing gown and pajamas. Presumably he had slept on the sofa.

"Sorry about last night, Josh. My fault. Sorry."

She was. But not in any way he would understand.

"You finished your coffee?"

"Yes. It was good."

"Are you all right? Not hung over?"

"No. I'm fine. I'll get up and have a bath in a minute and then I'll go. I have to change my clothes before I go to the office."

Josh said, "Did you mean what you said last night?"

"What? Oh. I'm not sure. Perhaps."

Josh very slowly took off his dressing gown and then his pajamas. "I just wanted to be sure."

Jill couldn't resist it. "I can see you're pleased to see me!"

He laughed and so did she. And it was very good, easy and loving between them, and she squeezed him and locked herself around him and felt more delight and love and thought I love him I love him I love him and this is what I want and I love him . . . and she felt his urgent throb inside her and the thrust of him and her own wetness and she came again and again and they both laughed a lot and she told him she loved him and did he love her and he was shy and said I must, and they lay side by side in the soft morning light filtering through the curtains and she said, laughing, "You still think it's such a bad idea?"

He grinned faintly. "No. I think it's a good bad idea."

She kissed him with passion and wondered if he was joking.

MAGGIE stood in her sitting room, the cable from London in her hand.

It was a hot summer day in New York City. The air-conditioning made the room pleasantly cool, but she ached to be out in

135

the burning streets, able to walk freely wherever she liked. Maggie had not been out of the house for five days, and she was beginning to feel the strain. Madge, the nurse, who was coming in days now, looked into the room. She saw the cable. "Not bad news, I hope?"

Maggie shook her head. "No. It's the people in London. They have plans that look like a September start."

"Will you go?"

"How can I?"

The nurse said nothing to that except, "He's awake now, if you want to go see him." As Maggie moved to the door, the girl touched her arm. "He's kinda drowsy. It's this bigger dose they're giving him."

Maggie shuddered. "All that dope. Poor man."

"It's that or the pain."

"Yes. I know." Maggie put on her stoical face (she felt anything but stoical; she felt unutterably desperate), tucked the cable into her dress pocket, and went up the stairs.

Philip lay back on the pillows, his face very waxen indeed. He was even thinner, and the sparkle had gone forever out of his eyes. It was the dope. The doctors said it was the kindest thing. They had suggested he be moved into a hospital but she had refused. They had been sympathetic but firm; she would need an extra nurse, somebody professional with him all the time. There was no way of knowing how long. He had a good, strong heart, that was the trouble. It was keeping him going, prolonging his agony. Maggie smiled and sat next to the bed and put her hand on his.

"How are you, my love?"

"I'm all right. A bit dozy."

"You've slept. It's almost evening."

A small smile appeared on his face as he looked out of the window. "Yes, but which day?"

"It's Tuesday, Phil."

"I know, but which Tuesday?"

"Oh, my love." Maggie kissed his cheek and plumped his pillows. "It must be awful."

"Sleeping my life away, what's left of it, courtesy of the pharmacists."

"No, you aren't. You're much better these last days."

"These last days I'm doped to the eyeballs. These *are* the last days, Maggie. Please be honest with me. I'm not an ailing baby. I still have a mind." Again, the effort at a smile. "I still have a rather dozy, dopey mind."

"Oh, I know, I know that, I'm sorry." How, Maggie thought, will I live without him? He's been part of me, all of me, for so long. She poured him a drink he didn't want and held it to his lips.

"I don't need drinkies. Talk to me. Don't mother me. I'll live." He laughed. "I'll live. That's funny."

"All right." Maggie swallowed the sob and blinked back the tears. "Guess what arrived? A cable from Jill Viner. They want me to be ready to start in September."

"They have a London theatre?"

"Must have."

"If they're going in September, they'll want you August." He stirred. His interest was caught, as she knew it would be. "It's what, the third week in July now?"

It was the last week but she didn't contradict him.

He added, "Means any week now you're off."

Maggie turned away and looked out of the window. Several well-dressed people were walking their dogs. It was that kind of street. Oh, how wonderful it would be, if Philip were still well, and she were doing something as ordinary as walking a dog, knowing he was sitting in the house, reading his *New York Times*, and that he'd look up from his chair and say, "Hello, darling. . . ." Oh, my God. Stop it. Stop it. He isn't well, and that ordinary little thing is never going to happen again. Maggie turned back from the window.

"No, I'm not going. I'll have to cable them later."

"Why aren't you going?"

"You know why. I can't leave you."

"Yes, you can."

"All right then. I *won't* leave you."

"I'd rather you were there. Working. Happy. I'd like that."

Oh, my love, she almost but didn't say, you can't know what the doctors said—three or four weeks, possibly even six, but really anytime, you never know in these cases. "You might be happy but I wouldn't be. So you'll have to do what I want for a change, won't you, Philip?"

Philip took a deep breath. It was painful to hear.

"I told you. It's all settled. You go."

Maggie tucked the bedclothes in. "Let's wait and see, shall we?"

"Maggie, I mean it. You've had everything your own way all your life. You want it your own way now." He pushed himself up. "But this is my decision, not yours. I'm dying. Not you. And I say you go to London." Philip fell back on the pillows, exhausted. She moved to him but he waved a thin, waxen hand. "Leave me. I'll be all right. Tired."

The nurse looked in and said, "I'll sit with him."

"No. It's all right."

The nurse said quietly, "You have a visitor."

"Oh?" Maggie was about to ask who, but the nurse put a finger to her lips, indicating Philip, whose eyes had closed. Maggie tiptoed out of the room and went downstairs, slowly.

It was Austin Ames.

"Austin, how wonderful to see you!"

They embraced and kissed on the cheek. It *was* nice to see him.

"I should have called up." He looked sheepish in his jeans and sneakers and shades. He held a bunch of roses in his hand, and carried a bottle of champagne. "Here. Take this shit, Maggie. Jesus,

I'm sorry about Philip. I knew he was like ill but your nurse tells me he's in really bad shape. Jesus, a nice guy like Philip. I'm sorry. I won't stay. I was in the city and I thought, Well, shit, I'll grab a cab and go over and see old Maggie, see how she's doing. And now this. Fuck. I hate life."

"Give me the roses, I'll put them in water. You open the champagne." Maggie felt cheered. "I have some glasses here." She put out her Waterford crystal goblets and went out to the kitchen and found some caviar and some plain biscuits, first putting a lace doily on the tray, and thought: They're right, I'm ice-cold, I don't have real feelings, I'm not sloppy and slipshod like other people, I wouldn't have bothered about the doily otherwise, I'd have been too upset. But she had, so she carried the tray into the living room and there was Austin pouring the champagne lavishly into the goblets and, ice-cold or not, she felt a surge of pleasure just to see another human face, one she could look at without pain.

"Well, shit, Maggie," said Austin. "Nobody but you would have caviar." But he laughed as he said it. It was kindly meant.

It was also, Maggie thought, true.

"I don't suppose I could take Philip a glass upstairs?"

"Not now. He's asleep."

Austin hesitated. "I suppose he's . . ."

"A matter of days or weeks or whatever."

"And you've been nursing him how long?"

"Oh, just a few months, that's all."

"Just a few months? That's all?" He raised his glass. "Well, lady. Here's to you."

They talked of all kinds of things, for they hadn't seen each other since the Oscars. Austin told Maggie about the shitty westerns he'd been offered and of his refusal to do them. Maggie said she had turned down everything to nurse Philip. She added, so as not to sound too self-righteous, that there hadn't been anything she'd wanted to do anyway. As soon as you won an Oscar, replied

Austin, everybody in the world sent their soiled and shitty scripts to you. "The dogs I've read." He shrugged despairingly, looking, to Maggie, even smaller and more vulnerable than he had seemed in *Good-bye.* "That's why when *Queen* arrived I took it seriously."

He sipped his champagne and looked at her in the darkening room.

"You get a cable, Maggie?"

"Yes. It came a couple of hours ago."

"Me, too. You going?"

"How can I? With Philip this way?"

Austin nodded. He seemed to accept her decision. That was one of the things she liked about Austin. He didn't press and he didn't judge—unless it directly concerned his work. She had enjoyed working with him. He had seventeen ideas a day, sixteen too many, but the final one was always very, very good. He would be a tiring partner, but she didn't mind. Usually she just played her parts naturally, hardly moving from a direct line once she was on it. Austin's ability to work and prepare always made her feel guilty. She was not surprised to hear he had been to Washington to catch as much as he could of the president.

"I reckon I know the guy in the play now," Austin said, squeezing a tiny rubber ball to improve his handgrip. "I think I might get him somewhere near right."

"I'm glad," Maggie said. "I know you'll have a big success with it."

"The queen's a helluva part, Maggie."

"I know it is. But how can I go?"

"Sure, sure, I know."

Maggie laughed at herself and told him she'd been looking at film clips of the queen. Studying her manner, style of speech, the way she stood, all that. "She's European, you see, Austin. She might be a queen but she's still a woman. There's a wall of reserve. American women don't know anything about that wall. They don't know it exists. They speak up for themselves. It doesn't occur to them there's any other way to be. We don't need the women's movement here because we've always had it. It's a good country to be a woman in. In Europe, in England, it's very different. It's a male-dominated society; everything's much more formal. Ordered. I've been thinking about it a lot."

"Yes, I can see that," said Austin. "You want it very much indeed. Be honest with yourself. Even if you aren't going to take it, right?"

"Yes. Yes, I do." Maggie stood up. She could hear Philip's low voice, upstairs, talking to the nurse. "Look. Come upstairs just for a moment and say hello to Philip."

"You sure it'll be all right?"

"He'd be furious if you didn't." And besides, she did not add, you'll never see him again, will you?

PHILIP gave Austin a wan smile, but he meant it. "Hey, fella. Nice to see you, Austin."

"Jesus, Philip," said Austin, putting a brave face on it. "I'd no idea."

"Yes, well. You know what the Book says. You never know the day nor the hour."

"Christ," said Austin, tears in his eyes. "If that isn't fucking true." He embraced Philip without embarrassment and Maggie thought, not for the first time, what a really nice man Austin was, beneath the bantam-cock belligerence and the talent. "You're gonna be out of that bed and jogging around Central Park this time next year if Maggie has anything to do with it!" He beat the tears back and grinned at them both. He was a good actor. "Great girl you got here, Phil."

"I know it," said Philip. "But stubborn, right?"

"Man, you haven't acted with her. Steal the scenes, steal your eyeballs. You got to work, you go to bat with Maggie, I tell you."

Philip raised himself on his elbows. "You see she does this play. Will you do that for me, Austin?"

Austin looked quickly at Maggie. "Why sure. She has to. Part of a lifetime, am I right?"

Philip said in a faraway voice, "Just see she does it."

"She will, don't you worry," replied Austin quickly. "Hey, we have champagne downstairs, are you allowed a glass?"

But Philip had closed his eyes and his breathing was shallow and uneven.

"Jesus." Austin looked shattered. "What can I say?"

They tiptoed out and the nurse said, "He's just had some medication. He'll sleep awhile."

Downstairs, Austin was quiet and just said "Jesus" several times in a low voice, to himself. Maggie put on her cheerful air and suggested that since it was time to eat she cook them both an omelette. Truth to tell, she wasn't hungry for anything but human company. A great coldness of which she was very much afraid was growing inside her, preparing her, she supposed. But what if she were to lose the capacity to feel? What kind of an actress would she be then? People said bitter experience taught people about life, but she doubted it. Bitter experience made people bitter. It was as simple as that. "So. An omelette. And *filtre*-coffee and maybe a brandy?"

Austin protested. "Look, I'm in the way here."

"No, you aren't. I need to do something. All I'm doing is waiting."

"In that case, sure, an omelette would be great."

So they talked and ate, and sipped brandies and time went by. Normally Maggie did not drink at all, but somehow meeting another actor and talking silly shop (they even laughed a few times) released her anxieties, and she felt better than she had for a long time. Austin had many anecdotes of his Hollywood experiences (he left out Carmen) and told them well. They both felt superior about Hollywood because they were really Broadway players, they had done good things with good people, they had been artistic and tasteful and all the things Hollywood was supposed not to be. They smiled at their own superiority, but Austin insisted, "In the theatre you can say what you like, there's no censorship, there's no editorial power like in TV, telling you not to say this or write that because it might offend somebody. Likewise, there's a good, or anyway as good a script as the author can make it, which—Jesus you should *read* it!—*Massacre at Moonrise* certainly wasn't. A mishmash like most movie scripts. Theatre is small, but it's *free*. That's why I'm doing *Queen*."

They fell silent. Maggie said nothing. Austin sighed, feeling he had said too much, let his enthusiasm run away with him.

From upstairs came a quick stirring of noise, a chair scraping, a hasty footfall, a low call. Maggie got to her feet in a quick movement—oh, *God*—and went up the stairs two at a time.

It was too late.

The nurse turned to her, shaking her head.

"No, no," Maggie said. "No, no, no, no. . . ."

She didn't throw herself on Philip as he lay still and waxen and somehow *different*. Women did that in plays and books and movies. In life you stood, stunned in the presence of something so elemental that no gesture you made meant anything at all. Words, actions, movements, nothing had any relevance to the finality of the event. To the cold pain, the tightness, the relief, and the rage, all mixed together and no way to release it, not even tears.

Philip, ah, Philip, how will I live? she thought.

Austin put his arms around her. "I'll do everything, fix every-thing. Don't worry."

She didn't hear his words. She didn't hear anything.

Philip.

SIR Harry met them in his drive. Patrician. Smiling. Debonair in hacking jacket and silk cravat. The great nose sniffing the air. Like an old and unsurprisable hound of impeccable parentage. Which he was.

A very good-looking young man was at his side.

Josh said, peering out of the taxi, "I must say the old boy looks well."

"There, I told you he'd be interested. He wouldn't have invited us down unless."

"True." Josh looked at her sternly as the taxi rolled to a halt. "And remember, let me take him off and chat at some point. He may have some suggestions about his part; that is, if he's read the script yet."

"Say yes if you can. We need him."

Josh dropped his voice. The cab had stopped. "Let me handle it, Jill. I really do know how."

Jill pressed his arm. "Of course you do, darling. I'll confine myself to business."

"I wish I could believe that."

They got out and tried to pay the driver. "No, no," said Sir Harry. "I'll put it on my monthly bill, it's enormous, you wouldn't believe, I'm sure they improve it, the bill, you know." He beamed at them benignly. "Johnny, dear boy, how nice to see you."

"Josh," said Josh.

"Josh? Of course. That's what I said, isn't it?" He looked round quizzically. "Wasn't it? Forgetting my lines again, am I? Oh dear." He turned to Jill and bowed in courtly fashion. "And this is, er, ah, yes?"

"Miss Viner. Jill Viner. Our producer," said Josh.

Sir Harry looked blank. "Our producer? Is she? I mean, are you, my dear? Well, nothing against that. Absolutely nothing. Miss Horniman was the first woman producer who ever made a real impact in the English theatre. Wonderful old lady, some people say." He kissed Jill's hand in the French fashion, and held her hand after he had done that. "My dear Miss Villiers, you have no idea how nice it is to have new people in the theatre. All the old bulls and buffaloes one had to deal with in the old days. So very grasping, a lot of them. So very greedy. Yes." He beamed again. "I should think you'd like to see the house, wouldn't you? I suppose that's why you're here."

The old boy's forgotten who we are and why we're here. Josh knew Sir Harry's reputation for absentmindedness. And for acuteness—a surprising, and some said well-rehearsed mixture.

"That would be very nice," Jill said. "But aren't you going to introduce this young man to us?"

"What? Oh dear. Didn't I do that?"

"No, you didn't," said the young man. "I'm Tony."

"Yes, that's right," said Sir Harry. "He's Tony, and er . . ."

"I got their names, Sir Harry," said Tony. "I'm Sir Harry's secretary. Will you be staying overnight?"

"No, really," Josh said. "We must be back in town tonight."

"Lunch is at one o'clock." Tony looked at his watch. It was a very large gold digital and went with his yellow silk shirt and immaculate blue jeans. "That's in twenty-five minutes. If you'll excuse me?"

"I say," protested Sir Harry, "where are you orf to, Billy?"

"I'm going to type your letters," said Tony. "And it's Tony."

"I know that, my dear, it's what I just said, isn't it?"

"No, and you know very well it isn't," said Tony, without raising his voice. He went into the house.

The sun beat down on the beautiful garden and the old white house.

"The boys are so difficult these days," said Sir Harry, not at all put out. "And so greedy, too. Have you noticed that?"

Josh said, "It's the cost of living. It's going up." He smiled. "Like everything else."

Sir Harry beamed. How old was he really? Nobody knew. "Going up? Like everything else? You naughty man."

Jill said hastily, "What a lovely house, Sir Harry."

Sir Harry said, "Full of woodworm, me dear. Beetles. Field-mice this time of year. The insects and animals invade you and the costs bleed you white, the same as the boys. The locals take advantage every chance they get. Everything in nature conspires against you." He looked round the garden. The roses stretched along the borders in deep rows. "I used to think that the country was all right provided somebody covered it all over with six inches of concrete. Not sure I wasn't right, y'know. Not sure I wasn't right, what?"

Jill said as they walked around the house, round toward the orchards, "I'm sure you're wrong. This is the most beautiful place. What is it, Georgian? And all genuine by the look of it."

"Oh yes, its genuine, that's the trouble. Takes more upkeep, continually crumbling away and so on. The odd Victorian extension wouldn't need looking at. Very solid builders, the Victorians. Splendid people in every way. One meself, so I should know." He saw Josh's enquiring eye on him. "Well, very nearly, dear boy, very nearly. Now the Victorians could act, what? Take Matheson Lang. When he went to Jamaica to do a tour, he knew practically every big Shakespearian part orf by heart. Othello, Macbeth, you name it. When he stepped orf the boat at Kingston, the blackies chanted, 'Bang, Bang, Matheson Lang.' Wouldn't do that for an actor today. Might for a pop star."

"I think you're very wise living out here." Jill looked at the ripe peaches hanging on Sir Harry's south wall. "Much better for you than London."

"It might be better for me," said Sir Harry, "but I'm bored out of my crust with the place. Can't get away from it fast enough. I really look forward to company. That's why I'm so delighted you're staying the night." He stook a small peach from the wall, and Jill had her face ready to smile acceptance, but Sir Harry popped the fruit, whole, into his mouth. Juice squirted out of his lips, and he dabbed them with an immaculate linen handkerchief. "They get a little overripe, you know." He directed a none-too-happy gaze at his apple orchards. "Costs the earth to keep the damn things free of pests and properly pruned and so on. Don't eat the things meself. Too acid. My old pater often used to eat an apple on stage. Peel it and eat it." He paused, in communion with his vast memory. "Seen him do it, playing Falstaff. He was a good Falstaff. Used an ordinary penknife, totally out of period, of course. No-body noticed. Nowadays, the *Observer* would take him to task. Oh dear. Those were easier days."

They followed him into the house.

It was cool and airy like all Georgian houses. Josh remarked on that.

"You should try living here in winter, dear boy. Huge rooms as you can see. Fuel bills are astronomical, yes." He paused in the middle of the splendid drawing room, and looked at them vaguely. "Ah yes. Excuse me." He crossed to the door and called, in a complaining voice, "I thought we were having sherry, Silvio?"

147

A quite new voice called back, Italian-accented, "It's in the decanter. And it's Mario."

"Well, yes, that's what I said, my dear," Sir Harry replied indignantly. "I don't know, they never tell me what they're doing. Ah here we are."

Sir Harry poured them both large glasses of Tio Pepe.

Jill sat down in a Chippendale chair and Josh on a chaise longue. Sir Harry stood in front of the Adam fireplace. "Ah, so you're an impresario, me dear Joan? Well, it's splendid work. Nothing against a woman doin' it." Sir Harry sipped his sherry. "I remember Irene Mayer Selznick was one. She put on *The Chalk Garden* by Enid Bagnold with Edith starring. Edith Evans. Dame Edith. George Cukor directed, too. Disaster y'know. Oh, absolutely."

"Shouldn't have been," said Josh stoutly, "with all that going for it."

"Can't tell," said Sir Harry, "can yer, in the theatre."

It was a statement, not a question.

"Then there was Lilian Baylis. Wonderful old lady. Literally invented the Old Vic. Ran it with a rod of iron. Yes, my dear, you're in a splendid tradition, yes. Of course, she had her share of disasters too."

"Both Miss Horniman and Miss Baylis had reps to run. They could afford an odd failure. Ours is a one-off. So we can't afford disasters," said Jill sweetly. "That's why we're trying for an unbeatable cast."

Sir Harry did not seem to hear that.

"Broadway *has* produced a few lady producers. Natural, I suppose. American ladies are very forward, what? There was Ethel Linder Reiner and of course Lucille Lortel and Averil Logan. Splendid, yes." He dipped the great nose into his sherry glass. "Most of the successful managers seem to be men. David Belasco, Al Woods, Erlanger, Jacob Clore, David Merrick, Cochran, de Beer, Charlot. Wonder why that is, what?"

"Because we men have kept the women out?" This from Josh.

Sir Harry nodded doubtfully. "There is that, I suppose. I like the term *manager*. Impresario? Producer? My old pater called himself a manager. Actor-manager, naturally. Used to rewrite whole scenes, cut them, too. Shakespeare, anybody, didn't care. He had a real horse on stage in *Richard the Third*. He loved animals. If he could have sheep and rabbits on stage he liked nothing better. Caused an awful mess underfoot and backstage. He used to forget to have them corked, you know. Loved all that, real fountains with real water and lots and lots of trumpets blowing in all of Shakespeare. He would have loved *Queen* but I'm afraid he would have demanded a coronation scene and a royal funeral. Wouldn't have considered it otherwise, I'm afraid."

Jill said, "Do *you* like it?"

Again Sir Harry seemed not to hear.

"Of course, a very great deal depends on who you get for the queen."

Josh frowned. This was too early; but Jill would force things. "We have Maggie Stride."

Sir Harry nodded. "I had heard that, yes."

Good God, how? Josh wondered. But Sir Harry was sweeping on. All this was merely a footnote in a long, long life, and could not affect a great reputation and career one way or the other. "Y'know, she has a quality, that girl. Saw her on Broadway three years ago. Very cool. Very much in command. Then she lets go. Wham! I like that. What's her voice, not very Yankee is it, no? Well, she'll be splendid. Of course, she's young, long way to go. Actresses matured in the old days. Bernhardt was wonderful at seventy, playing leads, only one leg. Like a caged animal, marvelous. Duse the same, very different style, very quiet, tiny movements, such economy."

Josh thought: The old boy's seen the best. He judges everybody by the best, including himself. He felt awed. However, he thought, am I going to direct this old man who knows everything?

Sir Harry had divination.

"In those days nobody directed anybody, did they? I don't mean I approve of too much discussion, too much bowel-searching, but they used to have none, none at all. The important thing was to know your part, word-perfect, and the longer it was and the more word-perfect you were, the better. Nobody bothered about interpretation, except the very great ones, Irving and Irene Vanbrugh over here, and Tyrone Power and the Lunts in the United States. Oh, I like my little chats with my directors." He beamed at Josh kindly. "I'm sure you're a very clever young man, James."

Josh thought: I'm forty-six. To Sir Harry that's young.

He grinned. "The part is a very nice one." He relaxed. "How did your last movie go, the epic?"

Josh saw Jill glaring at him. Can't she see there's no hurry. Doesn't she *know*? He decided she didn't.

Sir Harry was delighted by the question.

"Oh, you heard about that? Absolutely horrid, dear boy. Of course, all Arab money, the epic, so naturally we went to the Sahara or somewhere to do it, I'm not sure where it was. Perhaps it wasn't the Sahara. Egypt, perhaps? Or was it Somalia? No matter. A hundred degrees and there was I, in a long frock coat and top hat, playing the British consul. It was so hot I nearly died." He beamed once more, a picture of robust old age. "Never been hotter, except when I did Toby Belch for Guthrie in the thirties, was it? I was padded, you know, pounds and pounds of padding all around me, bladders and such. So warm. That was a mistake, of course. I was quite wrong. I should never have taken the part, it isn't me, the Belch, is it?"

"How do you see yourself as the prime minister in *Queen*?"

Josh closed his eyes at Jill's directness but thought, Well, the old boy will have to answer that one.

He was wrong.

"Awfully difficult to play prime ministers, isn't it? I mean, whom does one use as a model? Disraeli perhaps—a bit foppish, very acute. I played him once, can't think when—oh yes, in the thirties, terrible play, didn't run, forget its blessed name. Where was I? Oh yes. Playing politicians. Well, I suppose this one's a Tory, isn't he? Doesn't mean I can't play Labour, they're so alike now, aren't they? But your author has given him long, beautifully written speeches and that sounds like Eton and Oxford to me. I suppose they'll still be there in 1995?"

Josh said, "I'm sure we can sort that out in rehearsal."

Sir Harry looked blank. "Rehearsal? Oh, yes. I see. Well. No doubt, whoever plays it, what?"

Another very good-looking young man, of Italian appearance, obviously Mario, came in and filled up their glasses and offered them olives and nuts and potato crisps. Sir Harry ate everything he was offered.

"We were hoping you'd play it," Jill pressed. "We hoped so very much. I talked to your agent. He likes the deal."

"Well, he would, wouldn't he?" Sir Harry chewed an olive. "He doesn't have to go on and do it, does he? He'd accept everything I'm offered, I'd be in four places at once if he had his way, my dear." Sir Harry smiled fondly at Mario. "Wouldn't I, Silvio, and then I'd never be here with my friends, would I?"

Mario looked militant and said, "Mario."

"But of course," sighed Sir Harry. "That is what I said. Is lunch ready?"

"In fifteen minutes. Perhaps your guests would like to wash?"

"Would you?" asked Sir Harry. "Of course. Mario will show you."

Jill went out with Mario, but Josh remained behind. "It's a long time since we worked together, Sir Harry."

Sir Harry looked blank. "Is it? Oh yes. Of course."

"At Brighton. Ten years ago. *Family News.*"

"Ah yes," said Sir Harry blankly. "Of course. You . . . er?"

"I directed it."

"So you did. I'd forgotten. I remember Bernhardt and Duse but I've forgotten *Family News.*"

"It wasn't a very good play."

"Wasn't it? I can't remember, you know."

"You were excellent. If it hadn't been for you it would never have got into the West End at all."

"Wouldn't it? No, I suppose not." Sir Harry chewed another olive. "And what have you been doing since then, dear boy?"

"I've been at the National."

"Ah, yes. The National. I do so wish I could work there all the time, but there's the flat in London and this house and the boys, y'know. Terribly expensive, everything, these days."

Josh talked on, names they both knew, with more stories from Sir Harry of the great and the not-so-great, the forgotten and the remembered, the dead and the living. They all seemed to be alive to Sir Harry, because he had known them all, worked with them all. . . . "Dear old Bobby Atkins," said Sir Harry. "Expected to read the Lesson at the local church at Stratford, always the done thing, leading actor always asked. Bobby wasn't, probably because of his bohemian reputation, met the vicar in the High Street, accosted him, asked him, 'Vicar, give me one cogent reason why I shouldn't read the fucking Lesson.'" Sir Harry beamed. "The dear man. Lovely actor. Ever work with him? No?" Sir Harry smiled reminiscently. "Then there was old Oscar Ashe, long before your time I know. . . ."

Josh sat and drank in the memories. Sir Harry was not just a great actor. He *was* the theatre, a living memory bank. He prayed the old boy would take the part but knew far better than to ask him.

"I WONDER"—Sir Harry was showing them to table, the lunch (omelettes, fruit, Soave) having arrived—"I wondered, dear boy, why you thought of *me?*"

"Because nobody else could do it."

Sir Harry swallowed a mouthful of Soave vaguely.

152

"How nice of you to say so, dear boy."

Jill kicked Josh under the table but Josh would say no more.

Sir Harry had not made his mind up yet and nobody could make it up for him. "I believe," he said, "you have a Mr. Ames playing the president?"

A Mr. Ames. Lovely, thought Jill.

"He won an Oscar last year," said Jill.

"Ah. Did he indeed?" asked Sir Harry.

Sir Harry had won everything but never an Oscar.

"What," he asked, "is an Oscar? I mean exactly."

"It's for movies. It's for the best actors and so on," said Josh, with a very straight face.

"Ah, yes." Sir Harry finished his omelette. "Of course. They gave Piers one once, I think. He's done a lot more movies than I have, of course." Sir Harry's mood seemed to change. He frowned. "Likes the damn things. Loves all the fuss and the makeup. Loves all the publicity, yes." He blew out his cheeks and selected a Victoria plum. "Do try these, they're out of the garden. Yes, lovely actor, Piers." He stared at Josh. "I think you said you were *considering* him for a part in this play?"

"Well, I didn't exactly . . ." began Josh. Then he swallowed and said, boldly, "Yes. Actually."

You lying sod, he told himself. He avoided Jill's smiling eyes.

Sir Harry beamed.

" 'Considering'? I like that very much. 'Considering.' "

"It wasn't how it sounded—"

"Did he read it, do you think? Piers? The newspaper article?"

"I hope not. I believe he's in Cannes."

"He would be. Pity."

There was a silence. Sir Harry was still smiling gently.

"Your *Othello* together was history," Jill said. "I wish I'd seen it."

"Lovely reviews, my dear. Well, some were. You should see them. Lost money. Of course we were a lot younger then. Piers got the Moor and I got Iago—well, he's such a *brute*, Piers, so of course he got the Moor. Not to say I couldn't have done it but of course nobody believed it. They said I was far too thin and of course they were right. Some people liked my Iago."

"They say it was the best in living memory," Josh replied.

"Do they? Oh, well, I suppose so, if they say so."

A smile went round the table, from the boys to Jill and back again. "It would be nice to play with Piers again but somehow we never have. I think he funks it, you know. Yes, I really do. I think he funks it." Sir Harry looked at his watch. "I say, you'll have to rush if you want to get your train, won't you?"

Jill looked quickly at Josh. "Could we talk—"

"The boys will run you down." Sir Harry beamed. "I think I'll have a little nap. I usually do after lunch. You can get coffee on the train and the next one's not for ages, is it?"

"Of course," said Josh. He got to his feet.

To hell with that, Jill thought.

"Look here," she began, but Josh had her arm in a grip of iron. They trooped out and got into the ancient open Daimler that Mario drove sedately round to the front of the house.

"Well, well, well," said Jill, under her breath. "So that's that!"

Mario revved the engine, his white teeth grinning.

"What," asked Jill, "did we do wrong?"

Josh said nothing at all. He waited.

The car began to move.

Sir Harry appeared at the door. He held up his hand like a patriarch of old. "Of course, I expect you'll be getting Piers for the Russian?"

"If we can, yes," said Josh firmly. Jill said nothing. She stared ahead miserably.

"We got to go," said Mario, "or we'll miss the fokkin' train."

"I wonder," asked Sir Harry amiably, "if by any chance you wanted me for the prime minister?"

Mario revved the engine loudly.

Above it, Josh shouted, "Of course we do!"

"So glad." Sir Harry waved a hand vaguely. "I wasn't sure you did. Good-bye."

Mario took the car out of the drive very fast, raising clouds of fine dust that settled over the rosebushes.

He was smiling.

Jill said softly, "The old devil."

"If we had rushed him, as you wanted to," Josh replied, "we would have lost him."

Jill had to admit he was right.

SHE sat in the train back to London and looked at Josh sitting opposite, reading his *Guardian* and fighting sleep. He dozed. Suddenly his head jerked awake and he blinked. She felt a surge of tenderness and love so strong she could hardly contain it. She knew that Josh said he didn't like to be fussed over but she couldn't resist doing it. She reached purposefully toward him and brushed ash from his jacket. He looked over his reading glasses. "What?"

"I love you."

He nodded, seemingly unsurprised. "So I've noticed."

She laughed. It was going at a pace, the thing between them. They had got into the habit of staying at Josh's place most nights, and they were missing a lot of sleep. Josh protested mildly, saying they had heavy days to come and they must be sensible and moderate things a bit, but they always ended up in Josh's bed in Glebe Place, full of burning affection and loud with laughter, usually a bottle of wine on the side table. Their lovemaking got better and better—Josh was a considerate lover and did not try to dominate her; she hated rushed, masculine sex without real caring. She wanted to have a say in how things were ordered; she hated piston-poking and blind want masquerading as love. Fortunately, Josh didn't do that and the blind thing wasn't him, either. He was affectionate and easy and it was all very natural between them,

155

and Jill Viner was blissfully happy. It all seemed to be going almost too well.

So, as usual, she pushed things along too fast.

"Look, why don't I move into Glebe Place?"

"What?" Josh stared at her blearily. He was, after all, half asleep, the poor darling.

"I'm always rushing out at six in the morning, back to my place. It's a great bore. If I was *in* the place I could look after you a bit."

"I'm all right," Josh said, somewhat defensively it seemed to her. "I can look after myself, you know. Been doing it for years."

"Yes, I know, but your place looks an awful mess."

"That's because I don't get a chance to clean it up. Or have my cleaning lady in." Josh had canceled his cleaning woman because he didn't want her barging in on them.

"Well." Jill felt foolish suddenly. "The offer's there. Take me up on it any time you like."

Josh didn't say thanks or anything else but merely stared out at the green English countryside. His silence irked her even more and she said, "Look, if you don't want me around at all, Josh, for God's sake say so!"

Josh looked startled at her outburst and reached over and patted her hand. He didn't even squeeze it, she thought; he just patted the bloody thing! "Josh," she began, very annoyed by now, but he had got to his feet and muttered, "There must be some coffee on this train somewhere. I'll see if I can rustle us up some." With that he was out of the compartment.

Jill sat and looked mindlessly at the countryside for a few miles. She reproached herself. I must stop pushing the poor man. He had a wife he loved and lost, he isn't ready for a great red-blooded thing, he doesn't want to totally commit himself, he doesn't really approve of what we're doing, he thinks it could harm *Queen*, he's even said the actors would be better kept in the dark, they might think he'd only got the job as director because he was sleeping with the producer! It had seemed like a joke when he said it, sitting up in bed sipping a large cup of tea, looking somewhat convalescent after a bout of lovemaking. "They'll think I'm your fancy fella and then they'll play me up. I don't want that, you see, Jill."

Nor did she.

She wanted the very best for him.

She loved him, didn't she?

Jill went back to staring at the wet green fields again, feeling a thoroughly uncomfortable mixture of love and irritation, satiety and hunger. The miles rolled by, Josh did not come back with the coffee (obviously he had decided to have his in the buffet car), and finally she closed her eyes and, despite the rolling lurch of the train, she slept.

Her last warm thoughts were how much she loved him.

BACK in the compartment, Josh sat sleepless now and looked at this tornado of a woman who had taken over his life. He loved her, he thought. Or as much as he could love anybody these days. She was ardent, and the sex between them was very good: better, he had to admit, than it had ever been with Alison, even. With Alison it had been a thing of youth. They hadn't needed any salt or spice. Their blood had run hot, for they were young. With Jill it was different. It wasn't pure mechanical sex as it had been with Maeve, a thing of positions and oddity and the feeling he could do *anything* to her and she wouldn't mind—far from it, she would approve. With Jill, just the same, the sex was important. She cried out a lot, and used words he could not have thought she knew, and said, "Oh, make me come" at the height of her passion, and he responded, feeling different from the cool, considerate lover Alison had taught him to be (her health had dictated she should not get too excited), and now with Jill he felt the boundaries burst and he tried more and more new things and Jill did not resist, she welcomed them.

It was a kind of rebirth.

The important thing was, they must not let it get to the actors and harm *Queen*. Josh stared out of the window at the green English countryside tearing soundlessly by. That was the important thing.

TOMMI Traceham was Cheltenham Ladies College, Lady Margaret Hall, and the Slade School of Art, and she looked it. Josh had heard she could be snooty, could be difficult, could be brilliant, but he had not heard that she was beautiful. *Svelte* was the word—nothing too arty, everything very expensive.

"I was interested when I heard you'd left the National." Tommi Traceham crossed one long leg over the other and looked around the production office of *Queen*. "I must say this is an improvement on the usual West End production office. Most of them are absolute shithouses."

"That's Jill's doing," Josh said. "She's done a good job. We have a bit of space, and we're bang on Shaftesbury Avenue."

"I hear she's a bright lady," Tommi said.

"Very much so. You know our cast?"

"She told me on the telephone. Terrific. How can it miss?"

Josh grimaced. "A million ways, as you know." He indicated the folder she carried. "What's that, a new show you're doing?"

"No, it's some preliminary sketches for *Queen*."

"Already?" He was astonished. "You haven't signed a contract yet. Or anything."

"Does that matter? If you hate my concept what's the use of a contract?" Tommi opened the folder. "These sketches are very rough indeed." She spread the large pieces of drawing paper on a long leather couch. The work was not rough. It was neatly executed, beautifully done; and Josh knew as he looked at it that it was dead right.

"I have a raised dais for the throne," Tommi said crisply. "It

158

can be out of sight when you do the scenes that aren't in the throne room. Keep everything functional. It's in the future—*why* are you staring at me, do I have some snot on my face?"

"Sorry." Josh fumbled in a drawer and pushed some sheets across the desk at Tommi. "These are roughs done by a man in New York."

Tommi looked at them. "Very similar. He's a good designer, whoever he is. Why don't you ask him to do the job?" She collected her drawings together and began to push them back into the large folder.

"Just a moment," said Josh hastily. "We have no contractual deal with this person. It's simply he . . . Well, he used to be a designer. He is . . ." Josh knew how this would sound and he hated it, but it had to be said, "He was Maggie's lover. He died very recently."

"I'm sorry," said Tommi. "What was his name?"

Josh told her.

"I've heard of him. He used to do good work." Tommi continued to put the drawings into her folder. "I see your problem, if you promised to put his name on it." She paused. "I know I sound a shit but I'm not. Either I design this show or I don't. I did that drawing before I saw his. Pity we had the same basic concept. But the choice is yours, I'm afraid."

She waited.

Josh knew he had no choice at all. He reached over and took the rough drawings made by the dying man and put them back in the drawer. "Take me through it, very carefully, point by point," Josh said.

She did. At the end he leaned back. "You're very good."

"So are you," said Tommi. "And a nice guy, too. I'd heard you were."

Josh laughed. "Go ahead and get finished designs out and we'll get the set built."

"Can't till we know the theatre. Which one is it to be?"

Jill opened the door from the inner office. Tommi looked up at her coolly. Josh thought he could smell instant animal wariness in the air. He couldn't think why. Maybe because Tommi Trace-ham was too smart, too cool, too obviously together.

"We don't know which theatre but we will by the weekend. At least, I hope so." Jill looked over at the drawings. "Did you do something?"

"Yes, just some roughs." Jill exclaimed over them enthusi-astically, Tommi Traceham looked pleased, and Josh was reassured. Not once did Jill refer to Philip's rough notes, or even look quizzically at Josh. He expected that, but it never came. Jill wanted Tommi. "I'm so glad you're going to be working with us," said Jill at last. Still, she seemed wary. Tommi Traceham was a little too enameled, a little too much her own style, for Jill to be absolutely comfortable with her, Josh thought. He got to his feet. "I think we could all use some coffee. I'll organize Molly to make some."

Let them make their own accommodations, he thought.

It was as well he did not hear what they were.

As soon as he had gone, Tommi lit a long cigarette in a holder and said offhandedly, "I don't know if you'd heard, but I'm not interested in gents. I just thought I'd mention that." The cool smile. "I rather take it you are, dear. In one particular gent."

Josh did hear Jill's laugh.

He wondered what on earth those two had found to laugh at.

MAX Heston was very young for a stage manager but he had done a lot since leaving school at sixteen. Two years as an assistant stage manager at the Belgrade Theatre, Coventry, then a spell at the Royal Shakespeare, a stint in TV (which he hadn't liked), and back out to Shaftesbury Avenue. He was now twenty-three—sweatshirt, jeans, granny glasses, and long but shining hair. We need somebody young-looking, Josh thought. Everybody in *Queen* is simply creaking with experience.

"You've told me what you've done and I'm impressed," Josh said. "What's your background, are you from a theatrical family?" Josh was so used to stage people being that, he was always surprised when they were not. Max Heston wasn't. "My dad's a laborer in a fertilizer factory, about the worst job in the world," said Max unmoved, sitting in the office of *Queen*. "I didn't know a single person in the theatre. Just wanted to do it, after I'd seen a few plays. Wanted to be backstage—no interest in being an actor, no talent either. So I left school and begged a job and here I am. If I'd gone on to Oxford or Cambridge and got into OUDS or the Footlights I'd be a director at the Vic or the National by now. They all get noticed, those boys, if they have any ability at all. It's the English snob class-system operating. Everybody who picks people has been to one or the other, so they do the old alma mater a good turn, right? It applies to cricketers, and rugby players so why not actors or directors and writers? Me, I've had to clout my way up, every step of the fucking way. Why do I do it? Because I love the bloody theatre is why." He looked at Josh as if he were a thousand years old. "Of course, I'll naturally understand if you want one of those or some well-known actor's son."

"You'll be dealing with a star cast. Feel you can?"

"Sure. Why not? They're only actors, right?"

Josh liked his nerve and gave him the job on the spot. He was chip-on-the-shoulder but that was a fashionable thing to be.

"Nothing for you to do yet, except hang around the office, liaise with Tommi Traceham—she's designing for us—and generally make yourself useful and get your sleep. You won't sleep again until we're back in town for the first night, nor will I."

"I hear you're good," said Max easily. "I hope to learn a bit."

"Not an old theatrical buffer?" asked Josh straight-faced.

"No, but what about your cast?" came the reply. "Total age of a million, right?"

This young man and Sir Harry should be something to see, Josh thought.

"We aren't finished casting yet," Josh said. "We have an old actor and a young actress to cast."

"Who's the young actress?"

"The princess's part. We've no ideas. Any would be welcome."

"Let me have a think, right?"

Josh knew that young stage managers always kept a personal dossier on the younger actresses, sometimes through sleeping with them but mainly because they went to the same parties. Good young actresses were always rare. Girls used to become actresses because of their good looks. Now, they were all very plain or trying very hard to be. Critics rarely gave good notices to pretty actresses, not in the theatre. They were thought to be frivolous. Well, the part of the princess was frivolous.

"It's a good part. Make somebody's name, Max."

Max stood up. He'd got the job, there wasn't a lot of point in hanging about. "Like I say, I'll give it some thought. Thanks a lot, Mr.—"

"Josh will do. Nice to have you with us."

When Max had been introduced to Jill, he nodded, said "Hi!" and, taking his copy of *Queen* (with instructions that nobody, but *nobody*, should see it), sauntered whistling into sunlit, noisy Shaftesbury Avenue. Jill asked, "Isn't he very young?"

"Yes, but well recommended. He'll be fine. We could do with some young blood. We're getting geriatric." Josh looked at the budget breakdown for *Queen* on Jill's desk. It was long and complicated.

"How's it coming? Are we going to have enough money?"

Jill grimaced. "I hope so. A lot depends which theatre we get." As Josh raised his eyebrows, "And don't worry, I'm working on that."

"You don't want a barn for this play," Josh said. "It's only got a cast of five. We don't want the Coliseum or Wyndham's, they'd be too big. Something more like the Duchess or the Fortune."

"Both full with long-runners and likely to remain so. Leave it with me, Josh. As I said, I'm working on it. Can you sit down and go through my rough estimates with me?"

Josh said, "Now?"

"This evening. My place. The telephone won't be ringing with actors, and actors' agents who've just heard of Queen Productions. Molly has been putting off the poor dears all week."

Molly looked over her glasses. "Eighty percent unemployed, who'd be an actor?" She sighed. "But the angels' checks are coming in nicely. All is going very well, I think." The telephone shrilled. "Oh, dear." She picked it up. "Oh, hello, Annabel, this is Molly. Yes, I'm working here now.... Sorry dear, we're all full up, nothing for you anyway, really. How's Maurice? ... Oh, dear. I'm so sorry. Well, if I hear anything. Nice to talk, dear. 'Bye-ee."

She looked up at them. "Aren't we lucky to be working? And on such a nice play as *Queen*. And now I really do think we all need a cup of tea."

Josh sat down at Jill's desk and stared at her rough budget breakdown of *Queen*'s costs. It was nothing he wanted to face but it had to be done. He was a partner in Queen Productions. He was always going on about being consulted. Jill was consulting him. He'd been reasonably free of all this at the National. Now, he was in the marketplace. "I don't see why we can't look at it here," he said. "Molly can ply us with tea, and we can send out for sandwiches."

Jill pouted a bit. "It would be easier at my place. I could cook a light supper. More civilized."

"Might be," conceded Josh. "But I'd fall asleep. I'm beginning to eat, sleep, drink *Queen*, as a piece of drama." He laughed. "I'm shit-scared of my cast, too. They're dynamite." He looked at the lists of figures. His head ached just thinking about costs. "Let's have a go now, see how it works out."

Josh told himself he did not want to spend an evening in Jill's place. He wanted to slow the pace down a little. They had a lot on their plate; this emotional thing between them could get too much.

They were under quite enough pressure without the bed games. Their days were passing in a welter of telephone calls and interviews and the studying of actors' contracts. Manny's contract for Austin Ames was a prize, being no less than thirty-four pages long, and Josh had advised, "Just sign it. All American contracts are as long as the Koran." But Jill wouldn't. She sent it out for a legal opinion to an expert theatrical solicitor, in case Manny had inserted some tricky things. (He had, but not as many as he might have!) Another hundred pounds down the drain, Josh had said, but Jill insisted it was what Joe Dancy would have done, so it was probably the right thing to do. Maggie's contract had been easily dealt with and so had Sir Harry's. Josh could see why. They were going to be rich if *Queen* ran.

"How about us?" He sat and stared at the lists and scraps of paper on Jill's large and, inevitably, new desk. "Where's our investment showing?"

Jill sat next to him. "No calls, Molly, none. We are going to educate Josh."

Molly's eyes flickered from one to the other. "Wouldn't be the slightest bit surprised, dear." Before either of them could reply she was typing loudly. Josh thought: Surely the way I sometimes look at Jill isn't as noticeable as all that. And anyway, it's only sometimes. He took up the papers with an air of concentration. "Tell me what are your figures so far?" he asked in a businesslike voice.

THREE hours and four cups of tea later they were looking at a list of figures, the nearest they could hope to get to final numbers at this stage. Josh rubbed his eyes wearily. "Read it out, Jill. I can't see these figures anymore." He closed his eyes and tried to concentrate.

Jill recited in her best actress's voice, "Our capitalization, the money we actually have, is one hundred throusand pounds. . . ." She took a deep breath. "The rest is just an estimate but here goes. . . . Building and painting scenery, per Tommi's design, ten thou-

164

sand pounds. Furniture for set, three. Wardrobe—men's suits, queen's robe, princess's outfits, all that—six. Various props, one."

"How much is that up to now?" Josh asked.

"Twenty thousand."

"Good God. Go on."

Jill said, "Fees now. Tommi Traceham, designer, three, and lighting man another three. Brings us up to twenty-six." She took a deep breath. "Rehearsal expenses now. And they're big. For our stars, ten thousand pounds for three weeks' rehearsal, including two for understudies."

"Whom we haven't cast yet. Oh God, that's a rotten job." Josh breathed in. "I'll start on it tomorrow. Jill, our stars' money is too high, it's enormous."

Jill ignored that. "Stage management, eight more. Taxes, one— I'd forgotten them."

"I'd forgotten them too. Go on."

"We'll have to spend at least five on publicity and newspaper advertising. Our printer's bill for programs and posters will be two, sign-writing outside the theatre one more, and about five hundred on photographs of the artists and typing of scripts. What have I missed?"

Josh said, "Press agent?"

"I've got Tom Tully working for expenses only. Say another thousand. He wants a lot more if we get into the black."

"Wouldn't he take a flat fee?"

"Not now we have Sir Harry."

"No. I suppose not. Wily sod."

"Well, he took a risk. He's entitled."

"I suppose so. You haven't mentioned travel and out-of-town expenses."

"No. I know." Jill hesitated. "If we do two weeks out of town at a different place each week it's going to cost us four thou for travel and hotels. No way we can do it cheaper with our distinguished cast."

"Hopefully we'll be getting our costs back on tour," Josh said. "Maybe more. Audiences will come to see us. We could do well. We could be in profit."

"We could. Depends where we go. Let's leave that item out. Let's say two for preproduction costs, and the grand total is . . ." Jill sucked her pen. ". . . Fifty-six and a half, call it fifty-seven."

"All right," yawned Josh. He was beat. "The last and most important question. Where do we rehearse? Everyplace I know that I could respectably take Sir Harry, Maggie, and Austin is going to cost us two thousand pounds for three weeks. And that," Josh ruminated, "is not allowing for rehearsal-room fees and possibly out-of-town losses and the expenses of getting in."

"Lord, I'd forgotten the get-in. Shall we say three thousand?"

"It sounds as good a figure as any," said Josh ironically. "Where does that leave us? We haven't added management salaries, office rents, and the repayment of monies loaned by us and the American trip we made and the cost of flying our two American stars over here first-class, and I shouldn't wonder Concorde . . ."

"I've got all that." Jill stared at her calculations. "Say another fifteen thousand pounds." She paused. "Plus actors' salaries, ten thousand a week. We'll soon use up our hundred thousand if we don't make money."

Josh said, "I don't mind leaving our management fees out but I'm certainly going to be repaid what I put in to set us off. Aren't you?"

"Well, yes," said Jill doubtfully. "I suppose so."

"Are you debating not taking it?"

"I was."

"Look," said Josh kindly, "I'm going to eat while *Queen* is in production, I don't know about you, and talking about eating, I'm starved. Let's go to that Italian place and have osso bucco and a carafe."

Jill had her coat on at once, her eyes shining. Good Lord,

thought Josh. Where does all her energy come from? He felt all his forty-six years but the chianti and the osso bucco restored him, and smoking one of the havanas Jill had bought him, he said, "How much did we say again?"

"We're all right, so long as we have good houses wherever we get in."

"When we have a theatre to go *into*," said Josh pointedly.

"Don't worry. I'm working on it. I told you. There are over fifty theatres in London. We'll get into one of them, don't worry." Jill looked out toward the line of theatres bright with neon, names and titles, and the people, pushing forward with that air of expectancy only theatregoers have: fur and scent and cologne and leather and money, rain and shining pavements and lights, lights, lights. "It'll be wonderful to have *Queen* up there, won't it? Aren't you thrilled? Go on, say you're thrilled, Josh, be human, say you're absolutely thrilled."

"All right," said Josh, "I'm absolutely thrilled."

"So am I. I've always wanted that, without knowing it. Always. Lights up there, my name up there."

"Are you putting your name up in lights?"

"Well of course I am!" Jill grinned, and then said, "Any reason why not?"

"No," said Josh. "If anybody's name deserves to be up there, yours deserves to be." He put out his cigar. "Sorry, I'm still worried. I'm always like this before a production. I haven't your confidence, I'm afraid. Been in too many flops."

She put her hand on his. It was very warm. He looked into her steel-blue eyes. She was a lively spirit and he felt happy, if a little apprehensive in her company. Total extrovert, he reminded himself. Not good at the sympathies and sensitivities of life (unlike Alison), won't even see them; but staunch, loyal probably.... Good God, he thought, I'm thinking of her like a wife. He said, "For one thing, we haven't even talked to Actors Equity yet. Here we are, making all these plans and they could very easily refuse Maggie and Austin work permits, and we're done!"

"They won't. Not if we have both Sir Piers and Sir Harry."

"Want to bet?"

"I was keeping the good news until now."

"Oh, is there some?"

"Yes. We have two parts to cast, right?"

"The princess shouldn't be hard. I thought I'd get going on it right away."

"No." Jill sipped her coffee, looking far away, as if she were holding something back. Which, he thought, she probably was. "I have an idea there. At the back of my mind."

"That's what worries me."

She laughed her loud and hearty laugh. The Italians running the restaurant looked over admiringly. They liked a woman of spirit—not, perhaps, necessarily as a wife. Josh said, "Then there's Sir Piers. He's still in Cannes doing that movie."

"You fly to see him tomorrow. Here are the tickets."

She took them from her handbag, passed them over with a small smile. "All that sun. I wish I was coming."

Josh took the tickets, soundlessly. He thought, So do I.

But he said nothing. With Jill, that was always safest.

THE alarm call wakened Josh at eight o'clock. He got out of the rumpled bed with a slight groan and went to switch on the bedside light. Then he remembered that Jill was in the bed, too. He blinked across to see if she was still asleep, but the bed was empty. Plainly, she had gone home. She usually did that. He still steadfastly refused to go to her place. He wasn't sure why except he hated to slope out of a woman's flat in the early hours, like some stray dog. He was still a little astonished that Jill didn't seem to mind, but then women in love were always shameless. He yawned and switched on the bedside light and fumbled his way into the bathroom. Under the shower he began to come alive. He decided that he would drive to the airport instead of hanging around for a cab. The drive would relax him (he liked driving, one of the few physical things he did, most days, since he had given up squash), and he would be able to think about what he would say to Sir Piers. It would be tricky, but plainly the old boy had not taken total offense about the *Standard* item or he would not have agreed to a meeting with Josh in Cannes. There was hope that it wouldn't all be too embarrassing.

To work with both Sir Harry and Sir Piers. God.

Josh shaved, his spirits lightening, thinking, They may be household names but they're only actors, after all. There was nothing to get frantic about. As his father had told him, cigar in mouth, the week's takings and books in front of him on his desk: "The important thing with actors, my boy, is make sure you treat everybody exactly the same. No favorites. Never any favorites. And, despite the temptation, never never any whipping boys. Good actors, bad actors, middling actors, always the same. Good-tempered. No tantrums. Don't shout at people. No need for it. You're only the director. They do the work, remember. You only have to have a director because *somebody* has to read the *whole* play!"

He had laughed. His father was a manager and sometimes a director, but really he had been an actor, all the way. Josh had the reputation of being sympathetic, an *actor's* director, somebody who understood an actor's special problems. Well, if I don't, thought Josh, pulling on a shirt and a lightweight suit, I bloody well should. I've been around them all my life.

Queen, properly directed, could make his name, all over again.

In this business, his father had said, you need to make your name at least three times in your life. Otherwise you go under. Josh sighed. He missed his father. His mother, too. Alison, too. He missed them but he managed. He could look after himself, he'd grown used to it. For example, now he would make his own breakfast. Orange juice, muesli, toast, and coffee. He would switch on the radio for the news and read his *Guardian* while he ate, the way he always did.

Josh hummed a tune and went into the kitchen, leaving the bedroom a mess. He would tidy it when he got back. He was returning on a late flight, or more probably the next day, depending how things went with Sir Piers.

All the lights were on in the kitchen.

Jill stood there, in an apron, slightly flushed, her expression one of delight. Behind her, on the stove, frizzled eggs and sausages and bacon, and a large pot of coffee was percolating on the table. Fresh grapefruit had been sugared and quartered and stood ready to eat. There was no sign of his beloved orange juice or muesli.

" 'Morning, darling. I thought I'd get you breakfast. You must be starving, poor love."

"No, really," said Josh, blinking in the bright light. "I'm fine." He sat down. "You must have been up ages. I didn't hear you. I thought you'd gone."

Jill kissed him on the cheek and indicated the grapefruit. "Eat that first. I'll have the rest in a jiffy. It's fresh grapefruit, better for you than that awful orange juice."

"I'm sure." Josh ate the grapefruit, which he found a mite tart.

"Nice?" This from Jill.

He swallowed the remainder. "Delicious."

Jill looked pleased. "I wasn't sure if you liked it. I bought them yesterday. You had no fresh fruit in the place at all."

"No. I don't eat much fruit. It usually just goes bad."

"You should, you know. Good for you. And you shouldn't eat so much stodge. You'll get a pot."

"I'm too thin if anything," said Josh in defense. "I could probably do with a pot." He looked over at the stove. "I notice you've got a lot of food there." He was going to go on to say, "I hope it's for you, I never eat cooked breakfasts," but he didn't,

170

because Jill was serving up the food, and it looked very good indeed, grilled tomatoes too, which he had not eaten at breakfast for years. And her face was glowing with pleasure in her task. So he just said, "Don't give me too much, I have to rush out afterwards, you know."

Jill filled his plate with bacon and poached eggs. "It's all protein." Josh reached for his toast. "No bread," said Jill.

"I can't eat this without bread," protested Josh.

Jill relented and kissed him again. "One slice, no more."

Josh took two and ate his way steadily and silently through his food. Jill sat down and ate hers, darting anxious glances at him. He drank two cups of coffee and got up from the table. "That was very good. Must rush. I'm driving to the airport."

Jill swept off her apron. "No, you're not. I'm driving you."

"You're due at the office. I'll take my car."

She looked so disappointed, he kissed her and said, gently, "Look, I'll need my car for when I come back, won't I?" He kissed her again. "Thanks just the same. It was a nice thought. And thanks for the breakfast, it was terrific."

Then he was out the door.

She could hear him whistling as he got into his Volkswagen and then the noise of the engine starting, and fading away into the other traffic noises. She felt sad. She always felt sad when they parted. Silly fool. Calm down. Don't show your love too much. Don't scare him.

To hell with him, she thought, if he's afraid of my love!

Jill started to collect the breakfast dishes and put them in the sink. Her heart quailed at the idea of washing them and, on impulse, she rang his cleaning woman, Mrs. Megson, and asked her to come in and do the flat through. Mrs. Megson sounded somewhat affronted at receiving these orders from a woman she had never met, but she agreed. Jill stopped clearing the dishes, looked for her briefcase, found it, and went out of the flat, denying herself, for the umpteenth time, a search through Josh's drawers for letters to and from Alison.

Time, she thought, I have to give him time.

THE sun beat down on the Croisette.

Josh Williams sat and waited for Sir Piers.

He had telephoned the Metropole and spoken to the great man himself, from the airport at Nice. Sir Piers did not want him to come to the hotel. "It's full of people I'm working for, my dear fellow. Movie people. Never a moment's peace—you know how it is? Look, I'll tell you what. D'you know the little park at the end of the Croisette, palm trees and all that? I'll meet you in there at four o'clock. We will have a little chat, all right?"

Josh had been rather looking forward to the splendor of the ice-cake Metropole (especially after a boiling and thirsty flight) but of course he had agreed. It was impossible not to agree with that virile voice, one of the most famous in the world, a voice that had spoken all the great roles with aplomb: Macbeth, Galileo, Lear, and of course the famous Othello. Othello to Sir Harry's Iago. Josh looked at the deep blue of the Mediterranean and hoped without expectation that nobody had reported to the great man, word for word, the *Standard* diary piece. "Considering" Sir Piers. Good God!

Josh wished he were anywhere else but here, waiting for Sir Piers to turn up and embarrass him, more than he'd ever been embarrassed in all his professional life. And why was he here?

He was here because of Jill Viner.

Jill had set up the piece in the *Standard* to get Sir Harry. And to hell with what Sir Piers might think. Except that she wanted him as well. And who had to come to Cannes and try to get him? Why, he, of course. Josh Williams thought, Sometimes I wish I'd never set eyes on Jill Viner.

Just the same, the girl was a success.

Or he wouldn't be here, would he?

An old man tottered through the park, sandy and scrubby at summer's end. A crowd of locals were playing boule. As always they found a lot to argue about. Josh hadn't been to Cannes for years, sometime back in the sixties. It had been with Alison. They'd come as guests of a journalist friend who reported the film festivals. They'd stayed out at La Bocca, in a mosquito-ridden villa. They'd been poor and it had all seemed very exciting at the time. Free tickets to the festival (the movies had been uniformly awful) and long sessions losing small stacks of francs at the casino. All very innocent and pleasant and all a long time ago. Alison had seemed very well, the sun had suited her, and they had determined to come in September every year, when the French had all gone home. They hadn't even made it once. Like so many other things in his life, the idea had been buried beneath the demands of his job. Rehearsals or casting or meetings with designers or actors: the theatre.

The old man sat down at the other end of the bench. Josh felt irritable. They'd probably have to move when Sir Piers came. It was a conversation that would have to be very private. Josh tried to remember incidents of that fifteen-year-old summer, but only the jokes came to mind. Bernard once being talked into ringing up his paper and complaining about the shit floating in the bay, courtesy of the American Sixth Fleet. The Scots news editor had been less than impressed. "Bernard, are ye mad or what? Shit in the Med? And you're complaining? It's like an oven, here in the office. I'd take the fucking Med, shit an' all, and chance it, Bernard."

And Tom Warrison, who couldn't write his movie copy because he'd lost so much money in the casino he was in a state of shock. And who would eventually dictate it to the *Standard* telephonists, right out of his head, without a note, and then collapse and have to be given brandy, amid roars of laughter from them all. Then out to dinner at the Coq Hardi, the cheapest and best restaurant in Cannes, and then to the casino again.

Salad days, Josh Williams thought, and all gone.

He tried to remember Alison's face, how she had looked, as

they swam or danced or laughed, but he couldn't. The only face he got was that of Jill Viner, jolly and vital where Alison was sad and fragile, pushing where Alison was reserved, a totally different being altogether.

"I say, dear boy," said the old man along the bench, "you seem a long way orf."

It was, of course, himself. He was famous for this kind of impersonation, deceiving even those who knew him well. Josh said, "Good God, I watched you cross the park. How on earth—"

"It's the walk, old son. It's all in the walk." Sir Piers stood up and curved his back in a stoop. "Yer drag one foot. Not two. Two's too many. Just one. Leave yer coat open, let it flap like that, too old to bother. Hat pulled down, no curl to the brim an' glasses on the end of the nose."

"Marvelous!" It was.

"Glad you think so, glad you think so." The gray eyes twinkled. Sir Piers had loved that, as he did all japes and jokes and, indeed, life itself. Sixty-whatever-it-was, and still in love with everything, including his newest and latest wife, a very talented actress herself and, of course, young. A bear, Josh thought. The bloody woman's right. He's the Russian, he's the choice against the world. A little makeup to suggest the features heavier, more solid, more a man of committee and coup, rather than the actor. No problem there. Sir Piers was thought to be the best makeup expert in the world. As Sir Harry was thought to speak the purest English.

"Hear you've got old Hal for the prime minister."

"How did you know?"

"Somebody flew in with a *Standard*." The eyes twinkled innocently, making him seem twenty years younger. It was hard to realize that Sir Piers had once been the most handsome man in England and was now, when he wanted to appear so, the ugliest. The classic career of all actors, in the old days. Josh could hear his father booming it: "Juvenile lead until you're forty. After that, the looks go and yer a character man. Very rare to find any actor gets the best of both worlds."

Sir Piers had. All the great butch parts as a young man. Then a pageantry of character pieces, both on stage and in the movies. Josh listened hard. Sir Piers was talking. The famous, spine-chilling voice was still there, the balls were still there. The old boy had it all.

"Apologize for suggesting this place. My movie masters will think I'm sorting out my career on their time. I'm on call, d'yer see, and I've just slipped out. I read *Queen* and it's good, there's a nice set of parts there. I like the Russian. I think I could do him justice. The problem is money. Money and availability. I have several more movie offers. I'm trying to build up a nest egg for my kids when I go." He grimaced. "Got them all ages, y'know. Forty to six. Not bad, eh? Different mothers naturally. All cost money. Still, that's what money's for, hey? To spend, hey? Not much point otherwise in life, sit around countin' your pennies like old Hal." A long theatrical pause. "What kind of deal is he on, the old miser, what?" The smile was pure tolerance. Nobody could have suspected they had been deadly rivals for almost half a century—nobody knew why—except that it had seemed to start with that first *Othello* all those long years ago.

"I think," said Josh carefully, "that Jill Viner has given all the actors exactly the same deal. No doubt she's talked about it to your agent?"

"He said something, he said something. Odd, that. Usually you never know what other people are getting, do you? The management's way of divide and rule, hey? Must admit I used to do it myself when I managed. Too much, yer can't do both. So old Hal's getting the same as I'd be, hey? I usually get more, y'know? Usually get twice as much."

"I don't doubt it, sir," said Josh, even more carefully. "The thing is, here we have four splendid parts. Famous movie people playing two of them. Plus yourself and Sir Harry."

"The randy old sod," said Sir Piers. "Is the old gamester still up to it?"

"He looked very healthy when I saw him two days ago."

"Where was that?"

"On his farm. Well, not exactly a farm. Large house really."

"There you are, old Hal on a farm. He'll hate it!"

"I rather think he does. He seems keen to work."

"He will be. He'll want the money. Always does."

Sir Piers brooded on some inner thought.

"D'yer know he got more than I did when we did the Moor, all those years ago? 'Course, I was only twenty-two. Youngest Moor ever. Don't know how old Hal was, nobody does—including him, I shouldn't wonder. But one hell of an Iago. Don't let anybody tell you different. Hell of an Iago."

"So I hear. Before my time."

"Perhaps," said Sir Piers, "a touch prim. I dunno. Perhaps a touch. Anyway, he stole the notices, the old party. Absolutely stole them. Always had the press in his pocket. Don't know how he does it. Never buys a drink, you notice that? Never." Sir Piers coughed. "You've no say about money, I suppose?"

"None at all," said Josh firmly.

It was important with actors, even gods like Sir Piers, not to play favorites. The rest of the cast knew in two minutes flat.

"I'll tell you why I'm even debating this part, shall I?"

"It's a good part?"

"Plenty of them, or I make 'em good. No. It's dishing old Hal. It's stealing the notices from the cunning old sod."

"Difficult to do," said Josh neutrally.

Sir Piers's head turned, bearlike. "Think I couldn't?"

"If anybody could."

"Look," said Sir Piers, "I've been good to the old rascal. Never played with him since that *Othello*. Never showed him up. Let some fancy London critics think he was the greatest." Again the

176

twinkle. "Others, more discerning, thought I was that, hey?" Sir Piers drew in his breath. It was said that for Lear he swam two miles every morning to give himself the breath control for the big speeches. "He's never done the black fella, or Richard Three, or Lear, or any of the big ones, the adroit old master. Stayed with Polonius and the Jew." Sir Piers chewed his mustache, grown for the movie, torn between fairness and irritation. "Wonderful Shylock. I have to concede. Better than mine. Should be. Old Hal cares more about shekels than I do. Bound to do it better."

"I think you're both wonderful," said Josh. He did.

"I agree. I agree. But old Hal won't have it. Nothing I do will answer. Actors are funny about these things, what? There's old Bobby Atkins gets the CBE and he's furious he doesn't get a knighthood. Tells everybody there's Hal, a pretty poesy puff, and there's me, the 'Crucifier of Yer Verse'—you know Bobby always looked up to the sky when he talked about the Bard? Well, he did, always. Felt he had a private line to old Bill Shakespeare, did Bobby. Well, he says, to anybody who'll listen, 'There's Sir Harry and me—I *crucify* Shakespearian verse and Harry *minces* it!—he gets a knighthood,' bellows old Bobby Atkins, 'and all I get is a fucking CBE!' You ever heard that one?"

"Never," lied Josh.

"Perfectly true. Every word." Sir Piers looked pleased. "Bobby should have had a knighthood. You ever hear how he was doing this open-air Shakespeare and there's this thunderstorm and everybody rushes into tents and it's bloody dark in there and Bobby seizes this girl and it turns out he's one of the boys and Bobby drops him like a hot brick and shouts, 'Nothing like that about me, dear boy, nothing like that about me!' Ever hear that one?"

"No," lied Josh again. "No. I never did."

"Look here," said Sir Piers, standing up, "I'll take the bloody part just to demonstrate to the critics and the public generally the truth of what I've been saying for years. That the virile masculine actor wins out against the poetical one every time. In short, I will dish the cunning old sod." He twinkled at Josh. "Terms acceptable to you?"

"Any terms would be. It'll be an honor to work with you both."

"You're a bit cunning yerself." Sir Piers raised a warning finger. "I knew your father and he was cunning." He rubbed his hands together. "I think I'm going to enjoy upstaging and generally messing the old villain about."

That'll be the day, Josh thought—but with some dismay.

"Fear not." Sir Piers waved his stick. "It'll be all right on the night." He tottered off and among the multifarious noises of the park Josh thought he heard the muttered gleeful word, "*Considering.*"

Josh watched him adopt his old man's walk, and he stayed rooted in his seat, as Sir Piers paused at the boule players and engaged them in execrable French about a point of the game he pretended not to understand. When he had roused them to internal bickering and argument, Sir Piers looked satisfied and continued on his way, leaving chaos behind him.

Jesus, thought Josh, what have I taken on?

JILL was sitting in her office making her fifth long telephone call to British Actors Equity. Molly was watching her sympathetically, and had even stopped typing. If this went wrong . . . as Molly put it, they were all in the cart. Austin Ames was set, the Equity council accepted that an American actor was needed to play an American president. Of course, they thought there were many English actors whose accents were perfect ("Absolute bullshit!" declared Josh) but they saw her point. Where Maggie was concerned, they did not. The part of the queen should go to a British actress. It was quite wrong to think of an American actress for the role and the council were quite firmly against it.

Jill knew that if the council vetoed Maggie there was no appeal. The government department concerned with the issue of work permits wouldn't give Maggie one unless Equity said she should have it. Jill silently cursed all trade unions and their restrictive practices and agreed with the Equity official that a lot of London actresses were out of work. "I know, I used to be one. Look, I know I'm asking a lot, but if I don't get Maggie I will abort the show."

There was a shocked silence on the other end of the line.

"Do you really mean that, Miss Viner?"

Jill took a deep breath. "Yes, I do. I'm looking to take *Queen* to Broadway when it's had a decent London run. I must go with my original cast. Maggie Stride is a necessity for me, in both London and New York. While I agree there are one or two actresses who could do it on Shaftesbury Avenue, none of them would sell a ticket on Broadway. And the ones available wouldn't sell tickets here either. Maggie is a great international star. I need her for this most difficult of plays. And I should add, if I abort—and without her I will have to—then Sir Harry and almost certainly Sir Piers, who of course are Equity members, will not be seen in the London theatre this coming season, which would be a shame. Nor will several other Equity members, backstage and front. And that might not be popular with those members."

Another long silence.

"You are absolutely adamant the production closes if you do not get Maggie Stride?"

"Yes, I am."

"Miss Viner, I will put your thoughts before the council. We meet this afternoon. I will ring you at the earliest moment."

Jill put the telephone down and discovered she was shaking. Molly said, "What you need is a cup of tea," and Jill replied, "What we both need is a large drink," and poured two gin and tonics from the hospitality cupboard.

"Do you mean it?" asked Molly. "Would you close the show?"

"I don't know. Probably not. But I might. After all my trouble getting Maggie." Jill sipped her drink. "I'd hate to close it, it would be ruin."

"They don't know you," said Molly sagely. "With one of the old hands, they'd know they didn't mean it. If they couldn't get a work permit for Maggie they'd be depressed, yes, but they'd recover and get somebody else, and inside a week they'd convince themselves whoever they'd got would be better than Maggie."

"That kind of optimism," said Jill, "is what makes me both love and laugh at theatrical people. As far as Equity are concerned, I hope I sounded as if I meant business, because I did."

"Oh, you did, you did," said Molly, picking up a telephone to tell yet another young actress they were full.

Obviously, the council of Actors' Equity thought she meant it. They rang and said they would recommend a work permit be issued to Miss Maggie Stride for six months.

Jill said, "Thank you very much."

That was the moment another telephone rang. It was Josh calling from Nice airport to say Sir Piers was in, pending contract. "Josh," she whispered, "you're a lovely man."

"Always thought that," said Josh. "Got to rush. 'Bye."

He was, she thought, he was a lovely man.

But Molly's all-knowing eyes were on her. So she looked at her engagement pad and said, "Molly, will you ring Herbert Glass and ask when I can see him? As soon as possible?"

"Oh, we are rushing our fences, aren't we?" Molly reached for the telephone.

"This is a big one," said Jill. "See if he'll make it lunch. Suggest the Connaught."

Herbert Glass not only said yes to the Connaught, he suggested the next day.

"My my, we are making an impression," said Molly drily. Then she smiled. "You're doing marvels, dear. Marvels."

JOSH found a message on his Ansaphone.

It was from Sir Tom. Would he ring his private number at once? Any hour. Josh looked at his watch. It was ten o'clock. He was numb with tiredness. He intended to have a shower and go to bed. It wasn't every day a director booked Sir Piers into a show that already had Sir Harry. He poured himself a horse's neck (his father's ultimate pick-me-up) and stepped under the shower. Afterward, towel around his damp body and glass in hand, he rang Sir Tom.

Sir Tom was at home.

Would Josh like to drive over?

He knew where Sir Tom was. At his flat in Belgrave Square, where else?

Josh did just that and found Sir Tom nursing a cognac. He accepted one and sat down. Sir Tom was not alone. Sitting in another chair was a rather uncomfortable-looking Max Heston (still as scruffy, though, Josh noted) drinking beer, and a smart-looking young man in denim and a fringe, whom Josh did not know, but who was introduced as Paul Prinz. He recognized the name. Prinz was a sort of Professional Young Writer, who had tried many different routes to success: a detective novel set in Chicago, a sci-fi thriller, a documentary on British television about the Rosenbergs. None of it succeeded. He wondered what Prinz was doing there.

He was soon told.

"Paul," said Sir Tom, "is a friend of mine. He's writing me a play. And *he's* a friend of Max's. I say this because I want to be absolutely honest about how I came by my information about *Queen* and why I asked you over for a drink, Josh." Sir Tom smiled gently. "I always believe in absolute honesty, as Paul knows." Paul

Prinz smiled back at Sir Tom, who went on. "So you see, dear Josh, I had to ask Max how much more he felt he could tell me—he had told Paul you had Maggie and Austin cast already and Sir Harry too—"

"Look"—Max turned to Josh—"I did tell Paul. I mean, everybody knew. It was in the papers, right?"

Josh said nothing. He sipped his cognac and waited.

"I must say," purred Sir Tom, at his most dangerous, Josh knew, when most complimentary, "you have certainly surprised me with that wonderful casting." He warmed his cognac with his fingers and sipped it. "Absolutely first-rate, Josh, I must say."

Josh nodded but said nothing.

Max cut in, "Tom guessed about Sir Piers, Josh, honest."

"Well, I didn't need to guess very hard. It was obvious, once you'd cast Sir Harry." Sir Tom smiled modestly. "I mean, I had read the script after all, hadn't I?"

"And not liked it," Josh said.

"Did I say I didn't *like* it?" Sir Tom looked pained. "I don't remember saying that."

"You didn't want to put it on, Tom, did you?"

Sir Tom poured himself a little more cognac. "That wasn't *me*, dear old Josh. That was the board. They were worried. I put it to them that here was a delicate play and *they* were worried, d'you see?" He gestured with the cognac and Josh accepted a measure. He was beginning to enjoy this.

Paul Prinz said, "It's a terrific play."

Josh asked, surprised, "You've read it?"

Prinz shook his head too quickly. "No, no. I mean, it sounds like one."

Josh saw Sir Tom's sad eye on Prinz and thought, You'd better shut up, laddie, or there'll be no play at the National for you. He also cursed copier-machines, the thieves' friends. Sir Tom had obviously taken a copy. These days everybody did. "Have you read it again, then?" he asked Sir Tom.

"Again?" Sir Tom looked startled. "Er, well, it's been in my mind, Josh. In my mind. It's one of those rare plays that do stay in the mind." He lit his pipe. It was a moment, Josh knew, of extreme danger. "Maybe I ought to have fought harder for it. With the board, what?"

Josh said, "Maybe. But there you are."

There was a silence.

Prinz looked as if he might say something, but thought better of it.

Max Heston seemed thoroughly miserable.

So he bloody should, thought Josh.

Sir Tom puffed out a cloud of smoke.

"I could have another go," he said, "at the board. If I tried them again they might reconsider. If I put it to them the right way. That we . . . er . . . you . . . had the cast you have." He smiled apologetically. "Giving my apologies, naturally. Saying I was wrong and you were right, what?"

Josh said nothing at all.

Sir Tom's voice dropped an octave. "Naturally, you would direct." He coughed. "No question of any changes like that. You'd bring all your people over. Something could be worked out, financially, I'm sure."

Nobody said anything.

Josh said, "I'm not the producer, Tom."

"No, but, you see, I thought I'd try you first." A wave of the pipe. "Besides, I hear you haven't got a theatre yet, and if I took it into the National, well, it could always do its first run there and transfer afterwards."

There was another silence.

Max Heston looked at Paul Prinz and Paul Prinz looked at Max Heston.

"What," enquired Sir Tom, very, very gently, "do you think, Josh? Considering, that is, that you haven't got a theatre for your play in the West End?"

Josh finished his brandy.

"Considering everything, I'd say it's a very magnanimous and generous suggestion, Tom. And I appreciate it very much."

Sir Tom beamed. "Thank you, dear boy."

"But we've gone a long way and there's no turning back." Josh stood up. "Thanks for the drink." At the door he turned. "I did get Sir Piers today. I don't think we need to split our investment."

"No theatre, Josh." Sir Tom purred. "You have no theatre, do you?"

"Just the same."

"You'll put it to Miss . . . er, Viner?" Sir Tom still smiled. "The offer's open, Josh."

"I'll put it to her, if we don't get a theatre."

"The offer," said Sir Tom regretfully, "is only open for a very limited period."

"I must say"—Josh couldn't help smiling—"I like to be honest, so I must say I will have to advise Miss Viner not to accept."

"Oh, really?" said Sir Tom. "I'm terribly sorry to hear that, but thank you for being so honest, Josh."

"No trouble," said Josh. "No trouble at all."

He was smiling when he got into his Volkswagen and still smiling when he got into bed and still smiling when he went to sleep. He had ignored a telephone call from, he guessed, Jill. He was going to tell her nothing.

Queen was his. He wasn't giving it away to anybody.

"THEY say it's the best hotel restaurant in Europe," said Herbie Glass, refusing the famous steak-and-kidney pie. "And who am I to argue?" He was a good-looking version of his cousin, Lord Glass, but every whit as smart—some said smarter because harder. Others said not so smart because harder. There was a rivalry between the cousins, it was rumored, but in the end they kept it in the family.

"My cousin tells me you have a good play, and you tell me you have a great cast, so I'm listening." Herbie Glass smiled. He really was very sharp. "He also tells me he has money in it, a habit I've been trying to break him of for years."

"Please don't," said Jill. "I need him." She put it to Herbie Glass straight. "Which theatres do you have free in September?"

"All my theatres are full." Herbie Glass drank a little Perrier. He had a good figure to show off his excellent suits and he meant to keep it. It seemed such a pity, thought Jill, to come to the Connaught for Perrier. "One theatre might come free, though."

"Which one?" Jill knew she was being overeager but what the hell.

Herbie Glass looked pleased. "He said you were a hustler. All right. The Royal might—I said *might*—be available."

Jill thought: A medium-sized house, slap in the middle of Shaftesbury Avenue! Not too big, a trifle small if anything. It might take a little longer than she had anticipated to get their money back. Not perfect, but pretty damn near. She had seen Joe Dancy lose money going into the wrong theatre, because it was the only one he could get and it was now or never. It was now or never here, too.

"If we can do a deal we'll take it."

Herbie Glass sipped his Perrier and brooded. "I'd want a fifty-fifty split, Jill."

"Now, you know sixty-forty my way is usual, Herbie," she protested. "Just because I'm a new girl, please don't take advantage of me."

Herbie Glass held up his hands. "Just testing the water. We'll see, we'll see." He reluctantly ate a little smoked salmon. "So. We have a good play, nice cast."

"Star cast, Herbie. It's a star cast."

"All right. Star cast. As a bricks-and-mortar man I ought to be happy at the prospect. But it's been a long, hot summer. Tourist trade down. VAT on seats. Very bad, generally. Your angels don't know such things—my own cousin don't know such things—they're romantics. But I'm strictly business, Jill. If you come into the Royal and—let me see—less than five thousand a week is paid in at the box office, then I close the show. Kaput. No arguments."

"That's high, Herbie."

"I know it's high, but that's the deal, Jill. Oh, and I'll want, naturally, a cut of any film rights sold, or any other rights."

Jill let a moment hang. "All right. And I'll go fifty-five/forty-five with you."

"They told me you were tough," said Herbie. He hesitated. "All right."

Jill added, "Good. And we use the Royal to rehearse in, five days a week, before we go out of town, at say three hundred a week."

"You don't rest, do you?" Herbie smiled. "All right to that, too. But it's four hundred. Let's all get rich."

"In your case, Herbie, richer!"

Herbie leaned forward earnestly. "Everybody hates the bricks-and-mortar man! The producers hate us. They think we do nothing, risk nothing. All we do is buy or lease the theatre, and sit and take half the box office." Herbie blinked. He seemed sincere. "Look, you ever tried buying a theatre? They're all old, they're falling down, they were built a million years ago, there's always something needs doing. If it's not fire insurance and repairs, it's seat upholstery—you any idea what that costs today, to do the Royal right through, as I did last year? And sometimes I have to carry plays that aren't making money because I can't sack my bar staff and usherettes because if I did I'd never get them back again. Sometimes it's only the bar takings that make me show a profit."

"Don't go on, Herbie," said Jill. "You'll have me crying for you."

Herbie smiled. "All I'm saying is, it isn't a goldmine."

"Sometimes it just looks like it." Jill swallowed a little more champagne. Not too much. With Herbie, she needed her wits unfuddled. "How can you be sure the Royal will be empty for us?"

"I'll be sure." Herbie ate a small piece of brown bread in gloomy celebration.

Jill said, mischievously, "I'm sure you won't stop taking bookings at the box office by having the telephone permanently engaged, or allowing the adverts outside the theatre to peel off?"

Herbie looked affronted. "No. I'll just pull the play off. Like I'll pull yours off if it doesn't make money." He shook his head. "Besides, I haven't done anything like that for thirty years." He smiled, wistfully. "Used to be fun. The whole business has gone respectable these days. Or anyway, I thought so until I met you."

"What?" Jill was startled. "Who's been talking to you?"

Herbie seemed pleased at her reaction. "Just about everybody, dear. You're getting yourself a name."

"A name bad or a name good?"

Herbie Glass waggled his hands. "A bit of this, a bit of that. It's nice to know some producers get a name for being toughies. Takes the weight off the bricks-and-mortar men." He peered at the Connaught's magnificent sweets trolley. "Can I afford a crème caramel?"

"Have a rice pudding, they're back on the menu."

"No, no." He sighed. "Nothing."

"Then a glass of champagne. Just to celebrate."

"Celebrate what?" asked Herbie Glass. "I came to get fifty, I've got forty-five."

But he had the champagne just the same.

HALF an hour later, euphoric, Jill was back in the office of Queen Productions. She walked in to raised voices and a look of alarm on young Max Heston's face. He was sitting in the inner office reading the *Stage*.

"Max, what's going on in there?"

"Either the Third World War's broken out or Vercek doesn't

like Tommi's new ideas." Max smiled at the idea and went on reading. He looked rather white. She said, "Are you all right?" and he answered, "Has Josh said anything to you?" and she said, "No, why?" and Max said, "No reason."

Jill was too disturbed by the noise to question him further, except to say, "When did Vercek arrive?"

"Just walked in, half an hour ago."

"Oh, no!"

"Don't worry. Josh will look after him."

Jill took a deep breath and opened the production-office door. Inside was Josh with a large drawing in front of him, spread across the desk. Tommi Traceham sat smoking a cigarette in a tortoiseshell holder, dressed in the height of thirties fashion—high heels, ankle-strap shoes, midcalf dress, square shoulders—and with an expression of slight disgust on her face.

Vercek stood at the window, his back to them, wearing his old bomber jacket. He seemed to be trembling with mirth or rage, she couldn't tell which. He held one of his very strong Russian cigarettes in his maimed hand.

Josh was sitting mildly between them, like a referee.

"Look, Vercek old friend," he was saying, "there's no conspiracy to keep you in the dark. It's simply that we haven't really got going yet. I wouldn't have shown you our rough drawings—"

"They aren't rough." This, tight-lipped, from Tommi. "They're *it!*"

"I wouldn't have shown them to you if I hadn't been sure you'd like them."

Vercek said, very distinctly, not turning round. "They are musical comedy. The queen will look like a sugar cake, if you have red velvet. Black. She should be in black. Velvet if you wish. But black. It is a time for mourning, not rejoicing. It is a time of surrender. Not celebration. And a crown? This idea of a crown? Would she wear one? You say symbolic. I say, possibly, yes. But not a great big thing like a chamber pot with the jewels of India set in it!

Something small. Dignified. She does not need this pot on her head to tell the audience she is a queen. The words tell them that, Mr. Director. The words."

"If they listen," said Tommi Traceham. "Darling, it's what they *see* that matters most. In the first moment. What they *see*, dear. They don't hear the first five minutes of *any* play. They're too busy getting comfortable, getting adjusted to the light, breaking wind, all that. They aren't ready to listen, love."

Vercek said, "That is possibly true. All the more reason why the queen must look correct."

"She looks bloody marvelous, darling, and if you don't like it, I'm sorry but you can stuff your objections!"

Vercek turned round, genuinely shocked, it seemed to Jill.

"That is an incorrect way to speak to the dramatist."

"Shit, Vercek, you sound like a fucking commissar."

Vercek looked ready to commit murder. "I am many things, Miss Traceham. But I am not a commissar. Please do not call me that again."

Tommi said, icily, "Commissar or not, that's my set and costume. Finito, darling."

Josh looked questioningly at Jill. "Yes, Jill, can I help?"

Jill looked at them all, in turn. "There seems to be a problem. I more or less heard what it was. Do you realize you're all talking about something that doesn't matter at all? Unless there's a theatre to take the play into?"

"Well, is there?"

Josh was used to her ploys. She ignored him.

"Now, Mr. Vercek. You object to this design?"

"Yes, and I object to reading many things in the newspapers about my play, which I have not been consulted about."

"Like what?"

"Actors are talked about. But I am not consulted."

"Would you object to Austin Ames, Maggie Stride, Sir Harry, and Sir Piers?"

189

"Do you have them?"

"Yes."

"No," said Vercek. "From what I know they are excellent. I will have to see them in rehearsal to know if they are right."

Josh asked, mildly, "You will be coming to rehearsals?"

"I do not intend to miss a single one. This play is my life's blood."

"I see," said Josh, heavily. "Some writers never come."

"I am not one of these writers."

"No. I see that."

Jill was looking at Tommi's latest drawing of the costume the queen would wear. It looked good, but she thought she saw Vercek's objections. She said, "Look, Tommi, what if you used a tiara, rather than a full crown? And made the queen's dress of black velvet, really opulent black velvet?"

Tommi Traceham looked coolly at Jill a moment. Then at Josh. "If I had wanted to do that I would have done that, wouldn't I?"

Jill looked straight back at her. "All right. Let's leave it for now. We can talk about it later."

Tommi picked up her drawings from Josh's desk. "Call me, darling," she said icily to Josh, "when the producer has decided what *you* should do!"

And she left, in a hurry.

Vercek said, in the silence, "That woman is interested in fashion. She ought to be designing dresses for rich women. She is only interested in critics writing about her creations. She is a cheap person, interested only in effect, not art or truth."

Josh said, "That's why she's a good designer."

"I do not understand your reasoning," said Vercek.

"That," said Josh, "is why you aren't a director."

"We'll talk to her. We'll work something out." Jill smiled.

"No silliness, please," said Vercek. "This is an important play.

It must be staged with gravity. It is not something for socialites to croon and coo over."

"I might get her to change the crown into a tiara. I can't ask her to make the dress black as well." Josh sounded firm but reasonable. Vercek broke in with, "Red is too much, it is fancy dress—" but Josh just lowered his voice. "You will have to trust me, Mr. Vercek. I like the play but I make these sorts of decisions. Not Tommi Traceham or even Jill here. Or you. I make them. Or Miss Viner can sack me. But, until she does, I decide. Yours is a fine play. I will not let you down."

It was very skillfully done.

Vercek looked at Josh for a long moment, drumming the maimed hand ceaselessly on the windowsill. Then he nodded briefly, and left the production office. They heard the outside door slam.

Jill collapsed into a chair.

"Par for the course," said Josh easily, obviously not at all put out by the histrionics. "How did lunch go?"

"Herbie Glass is giving us the Royal."

"What?" He sat up. "Is it definite?"

"Absolutely!"

Josh got up and walked round the office twice, without saying a word. Then he took her in his arms, but he didn't kiss her, as she expected him to. He simply shouted, his eyes wide with excitement. "The Royal! We've got the Royal, terrific, terrific, hooray, Jill Viner, my darling, you're an absolute bloody miracle!"

Jill laughed and hugged him back.

She would rather he had said he loved her.

VERCEK left the office of Queen Productions in a sweat of anxiety and anger. He avoided the black plastic waste sacks littering the pavements. Another strike was on. He could not remember who it was this time. The strikers, like Josh and Jill and the silly woman Traceham, lived in a world far from reality. They did not know what reality was. They thought they were safe to go on with their silly games forever. He breathed in deeply to steady his nerves. These foolish theatrical people. They thought *The Queen of Finland* was just another unimportant production, a *confection* like most of the plays in the West End of London. It was to be expected. He had no right to be surprised. Look at the productions along Shaftesbury Avenue at this very moment. All silly thrillers or sillier sex comedies. The West End audiences didn't want to think. *Six for Sex* screamed a Soho sex-cinema, as he passed by. Exactly. Box office. Everything was box office. Money was the only thing that mattered. Profit. Like *Six for Sex*, his play had to attract the paying customer. It was a part of the West's philosophy he found hard to accept. He had worked in subsidized theatre as a writer, everything paid for by a government, for ten years. That was before the nightmare. He had liked the freedom to work on the plays selected by the board. He had liked being able to get any actor he wanted, any director he wanted, any materials or props he wanted. All that he had liked. The censorship he had not noticed at first, but when he had noticed it, when it had struck him like a blow in the face, then he had realized that all the other things (the right actors, the excellent conditions, all that) were as nothing. Freedom was the only thing that mattered.

Freedom.

Only a man who had lost it knew what it was.

Vercek slipped into a doorway and looked back down Frith Street. Nobody. He resumed walking past the saunas and the sex shops.

You could tell these very nice Westerners, Jill and Josh and the rest of them. You could write a play about it. You could couch your arguments and experiences in the best language you knew, toning down, yes, actually toning down, things you knew to be true, because you also knew that the Westerners would not accept them, would label them propaganda. What could one expect from people who gave out huge grants from public money to other people who then put on plays saying what was wrong with the kind of people who gave them the money, and the society they represented? Unless a play was left-wing none of the subsidized theatres would put it on. None of them would put on *The Queen of Finland*, which was why it was having to be sold in a whorehouse like the West End.

It was a warning, and they were trying to turn it into something pretty to look at, a spectacle. Vercek felt the anger still in his chest. He would allow nobody to do that. Nobody. He would watch every minute of rehearsals. He would not rest or let them rest.

Vercek crossed Soho Square, walking past the winos and the walkers. He looked at them without sympathy, averting his eyes. He had seen many like them on the streets of Moscow, away from the tourist routes. Alcohol was a way out. He had to admit it. Only when he was in one of his deep despairs, which he felt coming on, did he succumb. He doubled back quickly along Charing Cross Road to the Leicester Square tube and got on not the first train west but the second. He looked up and down the platform. Nothing. Everything seemed all right.

Vercek sat in the swaying compartment, brooding. These people were all right. They meant well. He must be reasonable. Josh Williams was a good man. He had integrity. The Viner woman was a Western tart full of the independence that socialism had talked about for women but never gave them. Such a woman, full of juice and opinion, would certainly be gazed at askance in some of the councils in which he had sat in his time. He smiled wryly and lit one of his brackish cigarettes. A fat and foolish young woman in an Indian kaftan (she, of course, was white) pointed to a No Smoking sign. Vercek stared at her hard. The woman noticed his maimed hand and looked away. Yes, thought Vercek, look away, my baby, with your silly Western fashion (dressing like an Indian peasant, was she mad? were they all mad? was it too late to save them in their headlong frivolous chase after sillier and sillier fashions?), look away from anything that offends you. You are able to do that today. But tomorrow, who knows?

Vercek changed compartments at Hyde Park Corner very quickly, glancing first along the entire length of the long platform. Nobody.

He sat in another nonsmoking compartment, the cardboard cigarette still in his hand. He had learned to smoke them in the camp. He could not now smoke anything else. Nothing else was strong enough. The harsh scent of the tobacco kept him in touch with the freezing cold and the dirt and the hunger. It reminded him who he was.

Vercek got off at Baron's Court and paid the excess on his ticket to the black ticket collector. He could not understand the West. England left her borders open. Anybody could come in, whether they had a job or not, whether they were friend or enemy. The English behaved as if they didn't care, as if nothing in the world could ever change, as if nothing was worth worrying about, worth defending, as if somebody else would defend it for them. He wondered if they were redeemable, with their open, trusting, pink faces and their easygoing ways. Innocents, all of them. And the Americans, quite possibly, were even more innocent. Perhaps *Queen* would open their eyes, just a little, one or two of them. It was as much as a playwright could do. He was not a politician.

Once perhaps he might have been.

But not now, not after the nightmare.

He bought a bottle of vodka at the off-license near Baron's Court tube station and a lemon and a loaf of dark rye bread at the delicatessen run by Asians that was still open, long after the fun-loving English all around it had shut up shop and gone home to watch their televisions. He walked all the way, over a mile, to his bed-sitter, off the North End Road, let himself in, and went straight to the window. Not moving the curtain at all, he looked quickly down into the street. A few black children played football. Otherwise nothing. Vercek sat on the single bed in the cold, bare room and sighed, very, very deeply. He tore off a piece of rye bread from the loaf, cut the lemon into slices, and put it on a plate. Getting up, he double-locked the door. He had screwed two new locks on it, without the landlord's permission. Then, and only then, did he open the bottle of vodka.

"WE start rehearsals tomorrow." Josh tried to keep the edge out of his voice and only half succeeded. He was well aware that Tommi Traceham and Max and Molly were in the production office and could hear every word. "Jill, I must have the cast fully assembled. I'm going to look a total idiot if I don't."

"You'll have your cast, darling. The princess will be a day late, that's all." Jill was smiling calmly from behind her desk.

"We haven't even got a short list of possibilities yet. We'll finish up taking somebody from *Spotlight*."

"That's exactly what we won't do, darling."

"What?" He stared at her.

"Tom Tully has fifty girls coming for audition to the Royal this afternoon. Two o'clock exactly."

Josh sat down. Here he was, strung up to shrieking point, preparing himself to take on Sir Piers and Sir Harry, not to mention Maggie and Austin, and now this crap! He should be sitting down calmly somewhere—of course he should!—absolutely alone, thinking about how he would approach each individual actor, what he would say about each individual part. A feeling of total unreality came over him. It was simply insane.

"You don't expect me to be there."

"Of course I do. These girls have been writing in for two weeks."

"You promised me," Josh said icily, "that it was just a publicity stunt, to draw attention to the show."

"So it was," said Jill reasonably. "But it's got big. The papers are interested. Television is going to be there. Look at today's *Mail*. The *Express*. Even *The Times* has a piece about us. Look. . . ." Jill held up the newspapers.

"How did you get all these girls together?"

"Tom Tully sent telegrams to them. Of course, they may not all turn up."

"They will. And a lot of other people, too. We don't need this kind of publicity. We have the sirs."

"We need the general public to come, the ordinary theatregoer. All right, there's a public, an up-market public for the sirs. But Mr. and Mrs. Average will read about this little unknown girl who gets the big part—"

"What do you mean, unknown?" Josh asked harshly. "You can't put an unknown actress in with our cast! Have you gone absolutely bloody mad, woman?"

Jill froze. She said, "Josh. Be reasonable. Max can take the girls through a reading or something and when he has them whittled down to half a dozen you can come in and make the final choice."

Josh wondered if he was hearing all this correctly; but he knew that he must be, because it was of a piece with everything that Jill had been doing over the last three weeks. Every day there had been some item in one newspaper or another: about Austin's habit of pumping iron between takes and his general fitness-and-diet-craziness; about Maggie's tragic loss of a lover; about Sir Harry's wonderful house out in the country (this had a spread in *The Sunday Times* color magazine); about Sir Piers's latest family, who had followed him out to Cannes for his last week there; and about the way they were all preparing themselves for the event of the London theatrical season, indeed for the event of their lives—to wit, the rehearsals and eventual West End production of *Queen.*

It was a brilliant press campaign. No doubt about it.

The trouble was, it was too brilliant.

"Can't you see what you're doing? You're raising too many expectations. Both in the press—where the critics will expect it to be a cross between *My Fair Lady* and *Mother Courage*—and with the public, who'll expect it to be a sex comedy like everything else on Shaftesbury Avenue this season! This is a serious play; it won't stand this Barnum and Bailey treatment!"

"We have to sell tickets," Jill said flatly. "Do you know what our block bookings with the ticket agencies are?"

"No, I don't, and I don't care!"

"Well, I do, and they aren't good enough, Josh." Jill was still being sweetly reasonable and that made him angrier. "They aren't convinced—Keith Prowse and the others—that the play will pull in the customers. I want them to take a third and all I can get is a fifth!"

"Look, it's got Piers and Harry and—"

"They know who's *in* it. It's the play that worries them. They think it may not take. That the public may not like it. They find that very worrying and so do I."

Josh said steadily, "You've never said that before."

"I know I haven't, but we have a big investment here, Josh, and I must look after the investors' money." Jill stood up and held out a hand to him. "Come on, Josh. Be a trouper. Say you'll come along to the Royal at four o'clock and pick your girl."

Josh stood up, but he did not take her hand.

"I will not be at the Royal at four o'clock for the bloody meat market. You can go there and pick the girl yourself."

"You don't meant that."

"Indeed I do."

Josh picked up his briefcase and walked slowly to the door. "I'm going home. Call me with your decision. I can get my own first choice on the telephone tonight and she'll be there tomorrow morning."

"And who is that?"

"You know very well: Pat Woods."

Jill said, "She's all right but there's no charisma, Josh. She's been around, she's a bit known. We need more. What's the good of raising all this interest and then casting somebody all the press know about already because she's been in a milk commercial?"

"She could do it. I can't think of anybody better."

With that Josh shut the door and walked down the stairs into Shaftesbury Avenue. He half expected Jill to follow him, but she didn't. He took a cab to Glebe Place and found his flat neat and tidy for once. His cleaning woman had been. Just as well. Jill usually left the place looking like a rubbish heap. She loved to cook but hated to clean. His father had always said, That's the choice: the cooks or the cleaners. Nothing in between.

Well, he hadn't chosen Jill. She had chosen him. He poured himself a large Scotch and sat on the sofa. Hadn't she? Of course she had. Women always did the choosing. He liked her, perhaps he even loved her. He wasn't sure he knew what love was anymore; but today was something different. Today Jill Viner was ruining the casting for *Queen* and that he could not allow. He sipped his Scotch and wondered if little Pat Woods would be right. Good looks, thin almost, young enough or very nearly—well, be frank; perhaps not quite young enough but what the hell, how many seventeen-year-olds could act at all? Pat was twenty, maybe twenty-one or even -two, but she could convince an audience she was seventeen. The theatre was an illusion. Pat Woods was a pro; she could provide the illusion. She could also take direction; she would know what he meant when he gave her a note. Some seventeen-year-old just out

199

of RADA thrown in with sharks like Sir Harry and Sir Piers! Good God. They'd eat her. He'd spend half his time seeing she got a look-in. The thing was impossible. Now that he had given his ultimatum, Jill would see that he was right, and change her mind.

Or would she?

Josh sipped his drink thoughtfully and wondered.

He had slept with Jill fifty times, had had sex with her twice that number of times, had talked and talked and talked *Queen* with her—costs, production, design, lighting, everything—and he could not be absolutely sure what she would do. Not absolutely sure.

To hell with her. He could live without *Queen*. The whole production staff had heard his words. He could not go back on them now and hold up his head. Could he?

No, he couldn't. He wouldn't.

He poured himself another Scotch and put his feet up on the sofa. He hated rows and he usually never had them. Since Jill had come into his life he seemed to be living on the edge of an emotional volcano. It wouldn't do. It would have to stop, whatever happened to the casting of the princess. That issue was only a symptom. It was the feeling behind it that mattered. They were simply not suited to each other. They didn't think the same way about anything, anything at all.

Except that bed was good between them.

He had to admit it was.

Bed wasn't everything. It was a lot, but it wasn't everything.

Josh sat and drank his whiskey and waited for the telephone to ring. And for Jill to say: It's all off. Forget it. You've won.

The telephone did not ring.

MAGGIE sat in the Savoy Hotel and looked from her room down over the Embankment and across the Thames. The river glittered in the summer sunshine and tugs moved along it in a timeless chug. Clerks ate their lunches on the green lawns of the Embankment

Gardens. It all had a look of peace and calm. None of it reflected Maggie's mood.

The words simply would not go in.

She supposed that it was jet lag; but some of it had to be prerehearsal nerves. It wasn't usual, but nothing about *Queen* was usual. For one thing, she had never played in London before. For another, she was facing a cast of phenomenal ability—and an audience who expected her to walk away with the play. And here she sat, trying to memorize her lines, and the words simply *would not go in*.

Maggie had never had this trouble before. She had always been a quick study. Now, the words of the script of *Queen* were simply a blur before her eyes. She felt a cold sweat of anxiety. She made another effort to drive the main speech of act one into her head. Nothing happened.

She lay back on the chintz covers of the deep sofa and closed her eyes. The suite was quiet and comfortable, one of the best in the hotel. She had asked for no calls to be put through to her and none had been. It was all as it should be, and yet the words would not go in.

On impulse, she picked up the telephone and rang Jill Viner at her office. Jill was not there, a young English voice said. He was Max, the stage manager, could he help? No, she told him, she was fine. Was Josh Williams there? No, said Max, Josh Williams wasn't there either. He thought Josh Williams was at his home. He could give Maggie the number. Maggie said no, it was all right, nothing to worry Mr. Williams about. Max asked if she was sure he could do nothing. She said no, she was fine, and rang off, feeling worse than ever.

God, she had to learn these words by tomorrow.

She had never gone into a rehearsal in her life anything but word-perfect. It was the way she worked. Other actors learned their lines as they rehearsed. She could not rehearse and worry about her words at the same time. Her hand reached out for the telephone again: she would ring Austin; he was only just along the corridor, he would help.

But she didn't.

Austin had his own problems, his own preparation to do. He too was facing a big challenge the next day. It wasn't fair to involve him in her difficulties. Anyway, he'd done enough already. Far too much, in fact. He'd arranged the funeral while she was prostrate with grief, sedated but still screaming inside. He'd written to everybody, going through her diary for addresses and telephone numbers. He had talked to her doctor and her agents and the press and he had generally protected her. When she had come around from the first raw shock of it all (by this time Philip had been buried), Austin was still there. She had disgraced herself at the funeral, stony-faced, unable to weep. The picture in the *New York Post* had shown her as cold and heartless and uncaring, whereas she was simply stunned, hanging on Austin's arm, in the graveyard, the sun blazing down on the coffin and the open grave, the barbarity of it all an affront to everything she remembered about Philip, the civilizing effect of him, his easy presence, his love.

All that was over. It was over two months now. She was in London. She was a professional. She had lines to learn. Why wasn't she able to learn them?

Philip, was it the memory of Philip?

Did he so fill her mind with mourning that there was no room for anything else?

So much for the ice-queen image!

Maggie reached for the pills and shook one out of the bottle. She had it halfway to her mouth when she hesitated: barbiturates sent her to sleep, and all that would happen if she took the pills would be that she'd lose two or three hours of valuable learning time. A feeling of panic came over her and she reached out for the telephone. This time she did ask for Austin.

"Hi, Maggie, how are you?"

"Austin, I'm in trouble."

"Huh?"

"Can't learn my lines. They won't go in."

"Relax, Maggie."

"Austin, will you *hear* me?"

"I still think it's an old-fashioned way to do things, Maggie, but you're an old-fashioned girl, I know that."

She laughed. Austin ribbed her about her background and propriety. He did it nicely, like an affectionate brother. "Thanks," she said. "I'm getting really worried."

"You got some grass in there?"

"No, I haven't. I don't use it much."

"It's only that I hate hearing other people's lines."

She was shocked. "Austin, if it's going to throw you or anything—"

"Shit, I'm only joking. Be there in two minutes flat."

And he was, sweatshirted and grinning, doing his Canadian exercises, bobbing up and down in his Adidas, flexing first this muscle, then that, in a varied series of contortions that made Maggie actually laugh. "Sit down, Austin! You'll strain something and then *you* won't be able to work tomorrow." She grimaced. "I have the character but I've lost the words."

Austin had brought the English newspapers. "They all got us at Heathrow." She looked, and there was her face, set and unsmiling, the long blonde hair falling softly on her shoulders. Austin had done all the talking, as they were hurried into the VIP lounge, keeping the newspapermen happy with cracks about his height. "You didn't think I was actually a genuine dwarf, right? Admit it, fellas, you thought I was just kinda short like Paul Newman, you didn't know I was the real thing, go on, admit it! How's this for a headline? DWARF TO STAR AS PRESIDENT. That would be nice." The journalists laughed, making no notes. "Or better yet, DWARF AND ICE QUEEN TAKE LONDON BY STORM. 'Indecent,' says *The Times*. This show is cruelty to dwarfs. It should be banned.'" The journalists had laughed again. There had been no mention of Austin's height in any piece in the London press. He had drawn their teeth by fronting it out. Maggie felt admiration and a tug of sympathy for Austin.

When Jill Viner met them in the VIP lounge Austin had still been halfway through his act. "I'm no male chauvinist," he told the press. "I just think women should all be home making the dinner, right?" Jill had smiled, but Maggie had thought it was a strained smile. She had greeted them with even more carefully selected members of the press corps, and they had done a number of photo sessions and television chats there and then. Plainly, she knew what she was doing. There was an air of success and style about her. Maggie had been impressed.

Austin sat and rolled a joint and lit it.

"You bring that through customs?" asked Maggie.

"Sure."

"You took a chance."

"Shit, I don't know anybody in London, do I? How would I get my supply? Here, try it, it's good stuff."

Maggie accepted a token drag. "I've never gone in cold before, with a director I didn't know. Maybe that's why I'm like this."

"Come on," said Austin, "let's hear the words." Slowly Maggie began to read her opening speeches.

The words would not go in. After a few tries she halted.

"It's no good. Nothing's happening."

"It's a block, love. That's all." Austin stood up and did a few exercises. "It'll unblock. You need to talk to the director. Or something. You aren't ready. It's like sex; you have to be ready or it's no go. Am I right?"

He stood there in the comfortable room, and she felt better just because of his presence. Austin was a sweetie. "Look. I'll give up. I'll go in tomorrow and see. I'll wing it."

"That's sensible," said Austin. "Of course, you could try the sex."

"What?"

"With me. Now. I'm game."

Maggie laughed. "Austin, you're a fool."

"I'm not fooling, Maggie."

Maggie stood up. She liked Austin, but not that way. She doubted if she would ever like anybody that way again. "Thanks for the offer. You're nice." She kissed him on the cheek. "And I know you're the greatest stud on the Coast. I've heard all the rumors."

"Hey," said Austin, "who told you?"

"Let's stay friends. You're nice."

"Don't keep saying 'nice,' Maggie. I do like you. More than like, you want to know." As Maggie just stared at him, feeling surprise and a little shock, he just grinned and kissed her cheek. "Forget it. You want to go to a show tonight, go on the town, that kinda thing?"

Maggie shook her head. "I need my sleep. Jet lag. Big day tomorrow. All that."

"Your decision, Maggie. Me, I'm going on the town."

"Sorry. I feel I'm being a spoilsport."

"No, no. You have your grieving to do, and it isn't over yet." At the door Austin paused. "Make it soon, huh?"

And he was gone.

How nice of him. How sweet he was, Maggie thought, picking up the script of *Queen* and settling down to try to get at least the opening pages off pat. After an hour, she gave up and in an unnerving panic took two pills. Thirty minutes later she was asleep on the sofa, the word *Philip* on her lips and in her soul.

AT three-thirty in the afternoon Jill Viner came into Josh Williams's flat.

He was sitting at the table, looking through *Spotlight*.

"Put that away," she said. "I've just come from the Royal and Max is cutting the girls down to a short list of six."

"I told you what I think about that."

"The press are there. And the television."

"Well, they would be, Jill, if you were organizing things." Just the same, he felt a pull of admiration. The girl was a goer.

"I told them *you* were coming. And, Josh, before you blow your top, I have Sir Piers there, too."

"Piers? He's there *now?*" Josh felt baffled.

"He's loving it. He's agreed to be photographed with whomever you pick. He isn't upset at all by the publicity. He thinks it's good for the show." Jill offered her face to him. "Darling, please don't ruin it."

Josh did not kiss her. He picked up his jacket and put it on. "I can see," he said, shaking his head, "that I have no choice. If Sir Piers is there, *and* the press. You've done a good job, Jill. On Sir Piers. On me. On everybody. Congratulations."

Jill's eyes flashed. "I don't deserve that, Josh."

"I'll see you there."

"I have a cab outside."

"You use it. I'll drive my car."

He walked out of the place and left her standing there.

She never cried, but he thought he heard, as he walked down the stairs, a sort of stifled sob. Probably blowing her nose, he said to himself. That's the nearest she'll bloody well get to a sob. Damping down his anger, he got into his Volkswagen and drove slowly into the West End. On the way he told himself, for what seemed like the hundredth time, that it was absolutely no use wasting emotional energy on Jill. She was what she was, a force of nature, and he hadn't a lot of control over her; nobody would have. So stop trying, he told himself. Stop expecting her to behave like Alison, because she isn't Alison. She's herself. Adapt to it, or get out of the game.

That did not seem such a bad idea. He had always thought it unwise anyway. Yet the idea of actually parting from Jill made him uneasy. He was getting used to her. Not only the sex, which had revitalized his emotional life. He had needed somebody like her, he realized, for a long time. Now he actually looked forward to the nights, whereas before he had found himself going to a lonely bed in what he thought was contentment, but he now realized was resignation.

Just the same, the price of Jill Viner was high.

He was beginning to think that perhaps it was too high.

THE Royal was in a state of siege.

There were girls everywhere.

Girls queued around the front of the theatre, three-deep, from the stage door onto Shaftesbury Avenue. Three policemen were attempting to get them into some form of order, and one of them looked askance at Josh's car as he drew up at the side of the theatre.

"Sorry, sir. You can't park here."

"Sergeant, I'm the man who's going to get rid of these girls for you."

"You what, sir?"

"I'm selecting one and I'm not going to be very long about it. Then the rest can go home."

"You leave your car where it is, sir. I'll see nobody tows it away. An' for God's sake get it over with. This is a bloody circus."

And that was exactly what it was.

The girls craned toward him as he walked in through the stage door. They were, he realized, mostly amateurs, but there must be some professionals among them, surely. A new surge of anger rose in him, but he beat it back and actually smiled for some photographer who seemed to know who he was.

"What are you looking for, Mr. Williams?"

"Just a good actress, that's all."

"Is it a sexy part?"

"Well, it was the last time I read it!"

"Will she be nude on stage?"

"Not if I can help it."

"We heard a rumor, that's all."

"The rumor's all wrong." Jesus, surely she hasn't told them *that*. "We have everything in this play *except* nudes." He smiled at them all. They looked disappointed to hear that. One asked, "Mr. Williams, any chance of a decision inside an hour?"

"Give me," said Josh, "thirty minutes and I'll have a name for you." He went into the theatre and walked down past the dressing rooms. A line of girls stood waiting to go up into the backstage area. A couple of stagehands were eyeing them. One said, "Any girl wants this part she has to sleep with me first."

"What does she have to do for an encore?" asked a tough-looking blonde, cheekier than the rest.

"Sleep wiv me brother 'ere," said the stagehand, winking at Josh.

"Is he your brother?" asked the blonde.

"No, I'm not," said Josh, "I'm the director."

"Then I'll sleep with you first, darlin'," said the girl. She seemed to be serious.

Josh said to the stagehand, "Tell everybody in this line and the one outside that unless they have an Equity card they can go home." A low moan of distress came from the girls. They didn't look like Equity members. They were wearing everything from fur coats to low-cut evening dresses, but the great majority were in jeans and blouses. Some were heavily made up and others wore no lipstick. Afro hairstyles warred with the long, straight, conventional look. The girls appeared, in the mass, positively dangerous.

"Loves," Josh shouted bravely, "I can't employ anybody who hasn't worked thirty days in the West End in the last six months. That's the rule."

The blonde girl yelled, "It didn't bleedin' say that in your bleedin' advert in the *Stage*, did it?"

"Do you have an Equity card?"

"No, I don't. I'm a dancer."

"Then I'd go home. I'm sorry."

"You're sorry? Who the bleedin' hell are you? The advert was signed Jill Viner. Where's she, the silly cow, whoever she bleedin' is?"

"Here I am," said Jill. She was standing behind him, having followed him in, looking cool and calm, which was more than Josh felt. He felt terrified.

"You tell them what I've just told them," he said. "Unless they've got an Equity card they might as well go home."

A renewed howl of rage greeted this remark, and Josh escaped, hastily going through the pass door into the darkened auditorium. Behind him Josh could hear a babel of voices, Jill's among them, as she tried to make herself heard. Serve her right if they lynch her, he decided.

"Thank God you're here," whispered Max Heston. He was sitting in the sixth row of the empty auditorium, with Molly at his side. Molly looked unflapped, but Max was, Josh was pleased to see, actually trembling. "This is an absolute shambles, Josh! Most of these girls think it's a musical."

Josh peered toward the stage. He could see half a dozen girls standing in line. "Who are they?"

Max shook his head. "I've had to bring them on six at a time. There's a line stretching around the whole block." Max lit a shaking cigarette. "The idea of picking one from that lot was driving me out of my mind."

"How many have you seen?"

"About a hundred, I should think," said Max.

"A hundred and seven, actually," said Molly.

"Any of them any good at all?"

"I've marked four possibles. One of them was Pat Woods. I knew she was your choice. She's much the best we've seen. I've put her in number one dressing room out of the way. Thought you might want to see her yourself."

"Max," Josh Williams said, "we might make a decent stage manager out of you yet."

209

"I'd be no good judging a talent competition, and that's for sure." Max moved gratefully from his seat under the light.

"Go and give Jill a hand with the other girls out there." Josh sat down in the vacated seat. "And, Max . . . where's Sir Piers?"

"In the foyer giving interviews to the press."

"Is he all right?"

"Loving it. He's been talking to the girls in the line. One bird complained he was feeling her up. I expect all that tit and bum drove him mad."

"Oh God, all we need is an indecency charge!"

"Well, I got him out and into the foyer. I hope that was right?"

"You're doing great, Max. Carry on."

"Thanks a bunch." Max blundered out through the pass door, into the backstage area. Josh whispered to Molly, "Do these girls have names?"

Molly passed him a list. "First names, that's all. No idea what any of them have done."

"Right. I'll take it on the wing." Josh cleared his throat and called toward the stage, "I'm sorry for the delay, ladies. I'm Josh Williams, the director. Now, I have your names here and I want to take you one at a time." He peered at the list in the pilot light. "First, Monica?"

"That's me," said a tough-looking little brunette in a leotard. A leotard, Josh thought wildly. What is she doing in a bloody *leotard*? "Monica," he called, "would you like to tell me what you've done?"

"Do you mean *today*, dear?" Monica had plainly heard some of the conversation and decided she had no chance. "Who I've done today, well, nobody yet, darlin', but if you're nice I might consider you."

The other girls laughed. All except one. Josh noticed her out of the corner of his eye: a flicker, no more. She was standing quite still, apart from the others, and she had very red hair. He laughed politely at Monica's sally. "This is a show you sleep with the director to get out of, love. Now listen, Monica, are you an actress?"

"Of course I'm not a sodding actress, dear. I'm a striptease artiste."

"Are you serious?"

"Come an' see me anytime, just around the corner in Frith Street," declared the embattled Monica. "Show every hour on the hour."

Everybody laughed, including Josh.

"It's no use, Monica. This is a straight part."

"Not what it said in the *Stage*, dear. It said anybody could apply."

"Well, not exactly anybody. I'm sorry, Monica. Good luck."

"Oh, I don't need good luck. I please the punters, dear." Monica showed him her bottom suggestively. It was indeed a splendid sight. "Come and see me sometime, darlin'. I might do things for yer. That is if you can still get it up which I doubt, dear, looking at yer." Monica waved a one-finger salute and swayed sexily off stage.

Josh let the girls stop giggling before he called out firmly, "Anybody on stage got an Equity card?"

One of the remaining girls, a tall brunette in a bikini—*a bikini?*—called out, "None of us has. I thought you was looking for an unknown?"

"You thought wrong. Do you have an Equity card?"

"No, I fucking don't."

"What have you done?"

"Been a beauty queen. Miss East End."

"I'm sorry, but I need actresses."

The girl stood looking at him, hand on hip. "I think you need a fucking enema, mate."

And she was gone.

The other girls just looked at one another and trooped off after her. Molly said, "I hear the noise of dissension."

Max slipped into a seat next to them. "Dissension, it's more like revolution. There's a bloody riot out there. The girls have gone mad and some of them are trying to break the place up. The police have sent for reinforcements."

"Did you lock the pass door?"

"Did I ever!"

The noise outside was very loud now: screams and shrieks and shouts.

"Thank God for that," said Josh, with feeling.

IN the corridors backstage the girls were fighting the police. The stage-doorkeeper had barricaded himself in his office and was staring out in alarm, as the policemen, helmets flying, dragged the screaming girls out, one by one. Jill was in the stage-doorkeeper's office, too, locked in, and glad of it: for the boldest and most enraged of the girls had hammered loudly on the door and one had smashed a glass panel with the heel of her shoe before being pulled by a constable, screaming and yelling, knickers in full view, out of the theatre into Shaftesbury Avenue. The girls had also torn down all the papers on the notice board and knocked over the fire buckets containing sand and water, and generally laid the place waste.

Jill could hear the sirens of police cars as reinforcements arrived, and she could see the gleeful faces of the press photographers, bored young men in dirty leather and Afro hairdos, who ran unmolested along the corridor and into the street, snapping as they went. It was all over in a very few minutes, but it seemed to last forever.

The elderly stage-doorkeeper said, "I was here the night they closed us for saying 'fuck' but it was nothing like this."

Jill tried to smile. "All publicity's good."

The stage-doorkeeper said drily, "You know what else

212

Barnum said? No man ever went broke underestimating the taste of the great American public."

Jill looked over the door, through the broken glass, at a young police inspector.

"You Miss Viner?"

"Yes, I am."

"Don't set up any more riots, madam, without telling us in the first place, will you? I've had to arrest ten of these girls."

"Oh, I'm sorry. Will I be wanted in court or anything?"

"No. Assaulting the police." The young inspector took off his cap and mopped his face, which was bleeding from a nail-rake and said, sadly and rather contemptuously, "You'll be in all the papers. If that's what you want."

After he was gone, Jill felt ashamed. Then she thought, hotly: He's only doing what he's paid to do. What's he being so holy about?

"I think it's safe to go out now, miss," said the stage-door-keeper, surveying the wrecked corridor. "What a bloody mess."

"Clean it up, will you," said Jill. Cheap at the price, she thought.

IN the auditorium Josh looked up from his notes. It was all a waste of time and it was over. He was surprised to see that there was still one girl left on stage, the one with the red hair. She was dressed in a white silk blouse and, surprisingly, a dark velvet skirt, cut to the calf. Most of the girls in the queue had been in trousers, of every sort, from satin to denim.

"Yes, dear?" Josh had decided he would put an end to all this. He was never going to do better than Pat Woods and Jill would have to accept that. She'd had her fun. She'd had her publicity. It was over.

"I do have an Equity card," the red-haired girl was saying.

"Glad to hear it. What have you done?"

"Coventry for six months. RADA first."

"You've only been out of acting school six months?"

"Yes."

"Never worked in London?"

"No."

Josh, wondering why he bothered, said to Max, "Go up on stage with two books. Do the scene in act two with the prime minister. Just feed her the lines."

"Will do." Max found two scripts. "Neat looker."

"Yes, she is."

Josh waited for Max to go backstage, and while he did so he called out to the red-haired girl, "What did you do at Coventry, what parts?"

"Everything from Mary Rose to Beatie in *Roots*."

"Did you?"

"I did."

"At your age."

The girl laughed. It was a nice musical laugh. She seemed at ease on the stage. Josh began to get interested.

"Only for three days. I was understudy."

"How did it go?"

"Well, I remembered the speeches all right."

"That was something, anyway." It was.

Max arrived, rather out of breath, and handed the girl the book. Josh called, "I'm sorry I can't give you time to do anything but glance at the speech. What's happening at this point is that the princess is the girl who's married the prince, the queen's eldest son, right? She's at this meeting by accident, but once she hears what's in the wind, she's for opposition to the prime minister's advice to give way, to submit. She's for fighting. One, because she's young. Two, because she's idealistic. She isn't born to royalty and she feels things like a commoner, an ordinary person. She's had total liberty all her life without particularly valuing it, because she's never had any reason to value it. Now, it's threatened, and she's horrified, astonished, she can't believe it."

The girl said, "I'm not sure *I* can believe it. I've always been free. Can you give me a note?"

Josh pondered a moment. "A young Jewess in Germany, around 1933. Couldn't believe the Nazis could possibly mean what they say. Then the Nuremberg Laws."

"What were they?"

"They reduced Jews to second-, no, tenth-class, citizens. Until it happened, nobody believed it could. People's astonishment was total." He shook his head. "Like France falling in 1940. Like Dubček arrested. Like Hungary. Total, utter power. And nothing to fight it with except words."

The girl thought a moment. "I think I see."

"What year were you born?"

The girl said, "Nineteen sixty-two."

"What do you feel indignation about? Vietnam?"

"No."

"Anything?"

"Ecology. Spoiling the planet. The Third World."

Josh shook his head. "That'll have to do. Think about starving babies in Africa. Something unbelievable. Have a go. Be indignant. Be horrified. Be, most of all, stunned."

"May I have two minutes to read through the speeches to myself?"

Josh said yes, and studied her. White skin, slim, graceful. A touch of Irish in the voice somewhere? A lot of confidence to ask for notes, at this point. He waited.

The girl smoothed her red hair. "All right. If you'll feed me the line?" This, to Max.

As the girl started to speak Josh sat very still. Her voice was soft and low and she took the whole speech without a breath that he noticed, although there must have been at least two, somewhere.

It was not only an intelligent reading of the lines, astonishing at first blush like this, it was an emotional one. *"I think we must fight even if it's with our bare hands. . . ."*

As the girl finished there was a silence while they all looked at her.

"What's her name?" asked Josh of Molly.

"Brigid Kelly."

Josh called out, wondering at his own nerve, "Brigid, congratulations. Equity allowing, and we may have trouble, you've got the part."

The girl looked shocked. Then she smiled. "Thank you."

"Max will take you front-of-house to the foyer. There's a press thing. Don't talk to anybody until you and I chat. Thank you for the best audition I've ever heard from a young actress."

"Thank *you*, Mr. Williams." The girl mock-bowed and went into the wings with Max Heston. Josh stretched his legs and lit a cigar. "Now," he said to Molly, "I have to explain to Miss Viner why I've decided to do things her way."

"No need," said Jill from four rows back. "I saw all that and I absolutely agree with you. The girl's terrific. And I'm not even going to say I told you so, Josh."

"Don't," said Josh, "because the chance of finding a girl like that at a mass audition is a million to one, at best." He coughed. "And who's going to tell poor little Pat Woods we won't be wanting her? She's in number one dressing room, waiting to hear the part's hers."

"I'll do it," said Jill easily. "Somebody has to, and you'd better go into the foyer and tell the press. They're getting impatient. If you go now we could make the last evening editions."

"Is Sir Piers still there?"

"Waiting anxiously."

"All right." Josh got to his feet feeling a bit foolish, but elated at finding talent, as he always was. There was something clear and direct about genuine talent. It was there, as real as rock. Brigid

Kelly had it, it could not be denied. "The problem is, Jill, we can't announce it today. This girl hasn't got the equity points for a West End part. We'll have to put it to Equity delicately, see if they'll accept her on merit."

Jill said nothing for a moment. "Could you talk to Pat Woods, after all? I'm scared the press will go."

Josh sighed. "All right. But be careful with them."

"Don't worry. Leave the press to me and Tom Tully."

Josh went backstage to see Pat Woods. It was something he always hated to do, tell an actress there was no job, that somebody else had been preferred. There was never any way of saying it nicely. It always came down to talent or looks, and in the end it was always somehow a rejection of the *person*. He loved actors. He admired actors. He couldn't be one, much as he tried. He didn't have the resilience, the sheer guts necessary to pick yourself up off the emotional floor every time you didn't get a job you knew perfectly well you could do. He poured Pat Woods a large sherry from the hospitality cabinet in number one dressing room (soon to be occupied by Maggie Stride) and kissed her on the cheek and said, "Sorry, love, you were the favorite but you've been pipped by an outsider."

Pat Woods drank the sherry in one swallow. "Is she a total newcomer?"

"Not exactly. She's been at Coventry."

"How old is she?"

"She's eighteen and a half."

"I see." Pat Woods collected her handbag. "Well, that's that."

"I'm sorry," Josh said. "She was just right, that's all."

"Right for the part?" asked Pat Woods. "Or right for the publicity?"

"Both, I suppose." Josh owed her honesty, at least.

Pat Woods paused at the door. "I don't suppose you could go against your producer anyway, Josh. After all, the advert's in the press. And the other thing."

"What other thing?"

"Well, the fact that you're screwing her, darling."

Pat Woods had plainly elected to do it the hard way.

Josh said, "I'm not certain to get Equity approval for Brigid Kelly. By that remark you've just lost yourself the chance of getting it if they refuse."

"Darling," Pat Woods said, icily, "I'm a pro, and I can lose gracefully. But I hate bed games that sod people like me about. Don't bother to give my love to Jill Viner. She promised me an audition and I got it. She kept her word but she's still a whore. Ciao."

And the dressing-room door slammed shut.

Josh poured himself a very large Scotch and drank it slowly. Bed games? Well, how else did it look?

Pat Woods had set her heart on the part and he hadn't even heard her. He had been wrong not to. But Brigid Kelly was *right.* He was sure of that. He finished his drink and went back into the auditorium. Max was sitting there, sorting out the lighting plot with Robbie Davis, the lighting man.

"Where's Brigid Kelly?"

Max looked up. "She's in the foyer. Went in with Jill five minutes ago."

"She did?"

"Yes. Big moment for her. What a dish, right?"

Josh didn't answer. He hurried along the aisle and into the foyer. As soon as he got there he knew what had happened. She had told them, the bloody bitch had *told* them! The scene was one of total pandemonium. There were at least twenty photographers and as many journalists—orchestrated by Tom Tully, obviously enjoying himself hugely—crowding about Sir Piers, who stood grandly, his arm around Brigid Kelly and his best profile to a BBC handheld TV camera, which bore down on him inexorably. Bulbs flashed and the noise was considerable.

218

"Brigid, this way, love, give us a smile!"

"Sir Piers, can I ask, how will it feel to play against such a new star. '

"Brigid, can you hitch your skirt up an inch or two, love, my paper likes cheesecake, or better, how about loosening that top button on the blouse, *lovely*, darling!"

There was a lot more of it and Josh stood watching it all, possessed by a slow and dull anger. Jill saw him and waved across the throng but he did not wave back. He just stood there, and waited.

Finally, Tom Tully held up a hand for some sort of order and said, "Fellas, I'm going to take Miss Kelly off to do one or two prearranged"—there was a low groan at this but Tom Tully carried on urbanely—"two or three prearranged interviews."

He smiled. "Most of you, I think, have what you need. I gave you a rundown earlier on Miss Kelly's vital statistics." That got a laugh as he knew it would. "If you want a more intimate view of them you'll have to get in line."

There was a good-natured howl at that, but nobody protested as Tom Tully turned to steer Sir Piers and Brigid Kelly back toward the auditorium, past a door guarded by two uniformed theatre attendants. Nobody, that is, except Sir Piers, who stood his ground, not unlike, Josh thought, Henry V at Agincourt. He raised a thespian's finger and his fabled voice was like magic.

"Just a word, gentlemen!" A silence. "In all my experience as an actor, I haven't known a better moment. Success is something we all learn to live with, but the first taste of it is sweet. Miss Kelly is tasting it now. Larry once said success was like oysters and champagne. Who could improve on that? Oysters and champagne Miss Kelly will have. I've sent my man to Bentley's for the oysters, and I always carry champagne in my car."

As if on cue, Sir Piers's factotum arrived, carrying plates of Whitstable oysters and accompanied by a man from Bentley's in a blue-and-white apron. There was another melee, to see Brigid Kelly swallowing oysters and Sir Piers drinking champagne. Tom Tully appeared at Josh's side. "The old boy doesn't need a press officer. He has a nose for publicity like a bloodhound. Oysters and champagne—bloody brilliant. Can't you see the headlines and the pictures?"

"Yes, unfortunately I can," said Josh.

"Why unfortunately?" asked Tom Tully.

"She hasn't got the points. She simply hasn't worked enough to get a big part in a London show. They'll reject her and all this will be for nothing."

"Balls," said Tom Tully, with certainty. "After this has been in every paper in the country? How the little girl from Dublin landed the part of the year? You have to be joking, Josh."

Josh pondered. Why hadn't he thought of it?

Equity would bleat a bit, but no organization would show itself as hardhearted (anyway, not in public!) as *that.*

"Jill," said Tom Tully, "has been very, very clever with this."

"Yes," said Josh, slowly, "I suppose she has."

Finally, Sir Piers and Brigid Kelly were separated from the ecstatic newsmen and shepherded by Tom Tully into the auditorium for the important personal interviews. Josh knew they would last some time.

Jill signaled to him that she would sit in on the interviews. He nodded bleakly. She crossed to him and said quickly, "It worked out all right, didn't it, Josh?"

"Yes. It worked out just fine."

"Will I see you later?"

"No. I need to work. See you at rehearsals tomorrow. Ten o'clock prompt."

"I'd been hoping we might—"

"Better get our rest. We'll need it, love."

It was the first time he'd said no to her.

"All right, Josh. I understand. How did it go with Pat Woods?"

"She was upset. And a bit nasty."

"Tough."

"Yes, it was. On her."

"I expect her boyfriend will want to take his money out of the show."

"Is that all it means to you? The girl was practically promised the part."

"No, she wasn't. She was promised an audition."

"You promised her that, did you, Jill?"

"Yes, I did."

"That wasn't right, either."

"Nothing I do is right." Jill's voice was low. "Well tough shit, Josh. But I'm getting this show on the road and right this minute I have to go and talk to the press. Do you want to come? You should."

"No, thanks," said Josh. "I'll see you."

"Yes. 'Bye, darling. Thanks."

"For what?"

She didn't reply and he walked out of the foyer to his Volkswagen and drove it home. His telephone rang several times during the evening but he did not answer it.

SIR Piers was having trouble with Lady Piers.

"I must say you seem to be enjoying yourself with that little tart."

The occasion was supper in Sir Piers's Mayfair apartment, full of silver-framed photographs of the famous and genuine and reproduction period furniture. Sir Piers's leonine head ached from the champagne he had consumed and his groin ached from the lack of consummation he hadn't derived with the little girl, Brigid. Lover's balls at his age! He sighed. "The pleasures of the hand and the eye," a phrase he recalled from some long-forgotten play, were not enough for him. He had wanted the little thing, wanted her very urgently, there in the foyer. Oh, it wasn't all over for him yet, but it was a mixed blessing, no doubt about it.

"Old Hal will be livid when he sees that," he told his wife with satisfaction, indicating that evening's *Standard*.

"Honestly, you and that silly old thing, what is it between you?"

Sir Piers hesitated. No. Best not.

"Rivalry, I suppose," he said, at length.

"Rivalry. You're both half a century too old for that."

Sir Piers reached out an exploratory hand under the table and it was slapped patiently by his wife, who was thirty-eight, and made up looked forty-eight, having dyed her hair gray to try to match his sixty-three years, and managed it almost too well.

"Stop that, Piers!"

"Later. We'll play later?"

"No, we won't play later. You're in rehearsal tomorrow."

"So I am. Oh dear."

"Are you going to wipe the floor with Sir Harry?"

"I am," said Sir Piers. "Oh, I am. Wait and see."

"Are you sure you didn't go home with that little tart?" asked his wife, with a knowing smile.

"Perfectly sure I didn't," said Piers, regretfully.

Lady Piers considered the situation. "Then we'll see about later," she said. She twinkled brightly at him across the table.

Sir Piers thought, Oh, there you are, gone and done it again, when will you ever learn, you marvelous old ham you, just when you were looking forward to drifting off to sleep thinking of the soft little velvety bottom of Brigid Kelly.

"Lovely, my dear. Thought you might change your mind!"

His old pater's words of advice: You want to be a successful actor, always *be delighted*. No matter what anybody says, asks, or

222

wants you to do, be delighted. Always be delighted."

"Delighted," he said, putting the famous catch into his voice, as he had been doing for fifty years or more. "Absolutely delighted."

BRIGID Kelly left the Royal Theatre, her head whirling with champagne, her body buzzing with adrenaline and a hollow feeling at the pit of her stomach that told her she had eaten nothing (Sir Piers's oysters excepted) for twelve hours. Max Heston followed her out into Shaftesbury Avenue and said, "Have you seen a *Standard* yet?"

"Will they be out, the last edition?"

"Of course they will." Max bought six copies from a newspaper vendor on the corner and handed them to her. "There you are, keep it for your scrapbook. Front-page news, you are."

Page one showed two pictures: one of the mob of girls fighting with the police; the second, even larger, of Brigid and Sir Piers drinking champagne and eating oysters, and it was captioned, "The Champagne Girl." Brigid looked at it a long moment, under the neon lights of the Royal Theatre, which was getting ready for the evening performance of the play currently running. "I can't believe it! Is it me? Or am I dreaming?"

"It's you all right."

She hugged his arm in a transport of shocked, disbelieving delight. "I'm high," she said, "I'm high on it. I see how people get hooked. If this is success, *wow!*"

She looked along Shaftesbury Avenue, neon reflected in the rain-shiny pavements. It was all—the cars, the crowds, the whole thing—all bloody marvelous.

"You hungry?" Max asked.

Brigid liked Max. He was young and he was her sort.

"Starving!"

"Let's go to Manzi's. Right?"

They went to Manzi's and ate crab salad and drank Chablis, sitting at the long counter, their backs to the room. Brigid still had an awful feeling of unreality. "I can't *believe* it," she kept tittering, knowing Max was smiling at her but unable to stop saying it because she really couldn't believe it.

"Somebody had to get the job." Max sucked a crab claw. "It just happened to be you. Why the surprise?"

"This morning, when I got up," said Brigid, "I very nearly went back to bed again. I thought, Shit, why should I bother? I've been to auditions when I had a real chance and never made it, so why this? I mean, it was so obviously a hype, right?" She drank some Chablis. "I tell you, Max, I really felt sick. I hate auditions and this was the bottom. What sort of a person is this Jill Viner lady to think of it?"

"She's okay, she just wanted the publicity."

"Well, she got it, but will I get my Equity permission?"

"You bet. She'll be talking to Equity committee members at their private number all evening. All strictly unethical, of course. But don't worry. It'll be fine." Max looked at her keenly through the thick fringe of hair that dropped almost into his eyes. "You've got the gods on your side today."

Brigid shook her head. "A few months out of RADA and this." She shivered slightly. "I found old Sir Piers a bit creepy."

"He is creepy," said Max, with unthinking but total contempt for age. "He's the original Dirty Old Man, is our famous Sir Piers."

"Yes, he had his hand on my bottom a lot of the time."

"Lucky it was only your bottom!"

They both laughed and Max added, "Can't say I blame him," and she said, "Can't you?" and he said, "No, actually, I can't," and she said, "Pervert," and they both laughed again, perfectly at home with each other and sure now how the evening would end. They went to Max's place because it was nearer, in Max's Mini (she had no car), and drank black coffee in Max's small living room-*cum*-bedroom (the walls all papered with theatre bills), and smoked a joint in easy contentment.

Brigid didn't know when she'd felt so happy.

"You're very young to be in charge backstage, aren't you?" she asked.

"Usually they have old guys, I know." Max drew the smoke into his lungs. "But they panic a lot and anyway this show's got all the age it needs. Everybody's a hundred."

"Josh Williams *looks* all right?"

She made a question of it, not knowing how Max got on with Josh, and she was right to do so.

"Josh Williams gave me the job," said Max slowly, "and I owe him for that. But he's about fifty or something, and I tell you Brigid, that's too old—the theatre's full of old guys like Josh, who've simply got out of touch." He brooded. "Even the play they're doing. It's political, but it's cold-war stuff. We ought to be worrying about how we all live on this planet, everybody on it, Russians, Chinese, us, not going on about eyeball-to-eyeball confrontation and Finlandization and all that. That empire stuff, that imperialistic stuff, it's over. The state of the upper atmosphere, half the world on a starvation diet, pollution of our lakes and rivers, nuclear pollution, they're the problems of the eighties, not war crap."

"I know." Brigid stood up, quite unembarrassed, and took off her white blouse. She unhooked her bra. "I only wore one because I was sure they wanted a princess type and bra-less princesses seem wrong somehow." She giggled and waited for Max to say something about her breasts, which were small but firm, but he did not.

"They're all hung up on this territory thing," he said, taking off his socks. "They don't seem to see we must love one another or die."

Brigid took off her skirt. "That's Orwell, isn't it?"

"Auden."

Brigid took off her panties, which were of black lace, almost transparent. She thought he might comment on them, but he didn't. She slipped into bed, and snuggled under the covers.

Max took off his bright-red jockey shorts. He said, "I've got a play for this management to do next."

"What's it about?"

Max climbed into bed. "The gypsies. The last nomadic tribe in Europe. It's a really important subject. Full of social comment. There's a rape scene and an abortion scene and this big final speech when this gypsy kills this Fascist policeman."

Brigid brushed the red hair from her eyes. "Who wrote it?"

"Me."

"Oh, how marvelous. I wish I could write."

"Don't try. It's hell."

They kissed. It was a nice kiss, Brigid thought.

What a day it had been. First the part and now *this*.

Max touched her between her legs. She was moist. "Don't say anything about my play, will you?"

"Huh?" Her hand found his member and caressed it expertly.

He began to move his finger gently.

"To anybody. I'm hoping to flog it to Jill Viner as her next play."

"Will there be a next play? Will this one run?" She put her lips on him, and kissed. After a moment she looked up for an answer: but he was lying back, his head on the pillow, eyes closed in ecstasy. Or was it sleep? She could not tell. She thought she must write home to Ireland—no—cable, first thing tomorrow morning, there would be no time to telephone. She resumed her task and then, suddenly, he turned her over and entered her and she thought dreamily, the alcohol and pot working in her, This is lovely, really lovely—six months out of RADA and I'm going into the West End.

"I'm going into the West End," she cried aloud.

"I'm in Ireland," he replied.

226

She laughed and laughed and thought: I did take my pill this morning, didn't I? I can't remember because of all that bloody rush.

SIR Harry read the *Standard* story in the bar of the Savile Club.

He was not pleased.

"There he is, old Piers, at it again." His remark was addressed to Mario, handsome and bored, in a tie and suit for once, casting a lascivious eye over a naval-looking member. "Watch it," said Sir Harry. "That chap's on the committee, I think. Or is he?" He returned to the offending article. "Just like Piers to get into the action. Quite typical. Always been the same. Look at that little tart with him, showing her tits. Bet he's groping her with that right hand you can't see, the randy old sod." Sir Harry sighed and sipped his Pernod. "I must say, it's nice to be back in town again. So uncivilized, the country, don't you think so, Carlo?"

"Mario," said Mario. "You 'ave just signed me in as a guest, for God's sake."

"That's what I said," said Sir Harry. "Isn't it?"

He brooded a moment as Mario looked hopefully round the roomful of leather furniture and dozing but ostensibly far too heterosexual men. "I think I may have to take Piers in hand. He's stealing the notices before there are any."

"In hand?" echoed Mario, on cue.

"In a manner of speaking," said Sir Harry, with a mischievous glint, well known to Mario. Mario sighed. It was not an easy life, his.

"I think," said Sir Harry, "we might toddle home, eh, Pietro?"

"Anything you say," said Mario. There was nothing to stay for. The attractive naval person had fallen asleep over his *Times*.

AUSTIN Ames sat at the bar in the Savoy and drank a cocktail, superbly served by Vic, that he didn't want. What would Singh say if he knew he was sitting drinking cocktails? Singh would be displeased with him and rightly so. But Singh seemed a long way off. L.A. was another world and one Austin had not really become a part of. He was still, at heart, a Broadway actor. But he had been away from the theatre a long time, too long: away from that living, breathing, and sometimes terrifying animal, an audience. It was all O.K. saying his movies had been acting, and in a way, of course, they had: acting to a director, a bald and ballsy hair-assed Hollywood old hand, acting for *him*, not for the audience, doing it for the director. The theatre was something else. The English director would be an artistic middle-manager. He would not be behind camera, cheering you on, making a love affair of it. He would be in the wings, at best, maybe even out front making notes on what you were doing wrong. Austin sipped his cocktail. Shit, he had nerves. Maggie had done that. She had infected him. He was sorry for her, too sorry; he was beginning to feel something like protectiveness toward her. He supposed it was in some way connected with the death of Philip. He had done a lot of things for her then, arranged the funeral details and so on, sure; but was that anything anybody else might not have done? No, it wasn't. He had never done anything like that before, not even for Betty, his first wife (whom he loved but who had not loved him) and certainly not for Minna, his last one. Protective? Was that all? Maybe not. He could not be sure. They had worked closely together on *Good-bye*, of course, but he had been having trouble with Minna at the time and his libido had been low.

The one thing certain was that Maggie was in trouble with her lines and he had not been able to do very much for her. He debated going upstairs and seeing how she was, but what the hell, she didn't want him; she had made that plain enough, hadn't she? Right. He signaled Vic for another of the same, glancing round the bar as he did so.

What he needed was a night out on the town.

Get his cock in gear and his mind off tomorrow.

Tomorrow he had to face a director he didn't know, the guy Josh Williams from the National, for God's sake. No wonder he felt queasy. He hadn't been on a stage for two—no three years. As long as that? He shivered.

What he needed was some action.

Austin had not been in London for five years but he had heard there was a lot of action. The London broads were liberated, that was the word. English reserve was a thing of the past. Morals, too. Singh said all this was purely technological. Liberty and the women's movement was shit, Singh said. The Pill had done it, quite simply. Women had started to fuck around, something they had always wanted to do but had been afraid to, in case of pregnancy. Now, he had opined, sitting in his Long Beach temple, the Pill made it possible. The liberation stuff was purely rationalization, just crap. Singh said women should be pure and cleave only to one man, several to one man. Austin sighed and looked around for any sign of a woman rationalizing the Pill.

He could see plenty of girls in the bar, but they were all escorted. Also they looked very unapproachable.

"Hey, are you Austin Ames?"

He said, "Wish I was, I'd be rich, right?"

"You're awfully like him though."

The girl was tall, good teeth, good tits, long blonde hair. She could be a million girls. The voice apart. The voice had command in it. It reminded Austin a little of his ex-wife Minna. He hesitated. A glutton for punishment, Singh had said.

The girl wore a simple red dress and red shoes. No jewelry or rings or anything. Yet the word was: *class.*

Austin pondered.

Shit, he was on the town, looking for fun, trying to forget tomorrow, trying to put the cold fact that he had to face the part of the president, before a new director, in great company (Sir Piers and Sir Harry, Jesus Christ!) and not crap himself. Maggie did it by going to bed with Seconals inside her. Not him.

"Wanta screw, darlin?" he asked, very quietly.

She moved closer, interested. "*What* did you say?" The voice was very crisp.

Austin replied, "Can I buy you a drink?" After all, it was London, not New York.

"That would be lovely. Thank you. The same as you're having would be nice."

"Vic, two more of these."

They sat at a table and she told him her name was Sarah Jane. She did not volunteer her surname, and when he asked her what she did for a living she said, "Oh, I'm at this bloody stupid finishing school."

"School?" Austin looked around nervously. School, for Christ's sake!

"Finishing school. To sort of learn to be a lady. All that stuff. Cordon bleu cooking. Typing. Fashion. It's all crap but if I don't do it I'll have to go home and help Mummy with the house or get a job. I don't want a job yet. I come up to town once a week and stay at the flat."

"You have a place in town?" Austin began to feel hopeful.

"Eaton Square. Family flat."

"Are you with friends?"

"My parents were eating here. Just said bye-bye to them."

Austin drank his cocktail with rising excitement. And, for that matter, rising cock. He wondered if he should indicate this interest to her but decided it was too early. Nonetheless, he navigated his jeans so she could see his interest.

"I say, you've got a hard, haven't you?"

Austin was gratified. This began to seem like an excellent evening.

"It's you. I wanted you as soon as I saw you."

"How quaint." The girl casually averted her eyes and waved to an acquaintance across the bar. "You aren't really Austin Ames, are you?"

He debated telling the truth and decided against it. "No, but I'm often mistaken for him."

"If you were Austin Ames you wouldn't get a hard just looking at me."

Austin was very near to telling her at that moment.

"No," he said, sadly, "I guess not."

"Never mind, I like you." Sarah Jane, still looking away, touched his jeans, and his cock registered an electrical impulse. Austin felt very cheered. This was better. This was a whole lot better.

"Baby," he said hoarsely, "let's go screw, whaddya say?"

Sarah Jane tossed her lovely blonde hair. "Don't be boring, please."

"Boring?" Austin considered this and shrugged. When in Rome, old boy, he said to himself. When in Rome.

"Let's find somewhere nice and dance for a while," said Sarah Jane.

"Why not?" said Austin.

They began by taking a cab from the Savoy. "Annabel's," he said. "I hear it's a good place to start the evening."

"I wouldn't know, sir," said the cabby. "I never held my birthday party there."

It was said drily and Austin remembered when he used to be an out-of-work actor in New York City and how he once hacked nights for a guy he knew. One fare had almost had a heart attack when he ran out of gas on a deserted street near the Queensboro Bridge. The guy had seen the driver's photograph, which wasn't of Austin, and Austin had difficulty convincing him it wasn't a stick-up. The guy had shown reluctance to believe a genuine cabby would run out of gas. "I'm no regular cabby," Austin had told him. "I'm an out-of-work actor." The guy had been rich, with Abercrombie and Fitch bags and a Brooks Brothers suit, and Austin had no sympathy for him. So alright, this London cabby felt like that about him.

Well, no shit.

He told Sarah Jane the story: she seemed not to understand it. "All cabbies are villains, darling."

Austin overtipped the man, just the same. Hacking was a lousy number.

"You gave that man far too much," said Sarah Jane. "You shouldn't. They get spoilt."

The place was dark and noisy. They had no difficulty getting in. Sarah Jane seemed to be known. Tips changed hands, and here he was, sitting under lights with the music slamming out, and being deafened at the same time. But of course he did have this astonishing blonde with him and they were drinking champagne by now. They danced for what seemed, to Austin, several hours.

Finally it was over. He thought: I'll sleep tonight; when I crash I'll really crash. Tomorrow I won't even think about it.

Sarah Jane seemed to know everybody; when they left the club the doorman called her "milady." Austin said, "What's your real name, honey?" to which Sarah Jane replied crisply, "None of your fucking business, darling," and stepped into a car that had drawn up without her needing to signal. It was a Daimler and had a liveried chauffeur. Austin asked uneasily as they drove swiftly through the quiet West End streets, "Is this automobile yours?"

"Belongs to m'father, actually."

She settled back against the leather upholstery. "I thought you were randy," she said.

Austin looked quickly at the chauffeur.

"It's perfectly all right. Briggs never looks round."

"You sure of that?"

"I can see him, can't I, darling?" And with that she raised her dress.

No panties: a triangle of black hair.

Austin gulped. Jesus. This was what he'd come out for, right? He unzipped and mounted her, kneeling. She wrapped her legs around him, and moved expertly. Here I am, Austin thought, here I am in London only one day, and I'm fucking a milady in a Daimler. This, he told himself, is living, this is certainly living.

"Darling. Take your time. No hurry to get past the post, is there?"

"Sorry," said Austin, slowing down.

She was right. Make it last. Think about it now, to remember it later. Austin felt that life, sometimes, was all it should be. This was undoubtedly one of the moments.

"You okay?" he asked.

"Certainly I am, darling, why ever not?"

Her laugh was silvery and her movements adroit and Austin wondered if it was possible to fall in love at first fuck. He glanced up quickly from his labors, full of affection and gratitude, and saw her ecstatically grinning face. It was not directed downward at him but at a point behind him. Puzzled, he half turned and saw, in the driver's mirror, the face of Briggs, the chauffeur. It too was smiling, in complicity.

Austin pulled away from the girl.

"Stop this fucking car!" he yelled.

"What," said Sarah Jane icily, "are you bloody talking about, you silly man?"

"Stop the car, you lousy voyeur," shouted Austin who, if there was any voyeuring to be done, did not wish to be the subject of it. "Let me out of this thing."

"Briggs, stop, please," said Sarah Jane languidly.

The car stopped and Austin got out.

"Good-night, Mr. Ames," she laughed, "did you think you'd fooled me? Silly boy. We could have had a nice threesome."

Briggs, the chauffeur, smiled.

"Pouf!" yelled Austin, as the Daimler rolled into Eaton Square, depositing a huge wash of dirty gutter water on his new Calvin Kleins.

A threesome?

What had he passed up?

Austin shook his head and turned to find himself looking into the unsympathetic eyes of a London bobby. The man was looking down at Austin's member, hanging, now half limp with indignation and shock, for all to see.

"Look," said Austin, fumbling at his zipper, "a silly bitch just threw me out of her car, right in the middle—"

"Sir," said the bobby, without a smile, "I don't think it's your night."

JILL was asleep when the police rang.

She had given up trying to get through to Josh on the telephone and had finally taken a sleeping pill. The day had been a success but she felt wretched. Nothing was worth the upset with Josh, not even *Queen*. Was it? Now, she felt very woozy, blinking in the light of the bedside lamp. What time was it? She opened her eyes with difficulty. The bedside clock said 3:45.

Three forty-five in the morning, for God's sake?

The sergeant at Marylebone Police Station was very direct. "Madam, is your name Jill Viner?"

"Yes, it is."

"We have a gentleman here who tells me he is employed by you. He was most insistent we ring you. It's not a thing we would normally do until morning."

Jill said, feeling suddenly very awake indeed, "What is the man's name?"

The police sergeant said carefully, "A Mr. Austin Ames, madam."

"I see." She didn't, she didn't see anything. "What is the problem?"

"There's the possibility of a charge, I'm afraid."

"A charge?"

"It might help if you came down to the station, madam."

"Right. I'm on my way. And sergeant—"

"Yes, madam?"

"You haven't . . . talked to anybody . . . the press?"

"No, I haven't."

"Thank you. I'll be twenty minutes."

Jill was there in fifteen, in slacks and sweater, facing a bewildered Austin Ames. "Jesus, they just threw me in the can." He gazed around the interview room. "What the fuck am I *doing* here?"

"What happened?" Jill demanded.

"I met this crazy broad. We were doing it in a car and she threw me out. This cop sees me."

Jill Viner thought she understood. "You exposed yourself?"

"No!" yelled Austin indignantly. "Not this time! Sometimes I do, yes. In selected sexual situations, yes, I admit I do that. But not this time!" He shook his head. "What a night!"

"I'll go and talk to the sergeant," said Jill.

The sergeant listened to all that she had to say. About how if this story got into the papers it would ruin a great first night for which many people had been working for months. Jill talked and talked, the sweat starting up on her forehead, and the sergeant (who was fifty years of age and had World War Two medal-ribbons on his chest) listened impassively.

At the end, when she had finished talking and could think of nothing more to say, he leaned back in his tall chair behind his tall desk and yawned. "Madam, you're very persuasive and you've persuaded me. We don't have any witnesses, except young Evans, the police constable who brought him in." He smiled. "You'd probably have Lord Goodman or somebody at us by morning, am I right? Big case, lot of fuss, and he'd probably get off." He sighed. "Take him home, miss, and tell him to behave his bloody self in the future, and don't talk to anybody about any of it."

Jill felt a great tiredness. "Thank you, sergeant. And there'll be two circle seats for the first night."

The sergeant smiled. "Make them stalls, miss. My wife doesn't like heights."

Austin was not grateful.

"Jesus H. Christ," he said, as she drove him back to the Savoy Hotel. "The nerve of that bitch!" He glanced at Jill sideways. "You don't believe me, do you? You think I was flashing, don't you?"

"Yes," said Jill Viner, "I think you were."

"Shit," said Austin, staring at the wet streets. "Shit, shit, shit!"

IT was almost five o'clock when Jill dropped Austin off at the Savoy. She debated driving back to her flat. No. She was awake now and doubted if she would sleep again. She thought of going over to Glebe Place and ringing Josh awake and telling him what had happened with Austin, and saying she was sorry about the way things were seeming to go wrong between them. She loved him, she slept with him, they enjoyed each other, surely they did, he as much as she? Somebody had to be the producer, somebody had to have ultimate control. Was that the problem? She hoped not. Josh hadn't seemed to mind at first, when it was a purely business deal between them. The resentment seemed to have begun as soon as they started sleeping together. Was it—perhaps—some kind of sexual hang-up Josh had about her being the boss? Surely not. Josh was too big a man for that; he'd done too much to be affected by that.

Surely.

She loved him, that was the important thing.

He would see it. He would be too busy tomorrow, once rehearsals started, to think about it. He would be glad to know she had booked two adjoining rooms on tour, when they went on a prior-to-London swing, north to Yorkshire and south to Brighton. He'd like that. Wouldn't he?

236

Jill felt troubled. Josh had seemed such a nice, quiet, easy man, but he had an unexpected stubbornness, a steeliness.

She stopped her car and found she was in Fleet Street.

The next day's papers were on sale and the Brigid Kelly story was on every front page. Tom Tully had done a great job. This should help the early box office, get the ticket agencies in line. Leafing through the sheaf of newspapers, the *Mail*, the *Express*, the *Sun*, the *Mirror*, even the *Guardian* and *The Times*, Jill felt a thrill of triumph so pure it shocked her.

It'll be even nicer tomorrow, she thought, tomorrow it all *starts*.

Jill walked back to the car. The first light of dawn was beginning to break, bathing Fleet Street in a rosy glow.

Tomorrow was here.

THE actors sat in a ring, watching Josh.

He smiled at them all.

This was the test, the animal liking or hating.

If a single one of them felt bad vibes from him it was going to be a disaster.

Just one. One was enough.

With a star-studded cast like this it would spread like fire.

Each and every one of them had had directors sacked. Only the previous year, Sir Piers had got rid of the Old Vic's most up-and-coming directorial talent. "The fella was trying to tell me how to play the Bard," had been Sir Piers's sole comment. Now he sat, lugubrious in heavy tweed jacket and horn-rims, his hand resting absently on the be-jeaned thigh of little Brigid Kelly. At least, Josh didn't have to worry about her. Maggie and Austin had been the Hollywood route and could select their directors. Sir Harry was director-proof and did not appear to notice one was there.

"Good morning, everybody," said Josh.

They all mumbled good mornings, watching him closely.

"I think we all know one another." Josh shifted his weight on the bentwood chair, which creaked rudely. The actors laughed. Josh moved the chair again. Again, the farting noise erupted. The actors laughed louder.

Sir Harry, elegant in dark suit from Savile Row, shirt from Turnbull and Asser, shoes from Lobb, said, "Why does everybody laugh at a fart? Odd, that. My old pater had a donkey in *The Merchant*. It came on and farted horribly and then did its business, very slowly and beautifully, in the middle of the last act. My pater said it was the best critic in London."

The cast laughed, all except Sir Piers, who said grumpily, "I always thought that was Tommy Beecham."

"Piers," said Sir Harry, in dulcet tones, "does it matter?"

"No, I don't suppose so," said Sir Piers. "Bloody drafty in this theatre." The others nodded and said, yes it was, all except Sir Harry.

"I think your blood must be getting thin, dear, it's a heat-wave outside. But of course it would be, wouldn't it, at your age?"

The cast laughed kindly, delighted, and Sir Piers glowered.

Sir Harry winked at Josh almost imperceptibly.

Thank God for the old boy, he thought. He engineered that laughter by design but I have to show I can run the ship or he'll be doing it or Sir Piers will or Austin will. He coughed. "Yes, well, let me go quickly round and then we know where we are, right?" He rushed on. "First, there's Maggie. You all know her, I expect. She's our queen of course. Maggie?"

Maggie sat quite still, the pilot light converting her hair into a golden aureole around her head. "Hi, everybody. I'm proud to be doing this, and in this company."

The cast smiled at her and she dropped her eyes.

People had been smiling at her all her life, Josh decided. She had been dropping her eyes like that all her life. It was a kind of apology for her beauty. He noticed her foot was tapping the leg of the old armchair (they were working with tat until the designed props were ready) and realized she was nervous, but that was to be expected.

"Austin Ames, the president, of course."

Austin shifted his small feet encased as always in Adidas. He wore a T-shirt with a gold crucifix around his neck. A suspiciously pungent, hand-rolled cigarette burned in his hand. A drugs bust is all we need, Josh thought. Austin rubbed his heavy beard (plainly he had risen late) and yawned.

"Hi, people," he said.

Josh asked, quietly, "You all right, Austin?"

"Sure, sure, I'm fine." Austin looked morose and then, with an effort obviously summoned from his boots, found his smile. "I was as nervous as hell last night, so I went on the town. I'm still recovering. I had quite an introduction to your London bobbies, I tell you."

"No?" Sir Piers was entranced. Anything dramatic entranced him. "What happened, dear boy?"

"I was having sex in this car and I got out too soon. This bobby thought I was flashing. Everybody!" Austin looked out into the darkness behind Josh, where he knew Jill Viner to be. "Everybody thought I was flashing, for Christ's sake!"

The cast was silent for a moment. Then the laughter, almost hysterical, went on and on.

"My dear boy," said Sir Harry with deep sympathy, when the laughter had subsided, "it could happen to anybody."

Jill called over. "Austin, stop sending everybody up. That didn't happen and you know it."

Austin sighed and smiled crookedly. "No. Of course it didn't."

"What a shame," said Sir Harry. "Lovely story."

Josh half turned to Jill, who was now sitting behind him, and whispered, "*Did* it happen?"

240

Jill spoke back in the same low voice he'd used. "Austin's a kidder."

Her voice was ironic and Josh felt a surge of annoyance. It was his show now. He had to know everything about his cast. Their worries, anxieties, the state of their marriages (if any), the state of their boyfriends (if any) and of their bank balances. He had to be psychiatrist, father-confessor, and headmaster to the whole lot of them. Jill was new to it all. This was her first production. He must remember that.

"Sir Piers is doing the Russian for us," said Josh, swinging back to his cast. "And how lucky we are."

"Haven't played a Rooshian since I was in a James Bond," said Sir Piers. "Ever noticed this about our friends?" He got to his feet. "It's not long since they had their feet bound in rags, since they were serfs, hey? Well, boots are a thing of the last generation to them, they like them big, they like to put their feet down like this, hey?"

Sir Piers hunched his shoulders, until his neck had disappeared. He stumped toward Maggie. *"The point, Madam, is not do we occupy your Sceptred Isle or don't we? It is that we don't need to. Your own ordinary working people have made their choice. Their elected government wants to come into our sphere of influence. That is an historically correct decision on their part. Anything else would be incorrect. Of course, some antisocial elements must be controlled, inside your Sceptred Isle. We cannot continue to be insulted, for example, by your capitalist press. That must naturally stop. The newspapers must belong to the people. War-mongering by certain army officers and generals must also end. These elements must be pensioned off. Your own office we have no strong feelings about. It is for the ordinary working people of England to decide if they want you. It could be that you will be a stabilizing influence, but I personally doubt it. If I were you I should prepare myself, Madam, to go. Preferably to the United States. I am sure they would be pleased to have you."*

Josh felt a thrill down his neck. It was a speech from act two.

Sir Piers was obviously word-perfect. Josh waited for Maggie to reply, to utter the queen's speech beginning, *"Sir, I am going no-where. These are my people and I stay to share whatever is in store for them. . . ."* Josh knew the speech by heart (he knew the whole script, in a rough and ready way, by heart), and he let the moment hang a long time, as Sir Piers, obviously disappointed, muttered "Hey? Hey?" a couple of times.

Maggie shook her head, the long blonde hair dancing down over her face. "That was wonderful. But . . . I . . . I . . ."

Sir Harry came to the rescue again.

"Ignore the old ham, my dear. It's just Piers grandstanding again. He's always been like that, you know."

Sir Piers harrumphed and made his way back to his chair. But not before he had reached out and touched Maggie's arm in a sympathetic gesture. "Didn't mean to embarrass you, me dear. Sorry if I did. I always turn up knowin' me part, d'yer see?"

Sir Harry said, "Really, what a terrible fib, Piers. When we played *Othello* together all those years ago, he didn't know a *word* at first rehearsal, take no notice of him, dear." He beamed guilelessly at them all. "My old pater never knew his long speeches, he used to import whole chunks from other plays, a lump of *Much Ado* stuck into *Lear*, that kind of thing. The audience never noticed, never noticed." He added, "Only knew one actor ever know everybody's part besides his own and that was Noel Coward. Of course he'd written it." He beamed at Austin. "No idea you were so *small*, dear boy." Austin started in alarm. Sir Harry careered on, "Of course, Irving was small, very small, about your height I should think. He had all his stage furniture made about half-size and he scoured London for midgets to play against him." Sir Harry seemed to think this information would be useful to Austin.

"Hal," said Sir Piers, "you have just put your foot in the shit again."

"Oh, have I?" asked Sir Harry. "Really? How?"

Austin shook his head, bemused. "How tall are you, sir?"

"I'm six feet one," said Sir Harry. "I used to be six-two but I shrank. It's the spine, you see? The spine bends, you see."

"Wonderful," said Austin. "Six-one. Marvelous. I *will* look like a fucking midget."

Brigid Kelly got up and crossed to Austin and kissed him on the cheek.

"Never mind, I love you!" she said. And sat down again.

"For a flasher," replied Austin, "I'm doing all right, yes?"

Everybody laughed. Josh relaxed, forcing himself to sound easy. He looked round. "You won't all know Brigid Kelly but you'll all have read about her in the newspapers this morning. She's more famous than any of us."

"Yes, today," said Brigid, ruefully.

"Not at all, my dear," said Sir Piers, gallant to the last. "Great future before you, no doubt of it." His hand caressed her thigh, innocent-seeming, and Sir Harry's voice, pitched with immense skill to be just audible, said, "As randy as ever, I see, the old gentleman."

"For the right kind of thing," retorted Sir Piers, who could hear a fart in a theatre at fifty paces.

"Oh, changed, haven't we?"

"What the hell," demanded Sir Piers, "do you mean by that, you silly old pouf?"

"You know very well!"

"What?"

"I said, you know very well—"

The voice of Vercek came from the darkened stalls. "This is incorrect behavior from actors who should be giving themselves to their work. Ten minutes have gone by and nothing is done. Mr. Director, you are behaving improperly in allowing this!"

Josh looked into the darkness. "I'm sorry, Mr. Vercek. I didn't know you were in."

"No, so I see."

"Who on earth," enquired Sir Harry, "is *that?*"

243

"You can't see him, cast," said Josh, "but the speaker is our author, Boris Vercek."

"Vercek only, please. There is no need of unnecessary titles. We are here to work, yes?"

"Well, I'm damned," muttered Sir Piers. "Bloody little commissar, what?"

"I'd no idea the fucking author was here," whispered Austin to Maggie. "I hate authors hanging around. They never want to change anything."

Maggie shook her head. "He wrote a wonderful play here."

Austin whispered, even lower, "How are the lines?"

"I don't know a single one. It won't go in."

"Still?"

"Yes."

"No shit?"

"No shit."

"Jesus."

Josh gestured to Max, who sat behind him in the shadow of the pilot light. "Max, you take the book, right?"

Josh thought: The important thing is to ignore Vercek's interruption. Then the cast will, too. He said, "I think we'll have a read-through of the whole play, if nobody objects. It'll give us an idea of length and we'll all have an impression of what everybody else will sound like. I'm not asking for performances. That can wait. I won't be taking notes. That can wait, too." He knew that actors were always nervous of a director scribbling. He would try to remember, rather than take down, any points that occurred to him. That way it always seemed spontaneous and human—and with actors humanity was everything.

Max said, "The throne room, morning. Maggie is sitting on the throne—"

A voice from the darkness said, "That is incorrect. With respect, Maggie is not sitting on the throne. The queen is sitting on the throne."

Max, scandalized, said hotly, "Please, don't interrupt a rehearsal!"

Vercek replied, "You are a child who knows nothing. I speak to the producer."

Jill called out, "It is a small point, Mr. Vercek."

"Vercek only, please. No, it is not a small point. We should not pretend we are actors. We should slowly become the people in the play."

Jill said, "The director must decide. He is running this rehearsal."

"Thank you, I was beginning to wonder about that." Josh's mind raced. If he cut the author down to size now, it would be a cheap victory, and where would it leave him later when he might be asking for small rewrites and changes? Besides, there was a good deal in what Vercek said. A director could spend half his rehearsal time trying to remember actors' names.

"Stanislavsky always did it that way," Vercek said, with finality.

"Then"—Josh bowed gracefully to the darkness—"let's try it Stanislavsky's way. In this particular play, I think there's a lot to be said for it."

"Balls," said Sir Piers audibly, but he sighed as he said it.

"The guy's right." This, unexpectedly, from Austin. "He's pretty bright for an author."

"Wouldn't have done for Irving," said Sir Harry. "He called everybody else by their surnames only, including the actresses, and demanded they call him Sir Henry."

"This is the cult of personality in the theatre," said Vercek. "It is incorrect to have so-called stars. It damages the reality of the play."

"Yes," said Sir Harry. "I suppose we should get people orf the street to come in and do it. How nice that would be." He beamed at Austin. "You know, the Americans are terribly good like that. When the movies started, the English film-makers went to the theatre for their actors, but the Americans went to the gymnasia and the brothels."

Austin laughed. "I am an American actor, Sir Harry."

"Well, of course you are, dear boy."

"And Maggie is an American actress."

"Well, certainly she is. Did I *say* something . . . Oh, I do hope I didn't?"

They all laughed except Sir Piers, who muttered, "Can't we bloody well get on?"

"Yes, let's. Cue, please, Max," said Josh.

Josh was listening, hard. He was also looking and committing to memory, but mostly he was letting it wash over him. The actors read from their scripts, and stayed in their chairs. They reacted differently one from the other, but each one would, Josh knew, give an earnest approximation of what was to come in their full-fledged, final performances in five weeks' time. Even Austin, who mumbled and grumbled and was very low-key and hardly seemed to, as actors said, *offer*—even Austin could not disguise from Josh that he had done a lot of work, a hell of a lot of work, on the character of the president. . . . *"Ma'am, I have to tell you that my Congress is prepared to do anything for you, short of war. And if you reply to me, Madam, that anything short of war will not help you, then I have to say, uh, then I cannot help you. . . ."*

Austin was going to be fine. He had Nixon's stare, Reagan's easy smile, and something of his own. Josh felt a thrill of excitement as he listened.

Sir Piers he knew about, but he checked. Sir Piers, too, was fine. He was simply there, like a bear, dangerous, and in command.

Sir Harry had decided on Disraeli. He had even imported into the script a line of the great man's. Josh heard Vercek's anguished sigh in the auditorium but he thought the old boy was perhaps right. *". . . I was playing golf, Ma'am, when the, er, ultimatum came. If one could call it an ultimatum. I suppose our friends would call it an . . . invitation."* The old boy's going to get a laugh there. And a long

246

pause on *"As Disraeli used to say, never be absent during a crisis."* But then Sir Harry added naughtily, *"Even to go to the lavatory,"* and giggled and said, "No, that's too much, sorry, Mr. Author, oh, dear, he's upset with me!"

Sir Harry was going to be himself.

The surprise of the read-through was Brigid Kelly.

Josh could not think how: she had only been given the script the night before. He whispered to Max, "She's good. She's done a lot of work."

"Up at six reading the bloody thing."

"How do you know, you randy young devil?"

Max grinned and placed a finger along his nose. He was happier now, and plainly hoped the Sir Tom incident had been forgotten by Josh. It had not. Josh had told Max in no uncertain terms that he had been very much out of order, in discussing *Queen* business with the awful Paul Prinz. Max had looked miserable and finally mumbled an apology. Josh, after taking thought, had let it go at that.

An unhappy backstage management was bad news on any production. He lit a cigar. Brigid Kelly was going to be very good indeed. . . . *"Ma'am, we must do something, surely there's something we can do, surely there is, we aren't just going to surrender, are we?"*

Maggie read her answer woodenly, as she had been reading all the time. . . . *"We could have done something but we didn't, we cared too much for our comforts and we slept the deep, deep sleep of England that Orwell talked about and we haven't been wakened from it by bombs this time, we haven't wakened at all. We are still asleep and when we waken it will be too late."*

That speech, Josh thought, she should make it ring. It was, after all, the very last speech of the play.

He wondered what was the matter with her. She had been trembling almost imperceptibly all through the read and her voice had wobbled a lot. Josh felt a cold shudder of worry about Maggie.

He said, brightly, "Well done, everybody, that was absolutely terrific! Let's have coffee, there's lots of it, let's just relax and take our time, then I'll give a few notes on moves and we'll all have an early lunch."

Always tell them they're wonderful early on, his father had said, gloomily drawing on his cigar, counting the week's taking. Darling, you were wonderful. That's all any of them want to hear.

"What's the matter with Maggie?" whispered Jill.

"I wish I knew," said Josh.

"Wonderful," he called. "Wonderful, everybody!"

They all smiled and looked happy. His father was right.

Darling, you were wonderful.

Only, Maggie wasn't.

JOSH spent the rest of the first day blocking moves for the actors. Max chalked lines on the stage floor and gave the actors their positions, and slowly everybody began to see the shape of the piece. It was a great advantage to be rehearsing in the theatre at which *Queen* would eventually open. It meant the actors, after two weeks on the road, would be coming home. Josh harped on this point as they did a slow stagger through the script, but he deliberately did not ask anybody to put a lot of effort into the part. He put a stop to the acting because he was very worried about Maggie, and during the course of the day he realized that she was very worried about herself. The way the other players reacted to her told him they had seen what he had seen, and were as perplexed about it as he was.

The hours nonetheless flew and he was astonished when Max said, "It's six o'clock, Josh."

Josh called, "So it is. All right, everybody, that's it. Next stop the Salisbury, the drinks are on me!"

The cast uttered a small hooray at that. Josh was in the business of binding his group of actors together, and he knew the importance of ritual. He intended the swift drink at the Salisbury to become a regular thing in the three weeks they would rehearse at the Royal. Not everyone would come every evening, he knew, but it was much better than having the actors and stage management pair off (and possibly nurse grievances) in different pubs around Shaftesbury Avenue. The Salisbury, known to every performer in London as the "actors' pub," greeted them in its customary and unchanging fashion, by totally ignoring them. Actors from productions all over Shaftesbury Avenue stood shoulder-to-shoulder with actors who had not worked for months, and there was never a hint of patronage. Nobody even looked at Sir Harry and Sir Piers as they called for, in turn, hock and seltzer and Russian stout. "Oscar's drink, yer know," said Sir Harry to the barman. "Had it in his hand when they arrested him at the Cadogan Hotel."

"Had *what* in his hand, sir?" asked the handsome young barman.

"Oh, you naughty boy!" cried Sir Harry, delighted. "Aren't you sweet?"

Sir Piers sipped his Russian stout. "Old Esmé Percy got me on this stuff. Mustn't drink more than two at a time." He surveyed the thick, dark liquid. "I suppose vodka's the stuff the Rooshian would drink but I like this better."

Josh laughed. "No need to carry it that far."

Sir Piers tapped his skull with his forefinger. "It all helps. Gets the character. I start with the walk, yer know. You get the walk right, the rest will come."

"What nonsense," said Sir Harry. "I hardly ever move on stage. All this walking about and waving your arms. It's so tiring."

"The only reason you don't walk is because you don't walk—you mince," said Sir Piers, unabashed.

"Well, I must say, coming from you, that's rich."

"What the hell do you mean by that?" demanded Sir Piers.

"You know." Sir Harry fluttered his eyelashes.

"No, I don't bloody well know!" Sir Piers glared around him, like a baited bull. "What's the terrible old thing on about, does anybody know?"

Austin interrupted hastily to buy a round. He was drinking champagne, which astonished Sir Harry. "Me dear boy, it's simply an interesting mineral between drinks!"

Max and Brigid were standing slightly apart from the others, Josh noted, and their drink was vodka. It astonished him how much hard spirits young actors drank these days. He had been brought up on half-pints of draft bitter, all he could afford. His father had told him, "Don't drink whiskey until you're forty. You won't appreciate it. Brandy when you're sixty. Nowhere to go after that." Josh took all this in, stationing himself next to Maggie, who was insisting that he have champagne with Austin and herself. It looked like the beginnings of a ritual and Josh didn't mind that. Maggie was the one who needed help at the moment. He had no idea why, but he intended to find out.

"Rehearsal went well, I thought," he said.

Maggie grimaced very slightly and stared into her glass.

God, but she was beautiful. The ivory skin, the candid blue eyes, the neat breasts and slim figure—everything about her was physically perfect. He said, "I was so sorry to hear about Philip. I expect it's taking time to get over it."

"I sometimes wonder"—Maggie looked up and the eyes were truly wonderful, so perfectly shaped—"if I'll ever get over it."

Jose felt a sudden lurch in his stomach. So that was it.

"How long has it been now?" he asked carefully.

"Six weeks."

"Not long."

"No. Sometimes I feel him at my elbow."

"His ideas were astonishingly like our designer's. You'll be pleased when you see our set." Josh talked lightly on. "Tommi Traceham is building us a revolve. I went down to the workshop yesterday and had a look at it. I think it's going to be great." He smiled. "Standing on that will put you three feet above everybody else."

"I heard that," said Austin. "It means she'll be six feet above *me!*"

"I had thought," said Josh, "that you could play your scenes with Maggie walking around while she just sits on the throne."

"Three feet above me?" But Austin was smiling. "I'm glad you said that. You've made my day. I was getting very worried."

Josh knew Austin was only half fooling, so he just smiled and said, "I don't know what we do about Sir Harry. He hates to move around. We'll just play around him."

"That," said Sir Piers, "is exactly what he hopes we'll do."

"Yes, I know," sighed Josh. "And there's not a damn thing any of us can do about it."

Sir Harry intervened, saying, "I say, talk to me, will you, please. There's that dreadful bore Tony Bishop over in the corner waving at me, and I can't possibly go across. I mean, life's too short, isn't it?" He blinked. "I always pretend I can't see bores."

"Why," asked Sir Piers, "don't you wear your bloody glasses, you vain old creature? Then you would see them in time to take evasive action."

"They spoil my profile," said Sir Harry seriously.

"You don't think," asked Sir Piers, "that the boys are interested in your bloody profile. It's your wallet they care about."

"I consider that remark very unkind, Piers," said Sir Harry.

"Well, then I apologize," said Sir Piers, with a wink. "Barman, give this old party another pint of that awful piss he's drinking, and the same again all round, hey?"

Josh said, "No, really." He didn't want the rituals to become booze-ups.

But Sir Piers was insistent. "Hate actors who can't hold their liquor. D'yer ever hear about Willie Lawson? He was so drunk they couldn't get into his dressing room at the New. And Willie couldn't get out. Finally had to break the door down, two minutes before beginners. Willie is sitting there, makeup on, all ready to go.

I say, 'Are you all right, Willie?' And he looks at the others and he says, 'I'm very worried about Piers. He's drinking far too much these days.' Then he went on and was bloody marvelous."

Sir Harry was peering again at the elderly actor sitting, a half-pint of bitter in front of him, in the corner. "Good Lord," he said, going across. "I made a mistake. It isn't old Tony Bishop at all." Before they could intervene he had taken the actor's hand and said vaguely, "How nice to see you, dear boy. Do excuse me for not responding to your wave, but I thought you were that dreadful bore, Tony Bishop."

"I am Tony Bishop," said the actor.

"Well, that's what I said, isn't it? So nice to see you. Working?"

"Not at all, for months."

"Good, good," said Sir Harry. "I'm glad somebody is. I hear an awful lot of good people aren't. We have to count our blessings, what?" He drifted back to the group. "What a nice man, can't think of his blessed name."

"The old party," said Sir Piers, "is most definitely ga-ga."

"No," said Josh. "Just shortsighted."

They broke up in a roar of laughter. As he was leaving, Josh bumped into Jill escorting Vercek. She said, "Going already? Just had a few words with our author on the first day's work. He would like to discuss it with you."

Josh took Vercek's hand. "Can you come in tomorrow morning at nine-thirty instead of ten? We can talk then."

Vercek looked half affronted, then nodded. "Very well."

"I assure you, I really must rush now." Josh smiled.

Jill said, low, "Will I see you later? For supper?"

Josh debated. Maggie was out of the Salisbury and on the sidewalk, trying to flag a taxi. He had to catch her before she disappeared. "Better not. I'll see you in the morning."

Jill looked even more affronted than Vercek had.

"All right," she said crisply. "Mr. Vercek, what are you drinking?" She turned her back and ushered the author toward the bar.

"No, no." Vercek produced a worn leather pouch. "Please. I will pay."

Josh took a half-step toward them, and then stopped. Maggie was more important, a hell of a lot more important. He would explain to Jill tomorrow. The play came first. He ran out of the pub, waving to his dispersing cast, and caught Maggie by the arm. "Let me drop you off? You going back to the Savoy with Austin?"

Maggie shook her head. "I think Austin's going on the town again. He finds my company a drag and I don't blame him."

"Let's hope he doesn't get arrested again," said Josh.

"Yes, what about that!"

They fought their way through the traffic along Saint Martin's Lane, out of Trafalgar Square, and at the Savoy the uniformed doorman looked askance at Josh's battered Volkswagen until he saw Maggie in it. He touched his cap to Josh. "Don't worry, sir, I'll find a place for it."

Josh laughed. "Out of sight, I should think."

"Why do you have such an old car?" asked Maggie, thinking it merely an affectation. Josh knew it was no use telling her he couldn't afford a large car. It wasn't something she would understand, he guessed. "Oh, I like the old bus. But I might buy a Rolls-Royce once *Queen* gets off the ground."

"Oh, I don't know." Maggie walked into the Savoy, all doors opening before her. "I think the Volks suits you. You're not one of those crude people who have to look rich, are you?"

For some reason Josh was very pleased with that remark, because it sounded sincere. He knew that it was sincere because Maggie Stride had never felt the need to say anything insincere in her life. She said, "I expect you'd like to talk to me, wouldn't you?" as if it were the most natural thing in the world, and they took the lift up to her suite. There she rang for a bottle of champagne, and caviar and biscuits. "I'm not really eating much. I can't face dinner, but I expect you're hungry, will that do?"

"It will do very well," said Josh, wondering how he could

begin. He still hadn't found a way when the champagne and caviar arrived. They talked shop, Broadway gossip, and Maggie ate little and drank less. Josh was hungry and found the Beluga delicious and the wine numbing. It was perfectly all right to drink champagne at the end of the day but it was of course unwise to mix drinks. He could feel the lift of the alcohol and wondered if he was being wise in drinking quite so much. He coughed a couple of times but the words would not come.

"I expect you're wondering," Maggie asked quietly, "what I thought I was doing today."

"Not exactly," Josh lied. "I saw you were having trouble."

"It's the words," Maggie said flatly. "They won't go in, did Austin tell you?"

"No." Josh thought: So Austin knows. We have to right this, and soon. He said, "Why don't I hear you?"

"Now?"

"When could be better?"

He was tired, very tired, and so was she, but the champagne worked in them both, and they sent down for another bottle, and sandwiches two hours later, and Josh was still being gentle and trying everything he knew and hoping he wouldn't have to be harsh, but knowing too that he would, sooner or later, and postponing the moment. Maggie stopped twice and said, in despair, "The words won't go in, Josh," and Josh, knowing that only bullying could work now, knowing that it was too late for caution, said, "Maggie, he's dead. You've got a job to do. He's dead, say it, he's dead, he's dead," and Maggie whispered back, tears streaming down her lovely face, "He isn't, oh, he isn't!"

"But he is!" insisted Josh gently. "He is, he is! Keep trying, keep saying the words, darling, for Christ's sake!"

And, slowly, Maggie began to get the words half right, the early speeches at least. The tears were drying up now, the racking sobs ending. She wasn't right and Josh knew she wasn't right but perhaps the spell had been broken, he didn't know, he was damp with sweat and exhaustion and champagne, and it was midnight.

Finally, he kissed her on the cheek and said, "Maggie, you're going to be all right and we all love you—" and her arms were round his neck and the lovely hair was in his face and she was sobbing, "Oh, I'll never do it, I'll never do it!"

It was only with a great effort that he resisted the sudden male impulse to respond but that would have been insane, he was sleeping with the producer, for Christ's sake, as if that weren't enough weight to be carrying at this stage. Slowly, tenderly, he laid her down on the bed and took off her shoes. He spread a coverlet over her and smoothed the hair back from her eyes and waited for his erection to subside before he got to his feet, and said, "Sleep tight, darling. You'll be great tomorrow, we'll work this thing out together, I know it, 'night now."

Her eyes stayed closed and she called, sleepily and tipsily, "Good night, Phil, good night, my love," and he was out of the Savoy as fast as his legs would carry him, in case he changed his mind, and into his Volkswagen and back to Glebe Place. The flat seemed very lonely and cold and he debated ringing Jill but he had said no, and it was one o'clock. So he went to bed and tried to think about the play, but all he saw was Maggie's alabaster face on the whiter pillow and all he felt was his own sexual reaction to that, mixed with a fear for her and for *Queen*, that she might not be able to do it, after all. If that happened, what would he do *then?* Before he could think further, sleep claimed him.

JILL sat in her new penthouse in Bryanston Square, and waited for Josh to ring. About midnight she fell asleep and did not waken again until two. She reached out for the telephone, then resisted the temptation. Josh was being very difficult, one way and another. He resented her being the producer, all right, but did he expect her to tell him everything she did, to consult him about everything? He'd been annoyed about the Austin business, but she wasn't going to have him slagging her off in front of the cast, even if he was the director. She couldn't be sure that nobody had heard him reprimand her. Certainly Max had heard. Jill lit a cigarette and poured herself a large brandy and soda. If Josh wanted to play it all the hard way, then she had to be ready, that was all. She had worked a long time to get to this point and she wasn't going to be dictated to by any man, even Josh Williams. She knew how to run the production of *Queen*. She'd got the money, hadn't she? She'd got the bricks-and-mortar man, hadn't she? What did he want from her, modesty?

Two o'clock. The telephone did not ring.

Did Josh think her job was over, now the show was, so to speak, on the road? Did Josh realize what an evening she'd had with Vercek? Did he think it was her idea of a good time to sit for an hour in the Salisbury and listen to Vercek sounding off about the way that Josh was directing the play, that Vercek thought it was altogether too lightweight in style, that Josh wasn't giving it the seriousness it needed, that he seemed to be more concerned with how *Queen* looked than what was being said? Did Josh Williams realize that she had browbeaten Vercek into an appreciation of the fact that this wasn't a State Theatre production in Helsinki they were running but a very large commercial enterprise in the West End of London? Did Josh Williams understand that Vercek would be more pleasant the next day because of it? "Mr. Vercek," she had said, "I love your play but Josh Williams is directing it, and if you upset him I will bar your visits, and I mean that, Mr. Vercek!" and Vercek had seen that she did mean it and had retreated a little—not much; it wasn't in Vercek's nature to retreat much. But at least he had said stiffly, "I do not wish to usurp the director's power. I simply wish the play to be put on with a proper emphasis on the serious story that it tells," and had got to his feet and, refusing her offer of supper, disappeared abruptly into the night, leaving her sitting there, alone. Did Josh Williams know all this?

No, he didn't, and she wouldn't tell him because there was no point in telling him. Vercek was simply worried, as they all were. Vercek wanted everybody to hear every word of his text, because he considered the text the most important part of the play. Everybody thought their own contribution the most important one. Tommi Traceham had been to Jill complaining that Josh had asked her to take four inches off her revolve set. Did Jill know that would cost four hundred pounds, because the revolve was almost ready? The workshop had almost finished the job! Tommi wanted to know if Jill knew of and approved the expense, for one thing, and for another, did she realize the set would look less effective, four inches less effective because of it? Jill had told her that if Josh wanted four inches off the revolve then four inches had to come off the revolve, and Tommi had said, "I can see that the management don't care how much money we're spending but please don't complain about my budget in the future. I like directors to know their own mind but plainly Mr. Williams is a protected species around here!"

Did Josh Williams realize how contemptuous Tommi Traceham had looked, her long cigarette holder in her fingers, her head cocked on one side, the dark eyes knowing and the voice curt? Did Josh Williams think she would stand a lot of cheeky talk from that talented lezzy if she didn't have to? Josh had put her in that position without even telling her why he wanted the revolve lower. Tommi had supplied the answer, since Jill plainly didn't know. "He told *me* he wanted it smaller because of Austin Ames. He hadn't realized Austin was quite as small as he was. To which my reply, dear Jill, was, 'Why the fuck not!'"

Jill said, biting back hot words, "It seems reasonable, Tommi."

"So reasonable he didn't bother to tell *you*, did he?"

And with that Tommi had slammed out of the office.

Four inches was a lot to Austin Ames but to Tommi Traceham it represented the Pan Am building. She wanted the set noticed. Now there were four inches less of it to notice. God, Jill thought, give me strength to endure it all! She had sent Tommi a bottle of champagne as if from Josh with the words "Thanks, darling" on it, but she doubted if Tommi had been deceived.

Josh didn't care about anything except his actors, now.

That was how it had to be.

It was very hard on Jill.

She sighed and poured herself a brandy. Perhaps that was why she had rented the penthouse.

No, it was't. She had rented it because she liked it. For a penthouse it was small but it had a nice view over the square and it was quiet, being high, and she couldn't live in that bloody box in Kensington any longer. It was all right for an out-of-work actress or a personal assistant to Joe Dancy, but for the newest woman producer in London it was rubbish. Jill had felt naughty, paying the first month's rent with a check drawn on Queen Productions, countersigned by Molly. She had told Josh nothing about that either. Or about the furniture she'd selected from the little antique shop off the King's Road or the carpet from Harrods. Well, why not? He hadn't asked. He had never been to her old place, not once, and all he had said when she declared that she had moved was, "Oh, where to?" in a relieved kind of way, and he had merely nodded when she told him. He hadn't said, What did you do that for, why don't you move in with me? had he?

No, he had not.

Jill did not wonder now why she had rented the penthouse. She had rented it because Josh had not offered any alternative. She looked at her watch: two-thirty. He would not ring now. Jill began to take off her clothes in front of the huge mirror in the teak thirties wardrobe she had bought the day before in Shepherd's Market. It showed that her body was as attractive, her breasts full, her neck unlined, her lips sensual, as the day she had first gone to bed with Josh. So what had happened? Why didn't he want her now? Was it just because she was the producer and in overall charge of the production, of *him?* Or was there more to it? Could no woman take the place of the dead Alison? Would she become another short-time affair, like the little Welsh actress at the National he had told her about? Josh made love to her nicely and she felt wonderful with him inside her and she always *came* for him (something she did not always do with the other men she had slept with), and she realized, sleeping nude, pulling the crisp new sheets over her (everything in the penthouse was new, even the linen), that she had grown to need him, sexually as well as affectionately, and that he didn't seem, or anyway part of him did not seem, to want the commitment.

Jill stared into the darkness.

She had thrown herself at him, got into his bed, unasked.

What did she expect?

She had forced herself on him and he plainly didn't want her.

Very well. She would learn to live alone.

She'd done it before. She could do it again.

Jill pushed her thoughts away from Josh to the problems of *Queen.*

What to do about Maggie?

That brought her back to Josh again.

Jill sat up, fumbled in her bedside drawer, found two Mogadons. She had not taken sleeping pills since her affair with Jimmy Bolton had ended.

Was her affair with Josh Williams ended?

She was still trying to work it out when the pills took effect and she slept.

VERCEK sat late into the night in the café of Kristos the Greek.

Kristos, like all restaurateurs, did not eat or relax until he had shut up shop. The wife of Kristos had gone to bed with a complaining air, and Kristos had opened a bottle of ouzo—Vercek preferred vodka but Kristos was a friend, his only real friend in this polite but impersonal city, and besides he was Kristos's guest. Like Kristos, he was an exile. He longed not for the provincial spires of Helsinki, but for the onion domes of Moscow. After all, that was where he had chosen to go. That had been his Mecca. He could have gone to the West. He could have gone to Paris or London or even New York. A Finnish Jew was a rarity: but they existed. He existed. He was one of them: he had forgotten his Jewishness. His father had fought for Finland in the winter war of '39. He had almost forgotten all this. Finland had, by that time, lived down the disgrace of fighting with Hitler against the Soviet Union. He had been a boy, he did not remember that war. In school it had all been talk of Moscow. Of Leningrad. The propaganda had been good. It had not seemed like propaganda. It had seemed like the truth. How was a boy of eighteen to tell?

The old ones like his father, who remembered the field marshal, they had not seemed pleased when he had taken the scholarship to Moscow, to the university, and later to the school of drama. They still resented the Soviets. They fought again, during the dark winter, the glorious war of '39, when Mannerheim, the Old One, had led them in spirit, if not in person, to fight in their frozen woods and lakes, to halt and burn the red-starred tanks, to harry and kill the blundering but never-ending stream of armor and men across Lake Ladoga from Leningrad. He had been only seven years old at the time and it had meant nothing, except that his father was suddenly in a Finnish Army uniform, and came back in the spring minus an arm. The Finns had not asked if he was a Jew or not. If you could fight, you fought. His father had been a teacher, an intellectual. He had not been a devout Jew. He had been a Socialist, until the winter war. Then he had been a Finn. Then he had been nothing. He had died young, less than fifty.

Vercek looked at his own maimed hands. Like father, like son. He had been lucky. Many others had lost their lives in the nightmare.

He was an exile, all right.

So was Kristos, for that matter.

It was the reason for their friendship.

260

And like Kristos, who talked now of the glorious days of the war against the Turks on Cyprus, he felt a longing for what was over, the vast squares of Moscow—that cold, cold city—of being young, and of believing in the future. Vercek sighed. Over, all over. He must forget. The nightmare should have washed it all away, but it had not. One's youth was not so easily washed away.

Kristos was telling some story of a running battle with the Turks, in the dark and dangerous alleys of Nicosia. "Ah, how we ran, my friend, our hearts in our mouths, but they never caught us, and we were free." Kristos poured more ouzo. "I regret those days sometimes, Vercek."

"They are gone," Vercek said. "And you were terrified. They are nothing to regret."

"It is true," said Kristos, "I was terrified. I almost shot myself that night. I wouldn't like to have to live that way at my age. I do not think I could do it. All I am good for now is talk. Fighting. Struggle. It's a young man's business."

"Sometimes," said Vercek, "you cannot chose when you have to do it."

"That is true," said Kristos. "One can only pray it will not come upon us in middle age when we might disgrace ourselves by not being the men we were." He sighed and swallowed a mouthful of ouzo that would have stunned most men. "At least, here in London we are safe."

"Perhaps," said Vercek. "Perhaps."

Kristos looked grave. "You are not sure?"

"No. I am not sure, Kristos."

"Do you have any reason to say this?"

"No. Just a feeling."

Kristos was silent a long moment. "When one is—how to say—underground, then one has to listen to such feelings, yes?"

"I know," Vercek said. "I listen."

"Good." Kristos poured more ouzo. "It may be nothing but always listen. Is there anything I can do?"

"Nothing anybody can do." Vercek knew this to be true. "If action is decided upon it will be taken." He shrugged. "Nothing to do."

Kristos said, "The police?"

"They would not know what I was talking about."

Kristos dared a question. "You are an illegal?"

"In a way, yes." Vercek paused. "And in a way, no."

Kristos looked very grave. "I see." He ate a piece of cheese. "And how does the play go? I see much of it in the papers."

"It goes well. The people are nice and they mean well but they have no true knowledge of how the world really is, or what they have in their hands. They are like spoiled children, used to playing their private little games of make-believe, without any real sense that these things I write of are as real as a prison door or the bars of a cell. They live for praise and perhaps money and the admiration of their fellows and love of what they do, but they do not realize it can all change, very quickly. I wonder"—Vercek sighed—"if they would notice if it did change? They live in a kind of glasshouse. It is warm and comfortable in there and they have forgotten, if they ever knew, that icy winds blow outside and real snow falls and blood is not always synthetic."

Kristos asked, gently, "It does not go well, then, the play?"

"It goes as well as one could expect. They will make a drama of what should be a reality, but it will serve. The important thing is to do it at all. To bear witness. As Auden said, all a poet can do is warn."

Kristos did not know of any poet called Auden but he nodded sagely. He was proud of his friendship with Vercek, a man of deep learning. He knew very little else about Vercek except that he was frightened of something and they had the bond of exile, and that was enough.

Vercek thought, I must not talk too much, that would be foolish. He refused more ouzo and made his farewells. As the door of Kristos's Café closed behind him, and the bolts shot home,

262

Vercek felt a sudden chill of fear, standing there in the deserted North End Road, and he walked quickly toward his lodgings, only five minutes away. Twice he stepped quickly into shop doorways and looked behind him. Nothing. Once, as he turned a corner, and then looked back, he thought he saw a shadow farther down the North End Road, in a doorway, but he waited for almost five minutes and the shadow did not move, so he walked on quickly to his door and let himself in. He went up the stairs to his room two at a time, and it was not until he was inside the room and had double-locked the door that he noticed the cheap colored postcard on the floor. Slowly Vercek picked it up. It was a view of the Kremlin and it was not signed. Vercek looked at it for a very long time before he began to tremble, and to stop that he took out his vodka from the cupboard and poured himself a very large glass. He drank until the bottle was empty. He sat fully-clothed on his bed in the small, drab room, smoking his cardboard cigarettes and trying to decide how they had found out. He had been so careful.

In the end he gave up.

They had found out because they wanted to find out.

It was as simple as that.

Soon he would move again. Perhaps tomorrow.

It would at least buy time.

For *Queen* to prosper, to succeed, he needed time.

Of course. He had been moving about in the West End. He was connected with the theatre. They had seen that. Obviously they monitored everything in that area. Naturally.

To continue with *Queen* meant they would always know.

Vercek smoked and drank until the cold dawn light filtered into the room. He did not sleep.

JOSH was half an hour early for his rehearsal.

There was no sign of Vercek.

Only Max and his two backstage assistants, Bobbi and Bill—fifty, gray, cheerful, as alike as twins, although of different sex—were in the Royal, which seemed chilly after the sun of Shaftesbury Avenue. Josh hoped the warm weather would not last out until September. Rain, his father had often said, is the actor's friend. Josh threw his old blouson over a seat in the auditorium and, desperate for coffee, he called, "Any sign of Vercek?"

Max was shifting the tat furniture around and rechalking his cue lines. He looked up, framed in the pilot light, the only illumination in the vast auditorium. "No, were you expecting him?"

"Said last night he had some notes for me," Josh replied. "I can do without them but I'm here half an hour early to talk to him. Any message from him?"

Max carried on working. "Nothing at all. Mind, we've only been here ten minutes ourselves."

"Bloody, bloody hell! Authors! Max, any chance of coffee?"

Max said, "There's a kettle and some instant in number one dressing room."

"In that case," said Josh, "I'll have about a pint, black, with a lot of sugar."

"My people are working," said Max, again not looking up.

"Go and get it yourself then," said Josh.

Max did look up then. "You don't mean that."

"I bloody well do, Max, and don't try it on with me. I'm not in the mood for it."

"I'll get it, loves," called Bobbi. "Don't get your bums in an uproar." Bobbi was a darling. She had once been a dancer and she had a dancer's figure. From behind she looked eighteen. She was probably forty-five and lived with Billy, fat, breathless and fifty, who hardly ever spoke and did what she told him. They were, by common consent, the best stage-management backup team in the business. A sign of their professionalism was that they didn't resent Max, who was their titular boss, although they had probably been running bakstage shows in the year he was born. They were the kind of people who were never out of work, never rich, never really poor, whose life was the theatre, no job too small—going for coffee, or onstage holding a book—and who stage-managed shows, plays, musicals, you name it, year after year, with, as they said, their bare hands. Josh was lucky to have them and he knew it.

Josh slumped into a stalls seat and looked at his watch. Vercek was ten minutes late. Somehow that didn't seem like Vercek. He opened his much-thumbed script of *Queen* and squinted at it in the gloom. The stage electrician had run a light out into the stalls, at his insistence. Sometimes he liked to direct from out front quite early in a production. Most directors didn't, but Josh reasoned that the actors had to get used to the stage—it was *theirs*, not his. Most of them liked the system.

Max called, in a low voice, "How was Maggie?"

"She was fine." Josh's reply was curt. If Max wanted to play bolshie, that was the kind of reception he would get. Josh had been an ambitious stage manager in his time; he knew how it felt. But that didn't mean he'd stand for any rubbish from Max. Especially after that nonsense with the National.

Max seemed to get the message. He got up from his haunches and came to the edge of the stage. "Do you think she's got nerves, or what?"

"Of course she's got nerves. All good actors have nerves."

Max fiddled with the broad leather belt that supported his jeans. Above it he wore only a sweatshirt, presumably summer and winter. His boots, on the other hand, would have carried him across the steppes. "Do you want to do another stagger-through today, or what?"

"No," said Josh. "We'll begin on page one and work slowly through." Maggie was sitting on her throne as the curtain rose and she had a speech at once. Josh decided to throw her in the deep end. There was no point in protecting her, and no way to do it.

Max whistled. "Is that wise? Couldn't we start later? Give her time to feel her way?"

"She has to do it, Max. If she can't do it to an empty theatre then she can't do it at all."

"Did you talk to her last night?"

"A bit. Where's that coffee?"

"Here, my love," sang Bobbi. Josh took it and busied himself with his notes. Max hung around a few minutes but, when Josh said no more, returned to his work of chalking the stage. Josh smoked a cigar, which did not go down too well on an empty stomach. Vercek did not arrive. He felt very angry indeed at being deprived of his breakfast and some of his sleep, but he kept his smile on his face as his cast began to arrive.

The first was Austin Ames. He looked fit and rested. Accepting coffee, he informed Josh that he had gone back to the Savoy the day before, eaten an omelette and slept for ten hours. He felt fine and he had several ideas for script changes in the president's speeches to make them play easier. Josh listened to his outline of them, which was lucid, and made a few notes and promised to think about them. He told Austin, with a smile, that his only objection, on principle, to script changes, was that as soon as one actor obtained permission to change his lines everybody else wanted to do the same. The English tradition—the one in which he had been trained—was to try to play to the script as near as possible, especially in a straight play. A comedy would be different, naturally; if a thing didn't work, you changed it for something that did. You had laughter—or lack of it!—to help you decide. With a play like *The Queen of Finland* they had a text of great merit. How the man had written it, Josh didn't know, he said, still smiling; but they had to try it and see. Austin blinked and said, sure, as long as he could come back to Josh if it didn't seem to be working. Josh said, of course, he supposed he was too rigid; he'd been doing an awful lot of the classics, the English stage director's cross. Austin said, sure, then I'll leave it with you, and Josh said, let's play to script up to final word-perfect run-through and then see where we're at. This seemed to satisfy Austin but Josh knew better than to count on it.

266

Sir Harry and Sir Piers arrived together, having met at the stage door. Sir Piers was complaining about the accommodations. "In all my years in the business I've never had a decent dressing room. They're all slums. Rotten old armchairs, naked light bulbs, lino on the floor. Like a workhouse. Except for the National, of course, and that's nationalized."

"We're only thespians, my dear. We're mummers, troubadors, one step above the beggarman, the lowest of the low; anything's good enough for us." Sir Harry refused coffee with a shudder and opened his flask of Earl Grey. "I always bring my own furniture into the dressing room. My man does it up for me. I can't bear sitting around a lot of verminous old tat."

"Your man, who's that?"

"My driver. He looks after me."

"That young Italian chap, you mean?"

"Mario, yes." Sir Harry sipped his aromatic brew. "Or is it Silvio?"

"Good God, can't you remember?"

"Well, they're all so very much alike, y'know."

"Then why do you keep on changing them so much?"

"Do you know, I can't imagine."

Josh grinned to himself. Nothing to worry about there. The old boys were settling in. They would cunningly hold back any "improvements" in their parts until a later day.

Brigid came in like a mouse, and smiled shyly at everybody. She evaded a welcoming hug from Sir Piers and drifted to Josh's side. "Do you think my hair's all right for the princess?"

Josh looked at it. "Far too modern. We'll talk about it later. All right?"

"Thanks." Brigid tossed her hair. "It combs out nice and loose."

"Just the same, no decision yet." Brigid was not the star and Josh had to make sure Maggie was happy first. He had no idea what Maggie wanted to do with her hair and she took precedence over

Brigid. It would never do for them to have the same style. "We'll sort it out," he said. "No hurry, is there?"

"No, no, of course not." Brigid smiled her innocent little smile, but Josh decided that she wasn't as innocent as she seemed. He made a mental note of that. He also heard Max ask her softly, "What did he say?" and the girl's reply, "Leave it for now," and Max's laugh and even lower aside, "Probably has to ask Madam."

Maggie arrived ten minutes late.

Josh knew, just looking at her, that if his work of the evening before had helped, it had not helped all that much. Maggie had made up very carefully, and her embroidered blouse and jeans were chic and her boots Gucci, but her fingers trembled as she held her script and she had dark rings under her eyes. Josh made no special thing of her lateness but simply nodded. "Good morning, Maggie, we're going to go from the top and see how it runs. I'm not asking for performances unless anybody wants to give me one, and of course we'll be working from books. . . ." At this Maggie smiled wanly. "So, let's just try it and see what we have. Leave the moves in that we discussed yesterday or improvise any others you feel like, but please, nobody stop to discuss anything. I just want to see again what we are aiming for." He smiled at them all, purposely missing Maggie out of his range. "Let's go whenever you're ready."

Josh noticed Max looking at him questioningly. He was wondering why they were doing today the very thing they had done the day before. To Max, to any stage manager, it was time lost. Max wanted to know the actors' moves, so he could fix them in his script and in his mind. Josh knew that there were more important things.

The principal one was Maggie.

"I'm going to watch from out front," he said, offhandedly.

The actors buzzed at that, as he knew they would.

They had come expecting to drone boringly through their moves and their bits of business, and now they were being asked to give a *performance*. Josh did not let them have long enough to decide

268

they had objections, which he was sure they had. Sir Harry seemed to be speaking for them all when he said, "I say, this is novel, these days, what? My old pater used to do it all the time. Actually played with a book in his hand with royalty in the house. King Edward and Mrs. Keppel, I think it was. Nobody minded. So why not?"

"Because I'm not ready, for one thing," said Sir Piers. "I haven't got the character's walk right yet."

"You and your walk. Say the lines and don't trip over the furniture, there's a dear boy."

"Whenever you're ready?" Max called in the tough voice common to all stage managers.

The actors took their time finding their places and clearing their throats and generally getting themselves in a nervous state, so that the adrenaline would run and they would be able to *perform* and not just read. All except Maggie. She sat center-stage in the shabby armchair that represented the throne, and her script shook, very slightly, in her hand, although her face, calm and serene as ever, showed nothing at all.

Jill Viner slipped into a seat behind Josh. A waft of Mitsouko came with her.

"What's happening?"

"I'm giving them a run-through."

"This early?"

"No choice. Maggie's in a mess."

"You were with her last night?"

"Till after midnight." Josh dropped his voice. "I'm not sure she's going to be able to do this, Jill."

"Why?"

"Losing her guy. I think it's just hitting her now. Her emotions are frozen, I'd say, and she can't unfreeze them to work."

"So much for the ice lady!" Jill's voice was mildly indignant.

"Look, it's to her credit, she loved him."

"She's an actress, she ought to be able to act, no matter what."

"That's crap and you should know it, Jill. I'll try my best with her but my guess is she's not far off a breakdown. That's why I'm throwing this run-through at her."

Jill said, slowly, "What if it doesn't work?"

"Then we know, and we can replace her if we have to."

"Replace her, are you *mad*, Josh?"

Josh looked up at the stage. The actors were ready.

"It would be better than having her collapse on opening night."

"Wouldn't it be even better to go slow for a bit, let her feel her way into the part?"

"It would be one way, but if she broke down later—"

Jill's voice was low but harsh. "Then do it that way, for Christ's sake, Josh! Give the girl a chance! We have to open with Maggie as the queen. If we don't, we're dead!"

Josh felt the cold anger grow. But he said, reasonably, "I've told the cast we're doing a run-through and that is what we are doing, Jill. Now, please don't interrupt. I'm taking this rehearsal." He called, in a louder voice, "All right, Max, cue Maggie please."

Max said, "Curtain up on Maggie . . . er, I mean on the queen, sitting on her throne. She is alone."

Maggie sat, quite still, for almost a minute.

Max said, in a low voice, reading from his script, "The queen rises and walks down center-stage from the throne. Then she pauses. . . ."

Maggie got up from the throne and walked, very slowly and beautifully, down center-stage.

Max whispered, on one knee now, so Maggie could see his prompt-finger, "She turns stage-left as if in deep thought. . . . And then she goes back slowly to the throne and sits on it. . . ."

Maggie did all those things. Josh relaxed.

Max called, "Enter the prime minister . . . stage-left. . . ."

Sir Harry came on, panned a hard look at the audience as he

would look at it on opening night, Josh knew, waiting for the round of applause that would inevitably accompany his entrance (Josh resolved to give him a note *not* to do that, on the first night, ten minutes before the curtain went up), and then, and only then, Sir Harry turned to Maggie and said, *"Ah, Madam, what a sad business it is. It seems we may have to echo the words of the senior Scottish earl at the Treaty of Union with England. . . ."*

Maggie said, in a low voice, which seemed all right, *"And what words were they?"*

"He said . . ." Sir Harry paused as he would pause for the audience on the first night, secure that he had the first good line of the play and ready to milk it for all it was worth. *"He said, Ma'am, throwing down his pen . . . 'There gangs the End of an Auld Song!'"*

Josh felt his spine tingle.

It was perfectly said.

He waited for Maggie.

She said nothing. She seemed to have trouble holding her script.

Behind him, Jill whispered, "Josh, stop it. She can't do it."

Maggie spoke. *"This song is not yet over, Prime Minister."*

Sir Harry shook his head. *"I hope you are right, Ma'am, and I am wrong, but I am the outgoing prime minister and my successor is demanding total surrender. He has the country and I do not, not any longer."*

A very long pause. Far too long. The sweat gathered on Josh's back.

"Perhaps not, but I still do."

The line was woodenly said, and Josh sat back in his seat, in despair. He listened in total silence as the read-through went on, letting the lines wash over him, ignoring every actor except Maggie, watching the beautiful head as it sank lower and lower over her script, as the words got slower and slower and more wooden.

"Stop it, Josh," Jill hissed once more, halfway through the second act. "The others are just as bad as she is now."

It was true. Out of sympathy with Maggie's predicament they had all stopped acting.

"She's going to work until the end," Josh said. He wondered if Maggie could. She was not looking at any of the other players now, and her voice was almost inaudible. If she staggered to the end, Josh thought, at least she will have been through it once and we'll have something to build on. The despair he felt he did not allow to show, not for a moment. He rehearsed how he would tell them all to break for coffee, quite naturally, and then pick up the pieces and start all over again, very slowly, from the beginning. It was at that moment that Maggie started to cry.

For a moment Josh was paralyzed.

Jill was not.

She stood up behind him and called out, "All right! Take fifteen minutes, everybody!"

The actors all stood as if turned to stone.

Maggie sobbed, almost retching now, and Brigid Kelly moved toward her. Maggie shook off her arm and ran off into the wings. There was a deathly silence in the auditorium.

Jill called out again, calmly, "Everybody! Please just take coffee. Ready again in fifteen minutes." Josh felt her move from behind him, placing her hand on his shoulder as she went. "It had to be, Josh. It wasn't working, was it?"

"If you ever do anything like that again," Josh said gratingly, "I go."

That's the second time I've threatened to go, and I'm still here, he thought, through a red haze of fury.

"I'll talk to her," Jill said gently.

"You will not. I'm directing this play."

"And I'm producing it, Josh. Your way failed. Mine might, too. But I'm going to give it a try, darling. So sit here and let me talk to her. Woman-to-woman. All right?"

Josh knew he should have walked out there and then.

But he didn't.

He said nothing. He could think of nothing to say.

Jill was absolutely right. His method had failed.

It did not make him love Jill any more for having pointed it out. He lit a cigar with shaking fingers.

Jill looked at him pleadingly, but he refused to answer her stare. Then she sighed and made her way through the pass door, backstage.

Maggie was sitting in number one dressing room, staring at the wall.

She had stopped crying.

Jill closed the door gently. She sat down next to Maggie and took her hand and held it. It was cold and sweaty. It was possible that Josh was right. Maggie could be close to a breakdown, but Jill did not believe it. She could not afford to believe it. The success of the whole show rested on Maggie. There was no possibility of a suitable replacement. Jill put the idea out of her mind. But Maggie's first words chilled her just the same.

"Jill, it's no good. All I'm doing is embarrassing myself and everybody else. Replace me. There's plenty of time." Maggie seemed to be talking about somebody else, her words dull, like her performance on stage a few minutes before. "I'll get a plane home tomorrow. All that will happen if I stay is that I'll let you down and everybody else, too."

It was all so queenly that Jill almost wept.

Her woman's impulse was to say: Go. Go now. At once. You're right, of course.

But she said, "No need for a decision now. Go back to the hotel and rest. Stay away a couple of days. You're overwrought and upset. Anybody would be. Rehearsals can go on without you. We have two weeks before we go on the road."

Maggie said, tonelessly, "Jill, I don't think I can do it."

Jill put her arms around Maggie's shoulders. "Don't even think about it. Come on, let me get you back to the hotel."

"I don't know." Maggie shook her head, and the golden hair

fell across her perfect face. "I think if I left now, that would be the best thing."

Never, Jill Viner thought. She eased Maggie out of her seat. "Come on. We'll take a taxi to the Savoy. Let's get you to bed for a few hours, right?"

Maggie looked at her. "It won't help. I feel numb. There's nothing."

"That's nonsense. What you're feeling is guilt. You don't think you should be alive when Philip's dead. Everybody feels it when they lose somebody."

"I never lost anybody before." Maggie shook her head. "Maybe you're right."

"My mother died when I was ten," Jill said. "I loved her more than anything in the world." It was true. "I had to get over it and I did. So will you."

Maggie shivered. "I wish I thought so. I hate to let everybody down. I've never had trouble with my lines before."

Jill thought, No, or anything else in your life.

Maggie lit a cigarette with trembling fingers. "I've done my homework on the queen. I've looked at hours of newsreels." The tears came to her eyes. "Philip got it for me, he was such a nice man." The tears ran down her face and she didn't wipe them away. "He made sure I took this part, you know. He died so I could do it, I think."

"There you are then. You can't let him down, can you?" Jill took her arm and they walked out of the Royal, past the stage-doorkeeper, who courteously averted his eyes, and into the street. Jill flagged a taxi and ten minutes later they were in Maggie's suite at the Savoy. Jill rang for coffee and some scrambled eggs but Maggie could not eat, so Jill ate them herself. She had had no breakfast, having wakened early worrying about Josh, then fallen asleep again, and out with a rush. She really had something to worry about now. Maggie sat in a thin kimono on the huge silken bed and sipped her coffee. If I looked as beautiful as that, Jill thought, I wouldn't have a care in the world. That fragility, men must go crazy for it. She glanced at her watch—almost noon—and asked, "Do you have any pills?"

"Pills?" Maggie's eyes were so wide and so blue.

"Tranks, that sort of thing?"

"I never use them. All the time I nursed Philip I had to keep half awake in case he needed me."

"I'm not surprised you're exhausted. You've been an angel, but now you have to think of yourself." Jill wondered whether she should send for a doctor but dismissed the idea. If it got around Fleet Street that Maggie Stride had collapsed on the first day of rehearsal, that would be publicity of the worst possible kind. No. Maggie would be all right. All she needed was care. "Are you going to promise me you'll rest all day and see how you feel tomorrow?"

Maggie nodded her head like a little girl.

"All right, if you think so."

"Of course I think so. You're going to be fine."

"I'm not so sure, Jill."

"Well, I am." Jill leaned forward and took Maggie's hand. "You said earlier that Philip wanted you to do this part. I'm going to make sure you do. But . . ." Jill forced a smile onto her face. "Not the way Josh was doing it today. I'm going to ask him to work with you on your own for a while. Not necessarily tomorrow. Or the day after. When you feel good and ready, and not before. What do you say?"

Maggie looked at Jill sadly for a long moment.

Then she smiled. It was a wan smile but it was the first Jill had seen that morning. "If you think it will work," Maggie whispered, in a low voice. Then she closed her eyes and lay back on the soft pillows, and Jill walked across and pulled the curtains, shutting out the view of the Thames and the sound of the hooters of the tugs and the rumble of traffic along the Embankment.

"It'll work," Jill said softly. "You'll see. I'll call in this evening and see how you are. Rest now. Ring for anything you want." At the door she hesitated. "You sure you'll be all right?"

Maggie did not reply. She seemed not to hear.

Troubled but hopeful, Jill Viner let herself quietly out of the room.

Maggie Stride had to be all right.

She simply had to be.

JILL took a taxi back to the Royal.

The rehearsals were going on as if nothing had happened. The assistant stage manager, Bobbi, was reading Maggie's part, and Josh was on stage himself, having abandoned the performance experiment and reverted to staggering through the play in a conventional way. Jill stood in the wings until there was a natural break.

"Josh, can I have a word with the cast?"

Josh said, "All right, everybody. The producer wants your attention." He did not look at her, but took his notes and his script and went out into the darkness beyond the pilot light. She couldn't see his face but she felt a sudden shaft of hurt. Surely he knew she loved him. Did he think she had enjoyed doing what she did? A feeling of hopelessness flooded over her, and she let it subside before she addressed the company, who waited, curious and expectant, on her words.

"First of all, Maggie is all right." Jill was surprised at how brisk her voice sounded; she was always surprising herself. "She's very tired and she's only just over a bereavement, as most of you know. She may not be in tomorrow, depends how she feels. I don't think there's any more to say except that Josh will work around her, I expect?" She looked out into the darkness toward Josh, but he did not reply, so she smiled to mask the snub. "Except one thing, and that applies to backstage as well as cast. Please, not a word to

276

anybody—and I mean anybody!—about Maggie. She's a famous person and it would make news and I don't want her upset. So, absolute discretion, if you please. Thank you. That's it. Unless anybody wants to say anything?"

Austin cut in. "That outburst looked pretty hysterical to me. Did you get her a doctor?"

Jill was wondering how to answer that when Sir Piers said, "What could a doctor do, old boy, for actor's palsy? I've had it a hundred times meself."

"Rubbish," said Sir Harry. "You'd be a bloody sight better actor than you are if you'd had it *once*, dear."

"I'm as nervous as a fool every time I go on," protested Sir Piers. "Ask any of me wives!"

"Poor Maggie," said Brigid. "Is *she* . . . ?"

"She's sleeping," Jill said, evenly. "She's going to be fine."

"No doctor at all?" Austin repeated.

Jill asked, "What had you in mind, a shrink?"

"I don't see why not. It's emotional, anybody can see that. Maggie needs help, I'd say."

"Austin." Jill smiled. "She doesn't even have a tranquilizer in her handbag. She tells me she's never taken them. Or anything. So what could I say?"

Austin nodded his head at that and said, "Sure, sure," but he looked unconvinced.

"This is London, dear boy," Sir Piers chided him. "We don't send for those sort of fellas until somebody starts chewing the carpet, what?"

Austin said, "She looked pretty bad to me."

"All right, folks, can we get on?" Josh's voice came out of the dark. "We have a lot of work to do."

"Right! Top of page sixteen, line four, the prime minister's speech. Places, please!" shouted Max briskly. The actors coughed and shuffled and got into their places.

Jill walked into the dark to Josh and put her hand on his shoulder. "Josh, I think she'll be all right. I did all I could. I'm sorry if it seemed impulsive."

Good God, Jill asked herself, what are you apologizing for? You did the only possible thing, what else could you have done?

"It was impulsive but it may have been right. Time alone will tell." Josh turned away from her toward his cast. He was a talented man and she had cast a reflection on, well not his talent, but his judgment. Jill thought, What else could I have done?

Jill said, low, "Can we meet tonight?" When he didn't reply, she added, "For supper? There are one or two things we should talk over."

"At least I agree with that." Josh's voice was grating. When he stood up and brushed past her, she smelled his male smell that she now connected with sex and she melted a little and hoped he would at least touch her hand. But he simply said, "See you in the office at seven," and walked out of the dark toward his actors.

Jill left the Royal in a fever of fury, seeing nothing—the crowds, the billboards outside the theatres—nothing, until she was in her office, staring at a list of costs for *Queen* and a letter from the Arts Council offering to assist (in principle) with the first production on tour of *Queen* when it went to Wallingford, in the north of England, for the first week. Wallingford had a subsidized theatre in a new town, an excellent venue for the first and probably ragged week, since nobody important would come that far north to see it. Which was just as well, Maggie being in the state she was. Jill rang the man at the Arts Council and made cooing noises and suggested lunch at the Ivy, and the man at the Arts Council, who was used to cooing noises from producers but who also liked his Ivy lunches, said why ever not, and they penciled in a date for the following week. Jill then talked to the manager at the Wallingford Civic Theatre. She told him about the cast (which he already knew) and the technical details of the revolve set, which he didn't. He asked, rather apprehensively, if they were traveling their own carpenter to erect the set, and seemed relieved when Jill said they were. Jill asked him why, and he said, "Well, we have a pretty bolshie crew up here. They don't like extra work."

"Don't worry," Jill told him. "Our man is a master."

Then she took a call from Jack Millard, also from the north of England. He was ringing to tell her that he thought her treatment of young Pat Woods (who happened to be a dear friend of his, as she knew) diabolical, and he was, accordingly, with regret, asking that he be allowed to withdraw his fifteen thousand pounds already invested in *Queen*.

"Not a chance," said Jill. "And just as well for you, Mr. Millard. This show is going to make you a lot of money."

"I still think you were hard on Pat."

"It's not me, Mr. Millard, it's the world."

"Still, it was rough."

"Pat isn't complaining, is she?"

He hesitated, and laughed. "Only about you and the director sleeping together. She seems to think it cost her the part. I mean . . ." He hesitated, since Jill had not replied. "I expect she's got it wrong. But she seemed to think the unknown girl, Brigid Kelly, got the part because the director, Josh Whatsisname, wanted her, and you agreed. . . . I'm sure she's wrong but that's what she told me."

Jill said, "Mr. Millard, your check for fifteen thousand pounds is in the post tonight."

"Now listen—"

"No, you listen. Josh Williams is a first-class director. He picked Brigid Kelly. Not Pat Woods. I'm sorry you don't like it. But I don't want investors who aren't happy. So your check is on its way. Good-bye, Mr. Millard."

She slammed the telephone down.

Molly looked across at her curiously. "Trouble, darling?"

"Oh, that? Not really. We can live without his fifteen thou."

Yes, Jill thought, we can.

But can I live without Josh Williams?

JOSH came in at exactly seven o'clock.

Molly saw the expression on his face, hastily gathered her handbag and lunchtime shopping together, and escaped with a muttered "Good-night, all."

Jill was determined to play it cool.

She poured them both a large gin from the hospitality cupboard, and then sat down behind her large new desk. If Josh wanted to play it tough, then she was the producer and she had the last word. If the ploy had succeeded, there was no sign of it.

"You and I have to get some things straight," Josh began.

How very nice his hair was, so thick; but it needed cutting, as usual.

"If you're going to tell me I was out of order with Maggie, I've already apologized, Josh."

"It isn't that altogether. It's the general principle. If you keep making decisions concerned with the acting part of the production, as you did today and as you will continue to do, I imagine, unless we can work something out, then my cast will believe that I am simply your office boy or whatever and they will cease to respect me. And if that happens, and I believe it could, then I'm afraid I will have to go, Jill."

He was so cool. So polite. It was as if he were talking to a stranger. If he would only shout, she could understand. Didn't he see how much all this hurt her? All she was trying to do was to keep *Queen* afloat, didn't he see that?

"I can see I've really upset you. What else can I say?"

"I don't want you to say anything. I want you to do your work and let me do mine, that's all."

He looked at his watch. How very sensitive his hands were.

How very nice he was really, despite his coolness. Poor darling. Her heart warmed to him in a wash of sympathy. "I had a call from Pat Woods's boyfriend. He's taken his fifteen thousand out of the show. I told him we can do without him."

Josh looked startled. "Did he say why?"

Feeling happier that they were moving away from the Maggie business, Jill said, "It seems he was upset Pat Woods didn't get the part."

Josh looked suspicious. "Did he say anything else?"

He seemed angry again. Jill wondered how she could placate him. It didn't seem that anything she said was right. Oh, dear. She smiled and said, offhandedly, "Not really. Just he wanted out."

"He must have had a reason."

"I told you. He thought Pat Woods should have got the part, not Brigid Kelly."

"Had he any reason for thinking that?"

"I don't know what you mean?"

"Yes, you do, about you and me. Anything about us?"

Jill felt a wave of fear. "Only that—"

"Only what?"

"That you and I were friends. That Pat Woods thought I made the decision, not you. That's all." The fear came into her throat and almost choked her, but she could not break down and cry and throw her arms around him and plead that she loved him. She was not made that way. She would not beg. She bloody well would not beg.

"Pat Woods was a lot more forthright than that." Josh was really angry now. "She said I was getting my own way because I was screwing you."

"Well," said Jill, bravely, "you don't seem to be doing much of that lately."

"No, and I don't think it would be a very good idea if I started again, do you?"

Jill just stared at him, suddenly cold.

Oh, my love, how can you say such a thing?

But he was saying it and he seemed to mean it.

"That's your decision, Josh" was, just the same, all she could force herself to utter.

"No." Josh stood up, probably so that he did not have to look at her, and stared out of the window down at the early evening theatregoers. "It's yours, too. It is simply that I can't afford for people to think I was given the job because we are sleeping together. That's all, you see?"

Then why, she wanted to scream, did you get into bed with me?

Probably, she answered herself, because I got into bed first.

Josh let the silence hang a moment. "So I think, for the good of the show as well as for ourselves, we should give it a rest for a while, don't you think?"

His voice was low and reasonable and it tore her to pieces.

"Whatever you want to do, Josh, I'll do."

He didn't turn round but when he answered, his voice sounded relieved. He probably had expected a scene, she thought, and he's looking at his watch now, so that he can escape, so he won't have to look at my face, because he knows, he must know, I love him, I must have shown it to him so often, in and out of his bed. She wanted to say some of this but she could not. The words, like the tears, would not come. All she felt was total misery.

The telephone rang. Josh picked it up and listened. He said, "All right. It's going fine. Come in when you can." He put the instrument down. "That was Vercek. He's moved his address or something. He's going to come in to rehearsals as soon as he can." Josh sounded puzzled. "Do you ever get the feeling he's scared of something?" Jill shook her head, she couldn't think about Vercek. She had her own problems.

"It's as well he didn't see Maggie." Josh reached for his leather jacket and put it on.

"How about supper?" Her voice sounded plaintive to her.

"I'm sorry. I have this chap I must have a drink with, must rush. 'Bye, darling."

And he kissed her lightly on the lips and escaped out of the office. Just like *that*. He could shrug it all off, just like *that*. Jill could hardly believe it. She poured herself another gin and drank it, slowly. So cool. So determined. He had known exactly what he wanted to do and he had done it. It was the kind of quality that made him a good director. He didn't let his emotions rule him. He kept them in order, in their place. Not like her. Jill drank most of the gin at a gulp. She was a fool.

That's what she was, a fool.

It must stop. It must stop now. *Queen* was all that mattered.

Shaming tears ran down her face, suddenly, from nowhere. She sobbed and sobbed and blew her nose and sobbed again. At last she stopped. It was no use. No use at all.

The telephone shrilled. She answered it.

It was Austin Ames and his voice sounded very strange.

"Jill, I'm ringing from the Middlesex Hospital. Maggie's just been admitted. She's taken an overdose."

Jill said, "Do nothing. Speak to nobody. I'll be there in ten minutes."

Outside, the sun was still shining, in the late evening haze. In the theatres without air-conditioning it would be sweltering. The cabby said, "Nobody's taking cabs, miss. It's so nice, they walk."

Jill nodded. Rain, as Josh had once said, was indeed the actor's friend. She looked at her tightly entwined fingers. Who was the producer's friend?

Nobody.

AUSTIN waited for Jill on the forecourt of the Middlesex Hospital, in a sweat of anxiety.

As soon as Jill got out of the taxi he took her arm and walked with her to one end of the doctors' car park. Looking around warily, he said, "If I hadn't gone into her room to see how she was, she'd be a stiff right now." His fingers shook as he tugged at the fringe of hair drooping into his eyes. "The hotel doctor was great. He got her here fast. She's had the stomach pump and she should be okay. I haven't talked to anybody except the doctor. I told him you'd be coming and, shit, that's all there is to it, Jill."

But he stubbed his sneaker toe on the ground and wouldn't meet her eye, and she knew he was thinking she should have called a doctor earlier. Well, he was right, obviously, but there was no point in thinking about that now. What was done was done. The problem was how to get Maggie Stride out of the Middlesex into some more discreet place, away from newspaper reporters and the rest.

"Where's the doctor now?"

"I'll take you. Come on."

Austin led the way into the casualty ward. He was not an unlikely figure among the people sitting there, with bloodied hands and patches over eyes damaged in accidents, or lying broken on stretchers. Most seemed to be dressed much as Austin was, in sneakers and jeans. Jill felt herself wildly overdressed, and was glad when she met the senior doctor, who was a very tired man of about fifty and took in her looks with approval. He was plainly busy and she wasted no time. "Doctor, I'm Jill Viner, your patient's current employer. How is she?"

The doctor said, "She's not going to die. She hadn't taken quite enough to kill herself."

"What is your usual procedure now?"

"We'd keep her on the wards a day or two until she's fit to talk to a psychiatrist, if she agrees to do that. It's normal practice. No point in her going out and doing it again, successfully next time."

"None at all, and I hope she won't try."

"Something," said the doctor, "brought this on and any competent psychiatrist would want to know what it was, in the best interests of the patient."

Jill thought hard. "I'm sure the best interests of the patient won't be served by having her here in a public or even a private ward, Doctor. You know who she is?"

The doctor nodded.

"Good. Then you see the problem. I want her in a very private clinic, where she can get all the attention you say she needs. I want you to help me. I want you to arrange it now. Expense is no object but discretion is. I am in your hands and so are the jobs of a great many people, and a great deal of invested money."

The doctor merely nodded as if he had expected something of the kind. "I can make those arrangements if you wish me to. I'll make a call now." He made to move off, but Jill said, "Can I see her?"

The doctor thought. "No. Best not. Let's get her away and then you can see her at the other end."

Austin was impressed. "Jesus, you handled that pretty good."

Jill said, "Austin. Can I rely on you?"

"Sure, how?"

"Not a word about this to anybody. The cast. Nobody. As far as they are concerned, she's overtired and gone into a clinic for a rest. Just for a few days. Capiche?"

Austin nodded his head. "Whatever you say." He hesitated. "So long as she gets the best treatment."

"She will," said Jill. "Come with me if you like."

He shook his head, looking very small and uncertain. "No, nothing I can do. You have the ball now." He looked close to tears. "I'll go see her when she's better. Jesus, I love Maggie."

The over-intense way he said it, and the way his whole body was shaking made Jill wonder if he meant it. Watching him walk out of the Middlesex Hospital forecourt, into the warm summer evening, she thought possibly he really did. Or was he only indulging in the traditional overstatement of the actor? There was no way of knowing.

"The clinic will send an ambulance round in five minutes." The doctor was at her elbow. He rubbed his eyes. There was a smear of blood on his white coat and his shirt cuff was frayed. "Wasn't that fellow Austin Ames?"

Jill nodded.

"I liked him in his movie with Miss Stride," the doctor said. "They should do another one together."

"They have a play to do first."

Jill sat in the ambulance all the way to the clinic in Harley Street, holding Maggie's hand. Maggie's eyes were closed but she was not unconscious. Jill felt a relief, in a way, that this had happened. A crisis. Somewhere she could help. Anything was better than silly crying over Josh Williams.

JOSH sat in his Glebe Place living room and drank most of a bottle of Glenlivet.

He was a shit, that was the trouble. He had behaved like one and he didn't like it.

The girl loved him and he wasn't sure he didn't love her. The urge to pick up the telephone, call her to come across to the flat, all was forgiven, was very strong. She had been good to him, a kindly and tolerant lover, and he had started to feel about her, lately, as he had felt about Alison. Yet, he had to face it, she wasn't Alison and would never be Alison or anything like her. He did not know if he could live his life with a woman who constantly went her own way, who did not so much dispute his decisions as ignore them. It was asking a lot of a man who had had a compliant and sympathetic partner for fifteen years and nobody at all for three. He might have been able to accept her nature if they had not been so closely bound together by *Queen*. Working side by side for weeks and months on end, sooner or later something would have blown. She was too hot-blooded, too definite, she was taking his life over, not that he objected too much, his personal life had been a vacuum, and she had filled it splendidly; but his professional life was something else.

So here he was, lonely and miserable and drunk.

He raised his glass to the smiling face of Alison in the photograph.

"Wish you were here, love," he said, softly.

But he wondered wryly, Was it Jill Viner he was really talking to?

THE cast got off the Inter-City express at York and climbed into the waiting hire-cars. They joked and chattered at one another like children. Everybody was present except Maggie and Austin, who were coming up north by car from London. And Jill, who had stayed behind to fix the final arrangements for the opening of *Queen* at the Royal.

Or that was what she said.

Whatever the real reason, Josh was glad she had stayed away.

Since they had split up he had studiously avoided contact with Jill unless other people were present. He felt disturbed just looking at her. It was no good, no good at all. Besides, he needed to be alone with his actors. Everything, now, depended on the rapport they all had with one another, the loyalty, the team spirit. That was why he had brought them all up north on the train, instead of by car, the way most companies traveled these days. On the train, tearing through the sunny fields of the south and the murk of the Midlands, the cast had made merry, Sir Harry explaining, "When I first began, we always traveled by train. Everywhere. Every actor in the business spent his Sundays in Crewe Station. Going from one job to another. The other six days you worked. Six hundred theatres in England in those days, how many now, no, don't tell me, it's too depressing. Of course, it's television. It astonishes me that people will leave their living rooms to see us, in the flesh. I mean, why should they bother?" The diesel train had lurched soundlessly on, and Sir Piers had replied, "Because we are in the flesh, we're real, and those people on the box are just shadows."

Everybody had agreed with that.

This cast, Josh thought, crowding into one of the hire-cars with Sir Piers and Sir Harry and Brigid Kelly, liked one another. And that was rubies beyond price. The weeks of rehearsal had gone astonishingly well. It was as if they all knew that Maggie was the problem and one problem was enough. Nobody had been difficult—yet! There had been a quiet seriousness about everybody during the last week of rehearsals, when Maggie had joined them, even paler than usual, full of Valium, he guessed, and determined to work, it seemed. He had not visited her at the clinic, at Jill's insistence, and he had been relieved not to, because he had the rehearsals to run, and they were exhausting, and he was no longer twenty-five years of age. Jill told him that Maggie was going to be all right, not to worry, to work round her, and this he had done, controlling his anxieties and hoping that Jill was right.

Even now he wasn't sure.

Maggie had given a good reading of the part in the week that he had her and, to his immense relief, she had come to the rehearsal knowing most of her lines. She had seemed relaxed and able to do what any competent actress could do, at that stage: be in the right place, say the right words in the right order.

Yet something was missing.

Josh stared out of the window of the car, at the green fields that had succeeded the streets of medieval York, and fretted. Maggie was a great actress but she was not, as yet, giving anything like a great performance. She was mechanical, inhibited. He had whispered this much to Jill, as they sat together through the final run-through in the Royal. "Be grateful, Josh," Jill had said. "Just be grateful she's up there at all."

Josh had wanted to ask more about Maggie's real condition but he had put off the question. Better he knew nothing of all that. Maggie was back with the play and she had to be treated and judged simply as another member of the company. He could not afford to work any other way. Sometimes, when he was giving Maggie private notes on her performance (and he had kept them to a minimum), Josh had felt an urge to ask her how she really felt, plus a sense of protectiveness so sexual as to be overpowering. Maggie had probably been attracting that all her life, he decided. She didn't need it. So, he had given his notes gently and encouragingly and gone back to his place and watched her rehearse and wondered if she would ever give the performance of which she was capable, the real queen, not the ghostlike genteel version she was showing up till now. Give her time, Jill had reassured him, she's been ill, remember. Give her time.

Time was something they had only two weeks of.

One week here—the new town of Wallingford was looming into view—and one week at Brighton, and then into town. Two weeks, and Jill Viner seemed to think it was something to be grateful for. He wondered again just how ill Maggie had really been.

Sir Harry viewed the high-rise towers of the new town, as if it might be Central Africa. "Just like New York but set in the Yorkshire wolds. How very strange it all is." He looked questioningly at Sir Piers. "Have you ever worked in this place before?"

Sir Harry was word-perfect as the prime minister and plainly leaving his best—and surprising—effects for the first night in London. Josh feared and yet looked forward to these moments.

Sir Piers stared gloomily at the vast new town, a vista of

deserted freeways and sparsely peopled shopping centers and empty, drab palazzos. "Does anybody *live* here? Place seems like the moon. Reminds me of H.G. Wells."

Sir Piers was getting the Russian very right indeed. The walk he had at last perfected and the rest of his characterization was falling into place; unstoppable, ruthless power was the quality he now projected. He had done a lot with his makeup—a heavy mustache and beetling brows—and promised to do more. Josh hoped he wouldn't overdo it, and made a mental note to watch the point.

"I've been here before," offered Brigid Kelly. "I did a week here with a sex comedy that never got into town. The audience was very nice to us."

Sir Harry asked, "Was the sex comedy a television spinoff?"

"Yes, it was," answered Brigid.

"That explains it," said Sir Harry. "Everybody knows those television people when they've done half a dozen performances. Somebody like Piers and meself, they wouldn't know us if they fell over us."

"Speak for yourself, old son," boomed Sir Piers. "I'm always getting stopped by people in the street."

"That's because you're always in a lot of rotten old movies." Sir Harry's reply was spirited. "They know your face because of good attendance in a load of rubbish. I have always been highly selective in my film roles, y'know."

"Nonsense, nobody asks him, m'dear." Sir Piers put a hand on Brigid Kelly's be-jeaned legs and left it there. "That's what he's so bitchy about. The movies need people who can move, not theatrical old things like him. They like the masculine actor, d'yer see?"

"Well, in that case they wouldn't want you," said Sir Harry, highly offended, "if they knew what some of us know, would they?"

"What on earth," exploded Sir Piers, "is the old darling on about, now?"

"*You* know, dear!"

"Look!" cried Brigid. "There's the theatre!"

"Good God," said Sir Piers.

"Is that thing a *theatre?*" asked Sir Harry.

The building looked, to Josh's eyes, rather like a large aircraft hangar. But he knew it had a magnificent apron stage, and no seat in the house was obscured by a pillar, since the roof was cantilevered. It was a modern theatre, like the National, and like the National paid for by public money. "It has a wonderful stage," said Brigid. "And they can hear you everywhere. The acoustics are terrific."

Brigid was developing marvelously, thought Josh. She had a natural stage presence, and she moved very well indeed. She had a clear, musical voice and an almost virginal quality, so beloved by audiences—a sort of inner purity. It only appeared on stage, which was the whole magic of it. Offstage Brigid looked like any other young actress: deliberately plain, no makeup, and fashionably scruffy.

Josh braced himself for the work that was to come. From tomorrow night *Queen* would be a reality. It would be seen in a theatre by living, breathing people.

Jill ought to be here.

It was her own fault she wasn't. He had asked her, hadn't he?

Josh felt a pang but he stifled it and said, "Well, here we are folks. All we have to do is knock 'em dead."

"I would say, at first impression," said Sir Harry, peering out at the vast expanse of stone on all sides, and the rare pedestrian, "that most of them are dead already."

THE Rolls, taking Maggie and Austin north, slid at a dignified seventy miles an hour along the M1. Maggie stared out at the land.

It was late summer and the leaves were still on the trees in the small green fields beyond the motorway. The few houses were small and the whole effect was patchwork. To anybody brought up in New England there was a reassuring similarity: the word was order. Maggie had been raised to admire order, and her life until Philip had been a testament to her upbringing. Until she had met him everything had proceeded in straight lines, like the motorway along which they drove. Their meeting had been, as Philip had remarked, like a road accident. Several people had been hurt, Philip's wife and children most of all. Then Philip fatally. Now, herself.

It all demonstrated the danger of living in a disordered, unplanned way.

Maggie stared out at the green fields and the small neat farmhouses.

She could not have done it any other way.

Austin stirred in his doze in the cushioned luxury of the Rolls. The driver had looked surprised at Austin's many questions about his working day, his family, his wages, and the way he voted. Austin always asked ordinary people questions. It was part of his attitude toward his work. Maggie had been with him the day before when he bought a new Italian safari suit (it was still very humid in London) from the Via Veneto, a King's Road boutique, leaving the delighted proprietor his own St. Laurent sweatshirt for a keepsake. Austin went around, Maggie thought, being a belligerent little cock-sparrow, when he was actually a linnet, with a talent for song.

For Austin was going to be very, very good.

Maggie wished she could say the same for herself.

The trouble was, the Valium was getting in the way. It relaxed her, as the doctor had said it would, but it blurred everything, brought everything *down*, and there was no kick of raw emotion anywhere in the work she was doing in *Queen*. She knew it and she guessed Josh Williams knew it. He had been very kind to her, cut his notes down to a minimum, and never once asked her how she felt, for which she was grateful.

If he had asked, she could not have told him. Numb, she supposed, was the nearest she could get.

The Irish doctor at the expensive and private Harley Street clinic had been most understanding. Realizing quickly that she had never regularly been in the hands of psychiatrists, he had determined to keep her away from them if he could and had treated her as he would any patient suffering from intolerable stress: with mild sedative drugs and rest. He told her that people in modern society had forgotten how to grieve—they were simply not allowed the time or occasion to do it—and that was a deep emotional loss. The rending of garments, he had explained, in his humorous Irish voice (he was fiftyish, gray hair, well-suited), had something to be said for it. So had the weeping and wailing. So had the wake. Maggie had been denied this easement. She had been expected to mourn privately and at no point show her distress. The Puritans considered that bad manners and she was plainly in the Puritan tradition, despite her profession. So, she had broken down. And what else, in the name of God, was she supposed to do? She loved the man and he was gone. His own mother had wept for days at his father's wake and so had he. He'd got drunk as well and it had helped. What did she think she was made of, ice?

"Some people think I am." She smiled, wanly.

He had patted her hand. "Not you. And you're going to rest here a week, and then we'll see."

"Can I at least learn my lines?"

"After a couple of days."

"You think I can go back and do the play?"

He shook his head, smiling. "Well, of course you can. If you want to. You're not dying. But rest first and then we'll see, all right?" He looked at her shrewdly. "This Jill Viner who brought you. She's keen to keep you in the play and so am I because I'm coming to the first night. But, if you don't feel up to it, then you

294

don't do it. The decision's yours. The world won't come to an end if you don't."

At those wise words Maggie had begun to feel better. The week had passed in a haze of drugged sleep, and the urge to cry had altogether gone by the end of it. Her only visitor (once a day, regularly for thirty minutes) had been Jill, who did not pressure her either (probably, she thought, on the doctor's instructions) but simply sat at the bedside and held her hand and told her how everybody was: that Sir Harry had perfected his part until he hardly needed to move at all; that Sir Piers now resembled Oscar Homolka; that Austin had tried to improvise some of his scenes in the manner of the Actors' Studio, but that both Sir Harry and Sir Piers had been so offended at this departure from the sacred tradition of English theatre that even he had given up; that Tommi Traceham's set and costumes were going to win her an award; that Maggie would love the queen's gown when she saw it.

That was, Jill had said gently, if she wanted to come back to the company. It was her decision and nobody would be pushing her, in any way. Maggie should sleep on it a couple of days more. Maggie had slept her dreamless sleep for one night, had awakened calm and refreshed, and told Jill on her next visit: Yes. And could she have a copy of the script? Jill had asked the doctor, and he had said, sure, she can, and Maggie had slowly, calmly begun to learn her lines. By the time she came out of the clinic (she had spent ten days there altogether) she felt weak and dull but she knew that she would not become hysterical again.

Whether she would ever give a good performance, as she explained to Jill, was another thing. She thought she would not, inside the short rehearsal time left to her. Now she was sure she would not. The firepower wasn't there. She had told Jill as much.

"So long as *you're* there I won't worry. The performance will come." Jill had been desperately relieved she was doing it at all, and it showed.

Maggie had said, sitting in the Salisbury, a tonic water in front of her, "Shall I tell Josh, or will you? I mean, about my not expecting to do it better than *this*. The poor man must be worried sick."

Jill had looked over at Josh, standing with his actors at the bar, laughing and apparently relaxed and happy. "I don't talk to Josh so much these days."

"No?" Maggie had been told there was something between them and had wondered at it. Jill certainly looked pale, and some of her usual abundant energy seemed to be missing. "Did you used to, I mean . . . ?"

"We've been lovers. We split up."

"No! Oh, I am sorry." Maggie was. The idea of anybody leaving anybody they might love struck her to the heart, at that moment.

Jill shrugged. "It's probably for the best, Maggie. I suppose I'm too possessive and I scared him off."

"No chance of it being on again?"

Jill had shaken her head. "None, I'd say. Josh has his sort of bachelor way of life and a woman's a complication to him." Jill had seemed moved, and Maggie had touched her hand in sympathy (after all, Jill had been very kind to her) but Jill had withdrawn her hand quickly and said, "I need another drink. Let me get you another of those tonics, and not a word to anybody in the company about Josh and me. I don't think anybody knows."

Jill didn't want pity and Maggie thought she understood that. Jill was wrong, however, in thinking nobody in the cast knew anything about Josh and herself. According to Austin, everybody knew. Max Heston was the one who had told him, he said, but he had guessed anyway. He thought Jill and Josh would be all right for each other. His reasons were psychoanalytical, as usual. "Look, one's an extrovert—Jill—a pushy lady, on the make, sexy, not too scrupulous, right? The other—Josh—he's thoughtful, kindly, self-contained. He's the only type of guy who could stand her. An extrovert like herself, they'd tear each other to pieces in a month."

"What about me?" Maggie had asked Austin, smiling.

He had touched her face very gently. "Maggie, you're a really nice Wasp girl under all that celebrity, sex, and success. You're innocent. You need some dude who could show you a good time but stop you getting hurt, know what I mean?"

Maggie had laughed. "You're going to say that dude is you?"

Austin had done his Bogart impression. "Who else, sister?"

Maggie had kissed him. "Austin, I love you."

"Me too." He hadn't laughed.

THE driver turned around. They had been off the motorway for some time now, and a bleak vista of brick and stone had sprung up, surrounding them as they drove into the heart of it. "Here we are, folks," he said.

Austin woke up and stared blearily out of the window.

"Jesus, where's this, Brasília?" he enquired.

SIR Piers was very impressed with his dressing room. Standing in it on the first night at Wallingford he boomed, "This may be Socialist architecture, but at least I have as good a seat as the feller watching me in the theatre."

"Yes," said Sir Harry. "And if they had *their* way, dear, you'd be paid the same money and that would never do, would it?"

"I dunno," said Sir Piers, who liked to think of himself as a liberal. "No reason why we shouldn't all be paid the same, in a perfect society, is there?"

"None at all," replied Sir Harry. "The trouble is, nobody's invented it yet, dear."

"I dunno." Sir Piers climbed into the thick, dark green suit he was to wear as the Russian, fussed over by his young dresser, on whom Sir Harry cast an appreciative eye. "There's something to be said for coming out here to the people and giving them something

297

worthwhile. Y'know what Clara Butt said. You can't live on fish and chips all your life."

"But they do, dear," said Sir Harry. "They like fish and chips. They won't understand a word of the play. The only reason we're here is because Jill Viner has got us a subsidy, we're being underwritten by the government, the dear fuddy-duddy old Arts Council, silly old things like you, who think everybody's equal, everybody's the same. We ought to be giving them *Getting Gertie's Garter*. They'd like that a lot better than our thing."

"You know"—Sir Piers carefully glued on his mustache in the dressing-room mirror—"you're a terrible old snob."

"We call ourselves elitists now, dear." Sir Harry was ready to go, dressed in his elegant morning suit from Huntsman ("Well, that's where the prime minister would *go*, isn't it?" he had asked Tommi Traceham). He was always ready half an hour early. "Gets you used to the feel of the thing, don'tcher see?" he had asked Josh, who was rushing around his cast, wishing them good luck and giving them last-minute notes. "Tell them it doesn't matter what happens here," Sir Harry had instructed him. "Nobody who matters a damn is going to see it."

Josh knew that was true, anyway.

He was glad of it. It gave him another week before Brighton, where some people of influence would be bound to see it. Their words would percolate to London, only fifty miles away, and influence a lot of other people, possibly including critics. He had seven days in this outlandish place and he had to make them count. He coughed and knocked on Maggie's dressing-room door. "It's Josh, darling."

"Come in, Josh, it's open."

Maggie wore the queen's red velvet gown. Josh hadn't seen her in it before: it hadn't been ready for the dress rehearsal (Maggie being in the clinic had held up the fittings) and her beauty stopped the usual cheap words of encouragement he had ready.

Tommi Traceham held the silver tiara over her golden head. It looked like the real thing. "What do you think, Josh?"

"Beautiful. Absolutely knockout, Tommi. Maggie, you look great."

Maggie nodded, biting her lip. "I only hope I do justice to it, Josh. I haven't till now."

"The performance is coming, love," Josh babbled, falling back on tradition: always encourage actors at curtain-time, it's too late to do anything else. "Just go out there, take it nice and slow. Let them hear the words. Don't go for the big moments, not tonight. We have two weeks before town. There's time."

Shut up, Josh told himself. The more you say the worse it sounds.

He kissed Maggie on her cool, alabaster cheek, and said, "Be lucky, love," and said, "Tommi darling, wonderful," to Tommi, and let himself out into the corridor. He was surprised to find that he was sweating. His nerves were not good, he was sleeping badly, and he was missing Jill, in and out of bed. That was the trouble, he told himself, standing undecided whether to wish the sirs good luck or not.

He decided not to. They would be fine. What else? Ah, yes, Brigid Kelly.

Josh opened Brigid's door with just a light preliminary tap. Max and Brigid were kissing and Max's right hand was caressing Brigid's left nipple, which was visibly erect under her wrap. She turned away quickly and Josh didn't say "Sorry" but fixed a basilisk eye on Max.

"I have to go." Max didn't look embarrassed. "Things to do."

"I would have thought so," said Josh, icily.

Max didn't look away. He smiled to himself and left, in no great hurry. I think I made a mistake, decided Josh, with that young man.

"Sorry about that, Josh." Brigid was scrambling out of her

wrap, skimpily attired now in tiny panties. A wisp of red-gold pubic hair showed above the pants. She had a very white Irish skin and with her red hair and china-blue eyes, and those tits, Josh could see what Max saw in her. "Max only popped in to wish me luck." She pulled her stage dress over her head.

"He had a comprehensive way of doing it."

Brigid laughed, glad to get the conversation on to a sexual level. There, any woman was equal to any man. "Sir Harry says opera singers are always having it off before their performances to steady their nerves." She smiled at him provocatively. She was without doubt going to go a long way.

"Never heard that before," said Josh, who had. "Remember, nice and easy, no hurry, you're going to be good." I'm wasting my breath, he thought, she knows that without me telling her. She's really talented, she doesn't need praise; it's water off a duck's back. He kissed her cheek. "Be lucky!"

Brigid nodded, looking at herself over his shoulder in the long mirror. "Thank you, Josh, darling."

She had very good breasts. Not as full as Jill's but nicely shaped. He missed Jill's breasts.

None of that. He had a job to do.

Josh hurried backstage. Max and Bobbi and Billy were bustling around, although the backstage work was easy on *Queen*, one set and a revolve. Bobbi was on the book, a veteran of a thousand soft prompts, to actors famous or unknown, alive or dead, and all one to her. She bobbed her head in his direction and said, "No problems, Josh. Maggie might be slow but I think she has the words."

It's all she has got, Josh almost said, but didn't.

He called to Max, "Everything all right backstage?"

"It is as far as I'm concerned. But you'd better talk to Ernie."

Ernie was their carpenter. He had traveled north by truck with the revolve set, a contraption weighing twelve hundred

300

pounds, made of wood, steel and cloth to the value of four thousand pounds, sterling. Ernie was very old, nobody knew how old, a theatre craftsman all his life, and proud of it. His cloth cap looked as if it had been nailed to his head, and his voice was undiluted Cockney.

"Trouble?" Josh asked, anxiously.

"You wouldn't fackin' nob it, guv'nor." Ernie touched the splendid cap with a gnarled forefinger. "There's a right fackin' Berk 'ere calls himself a fackin' shop steward, says I 'ave no right to do nothink else wiv the revolve than fackin' advise."

Max translated. "Union rules are vague here. Ernie can advise and help erect or just advise."

"Where *is* this right Berk then?" asked Josh, smiling.

"If yer talkin' to me I take exception." The speaker was a thickset man of thirty with a spotty face and greasy hair. He seemed aggrieved but not at Josh particularly: probably, Josh decided, at life. Josh knew him as Mr. Stribling. He knew the power of the Mr. Striblings of the theatrical world. He had not been at the strike-happy National for nothing.

"No offense meant, old son." He smiled. "I didn't know you were the person Ernie was talking about."

"*Advise?*" Ernie spat tobacco juice expertly into a sawdust bucket. "My fackin' arse. I near enough built that fackin' revolve. Your heavy-handed fackin' twats 'ere will make fackin' sawdust if they try to put it up."

"They're properly qualified stagehands and electricians, brother," said Mr. Stribling, impassively.

"A load o' fackin' wankers," said Ernie, "what I seem of 'em. They couldn't erect theirselves a fackin' erection, never mind erect that fackin' revolve!"

"I take exception to that an' all," said Mr. Stribling. "The rule book is explicit on this matter, brother."

"No, it fackin' ain't," said Ernie. "An' even if it fackin' is, you couldn't put the fackin' thing up, save yer fackin' life, yer big Berk."

"I'll be reporting your conduct, brother," said Mr. Stribling. He didn't meet many like Ernie in his daily rounds, guessed Josh. The backstage men had been underpaid and overworked when he was a young man in the theatre, twenty years ago. Now the boot was on the other foot. In the old days the actors and producers had trodden on them. They were kicking back. It was the old English story but very tiresome. Josh, however, knew the rules of the dance.

"How much remains to be done?" he asked.

"Needs knockin' into fackin' place, thass all," supplied Ernie. "Take me three, four minutes. Take this Berk 'ere and his wankers all fackin' night and even then it won't fackin' *revolve*, will it?"

Mr. Stribling inhaled. "You're in deep trouble, brother," he informed Ernie. "Definite noncooperation on your part. Definite."

"Take your fackin' cooperation," said Ernie, without raising his voice, "and stick it up your fackin' arse, you big twat."

"Abusive language won't get you far, brother. I seen men lose their union ticket for less than what you've done tonight."

"An' shove that up your arse as well," declared Ernie, and spat in the sawdust bucket again. Josh took his arm and led him away a few yards, as Mr. Stribling declared in a loud voice, "That's it! All work stops on this production! It's a dispute, everybody out!"

"Look," said Josh to Ernie. "Shut up. Not another word. I have to reason with this idiot or we'll have no show."

"He's fackin'—" began Ernie.

"I know what he *is*," said Josh. "You do what I say. No matter what I say. All right?"

Ernie contemplated the world and found it wanting. His nod was almost nonexistent: but it was there. He contented himself with "Fackin' norf-country, swede-bashing Berkshires."

Josh left him and turned to Mr. Stribling, who was still looking extremely affronted. "Look here, Mr. Stribling," he began.

"You and I want the same thing, this show to go on—"

"I don't care whether it goes on or not, Mr. Williams. I want an apology from that man there. And unless he gives me one the show won't open. And . . ." Mr. Stribling was very red and very angry. "That man there is not to touch that revolve or I call my men out."

Ernie was ready to shout at that, but he got no further than *fackin'* and Josh interrupted him, "Ernie, we have to agree. There's no point in doing anything else. You know that as well as I do."

"Who runs this fackin' country?" Ernie demanded.

"The unions do, mate," said Mr. Stribling. "An' you owe them your wage packet."

"I had a wage packet afore the Unions," said Ernie stoutly.

"Yeah, and what was in it, brother?" asked Mr. Stribling.

"Fack all," said Ernie, "but I didden 'ave to apologize to no fackin' pricks like what you are."

"That's the nearest you're going to get, Mr. Stribling," Josh said, low.

Mr. Stribling considered the matter, glaring at Ernie, who averted his eyes and spat once again, a squirt of tobacco juice, into the sawdust bucket. "Awright," he said, at last, "but the man advises. He doesn't touch. Is that understood?"

"Yes, it is," said Josh. "Curtain-up in ten minutes. Can we do it?"

"Certainly we can do it," said Mr. Stribling. "That's not the point, is it?"

"Gawd blimey ole riley!" said Ernie. "Let's go and fackin' do it then!"

Reluctantly, Mr. Stribling led the way. Josh followed and watched, as under Ernie's hoarse and desperate instructions the revolve containing the throne was agonizingly and slowly set in position by Mr. Stribling's stagehands. Tommi Traceham looked on in total calm ("I only designed the bloody thing, dear!"), but eventually Ernie declared himself satisfied. Josh glanced at his watch. It was three minutes to curtain-up. "Thank you for your cooperation, Mr. Stribling," he said.

"That's perfectly all right," said Mr. Stribling. "All some people 'ave to do is work to the union rule book."

Ernie put a fresh plug of tobacco in his mouth. "What he needs," he told Josh, "is a firework up his jaxy."

Josh darted around the front-of-house and found the house manager cheerful, in rusty black dinner jacket, in the foyer. The clientele's dress was not so formal. Most wore bomber jackets and denim and scarves. Josh wondered what, if anything, they would make of *Queen*. "We're three parts full," the house manager informed Josh. "Nearly as good a house as we had for *No Sex on Sundays* last winter." He wished Josh good luck and, upon learning there had been trouble with the backstage crew, simply commented, "I told you they were bolshie, didn't I, Mr. Williams?"

The two-minute buzzer went, and Josh walked into the theatre, and stood at the back. *Queen* wasn't his anymore. It belonged to the actors from now on. He felt a wave of sadness but quickly repressed it.

There was Maggie. He had to remember that.

He stood and watched the curtain rise.

VERCEK sat and watched avidly from his seat on the aisle of the darkened theatre. He had made his way north from London by a succession of trains and buses—each stage shorter than the last, as was classic if you thought you were being followed and wanted to cover your tracks. He had reached Wallingford only minutes before the performance was due to begin. Wallingford surprised him (the looming, hangarlike theatre, the vast soulless tower blocks) but not because he had seen nothing like it before. He had, often. It was Socialist architecture, the Soviet Union was full of it. He'd seen towns very like Wallingford in Poland and East Germany and Czechoslovakia. At the time he had not thought them as deadly as he did now. Now, they were of a piece with the nightmare times, and he realized, looking at the vista of gray slab-housing, how far the disease had gone in England, and it troubled him. The workers, too, who had left their television sets to come and see his play: they didn't look so very different, to his eyes, from the people who had trudged through the snow to see his early student productions in Moscow. Better fed, of course. Better dressed and every one of them still with a vote. He looked around him: these were not learned or even educated people, that much was obvious. They had the cheerful physicality of peasants and workers everywhere. What could they possibly see in *Queen*? What committee of nameless apparatchiks had thought to build a magnificent theatre like this in which to show it to them? Vercek was much puzzled by that thought, but he put it out of his mind, as the curtain slowly rose.

Maggie sat there, on the throne, clad in the red velvet gown he had attempted to veto, and on her head was the glittering tiara that he had hoped for. Larger, perhaps, than it should have been, but an improvement on the full crown of the Traceham woman's early sketches. Vercek breathed in. So far, the production values were good. The backcloth of dark drapes enhanced the ivory of the revolve and the lighting plot seemed to him excellent. Tears came unbidden to his eyes. He had waited a long time for this. The other plays, the true ones, mostly unproduced but simply read to small groups in freezingly cold apartment blocks in the students' quarter in the arctic city, had taken him finally into the interrogation rooms. At first his questioners had been playful and reassuring. He was, of course, a guest of the motherland, a Finn anyway by birth, and as such they expected him to see things from a different, if incorrect angle. That was to be expected, after all. The Finns had a reputation for being difficult. They did not mention his Jewishness. He had become a known establishment writer and that was something, they considered, that outweighed all else. They had smiled and pulled on their Western cigarettes and offered him genuine whiskey and tried to cajole him out of his indignation. They had not wanted to think of him as *dissidenty* because he had such an excellent record, and his work for Socialist drama had been exemplary, quite correct in every way. They were prepared to overlook his contact with the antisocial elements with whom he had been associating, provided, naturally, that he gave them some facts, some names, some reports of conversations, and so on, most of which, again naturally, they knew already. Their smiles had been broader as they opened their notebooks and held their English ballpoint pens in readiness. His silence had saddened them, they said, closing the notebooks with a snap, but he had to realize he was in serious trouble. *Dissidenty* was not for such as him, a comrade with an excellent reputation who had been allowed to travel extensively in the other Socialist countries and to spend a particularly long period in his own birth-country, Finland. The establishment had been good to him, but his behavior was straining everybody's patience. He must take care. They would review his case in six months, or before, if necessary. He was free to go, but naturally his special work-status was ended, as of that moment. Suitable proletarian employment would be arranged for him, where he might reflect on the ways in which he had erred: the printing of *dissidenty* plays was forbidden and he knew that. When he gave up his Finnish nationality he took on a responsibility to his new motherland. There were other complications in his case: they meant his Jewishness. He had let the motherland down and he must accept the consequences. For a while he must live as the people lived, and ponder his behavior.

The suitable proletarian employment had been in a public lavatory on the subway.

When he had protested to his friends in the Writers' Guild they had smiled and said, "You haven't lost your card. You still have your apartment. Be grateful. They are playing with you. It's a joke they are having with you. Six weeks, a month, it will be over. Then appeal. And you'll see. All will be well. Be patient."

Vercek had not appealed. That was when he had started to write the famous little pieces, innocent satires on the stream of humanity that passed in and out of the pissoir in the course of one day. *Visits*, he had called it. It had been printed in *samizdat* broadsheets everywhere, and had made a lot of people laugh.

Somebody had talked and the nightmare had begun.

Vercek shuddered and brought himself back to the present. His play was on. That was what mattered.

Maggie was in a scene with the prime minister. The old man, Sir Harry, was an excellent actor of the old classical school and much as Vercek had seen the prime minister when he was writing the play. There were few actors of such style and class in his early seminars in Moscow. Russian actors used the voice a lot, they had power, but this old man had subtlety. One thing puzzled Vercek. Why had he waited, on entering, and simply smiled at the audience? Had he been expecting a round of applause? Perhaps. Anyway, he had not got one, and a good thing too. This was not the West End of London, where the cult of personality extended even to the actors.

It was a pity, but these people sitting watching the play had no influence at all. *Queen* had to be seen by the influential, the powerful, admittedly in their relaxed moments, to have been worth the sweat, the terror, the hidden manuscript in the snow, the house searches, the cells, the punishing work, and the soulless uncaring whether you lived or died in the vast penal settlements in the snow.

This play had been written in his own blood.

Vercek leaned forward. There was something wrong with the queen.

Vercek pondered: It was not that the actress was doing it badly. It was as if she did not understand the part at all. As if

307

nobody had said to her: This is the moment when you realize that you are the last of your line, that it has all been for nothing, all, *all* of it. Somebody, quite simply, had not told her who she *was*.

Josh Williams was the director. He should have done it.

The woman was beautiful. But she was simply *saying the words*.

Vercek sat in deep gloom throughout the rest of the play.

Everything was right, except the queen: and the queen was the centerpiece of the entire drama. He knew only a little of the actress's reputation, but the word about her had been good. He considered, the maimed hand tapping the program irritably. Possibly she was ill. It was the only explanation.

Vercek did not leave his seat at the interval. He did not think it likely that anybody was watching him but one never knew. The day after the postcard arrived, he had left his lodgings off the North End Road and had been sure he was followed much of the way, but tolerably certain he had eluded his tail in his circuitous three-hour flight. He was now holed up in a bed-sitter in Camden Town. His meetings with Kristos had been a luxury and could not last: he should have known that. Now he spoke to nobody, passing his days in writing his journal. His money was low but the advance royalties from *Queen* had helped and if it was a success he might go to live in America. Vercek no longer considered Europe safe. His contact in Whitehall (offhand, distant as only the English could be now that his usefulness was over) had told him that was only possible with money. *Queen* might give him that money. The actors were worried, he thought wryly, listening to the audience round him discussing the play, but only their reputations rode on it. Very probably his life did.

Around Vercek the audience was not impressed by *Queen*. They found it too full of long speeches, mostly about politics (in which, to Vercek's despair, they seemed totally uninterested) and compared it unfavorably with many of the other offerings of the season, most of them sex comedies. They seemed unsure whether the queen, as depicted on the stage, was their queen or not. Opinion was divided on it. They liked the queen's dress though, and wished for more action and a few laughs. They made no comment about Maggie's very slight American accent, possibly because, Vercek thought, they were so used to American accents on television. It was, anyway, very slight. Vercek felt something close to despair, and wished once again that he was a film-maker or a novelist, somebody who could reach a vast popular market rather than a disciple of an art that could speak only to a large roomful of people at a time. The English, he thought, they are in their biggest political crisis since their civil war and they don't know it.

He sat through the second half of the play in ever-deepening gloom. The queen was no better. He had not intended to make his presence known. One never knew. By the time of his third arrest he had become as clever at concealing his movements as he was now: and yet they had found him, crouching in the false wall in the freezing attic. Still, he would have to take the risk. He would have to talk to Josh Williams.

The audience filed out, after desultorily applauding the play, and no "God Save the Queen," was played, a symbol of the nation's lack of belief in itself, thought Vercek. He wondered if the English cared about anything except their football pools and their beer. He had talked much to Kristos about that. Kristos had said they had been on top of the heap so long they couldn't imagine being on the bottom. As a Finn and a Greek, they could understand. Only history, Vercek had said, could teach them: *and history to the defeated,* Vercek had added, *may say alas but cannot help nor pardon.* Auden, he had added, kindly. Kristos had looked respectful. Obviously this Onden was a great poet. The lines were embedded in *Queen*—spoken by the prime minister—but nobody in the audience had noticed them.

Feeling profoundly gloomy, Vercek made his way round to

the stage door and asked for Josh Williams. He could not give his name and, on being pressed by the stage-doorkeeper, finally declared that it was Smith.

JOSH Williams was not too pleased to see Vercek but he hid the fact under a warm welcome and the offer of a glass of white wine in the production office backstage. Only Max was in when Vercek arrived, and Josh had already been on his rounds, reassuring everybody, except Maggie, that it had gone extremely well for a first night to an audience not exactly in tune with a quality play like this, telling them to remember that the week in Wallingford was a week of paid rehearsal and they were not to expect huzzas or bouquets here.

The reactions of his cast had been typical. "They've never heard of either one," declared Sir Harry. "You'd think none of them had ever been in a theatre before, but you have to remember Irving died only fifty miles from here." Sir Harry had peeled off his crepe sideburns and added, " 'My dear boy, I am home.' His last words." He sighed. "Do you think they knew me? There was nothing at my entrance."

Josh said, "I wasn't terribly unhappy about that."

"Weren't you?" mused Sir Harry, taking off his wing collar. "I was, dear boy."

"I decided to up the volume a bit," boomed Sir Piers, "when I felt their attention wandering. Think it helped?"

"Not much, dear," opined Sir Harry. "Noise never helps."

"That wasn't noise, you old faggot, that was projection."

"Sounded like noise to me, dear, and I was there. I couldn't hear myself think for it. Quite disorientating. We all know you pretend to be ever so masculine and bull-like, but there is a limit."

"What the hell d'yer mean, *pretend?*" roared Sir Piers.

Sir Harry smiled.

310

AUSTIN Ames was being quite marvelous, Josh thought. His basic sense of the part was superb. "Nice, Austin," he said. "Tell me why you do it so softly."

"Softly?" asked Austin, deeply hurt.

"You know what I mean." Josh smiled. He wanted more aggression from Austin: he felt it was there for the asking.

Said Austin hotly, "I have based this man's walk, stance, and motivation on the president himself. I talked to him. I looked at him. In Washington, a couple of months ago. This man is him. Josh, you want an actor's performance?" Austin took a breath. He walked, cockily erect, yet modest, a facsimile of the president. He spoke Vercek's words: *"Ma'am, you have thrown out the United States Army, or anyway your new government has. What am I to do, except go? Your people think that Providence will protect them because their government, their welfare government, has been protecting them for fifty years. It won't. We were the Providence. The United States of America was the Providence. It protected Europe. It protected you, Ma'am, and your Sceptred Isle. Now you tell us to go. What can I do but go?"*

Austin lifted his eyes earnestly from the page. "The key word? 'Providence.' Right? 'Providence.' It's a religious word. He's a religious guy. I've been thinking about that a lot, Josh. It's the key word, isn't it?"

Josh said, "Is it? I would have thought perhaps yes. But surely that last sentence is the one you lean on."

Austin nodded. "Hey! That's *right!*"

"Well, so long as you're happy." Josh was not having as bad a time with Austin as he'd feared. What Austin needed, like all actors, was firm reassurance. Austin had, the first week in rehearsals, come to him with a totally rewritten second act. How he had found time to do it Josh couldn't think. It was full of clichés culled from every play Austin had ever seen or performed in. There had been a noisy discussion, because some of Austin's points were good. Josh had pondered Austin's scrawled pages of penciled script (with many crossings-out and balloons of second thoughts), had given

311

him a large vodka, and sent him on his way, promising to look at the rewrites and let Austin have his thoughts. Austin had kept his dignity. Neither of them had referred to the rewrites again. Austin had settled down to the script as written and was working very well. He had become used, now he was a star, to changing anything he wanted to, anytime he felt like it. Josh was slowly getting him unused to it, teaching him to be an *actor* again, an interpreter, not a creator. He was the better for it.

Now, all Josh needed to do for Brigid Kelly was kiss her cheek and say, "You get better and better, keep it up," and get out of her dressing room before she took *all* her clothes off. He felt a renewed pang of jealousy for Max Heston. Josh realized that always taking off her clothes when he was in the dressing room was a playful tease but it didn't make things easier. He must not respond to it because when he did have to utter a note of criticism, sex must not rear its head, even in jokey form. Brigid Kelly was a very clever young lady.

Maggie he had left until last, and was on his way to her dressing room when the stage-doorkeeper told him a Mr. Smith was asking for him. When Smith turned into Vercek (he had followed the stage-doorkeeper along the backstage corridor) Josh had felt irritability but concealed it with a smile. Vercek was the author, he was entitled to be here. But why hadn't they heard from him during rehearsals? He could have been useful at the early stages. Over the white wine (and conscious of the presence of Max Heston) he listened to Vercek's criticisms. They were reasonable enough. He simply didn't want to hear them at that moment.

"First, the thing that is most wrong is the queen. You must know this. She is walking through the performance like a zombie. I am sure you must know this, Mr. Williams."

Josh said, "I think I know what you're getting at, Mr. Vercek."

"Vercek only, please. I have many notes about small aspects of the play. I still think the red velvet is wrong. I still think your

312

players are not yet an ensemble. I believe they are all playing for themselves."

"English actors tend to do that," said Josh. "They weren't brought up in the ensemble school. They are private-enterprise actors. They know a bad performance will be held against them personally, not the group or the director, but *them*. So naturally—"

"This is incorrect," snapped Vercek. "But I am not concerned with it, Mr. Williams. I have only two questions for you. One, are you aware of the problems of the actress playing the queen? Two, do you intend to put this defect right before you open in London?"

Josh considered telling Vercek what had happened to Maggie, but decided against it. Plainly, his paranoia, for whatever reason, was well advanced, and reassurance was the best course. Besides, the fellow was right.

"Yes," Josh replied, "to both questions."

Vercek nodded. "That is a correct decision. I will say good-bye then and see you in London, hopefully on the first night." And he bowed stiffly, turned, and walked along the corridor. By the time Josh had put down his glass of wine, and followed him to the stage door, he was gone, swallowed up in the dark night of the new town.

JOSH decided he would not talk to Maggie about her performance that evening. He would let it ride and see what happened. The reason he came to that decision was because Jill telephoned from London to ask him how it had all gone.

"It was all right, Jill. Much as we expected."

Josh tried not to think of Jill's laugh and her merry eyes, now dark with a certain dull sadness, he knew. He added, "Before you ask, Maggie didn't *offer*. She knew her lines, that was all."

Jill said slowly, "Never mind that, Josh. So long as she's there we have the chance of a hit. Without her, we're dead. Remember that."

Did she think he was new in the theatre, or what?

"I'll have to talk to her sooner or later, Jill. I can't take her into London with this performance. If I do, she'll get murdered by the critics and so will the play."

Jill cut in. "Where are you speaking from?"

"My room in the hotel. Nobody can hear anything."

"Good." Jill sighed with obvious relief. "Is the hotel in the new town?"

"No, it isn't, it's five miles outside. Yorkshire stone and old oak beams, and open fireplaces."

There was a long pause. "Josh, I wish I was with you."

"No, you don't," said Josh harshly. "You only think you do. All you care about is *Queen* and all I care about is *Queen*. If we stay apart, it has a chance. Together, it sinks like a stone."

He wondered if that was true. Probably.

Jill seemed to be having trouble with her voice. He hoped she wasn't crying. That was all he needed, at that moment, nursing a total turkey. It would never survive the performance Maggie was giving, face it, it wouldn't run a week. Josh felt cold, just thinking about it.

"I'm sorry you feel like that about us, Josh."

"Well, I do. And, if you think about it, so do you."

A long pause. "I don't, you know."

It was said Jill never cried. It seemed to Josh she was crying now.

Bloody, bloody hell. Didn't the woman know what he was facing up here?

"Look," he said icily. "It's no good either of us getting upset. I have problems with Maggie. I also had a visit from Vercek."

That startled her, as he knew it would. "Vercek, is he there?"

"No, he's gone."

"What did he say? Where's he *been?*"

"No idea where he's been and I care less. What he said was what we're saying. Maggie is going to sink us." Josh felt black

314

despair overcome him. A decision had to be taken, and now was as good a time as any. Now was the only time. "Jill, I want to recast."

A long silence.

"You don't mean that."

No tears in the voice now, he noted. All of a sudden, no tears in the voice.

"I wish I didn't but she'll never do it."

"Josh, we *can't* recast—"

"Let me finish, please. Unless we recast the queen, the play sinks. Since the curtain came down I've been fooling myself I could do something with it, but it's no good, it's finished, kaput, over." There was no reply to that, and it irritated him (did the woman think he *was* fooling?), and so he added, "Like us," and was sorry the moment he said it.

Oh, shit. Let it go. Something had to get through to Jill.

Something did. Her voice was suddenly sharp and hard. "Josh, can you hear me?"

"I can hear you."

"Listen carefully. These are your instructions."

"My instructions?"

"Yes. Unless you decide to go."

"Go where?"

"Leave the show. Your contract is with me. With Queen Productions. I hold majority shares. I can ask you to go. I can fire you."

"Oh, really?"

"Yes, really. And I will if you don't do as I tell you." Her voice was very cutting indeed. Josh wondered if he liked it better than the tears. He decided he liked neither.

"And just what are you telling me to do?"

"Give Maggie whatever notes you like but mainly wait. Give her time to play herself into the part."

"She's never going to do it." Josh wondered why he wasn't shouting. "Never."

315

"Just the same. Under no circumstances do anything until we open in Brighton. Nothing, Josh, do you hear me?"

"I hear you." Josh bit the words off sharply. "Anything else?"

"Yes. I'll come to Brighton, and I'll decide what we do."

"You will? All by yourself?"

"Yes, all by myself."

"And if Maggie is still hopeless?"

"I'll take the play off."

"Just like that?"

"Just like that. I owe that much to the angels. At least they get some of their money back."

She sounded as if she meant it. All that work, and now this. "You owe the cast something, too! You owe me something! I want to recast Maggie now! Get another actress while there's time!"

"Like who?"

Josh said, "Vanessa Redgrave, Joan Plowright, Eileen Atkins."

"One's in a play opening next week, one's in rehearsals, and one's in a movie."

She had done her homework. As ever.

"Give me time. I'll think of somebody."

"No. It's Maggie or we close. I mean it."

He could hear that she did. He said, finally, "It will ruin Maggie's career if we go in on this performance."

"I won't take it in if she's bad, I've already said so."

Josh tried one last time. Deliberately lowering his voice he half whispered, "Jill, why don't you get on a train and come up here tomorrow? We can talk and you can see exactly what's happening. I don't want to alarm you too much, love, but it's hopeless, really it is." He waited, and when she didn't reply, "It would give us a chance to talk. I mean the two of us, personally."

He thought, You bastard. And he also thought, I'm right.

After a long pause Jill's voice, cold and distant. "Josh, the only reason I didn't come up—and I should have, I'm the producer, after all—was because I couldn't bear to be near you because I really love

316

you so much." There was a pause, then: "Obviously, I was a fool. I should be there. But I'm not coming up to screw with you and then change my mind and I think you are a shit, Josh, even to hint at it." Josh felt nothing but growing dull rage, at her, at Maggie, at *Queen*, at himself. "So please obey my instructions and I'll see you in Brighton in one week. Good-bye."

The line went dead and Josh slowly replaced the receiver.

He felt worse than at any time since Alison died.

MAGGIE looked up, surprised, as Josh put his head round her hotel-room door. She was dressed only in a slip, with a thin cotton wrap over it. Her hair hung loosely over her shoulders and she looked tired. A small bottle of pills was in her hand. She gestured for Josh to come in. "Just taking my nightly oblivion," she said apologetically. What a really nice, sweet-natured girl, Josh thought. What a difference from Jill, with her independent ways and her peremptory orders. Josh smarted at the recollection. Telling him she'd sack him. That would be the day. "I know it's late, but can I bother you for a moment, Maggie?"

Maggie gestured to a chintz-covered chair. "Sit down. Can I get you a drink?"

"Are you having one?" Josh sat, feeling better already. How nice it was for somebody to smile at him, some *woman* to smile at him.

"No. Doesn't go with my pills." She shook the bottle ruefully and put it down on the table. Maggie had a suite, one of two in the hotel. Sir Harry had the other, having beaten Sir Piers to it by the stratagem of ringing from London and making sure he had it. "Would champagne do?" Maggie was asking. "I have some here in the 'fridge."

"You do?"

"Keep it for visitors, it's all we ever seem to drink on this show! It's a good hotel." Maggie's magic had obviously worked on them. "They put the champagne in especially for me." Again, she looked and sounded apologetic, as if it were not her fault she was beautiful and talented and lucky. Which she had always been, until now.

"Champagne will be fine. Join me." Josh opened the bottle and poured.

"Better not. I wouldn't sleep."

"You need the pills to sleep?"

"Josh, I need them to live."

"The shrink said that?" Josh sipped his champagne. It was good and he needed it. "Stay on the pills?"

Maggie sat opposite him and the cotton wrap fell open, revealing the long smooth white legs. "No, he said to kick them as soon as I could."

"Then why not kick them?" Josh held out the bottle of champagne.

"I don't know. I feel I need them, I suppose."

"But perhaps you don't?" He tipped the bottle toward her glass.

"No, I couldn't really."

"All right." Josh put the bottle down. He drank more Bollinger and felt a little numb. They talked about the evening's performance in a general way and he drank even more, and felt even more numb. This went on for about fifteen minutes and then Maggie said, very calmly, "I suppose you're here to tell me you want to recast, aren't you?"

Josh sat up straight, shocked. The words were out before he knew it. "No, I'm here to sleep with you!"

It was true. Every word, he realized. He laughed, to cover up.

Fortunately Maggie was treating it as a joke. Or pretending to. "Josh, you're a fool. You and Austin both."

"You mean he's offered as well?"

"Twice a day, every day."

She was laughing, anyway.

"The cheeky fellow. And I thought I was first."

"No. He was. He wants it about as much as you do, which is not at all! Josh, be honest. I can't do this part, can I?"

"Of course you can do it. And marvelously."

"Thank you for saying that, anyway." She smiled. "I can work my way out of this without sex, you know. It doesn't unlock every door."

Josh looked at his feet. "No. I'm sorry. That was stupid of me. I had been having fantasies about you, just the same."

"Natural enough." Maggie smiled. "Damsel in distress. It's because you're a nice man."

"But I'm not," Josh said, steadily. "I meant those fantasies. I do want you. But . . ." He stood up. "I'll leave it for now. We're in Brighton next week. Last stop before London. The sea air should do you good."

"Might put a stop to your fantasies?"

He stood at the door a moment. "I don't think so."

"Josh, you aren't serious."

"I don't know. All I know is how I feel." He shrugged. "But I can understand how you feel. It was stupid of me to say what I did."

Maggie got to her feet. "What you could do is give me some time with you alone. Could you do that, Josh? Go over my lines with me? After supper each night? Up here. Quietly. Away from the others."

"If I come up here for supper every night the cast are only going to think one thing, Maggie."

"Let them. I need your help, Josh. I really do."

"All right. Why don't we start now?"

Maggie looked startled. "If you like. Have you eaten?"

"I had a sandwich. You?"

"I'm not eating much, anyway."

Josh picked up the telephone and ordered smoked salmon sandwiches and coffee for two. They ate as they worked. Josh

319

thought, beginning to sweat: This is right. This is how it must be, I can warm her talent back, slowly, line by line, if necessary, right through the whole bloody play, if need be. Maggie began badly, tonelessly, and he would not let her go on. "Let's see it as a mechanical exercise, Maggie. You speak every line *correctly* from now on. With the *correct* emphasis on every line. On *every* line. We don't go on to the next until you have that line right. Perfect. What we get will be mechanical as far as feeling is concerned, but it won't sound like that to the audience. It'll sound thoughtful. It'll sound correct. It won't have fire, but let's forget about fire, anyway for now." Josh put his warm hand over her cool one. "Just trust me. I think it's the way."

"Yes. Yes. I see." Her lip trembled. "It's an awful, untalented way to do it."

"Lots of actors never work any other way. They rely on their directors for everything. Every nuance. Every move. Everything."

"I know. I've seen them. I never thought I'd be one of them."

"Only for this play. Let me be your Svengali for this play."

She shook her head sadly. "It seems I have no choice."

"Not if you're waiting for a blue flash to strike, Maggie. It isn't going to happen, is it?"

Maggie was a long time answering. "No. It isn't. Let's work, Josh."

They worked. Line by line. Until one o'clock in the morning they worked, when Josh threw down the script and said, "Bed for us both. Seven hours' sleep. The same thing tomorrow evening and as long as it takes."

Maggie kissed him on the cheek in a waft of Calèche.

"I feel happier, more optimistic. Josh, you could be right, you know. This could work."

"I know it," he said, and kissed her on the lips, very lightly. The action sent a tremor to his groin, but he smiled quickly and got out of the room and went to bed in his room next door and slept dreamlessly until his eight o'clock call.

320

IT was going to be all right, he thought, looking at the day. Josh showered, dressed, and shaved, and ate a large English breakfast. He was hungry for something, and the food would have to do.

Rehearsals went well. Austin was still trying to break down Sir Harry's resistance to additional business and dialogue. Austin said, "Look, I'm the prez, right? I walk into the throne room, right? You're standing there waiting, right? My line is what?"

Sir Harry, who knew everybody's lines said, *"Is this to be the end of the special relationship? Two countries that speak one language? Mostly divided by it?"*

"Right," said Austin. "What if I take your hand then? I'm a grandstander. I'd take your hand, shake it, I'd shake any hand in sight, it's my job."

"No mention of handshaking in the text," said Sir Harry, frostily.

"I'll do it, though," said Austin. "It seems dead as it is."

"Dear boy," said Sir Harry, "you can get a laugh there, you know."

"Where?"

"On the line, *divided by it.*"

"Is my motivation wrong somewhere?"

"All you have to do," replied Sir Harry, "is stand quite still. Count to three. Take a pace backwards. Count to three again. *Then* say the line."

Austin said, "It's not me."

"Try it, dear boy," purred Sir Harry.

Austin did. He got the laugh.

"The old guy's a genius!" he declared.

"So much simpler than all that motivation nonsense," rejoined Sir Harry. "So exhausting, what?"

THAT night Josh and Maggie worked until one-thirty.

There was no doubt Maggie was improving. The cast knew it

and responded. By Wednesday evening Maggie had most of the first act technically pat. By Friday the second act was mostly right. Or it *sounded* right, which was all Josh cared about. He was exhausted, taking his ordinary rehearsals (at which he gave Maggie only the same attention as he gave the other actors) and working hard into the night in the private sessions in Maggie's suite. By the end of the week he was feeling drained but triumphant.

Maggie was better. A hell of a lot better.

The Saturday evening performance sounded almost there.

Even young Max Heston was impressed. "I don't know what you're doing, Josh," he whispered, at the final performance of the week, "but, whatever it is, it has to be right."

Josh checked a harsh reply. No point in it. "Maggie's a great actress, Max. And she'll get better and better."

"The special treatment she's getting, I'm not surprised."

"Smile when you say that, sonny," threatened Josh.

"I'm smiling, I'm smiling," said Max, who wasn't.

The audience enthusiastically applauded the last performance, and the whole cast was much encouraged. "D'yer think I got the walk right at last?" asked Sir Piers. "Was that what made the difference?"

Sir Harry said, "No, it wasn't, you silly old thing, it was Maggie, she's going to be absolutely wonderful in town, aren't you, darling?" And Sir Harry gave her a kiss. They all had champagne in the chintz and paneled lounge of the hotel, and Brigid Kelly whispered, pressing closer to Josh, "I wish I rated special treatment from the director. It would do wonderful things for me." She looked mock-sexily over the rim of her glass. "Might do nice things for the director, too."

"Give him a heart attack, I expect," said Josh.

"Really, Maggie," said Austin. "You're terrific. Great."

He seemed to be affected, Josh thought. There were actually tears in his eyes. Well, the more emotion everybody felt, the better *Queen* was going to be.

Later, Josh put his head in Maggie's room.

She sat, in her dressing gown, near the wood fire. The flames glinted on her hair. "Hi, Josh. Come in." The script lay on her lap, the Q shining in the flicker of flame.

Josh yawned. "Just looking in to say 'night-'night."

"We still have the last scene to do, Josh. It isn't right yet, is it?"

"I thought we'd leave it. I'm bushed."

"Please." She indicated a bottle in an ice bucket, and a pile of freshly cut smoked salmon sandwiches under a white cloth. "I'm all prepared."

Josh poured two large tumblers and drank his own straight down. "If I fall asleep on you, don't be surprised."

Maggie smiled a secret smile. "I won't."

They worked for an hour and a half, sitting on the large deep sofa in front of the fire, before Josh eventually shook his head, despairingly; his eyelids had all but closed. "I'd better go. I'm past it."

Maggie said, in a strange voice, "Close your eyes then."

"No, really." Josh struggled for the willpower not to. It didn't arrive. He closed his eyes; the heat of the fire and the alcohol sent him into an exhausted doze. When he awakened it was four o'clock and the fire was a guttering ember. He felt light-headed and strangely refreshed and somehow he was not surprised when he heard Maggie's voice, low from the bedroom, "Josh, I'm in bed if you'd like to join me."

As he was to say to himself ever afterward, what was he supposed to do, make his excuses and leave the room?

THE first evening in Brighton, just before curtain-up, Brigid told Max what she had known for ten days. She was pregnant.

Max sat opposite her in the coffee bar along the promenade

across from the Theatre Royal. She had chosen a semi-public place because she knew what his reaction was likely to be. She was right about that, anyway.

"You stupid cow!"

"Please, Max. People are looking."

"I hope they are. Jesus. How?"

"The usual way," Brigid said with asperity.

"Oh, clever stuff! What about me, what am I supposed to do?"

Oh, God. She should never have taken up with him. He was a child. She needed a man, somebody who'd made it, somebody who cared about *her*, not a boy with a lot of clever talk and nothing behind it yet.

"I'm not asking you to do anything."

"Ha-bloody-ha."

"No, the information is simply for your interest." Brigid's voice rose. Let anybody hear who wanted to. Fortunately, nobody from the cast was in the place. She had selected it for that reason, too. "You've been screwing me, so you're entitled to know, and that's all you're entitled to."

Max sat back in his chair and sipped his coffee thoughtfully. He seemed relieved, as she knew he would be.

"What are you going to do about it?"

"That's my business."

"If that's the way you want it, darling."

Brigid felt a surge of anger. It wasn't the way she wanted it. It was the way he wanted it. "It happened the first night. I rushed out to the bloody audition and I forgot to take my pill."

"Why make a fuss?" Max's voice was cold. "You just said it's your business." He rolled and lit a cigarette. He was trying to cut down on the tobacco, he disapproved of tobacco, but since he had mixed it with Jamaican Gold that made it all right. "Anyway, I don't know how I can help. I have about fifty quid in the world. You're welcome to it."

"Fifty quid? Is that all you have?"

"I never have more than that. I don't believe in saving money."

"What a useless jerk you are!"

"Thanks very much. You weren't saying that in bed up in Wallingford, were you?"

"We won't be in bed together ever again, buster."

"Suits me. D'you want the fifty?"

Brigid Kelly thought: He's sure I'm going to have it dumped. He's so bloody sure. "I'd thought of keeping it."

She had: for about ten minutes. It had seemed a nice idea. A vision of herself in a cottage, roses round the door, just herself and the baby. She had never thought of including Max in the equation and she had been right. A feeling of panic shot through her. She had twenty pounds and Max was offering fifty. That was seventy. Where the hell could she get a nice, quiet abortion for seventy pounds?

Nowhere.

"I'm going to have to talk to Josh Williams or somebody." The cold, numb feeling was growing. She realized that some part of her had been hoping Max would come through. At least try to help. At least show some feeling for her. Men. She ought to know men by now. Especially in the business.

"You are *not* going to talk to Josh." Max's voice was low.

"I have to do something. I can't let it go on."

"You are not going to talk to Josh Williams. He'll know it's me."

"So what if he does?"

"If he does, he'll use it." Max was leaning forward. "It'll go right round the company and I'll be the stupid git who got you pregnant and you'll be the idiot who let it happen. And let your great big chance of stardom"—Max's mouth twisted; he did not believe in stardom—"go to shit."

Brigid felt colder than ever. Every world he said was true.

"I have to find some money somewhere!" She paused. "How about your family?"

"I never see my folks. What about yours?"

Brigid thought of the semidetached brick bungalow in the Dublin suburb, and her father's bowler hat hanging in the hall, and the sound of children's voices and the television and the smell of an Irish fry-up lingering all over the house. She thought of the crucifix over her bed. "I can't even tell them. They think I'm still a virgin."

"That's a laugh anyway," said Max cruelly.

"I know you're hurt," she said. "I'm hurt, too."

"You must have some friends somewhere who could help."

"I haven't. Not that could do anything."

Brigid thought, You bastard, Max. And then felt guilty. It wasn't Max's fault, the prevailing theory said: it was hers. She should have taken her pill. She *had* been a silly cow, allowing the exictement of getting the job and a few glasses of booze to go to her head. It wasn't Max's fault and he owed her nothing, said the prevailing thought. Brigid felt shortchanged by it somehow, but she did not question it, for to do that would be to say her parents were right, their way of living was right, and she and all her friends (actresses like herself, students, people in fringe theatre) were wrong. A woman had to be herself, the prevailing thought said: She had to realize herself. She had to find herself. A man was an encumbrance and anyway he had his own problems. A woman should live with the consequences of her actions.

Well, all right, she was doing that.

Max looked at his watch. "We're due back."

"Yes, I know." She collected her tote bag. "Give me the fifty, okay?"

Max reached in his pocket. "Here." Without looking, he passed over all the notes. They were in a large paper clip.

"Is this the lot? All you have?"

"That's right."

"Here." Brigid gave him ten pounds back. "You have to get through the week yourself."

Max nodded and got to his feet, pulling at his heavy belt. Brigid found her eyes on the level of his genitals, which bulged provocatively in the deliberately overtight jeans. The sight did not now inspire her. She'd had enough of *that* to last her a very long time. "You go on." She tried to smile at him but found it too hard to do. "I'll follow."

"Don't be long or you'll be *off.*"

"I'll be there."

Max nodded and left the café without a further word. Through the window she watched him walk along the Promenade toward the theatre. He shouldered his way through the holiday makers in their bright shirts and summer dresses and, to Brigid, his step seemed light. He's glad to be rid of you, face it, she told herself. Face it. You're on your own. What's new about that?

What's new about it is you're pregnant.

Brigid smoked a cigarette, slowly. Cigarettes were supposed to be bad for kids, she remembered. She thought to stub it out, then smiled wryly to herself. If cigarettes could get rid of it, she'd smoke a thousand, and gladly. She looked at her cheap wristwatch. Thirty-five minutes to curtain. She'd better move.

There was a queue at the box office and the people waiting looked, compared to their audiences at Wallingford, like creatures from another planet. Here, dark blazers and striped ties were the order of the day, and smart summer dresses, and pearls. The Brighton audience was implacably middle class and knew its theatre. It saw most of the London hits before they were hits and most of the flops before they were flops. She felt a rush of excitement as she slipped into the theatre. This was her life. This was what she had worked for, all the way through drama school and at the northern reps, footsying with the bearded young directors, sleeping with them too, sleeping with a lot of people, everybody really, more or

327

less as a kindness, as a gesture. Holy Mother of God, how many had there been? She couldn't remember their faces, never mind their silly names, usually Joe or Bert or Jim or Les in the Socialist manner, to show they were of the people. Most had university degrees and came from middle-class homes and affected sweatshirts and granny glasses (again, to prove how proletarian they were) and they had been indistinguishable from Max. Max thought he was an original but she had news for him. There were a dozen young directors around his age who thought his thoughts: about fringe theatre, street theatre, socialism, sociology, black kids, nuclear power, the Bomb. She knew. She had slept with them.

Her mother would have thought that made her a whore.

Her mother knew nothing.

Brigid's pulse quickened as she walked into her dressing room. She was going to be a big success in *Queen*. She knew it. Nothing could stop her. Maggie was getting better every performance. She had asked Max why and he had replied crudely, "Cock."

"Whose?"

"Josh. Who do you think?"

"He's doing it to get a better performance from her?"

"I reckon."

Brigid had not been too pleased to hear that news. Even so, Maggie was not going to grab all the notices, however much cock she got or however much she improved. There was plenty of room for Brigid Kelly. And Brigid Kelly was going to see it happened. She was going to keep quite a lot back for the first night on Shaftesbury Avenue. Oh, yes indeed. Brigid Kelly could hear, through the dressing-room intercom, the pianist tinkling in the stalls as she took off her grubby jeans and sweater to change into the white satin dress that Tommi Traceham had designed for her.

Tommi?

Brigid wondered why the thought came into her head. Had it been lying there all through the rehearsals, nagging, insistent, as

Tommi's cool hand lingered a little longer than necessary on her bottom, as they stood in a fitting room, or touching her breasts unnecessarily while adjusting the cleavage of the white satin gown? Even an odd touch on her hair. There was no doubt really. Tommi was a likely friend. Tommi was the kind of cool person who would know people. Tommi was the kind of person who would know everything.

She opened her dressing-room door and called into the corridor, "Tommi, are you around?"

Tommi came out of Sir Harry's dressing room. She looked with frank appreciation at Brigid's sleek form in the apricot-and-cream-fringed slip she had stolen from a production of Coward's *Private Lives* at the Belgrade. "Nice thing, that. Needs a wash though, darling."

"I know," said Brigid. "I keep meaning to, but we've no time, have we, on the road?"

"Of course we do. Take it off and leave it with me. I'll see it's washed and ironed for you."

"Will you? That's lovely." Brigid pulled the slip over her head. She was now nude except for her pants.

"Lovely tits, haven't you?" Tommi lit one of her cigarettes and fitted it in her holder. "Wasted on young Max. I'm surprised at you, darling. He probably piston-pokes you and you pretend to enjoy it, am I right?"

"Tommi, you are naughty." Brigid laughed. "But yes, it is a bit like that." In fact, it wasn't. Max had been very experimental indeed but then so was she. No sense in telling Tommi that, however. "Look, I think this princess dress cleavage could go down a bit, don't you?"

"Put it on." She did.

Tommi pondered. "If I let you wear it lower, Maggie might object. Oh, not to you or me, dear. To the director. With whom, as you know, she is making time, as they used to say."

"I thought he was having it off with Ms. Viner?"

"He was, but like Sir Harry says, it doesn't count standing up or on tour."

Brigid arranged the white dress and twisted around. She could almost feel Tommi's temperature rising. It excited her too, in an odd way. The callboy called the quarter and that added to the fever of it all.

Tommi made some fast alteration to the cleavage, touching Brigid's breasts quite frankly, her nail caressing the nipples sharply, insistently. Brigid did not find it any worse than the touch of the older girls at the convent, nicer if anything. She looked at herself in the dressing-table mirror. "My boobs aren't falling out or anything, are they?"

"I'll get the wardrobe lady to sew it up for you at the interval. The pins will hold until then." Tommi turned to go. Brigid called lightly, "Tommi, I'd like to talk to you about something very personal."

Tommi almost stopped breathing.

"We can hardly discuss anything . . . personal here."

"Well, no. Later maybe. At the hotel?"

"I'm in room twenty-two, second floor. Come and have a drink before bed."

"Tonight?"

"Why not?" Tommi smiled. It was a very mannish smile, it went with the dark, cropped head and the tight, smart clothes. "And do see your tits don't fall out. And, if you intend to up-stage milady Maggie with them, leave it until the first night in town."

Brigid stood shocked as Tommi leaned forward and kissed her full on the lips and at the same time ran her finger along her mons. "Good luck, darling, show them how."

And she was gone.

Well, Brigid Kelly thought. Well, well.

MAGGIE was better than ever, that first performance in Brighton, and the house rose to her. Brigid held back in her scenes with Maggie, suspecting that all Maggie was doing was an actress's job, knowing that when there was emotion needed Maggie did not always have it on tap. Well, she had, by the Holy Mother, she had, but she would hold it, hold it, *hold it*, until Shaftesbury Avenue and the critics.

Sir Harry received his opening round of applause (to which he actually raised his hat) and Sir Piers got a big round at the curtain by throwing in half a dozen words of Russian nobody (including Josh Williams) knew he knew. "Freely translated," he told the delighted audience, "that means, God bless you!"

Backstage, after the show, Maggie looked exhausted. Brigid thought: She isn't fit and with any luck she won't be fit in a week. Cock or no cock. This play is mine, if I take my chances. "You were lovely tonight, darling," she told Maggie. "Better than ever."

"Thank you, darling, you're so nice." Maggie's eyes were large and round and she seemed to mean it. Silly cow never went without anything in her life, she doesn't know she's alive, all she needs is some fella to cling to, all she needs is cock. Well, thought Brigid Kelly, I don't need cock, ever again. I've had enough to last a lifetime.

Sir Harry said, "Lovely audience here. Always are. They all used to dress in the thirties, you know. You looked out and the whole of the stalls, boiled shirts, dinner jackets. Women in long dresses. Lovely. Even tonight, most people had a tie on." He turned to Maggie. "Darling, I'm so glad it's coming along. You're going to be wonderful. Must be the air here. Marvelous thing, sea air, what?"

"I went around the Pavilion today," said Austin. "Some place, right?"

"When I see it I think of Beau Brummell," replied Sir Harry. "Cut his own throat just by seven words. He'd fallen out with

Prinny, and the Prince was ready to make up, when Brummel asked his companion, 'Tell me, who is your fat friend?' Cost him everything, died in poverty." Sir Harry sighed. "But what an exit line!"

BRIGID Kelly went to Tommi's room very late. She wanted to be sure everybody else was in bed. She found Tommi in bed too, and nude, so she took a deep breath, took off her clothes, and joined her there. It wasn't like screwing, it was like an interminable preparation for screwing: but it was pleasurable enough, a striving of tongues and fingers and even eyelashes, and the climaxing was different, and there was no danger. She liked that, she had had enough of danger. Men were dangerous and she didn't need that. There was enough danger on stage, in the sweet, sweet struggle with such as Maggie. So Brigid kissed and was kissed and came and cried out more than perhaps she needed to and felt a sense of liberation (after all, she thought, this was where it all ended for most libbers, where else was there to *go?*) and, when it was all over, anyway for the time being, she was not taken by surprise when Tommi asked, "And what's the little problem then, darling?"

Brigid told her.

"That's no problem. I know a man. Do it for you next Sunday. You'll be at the opening Wednesday." Tommi leaned over. Her eyes were wide like a cat's. "I ironed the slip. Put it on for me, darling, will you?"

Brigid kissed her on the mouth.

AUSTIN took Maggie to the Pavilion in Brighton on Friday afternoon. There were no more rehearsals. Josh had decided there was no more work to be done. "It's all finished, people," he had said. "Go out and enjoy the sunshine this afternoon. Tonight as usual, and a matinee and an evening performance tomorrow. Then

332

nothing until we open on Wednesday, in town. No point in driving ourselves into the ground. I don't say coast, but don't knock yourselves out. We're there, or as near as we're going to be. Good luck and enjoy yourselves." Josh had hesitated, standing on stage, holding his tattered and dog-eared copy of the script of *Queen*. "Oh, and you'll be glad to know your producer is coming down for the last performance tomorrow night."

Max Heston had said, quite audibly, "That *will* be nice."

Nobody else had said anything, except Sir Harry. "Where has the dear lady been all this time?" He had gazed round plaintively. "Am I missing something?"

"For once," said Max, sotto voce. "Yes."

"I wonder," mused Sir Harry, "what on earth it can be?"

In the Pavilion, walking through the Regency treasure trove, Austin asked Maggie the question direct. "I know you're sleeping with Josh. But do you love him?"

Maggie turned the large and lovely eyes on him. Like sexual searchlights, he thought miserably. "Of course I love him, what a question! I wouldn't be sleeping with him otherwise, would I?"

"I thought," hazarded Austin miserably, "that it might be a sort of location thing. We've all had them. They're nearly always a mistake, right, like shipboard romances and vacation hot-pants."

"I've never slept with anybody on location." Maggie inspected the contents of the glass cases: Georgian silver and porcelain. "Aren't these things wonderful? I'm so glad you brought me here, Austin."

"Don't stand there," said Austin, "as if you're in Bonwit Teller wondering whether to buy!"

"Do I look like that? I'm sorry. I guess I'm starting to take an interest in things again."

God, she was lovely! The fragile head and hands, the long gold hair, the pearl-gray suit from Halston, no jewelry except a Georgian ruby ring she had bought earlier in the little shop in the lanes at the back of the Promenade. "A Georgian ring for a Georgian town!" She had refused to allow Austin to buy it for her. He suspected she wanted Josh to pay for it, or try to: then she could pretend he had. Austin knew Josh Williams well enough by now to know that buying a ring for the most beautiful woman in the world, with whom he also happened to be sleeping, would not be a priority high on his list. Now Austin's throat felt tight, just looking at Maggie as she drifted through the Pavilion, giving little cries of pleasure as if in the act of love. He was glad she was well again, or anyway very nearly: what he found choking was that he had had nothing to do with it. Austin took off his dark glasses and was instantly recognized by a matronly woman who asked him to sign her guidebook.

"Sorry, ma'am, you've made a mistake."

"And isn't that Maggie Stride with you?"

"No, ma'am. We are Mr. and Mrs. Paul W. Henderson from Pasadena, California."

"I'm terribly sorry. I do apologize."

"Not at all, ma'am. It happens all the time."

Maggie giggled as they moved on. "Austin," she said "you should be happy for me. Really, I'm disappointed in you."

"I'm disappointed, too. That that limey shit got there first."

"Austin!"

"Well, Jesus. He's about fifty, right?"

"Forty-six."

"Fifty, near enough. He hasn't a pot to piss in, look at that ratty little Volks he drives."

"Austin, the British don't put on a show, except in places like this. They have an aristocracy of talent and learning and class. They don't worry about money the way Americans do."

"You feel at home with the guy. Go on, deny it!" Austin felt this superior attitude Maggie was adopting was close to treason. "You think that kind of snobbery's better than the dollar kind. Right?"

"Austin, I love him." The words went through Austin like a

knife but he showed nothing; the actor in him was always paramount and he thanked the Studio for that. He remembered a note from Lee Strasberg. It had always stuck in his mind. When people were really hurt, they showed nothing. Nothing. Austin knew that was true, because here he was, listening to all this love shit and showing nothing either. I love him, I love him. Why was he standing here among all this culture crap listening to it? Talking to a woman who loves another man, his father had once told him, is like talking to the wall. His father had been a very ordinary type guy, very straight, all right, but Austin had never thought him a wise man. Now, he wondered about his dead father.

"Sure, you think you love him, Maggie," he declared. "But does he love you?"

"Yes, I think so, Austin." Maggie had two spots of color in her cheeks now and Austin could see the signs. Yet he pressed on.

"How do you know?"

Maggie said, in a low voice, "He makes love to me very nicely, Austin."

"He does? You surprise me."

"Very nicely and very gently, Austin. He isn't into all that macho nonsense."

They were sitting outside in the gardens by now. Austin gazed miserably at the yellowing lawns: the September sun beat down on them. "You mean," Austin said, "he lies back and you do all the work?"

"You know I don't mean anything like that." Maggie took a deep breath. "I mean he's considerate and kind and he thinks about me before himself. Also"—her voice dropped—"he lost somebody he loved. Just as I did. He knows what I'm thinking. I've never met a man like that before."

"How many men?" Austin asked, harshly, but he had to know—Jesus, he had to know everything about Maggie, it was becoming an obsession with him. "How many men have you slept with, Maggie?"

"Only Philip and one other person."

"Oh, yes, and who was that?"

"He was my tutor at drama school, if you must know."

It figured—shit, it figured. "An old guy," Austin said, flatly. "Bald, married, past it. Locked in this marriage he couldn't get out of?"

"He was married, yes."

"He introduced you to sex and then when you got to like it, he said good-bye, am I right, this wonderfully interesting old drama tutor?"

"He was a fine person, Austin, and I won't hear talk against him."

Austin shook his head. "He's imprinted you. Don't you see? First him. Then—excuse me—Philip."

"Austin, please don't talk about Philip." Maggie closed her eyes. She looked as she had looked on the stretcher, going into the hospital. Austin's heart turned over. All this had been coming on a long time. It had taken her thing with Josh Williams to force him to admit it. Shit, he had thought he was through with that love crap. He sighed. It seemed he wasn't. Otherwise why would he be here, listening to all this bullshit?

Austin said, gently, "Philip was married. You got him away from his wife and kids. You had to be ruthless to do that, Maggie. Don't play the sensitive plant with me. It probably killed him, the guilt of it, and it didn't do you much good either."

Maggie kept her eyes closed. "Austin, this is outrageous."

"Sure, but the truth generally is, right?" He plunged on. "So now you've found somebody who's older, who probably doesn't want a family—"

"He has a grown-up daughter," said Maggie icily.

"Right! So no need for all that family stuff. You have a new ready-made daddy just like Daddy and the tutor and Philip, if the poor guy had been up to it, which he wasn't."

Maggie's voice was almost inaudible. "Austin, will you please get off the subject of my love life! It has nothing to do with you. Please."

Austin sighed. He was trying to help, he was trying to explain Maggie to herself, shit, anybody with half an eye could see it, why couldn't she? He shook his head. "Surely you can see the pattern. Don't tell me you can't."

"What," asked Maggie patiently, "is wrong with the pattern? I like it. I like older men. Men with talent. Men who aren't—"

"Dangerous?"

"All right. What's so marvelous about dangerous?"

"Jung says American women like soft men, they play the mother. He says they need dangerous men and they can never find any, they have to come to Europe for them."

"That's a terrific generalization, even for Jung."

"Even so, the old guy had a point. You found an Englishman. You even took him off his girl friend, our producer, who, incidentally, is coming down here from London tomorrow."

Maggie sat quite still. She didn't know, Austin thought, he didn't tell her. Which means he hasn't told Jill Viner about her. Which means he isn't sure. Austin felt his heart lighten a little.

"How do you know she's coming?"

"Josh told us. You were at that dress-fitting or whatever."

"I see. Yes."

"He didn't tell you?"

"No." She bit her lip. It was a beautiful lip. Austin wanted to bite it himself. "No, he didn't."

Austin let it lie: and he hoped fester. "Anyway, I think you're going to run away with the notices."

Maggie didn't reply. She sat in the warm sun and looked troubled. So, let her be troubled, Austin thought. I'm troubled every time she moves her body, I'm troubled every time that curtain of fucking gold hair falls over her face, why shouldn't she be troubled too?

"You are going to be a hit, in London," he said, just the same.

Christ, love makes you feel lousy, he thought. It surely does.

"All I'm doing," Maggie said dully, "is going through the motions. I have the words, I have the inflections. My awful nerves are better, but I'm still waiting for the emotion."

"Nobody would ever know."

"You know. Don't you?"

"I'm on stage with you, Maggie. I'm so busy doing my own thing I can't even see you." It wasn't strictly true but what the hell. He knew Maggie was in some way faking it. She was working entirely to the director's notes—and it was brilliant, what Josh Williams was doing, he had to admit that. The way he was taking her through it line by line, getting the inflections dead right every time. That was great. Austin had to admit that, too. Maggie was giving very little of herself, it was all the director. Well, it seemed to work and meanwhile the director was having a hell of a time screwing this beautiful woman he, Austin, loved.

Maggie stood up. She looked tired. "Austin, I'm going back to the hotel. I think I'll have a rest before tonight's performance."

Austin felt a stab of guilt so sharp he almost gasped. "Hey, listen, Maggie, I didn't upset you too much, did I? I mean, I'm full of shit talking psychoanalysis crap to a lovely, uncomplicated person like you." He stood, in a sudden sweat, blinking at the bright sun. "It's just I know you need somebody who can be young with you, show you a good time, but on an equal basis, you don't need all these old guys. Maggie, they're fucking *teachers*, why not be your age, you're young, enjoy life, enjoy yourself, for Christ's sake!"

"With you, you mean, Austin?"

Her words were low and she was smiling. What the fuck, was he as funny as all that? Austin felt a fool, standing there in the Pavilion gardens and wishing himself anywhere else, like back in L.A. in the arms of little Carmen. Shit, at least he had been happy then. He had been happy, too, in Washington, talking to the president. He knew he was getting some of the feeling of the man's power into the part. He, too, had a success coming in London. He knew it. And yet it wasn't enough, it wasn't halfway enough. He wanted this woman, he wanted her more than he'd ever wanted a woman before, not just sex but that too, and here she was, the lovely ice queen, laughing at him.

"I suppose it had occurred to you he might have slept with you so you'd loosen up and give a real performance as the queen?" he asked, but already she was walking away from him, tall and regal, her high heels striking the ground in queenly measured paces, her gold hair swinging, a vision of loveliness, no other phrase would do, and all he could hope was that she had not heard him. He would never be sure of that.

JILL sat in the box and watched the Saturday night's Brighton performance of *Queen*. She had deliberately arrived very late, just before curtain-up, and slipped into the theatre at the last moment. It was a full house, which meant that anyway the local word-of-mouth was good. The audience was middle-aged and basically moneyed and might be expected to watch *Queen* sympathetically. Anyway, she hoped so.

She needed some good news.

Her life was bleak since Josh had gone out of it. She had never thought she would miss him so much.

All the work, the transatlantic calls to Broadway producers who were showing interest (and several were), advising them of the dates of *Queen*'s opening; talking possible money in a very guarded way; arranging billing details outside the Royal with Herbie Glass; none of this action took away the ache. Herbie had sent roses after their last lunch, and obviously he was smitten. Herbie was a sweetie but she couldn't think of him like that. She had sent a thank-you card and Herbie had telephoned again and suggested dinner at his Mayfair apartment. She had accepted—anything was better than sitting in the penthouse thinking about Josh—and Herbie had revealed himself as discreetly amorous. A manservant had served their dinner and then gone out. Herbie obviously ran his seductions in a Victorian manner. Jill had kept him busy talking money and business details of *Queen* until finally he had taken his Monte Cristo out of his mouth and said, "Jill, don't bullshit me, you've got a steady feller?"

"I used to have one. Not anymore." Jill could admit it to Herbie. He was sixty, and, as he said, "At sixty no woman expects anything of you. I like that state of affairs." He had sensed her grief and been very sympathetic from then on and had even relented on some points of the get-in money that she was pressing for.

Herbie's goodwill mattered. He was vital to the success of *Queen*. He could, by contract, close it anytime he liked, since he owned the theatre. But he seemed well disposed to her and to *Queen*. He had let her go to her taxi with regret. "Whoever he is, he's an ingrate. You're wasted on him. Forget him."

Easier said than done. She had worked like a fool these last two weeks. She had telephoned and argued and rushed about London, meeting the ticket-agency people again, trying to get them to up their block bookings for *Queen* (and failing; they were polite but a political play posed problems and they preferred to wait), and writing personal letters to the critics, sending them along with their invitations, hoping to get the number one critic from all the big papers. Money, money, money, work, work, work. None of it had blotted out Josh Williams's face or the loss she felt.

Jill had never thought she would miss anybody so much.

Somehow, she had nursed the hurt and the loss. She had kept away from *Queen* until now, until she felt she could bear to see Josh again and show nothing.

The curtain went up and there was the white revolve, with Maggie sitting on the throne and wearing the long red velvet gown, the tiara glinting in her hair. Jill hung on to the sides of her chair, in the long silence before Maggie spoke her first lines.

She had no idea how Maggie was going to be.

Josh had said very little on the telephone, except that she had improved. Jill wondered how much. She was not prepared for what she saw. Maggie was superb. Cool, very cool. There was room for fire in the performance (Jill noted it on her program) but there was no doubt at all Maggie was going to be all right. It was a miracle. She wondered how it had happened.

Jill stayed in her seat through the interval. She heard the buzz in the theatre and thought, They like it, they're excited, it isn't London, of course, but it's an omen. She made jottings about performances on her program and tried to compose her mind before meeting Josh again. And under it all she felt triumph. Maggie was fine. Everything was going to be all right.

There was solid applause as the tabs came down, and the audience shuffled, obviously pleased, out of the theatre. Jill felt suddenly warm and hopeful. She left by the front foyer (thanking the house manager) and went round to the stage door. She found Josh in the production office with Max Heston and the backstage staff, Billy and Bobbi and the electricians and Ernie the carpenter. Josh was talking. "I can *hear* that boat truck at the beginning of act two, Billy. And, Ernie, that revolve still creaks a bit, look at it, will you, and somehow those floats are too powerful, can we take them down a bit? We could use a follow-up spot on the queen in act one. Let's try it, shall we?" There was a hush as Jill entered and they all stared at her. Nobody spoke, which seemed to her odd, but she had interrupted them.

"Hello," she said, at last. "That went well, didn't it?"

They all smiled and looked at their feet. Still nobody spoke. Josh broke the silence. "All right, everybody. Nothing else. I'll give you any other notes first morning at the Royal. Okay. That's it."

They all nodded and left, except Max Heston, who sat down and made some notes in the working script, obviously last-minute changes. She wondered if Josh would ask him to leave, but Josh didn't. He sat on the battered desk and lit one of his cigars and talked to her in a very ordinary voice, the while pouring her a glass of white wine and handing it to Max to pass, in turn, over to her.

"Well," Josh asked, "what did you think?"

"Maggie is marvelous. What have you done to her?"

Max Heston looked steadily into his glass of wine. Josh stared hard at him. What, Jill wondered, was all this about?

"She's not absolutely there yet. It'll come. By opening night. We hope." Josh stopped looking at Max and turned back to her. God, he looked well: and he was wearing a very expensive shirt she had never seen before. It was just the sort that Josh would never buy for himself, and Jill found herself wondering. She said, "You look well."

"I'm fine. It's the cast I worry about. A bout of throat or flu. That's the nightmare." He rubbed his eyes. He looked well, yes: but there was a feverish glint in his eye. Tired, but well. He yawned openly and her heart went out to him. Now there was so little he could do. He had handed *Queen* over to his cast.

"You've done a great job." Jill tried to keep her voice neutral. "Maggie really is terrific. I feel we're over the biggest hurdle of the lot. I'll sleep well tonight."

"Max," said Josh, "would you excuse us?"

"Sure, no problem." Max stood up.

"I've booked a table for the cast at Wheeler's," said Jill. "Max, naturally you're invited."

Max stopped in his tracks and said softly, "Jill, that's really nice of you," and went on out, strangely subdued.

"He seems a bit quiet," Jill said.

"Oh, you know how it is with a cast on tour." Josh smiled. "Wheeler's is a nice idea. They'll love it. They've worked very hard." He went on, easily. "Have you any notes on the production? I could do with a fresh look. I'm too close to see anything now." He rubbed his eyes again and Jill's heart moved. The poor man. He'd been working himself to death while she'd been keeping away because of her silly bruised sensibilities.

"I didn't come earlier because I thought you might find it upsetting." She sipped her white wine. Josh said nothing, it was as if she hadn't spoken. Perhaps that was the way to play it, the English way, as if nothing had ever happened between them. That way, perhaps, something might happen again. Give the man room, she admonished herself. Don't crowd him. That's how you lost him. Give him room to come back again. If he wants to.

"I know a producer should be around but I didn't want to look over your shoulder all the time." She smiled, feeling nervous, a rare thing with her. "You seem to have done very well without me, I must say."

Josh stared at her as if she had just said something important. Then Max put his head in the door and asked, "Shall I tell the principals Wheeler's in fifteen minutes?"

"Please," Jill said. "Oh, and Tommi Traceham, naturally."

Josh closed his mouth and, whatever he was going to say, left it unsaid.

There was an embarrassed silence. Jill found that odd. She was never awkward with Josh. It was one of the nice things about him.

"I had a few notes." She held out her tattered program, much annotated.

"What are they?" Josh took up a pad and pencil, seemingly with relief. Obviously, she thought, he's as embarrassed by all this as I am, more so. We were in each other's beds and bodies a month ago, after all, and now we're talking like polite people in an office. Oh, Josh, she wanted to call out, please forget everything you said and everything I said and kiss me. Instead, she said, "Well, I have a note on the revolve. I know it's electrically operated, but I heard a distinct squeak. It might get a giggle if it isn't put right." Josh nodded. "And I thought the black drapes moved a couple of times."

"Probably backstage drafts. Performances?"

"Maggie, as I said, terrifically improved."

"I'll keep working. There's more to come. Austin?"

"Austin shuffles. He's very good but he's a bit too busy. I just think a president would be a little, I don't know, perhaps more *solid?*"

343

"Good point. I'll tell him. Sir Piers?"

"Terrific. Possibly a bit too heavy, a bit *too* menacing. He doesn't need to be. He has a hundred divisions behind every word."

"Good. Sir Harry?"

"Do tell him not to take that bow when he comes on stage at the beginning. The audience love him. We know that. He doesn't need to underline it, he's got nothing to prove. Otherwise, nothing really. He's Sir Harry, we paid for the performance and we're getting it."

"I think he'll do one or two new things on the first night. Piers, too. I can't think what." Josh sighed. "But I'm sure they'll both try something new on each other. I dread it."

"Warn them," said Jill, with asperity. "We don't want scenes ruined for old scores."

"Warning those two not to upstage each other is like warning sharks not to bite. Up to now they've only been sparring." Josh made a note. "I'll mention it, just the same. That leaves Brigid."

"Brigid's cleavage is far too low," said Jill. "She's a princess of the royal house, not a tart. She's very good, though. Perhaps too good. You may have to ask her to take her performance down a notch. Especially in her scenes with Maggie. She's trying, in a very nice way, to make those scenes her own."

"She'll find it more difficult, now Maggie's coming good."

"Just the same. She's a clever little lady."

"Yes. I can see that. I'll give her a note."

"That's all." Jill smiled. "Gosh. Isn't it warm backstage?"

"Been like that all week, a sweatbox."

"I see you bought a new shirt, Josh."

"Huh? Oh. It's so hot I change them twice a day."

"I like it—silk, isn't it?"

"Let's hope we get some rain. Or we'll be opening in a heat wave. Here it hasn't mattered." Josh didn't say if the shirt was silk or not. "The normal audience comes in here anyway. Local papers have been good to us. Here." He passed her a clipping from the

Argus and she read it quickly. "A play of real merit about a real subject, one that ought to be concerning us, perhaps, a lot more than it is, even in a holiday resort in the hottest September anybody can remember. Certainly the Brighton audience liked it." There were kind references to almost everybody in the cast. Josh Williams got a mention, too. Jill did not. Producers rarely do, she thought. Never mind. We put the whole thing together. Sometimes we even get rich doing it. Sometimes.

"The ticket agencies won't up their bookings. They're blaming the weather, too. Attendances in London theatres are down a third, let's hope it rains." Jill wondered if he liked her satin dress. It was low-cut but then she wasn't on stage, like Brigid Kelly. "I got this new dress," she heard herself saying. "Something cool."

"Looks good," said Josh briefly, not looking at the dress, but at his watch. "I think we should go. Do you have a car?"

"No," said Jill hollowly. Wasn't he going to drive her to Wheeler's? Apparently not. He said, "You go on in a cab. I have one or two last-minute things. I'll see you there, ten minutes?"

Jill went to Wheeler's alone, in a cab.

She looked out at the darkening Promenade, at the holiday makers strolling gratefully in the first cool of the day. She hoped the heat wave was going to break, soon. It had to. London that day had been an oven. She shook her head. She could not control the weather but she could control her feelings. She was a woman of business and she must behave like one.

The cast was already at a table and had broached a couple of bottles of the house Chablis. Sir Harry and Sir Piers stood up when she entered, but Max Heston did not, although he did smile nicely. "Do come and sit down next to me, Joan dear," intoned Sir Harry. "How very nice to see you, we'd been wondering where you were. Of course, not all producers cluck around after their shows like broody hens." Max had an attack of the giggles at that. "Have I made a funny?" asked Sir Harry.

"Yes, you have, do sit down, you silly old thing," said Sir Piers.

345

"You aren't playing the P.M. now. That ended forty-five minutes ago." Sir Piers kissed Jill on the cheek and held her hands in his vast paws. "Well, how were we, don't keep us in suspense, what did you think of us?"

They all stared at her: Brigid Kelly, sitting in the corner next to Tommi Traceham (Tommi's arm around her waist; how very odd, she wouldn't have thought *that*), and the two sirs.

Austin came in at that moment, having at first been refused admission by the waiter, who thought he was one of the town students, many of whom slept rough on the beach. Austin's sweat-shirts might be King's Road and his jeans Calvin Klein, but the waiter had not known the difference.

"Do come out from behind those awful glasses, dear boy," said Sir Harry reproachfully. "There's a good chap. It took some of us fifty years to get accepted as respectable, you know."

"Jill!" said Austin, seeing her. "Great!" He kissed her, looked embarrassed, and sat down, calling out, "Anybody ordered? I want cold lobster."

"Our producer, laddie," remonstrated Sir Piers, "is just about to tell us how we were." He turned to Jill.

Jill paused, looked at the expectant faces. They were all here, except Josh and Maggie. Maggie?

"Darlings," she said with a smile, "you were *wonderful!*"

It was all they wanted to hear.

Maggie? Jill sat very thoughtfully as the cast burst into an uproar and ordered crab cocktails and cold lobsters and Chablis all round, and Sir Harry said, "I've heard of plays that did wonderful biz on tour and died on Shaftesbury Avenue, just *died*, darlings."

"Tell us more!" urged Austin, mouth full of lobster. "Cheer us up!"

But Sir Harry was away. "Strangest hit ever was *Young England* by a fella called Walker Reynolds, fat chap, muttonchops, looked like John Bull. At the Victoria Palace, great barn of a place, 1931 or so. So bad everybody booed at the end, even up in the gods.

Whistled, catcalled, the lot. The old man was stone deaf, thought it was applause. Came on and took a curtain call, said, 'Glad ye liked it, I'll write you another!' Everybody started laughing, they all clapped, up in the gods. Stalls took up the clapping, whole deuced theatre in an uproar. Critics mystified, poor dears, went away and wrote it up as a hit. It ran four years." Sir Harry sucked a crab claw. "Damn funny thing, audiences."

Sir Piers said, "Biggest flops of all are plays with *real* people in 'em. *Beethoven* at Daly's in the thirties."

"*Beethoven?*" asked Austin incredulously.

"*Grimaldi*, the clown, another," intoned Sir Harry.

"What about *Houdini?*" asked Sir Piers. "Terrible flop. All real people, d'yer see? Audiences don't like it, dunno why."

"That's rot," said Sir Harry. "Plenty of plays with real people in 'em. Mary Queen of Scots. Cromwell. Dozens."

There was a silence.

"We have a queen *and* some real people, so who knows?" asked Jill. They all laughed, relieved, and went on to talk of that evening's performance and the many small things that made it different from any other performance of *Queen* or of any other play, anywhere, ever. Jill listened and laughed and smiled and nodded her head and ate her lobster and sipped her Chablis, and still Josh and Maggie did not come. The coffee was being poured when at last they did come in, Maggie looking radiant in a light cream suit, and Josh rather pale, wearing a different silk shirt. Oh no, Jill thought, feeling sick.

Josh said, "Sorry. We didn't feel hungry. We'll just have coffee." They had coffee and brandy and the cast fell silent for a few moments, most of them looking at Jill, and Tommi Traceham said, "Shit, the tact of some people," in a low voice everybody heard, and they all excused themselves early and left, protesting they had to pack for tomorrow, and at last only Maggie and Josh and herself were left at the littered table. Jill knew that it was true.

Oh, God.

Maggie fiddled with a cigarette. Josh looked at the tablecloth. Maggie said, "Josh has told me and I'm glad he has because you're a friend, Jill. I want you always to be my friend. I didn't know there was anything between you but Josh tells me it's over and so I feel I can say honestly that Josh and I have something going that I think can be very good. And I want you to know about it, because I think you'll be glad."

Glad? Jill just looked at her.

She opened her mouth to speak when Josh knocked over his coffee cup. She saw his eyes and knew it was a deliberate act. She looked into Maggie's beautiful wide eyes and thought, She's beautiful, so fragile, any man would want her, why not Josh? And yet the words, the insane biting words, *Bitch*, you knew he was mine, everybody in the cast knew he was mine, *bitch bitch bitch!*

Then she saw Josh's eyes: beseeching. Don't, he was saying. Don't. Please don't.

"*Queen* is going to be fine," he said, very slowly, drawing out each syllable. Jill hesitated, the biting, hating words, bitch bitch bitch on her tongue. Then she closed her mouth and said, "Yes, it is. Lovely performance, Maggie. I'll see you two at the Royal in London tomorrow. I must rush. I have a cab."

How she got out of the restaurant she never knew. Or got the hire-car or got through the journey back to town or into her penthouse in Bryanston Square. Or through the night. The only thing she kept saying to herself was: *Queen* is all right, *Queen* is all right. *Queen* is all right . . . *Queen* is all right. . . .

It didn't help the rending pain in her heart.

9

SHAFTESBURY Avenue sweltered.

It was 7:15 in the evening and still men carried their jackets over their arms and the illegal rip-off Coca-Cola sellers at Cambridge Circus were flogging their wares to thirsty people who were not even tourists. The old newspaper sellers had just closed down their pitches at the corners of Frith Street and Charing Cross Road and gone into the Victorian corner pubs to drink their nightly pints of warm bitter beer. The Chinese restaurants in Gerrard Street were empty yet, for most people would eat late, when it would—perhaps—be cooler. The whores in Old Compton Street stared out of their open windows and fanned themselves with newspapers. Nothing moved. It was too hot. All the way from Piccadilly Circus to Cambridge Circus, the whole length of Shaftesbury Avenue, nothing moved, except a desultory taxi or two, and the last commuter leaving the last bar on his way home to the suburbs.

The few pedestrians who walked looked neither to the right

nor to the left at the theatres displaying their wares in garish neon, and few of them noticed the new sign atop the Royal Theatre, halfway up Shaftesbury Avenue going north, which read simply, JILL VINER'S PRESENTATION OF THE QUEEN OF FINLAND. For these were not theatregoers but (if anything) cinema-goers or pub-goers and they passed this way most days and noticed little. The tourists had mostly gone from the streets (it was, after all, late September) and there was room at least to walk, and space on the red buses if you had lost too much sweat or your feet had given out.

Then something unexpected yet a nightly occurrence happened: the whole street suddenly came to life. The avenue was still empty at 7:30 but at 7:40 it was full of taxis, bumper-to-bumper, hooting irritably at pedestrians attempting to cross, in droves, at the lighted intersections. The pubs disgorged people who had been drinking short expensive things like whiskey and gin and tonic, and these people, like those in the taxis, were dressed formally, the majority of the men in dark jackets and trousers and sometimes even dinner jackets, and the women almost always in evening dress and carrying small handbags and some even fur stoles despite the heat. A general air of excitement eddied around them as they hurried toward the lighted theatres. There was a rise in the noise level, what with the slamming of cab doors and the cries of friends meeting one another in the foyers of the theatres and a general air of festivity and expectation.

Nowhere was this more evident than in the foyer of the Royal, where Jill Viner stood, in a smoky crepe de chine dress she had bought in New York at Bergdorf's, and greeted those of the audience that she knew. With her was Tom Tully, resplendent in dinner jacket with a carnation in his buttonhole, who made sure she spoke, however briefly, to those people important enough to be greeted by the producer. Among the early arrivals thus greeted were influential journalists and critics like Milton Shulman of the *Standard* and Jack Tinker of the *Mail*, and others she half recognized but had no time to speak to other than "Hello, I hope you enjoy it."

In the thick crowd in the foyer stood Herbie Glass and his cousin, Lord Glass. Lord Glass embraced Jill and said, "What a businesswoman, I wish she was working for me!" Jill said she was, she hoped *Queen* was going to get Lord Glass his money back and lots more. Lord Glass said he hoped so, and his cousin Herbie, the bricks-and-mortar man, shook his head and said, "Did you hear about the Jewish theatre owner who met his friend Maxie and his friend Maxie said, how's it with you, and Maxie said, the wife left me, and the girl friend's pregnant what could be worse than that, and the Jewish theatre owner said, *September?*" Herbie smoked his cigar and looked gloomy. He seemed to take the parable seriously.

Tom Tully moved Jill on to talk to a young lady from the *Observer* who wrote items for the gossip column. She was not in evening clothes but wore a long woollen dress in the style of a Victorian shopgirl, and a woolly scarf. "I hope I'm not going to hate this play," she hazarded. "It sounds pretty Nazi to me."

Tom Tully said, "Darling, I fought those bastards for four years and, believe me, they were nothing like our author."

The *Observer* girl peered out from under thick hanks of hair. "Right. Where *is* he?"

Tom Tully shook his head. "If I knew I'd tell you. He's Mr. Mystery Man."

The *Observer* girl looked very interested indeed. "Hey, listen, Tom, you get him for me, I guarantee a nice piece."

Tom shook his head. "Everybody says the same thing. No good."

"You mean he isn't here, at his own play?" the *Observer* girl asked incredulously, her workers' accent dropping away, revealing the tell-tale tone of a fashionable girls' school—Benenden, perhaps? "Tom, you get him for me, I'll guarantee it, I promise!"

The Misses Dobbs from Leeds were among the crowd and were invited to the stage party afterward as was Colonel Chase-Gordon and his pleasant wife. They were very delighted and excited by it all and were sitting together, placed by Molly, who knew how to arrange these things. They departed, talking loudly and expectantly. The last angel to arrive was Prince Ahmed, in immaculate dinner jacket and Arab headgear. He kissed Jill on the cheek and said, "Darling, I know this is going to run and run, I'm feeling very lucky tonight," and swept into the stalls, with Ali, his man, parting the crowd for him.

"Well," said Tom Tully, "can't say we haven't got everybody here, because we have."

The crush was by now intense. Actors and actresses began to arrive—Sir John Gielgud, Sir Ralph Richardson, Rex Harrison, Larry and Joan, Michael Dennison and Dulcie Grey; there were others, and inveterate first-nighters like Peter Cotes and, of course, Sir Harold Hobson. There were several American producers ready to cast a cool eye on the show, with a view toward Broadway, and there were Lords Grade and Delfont, who might even buy the film rights if all went well. She had words of greeting for them all, and still found time to be shaking with nerves as the second bell sounded and the foyer began to clear and was suddenly empty of everybody except herself and Tom Tully, who miraculously had two very large gin and tonics in his hand.

"Good luck, darling," he said.

Jill was shaking so much she almost dropped the glass. Behind her, in the auditorium, she could hear Maggie's clear, steady voice, answering Sir Henry's *"Ah, Madam, what a sad business it is. . . ."* and the hush of the audience throughout the entire theatre, as they listened to her reply.

She's a bitch, Jill thought, but thank God for her.

BACKSTAGE, everything was hushed, too. Josh stood there, knowing his place was traditionally out front, but unable to go, to leave his children and his baby. He just stood around at the side and got in everybody's way throughout the first half. There were no first-night nerves, although Brigid looked very pale and seemed without her usual attack and he saw her pressing her fist into her stomach quite fiercely, once or twice. Stomachache wasn't unusual at a first night, he thought, and said nothing. Sir Piers was pacing around his dressing room, getting into the feel of the part (or so he said) and Austin was hunched and white-faced but confident-looking.

Maggie was superb.

Josh watched her and felt proud. Of her talent and of the way he had warmed it back to life. He wondered if he loved Maggie. He supposed he did or he would not be sleeping with her. Or would he? It had all, anyway, worked out for the best. It had got Jill off his back. Jill was too much. He could not face *Queen* and Jill at the same time. He wondered, if things had been different, would he have run from her, as he plainly had, right into Maggie's bed? He felt uncomfortable at the thought. Maggie was pleasant and quiet, rather as Alison had been. Star or not, she had a sweet nature. Most of her emotions he guessed went into *this*, into her work, into the magnificent thing she was doing now, holding a thousand people in thrall. . . . *"I cannot believe that we have no alternative, Prime Minister. Surely there is something we can do. Surely things are not as bad as you tell me they are. Have we been a thousand years in this land, to come to this. . . ?"*

The interval came and the house buzzed. Josh worked around backstage, seeing that everything was all right, everybody was happy. He surmised there was a note of puzzlement, as well as excitement out front. This was not the usual West End fare. This was a serious piece, implacable, a warning as real as a cell door, as Vercek himself said. Was it what the audience would want to hear, resplendent in their satin and worsted, on the hottest September night for twenty-six years?

It seemed it was.

There were enthusiastic curtain calls and the dressing rooms were crowded after the curtain. Many of the celebrated people stayed on to eat smoked salmon and caviar and canapés and to drink riesling and beaujolais and to talk, long into the night. It was three o'clock when they all went homeward, and their voices hung in the stale air of the auditorium, crying of success and the long run that was doubtless going to happen, and the Royal Theatre absorbed the cries as it had absorbed the cries of countless other first nights over a hundred years.

Jill called out to the cast, "Go to my place, darlings, I'm off to Fleet Street for the critics," and left on her own. She could not bear to gaze any longer at Maggie hanging on Josh's arm, drained yet smiling, fending off the congratulations of well-wishers. Maggie looked too happy to live and enough was enough.

Jill found Tom Tully at her elbow in Shaftesbury Avenue, the streets warm even in the darkness.

"I'll drive you down to Fleet Street, love," he said sympathetically. She wondered if he knew about Maggie and Josh. She guessed he did. She got into Tom's Jaguar. She found she did not care. All she cared about was *Queen*. Wasn't it? She settled back against the cool leather of the seat and closed her eyes. Of course it was.

THE notices were mixed.

Jill sat in Tom Tully's Jaguar in Fleet Street and read them one after the other. Jack Tinker in the *Mail* thought it was a great play, the dramatic equivalent to Solzhenitsyn's novels. John Barber in the *Telegraph* thought it a very important drama indeed, touching on genius. The *Guardian*, however, felt it was a cold-war story and advised any reader going to see it to take a packet of salt along with him. Irving Wardle in *The Times* found it strangely irrelevant, as if the author were picking at old sores. It did not seem to him to belong to the moment. It could, he ventured, be almost described as an anti-détente play. The *Express* thought it good and timely but wished it was shorter and wasn't sure if it was a good thing for stage plays to portray the queen, even if they didn't say it was the queen.

The *Sun* was sure it was a bad thing, a scandal even, and that the producers were showing bad taste in cashing in on royalty. The *Mirror* hated it, thought it a disgrace that, at a time when we should be seeking to mend our bridges with the Communist bloc, such a warlike play should appear in London. We needed peace plays, not war plays, said the *Mirror*.

Every critic thought the two knights were marvelous. Everybody had reservations about Maggie's accent as the queen, but most conceded it was a "bravura performance" (*The Times*), and "wonderfully paced" (the *Telegraph*). The *Guardian* thought Sir Piers's performance "a marvel of authority, the like of which we have come to expect from our greatest actor!" Austin Ames was assessed variously as "very modern in technique but somewhat fussy" (*Financial Times*) and "a strong president but with a human face, brilliant" (*Mirror*). Brigid Kelly got a favorable mention from almost every critic: from "a splendid cameo" (*Times*) to "a sexy newcomer from the Emerald Isle" in the *Sun*, which also had a middle-page picture-spread of Brigid in a bikini, the caption of which read: "*Star Brigid Waits for Mister Right.*" The *Morning Star* described *Queen* as "a piece of Fascist propaganda, especially written and produced to deceive the working people of this country as to the true nature of capitalist society."

Every critic thought Sir Harry was wonderful.

Altogether, Jill thought, handing the copies around her penthouse, to which the entire cast had repaired for coffee, sandwiches, and the notices, the critics' reception of the play itself was not as good as she had hoped. Not fatal. Yet, oddly cautious.

"Could be worse," she said to Josh.

She was able to speak to him so long as she did not have to look at Maggie at the same time. Maggie was lying back in a deep chair, eyes closed, exhausted. She had just given a great performance, Jill thought, and she didn't give a damn what the critics thought, and rightly so. Just the same, she was still a bitch. The fact that she was an innocent one changed nothing.

355

"Could be a lot worse," said Josh, "for a play that all but destroys the liberal consensus!" He was sprawled on the leather couch and his eyes looked very tired. He was wearing a new silk shirt, and his hair was far too long and he looked vaguely unhappy. *She* is trying to make him over into something he isn't, thought Jill. Let us hope she has no more luck than I did.

"I think we did well, all things considered," said Sir Piers, eating a ham sandwich with appetite. "The critics aren't sure of the play. That's all, poor dears. They have a kind of Mafia, you know. They all meet in the foyer and sip their gins at the interval and give each other the eye and exchange the odd word and presto! Osmosis happens and in that instant they all decide to write it up much the same way. Otherwise a critic might be out of step too often, in which case he'd be out of work, once his editor noticed, what?"

"In that case," said Sir Harry, "it's obvious some of them went to the lavatory because they ain't agreed on the play, are they?"

"Well, of course they ain't," retorted Sir Piers. "And I must say I'm very glad none of them noticed your constant upstaging, dear old friend."

"If you mean," said Sir Harry sweetly, "when you very *accidentally* masked me in my important speech, then I must say I'm glad they didn't."

"Masked you? Never, dear boy!" Sir Piers winked at the company.

"Of course, it's very masculine to shout, but I do feel a falsetto note in your big speech, Piers."

"*Falsetto!*"

"I'm afraid so. Almost, if you'll excuse the word, *feminine?*" Sir Harry looked earnestly round. "Did anybody else find it so?"

"Absolute rot, Hal, and you know it!"

"I can't think why you should find it offensive?" Sir Harry enquired. "I mean, you did used to have quite a *feminine* streak in your nature in the old days, Piers, now didn't you? In *Othello,* for instance? All those years ago?"

"In my performance, you mean?"

"You know I don't mean in your performance, dear. I mean in your personal, your *very* personal life."

"What rubbish, Hal. You do talk balls sometimes!"

"I'm thinking of that young juvenile, the boy who was killed in the war? Weren't you and he, well, *friends?*"

Sir Piers was on his feet, waving the *Daily Telegraph* (in which he had a favorable notice). "Take that back, you awful old creature!"

"Absolutely not. I know you two had a *thing*, dear."

"How can you possibly know that, you dreadful old faggot?"

"Because he told me, dear. He and I had a thing *too*, you see."

Sir Piers roared and lunged forward. Sir Harry simply smiled as Austin and Max held Sir Piers's arms. "Liar! Bloody liar!" yelled Sir Piers. "Bloody lying old faggot!"

"I don't think so but let's not get our bums in an uproar," said Sir Harry, smiling at Brigid. "I mean, a lot of us *are* bisexual, after all."

"You're not bisexual," roared Sir Piers. "You're an old pouf!"

"I resent the word *old*, dear," replied Sir Harry. "Is there another sandwich does anybody know? I'm starving."

There was a buzz at the door. They all fell silent.

"Expecting anybody?" asked Josh.

"What, at four in the morning? Find out who it is."

Josh asked in a soft voice, over the intercom. He turned back to her. "It's Vercek."

"Here? How did he find out where I lived?"

"God knows."

"Well, let him in, please."

"Sure." Josh said, "Welcome. Come up. Penthouse. Press *P* in the lift." He turned back to the company. "Did anybody see him at the theatre?"

The cast, silent, shook their heads and yawned. Sir Piers sat down, muttering. Dawn was turning into day outside and tiredness was beginning to hit them as their adrenaline ran down. It had been a frantic day for everybody. Jill remembered it only in a blur of exhaustion. The last-minute snags inseparable from a London first night had of course happened: cancellations of important people who had promised to be present and their replacement at short notice by even more important people. The house had been full but (a secret known only to Jill and Herbie Glass) it had been a quarter paper. These comps had been given to people who could be relied on to keep quiet about it, since they wouldn't get any more tickets if they didn't. The Keith Prowse Agency had been polite but firm: they had not upped their advance bookings, despite a final plea in person from Jill Viner. They had been sorry, the hot weather didn't look like breaking, although it must soon, surely, and attendances generally were down by almost half, as against a third a week ago. Shows were closing all over town. Jill was unlucky in her timing. But things could change. If the notices were particularly good, especially in *The Times* and *Guardian* and *Telegraph* (the others mattered less), then they would certainly review the position.

But the notices had not been particularly good, they had been mixed: and, although the Shaftesbury Avenue audience had applauded, they had looked a trifle puzzled at the interval, and had filed out of the theatre at the end of the play (after the national anthem; Jill had decided to play it for *this*, of all plays) looking sober and thoughtful. Jill, listening in the foyer for any passing remarks by theatregoers, had heard a man say, "Not a lot of laughs," but others had said, "Very interesting," in the guarded way that people (especially people who wished to be thought thoughtful) had when they didn't know what to think or what they were expected to think. Even Herbie Glass had looked doubtful as he stood in the number one dressing room at the Royal, after the show. The room was full of cables—one from Joe Dancy, and that was nice of Joe—and flowers and bottles of wine in baskets and well-wishers by the score, other actresses (Joan Plowright, Glenda

Jackson, and Deborah Kerr) and actors and fellow impresarios, and altogether a feeling of success, success, success, and yet . . .

And yet the house had been one-quarter paper.

And the reviews had been mixed.

VERCEK was still wearing the old bomber jacket and corduroy trousers and heavy boots. He refused a glass of wine, asking, "Do you have vodka?" and Josh found some for him in the drinks cabinet. The cast smiled and shuffled and yawned. They were wary of authors by training and especially of foreign ones. It was a barrier that could be broken down only by constant attendance at rehearsals and the sharing of many in-jokes and a lot of flattery and shared experiences. Vercek had been noticeably absent and he was certainly no flatterer.

"Well, Mr. Author," Sir Piers boomed, "the audience called for you tonight, but you were not present."

"I was present. I was in the audience."

Sir Piers exploded. "But, my dear fella, they wanted to *see* you! They called out for you." He coughed. "One or two of them, anyway."

"I have no interest in their curiosity. They were there to see my play, not gape at me."

"They would have enjoyed seeing you, you know," said Sir Harry gently.

"Really?" asked Vercek. He seemed surprised.

"Anyway," asked Sir Piers heartily, "what did you think of us?"

"Adequate," said Vercek, after a long pause in which he seemed to be thinking deeply.

"*Adequate?*" echoed Sir Piers.

"Just so," said Vercek, and sat down.

"Well, I'll be buggered," said Sir Piers, and sat down too, shaking his head. He seemed to have quite forgotten his upset with

Sir Harry. "Between you and the critics this is getting more like a wake every moment."

"The critics," said Vercek, "know nothing."

VERCEK wondered why he had come. He supposed it was author's vanity.

He was a little disappointed in himself. He had supposed that he was over that cult-of-personality nonsense. He had been taught at his very first school of drama (taught most earnestly) that a writer was simply one of the team, as important as, but no more important than, any other member—the electricians, the newest young actress, the props girl, the director himself. In Socialist theatre everybody was equal and their contribution was judged solely on their adherence to and propagation of the Socialist cause. Nothing else. Which was why so many writers got into trouble: they could not accept this. He had not accepted it, in the end: and yet the vestiges of the training still clung to him (how could it be otherwise?) and he hated his display of Western egotism. He should not need to meet and talk to these people tonight. It was enough that he had written the play and that they had performed it, as he had told them, adequately.

The problem was: they were all stars, all victims of the Western theatrical cult-of-personality system. They had not been real people up there on the stage at the Royal Theatre that evening. They had been well-fed, well-known, excellently technical actors playing all out for themselves. He had wanted more, he had hoped for more. He had hoped for reality, something rarely seen in Western drama. But in the end it had been well enough. The actress playing the queen had improved enormously. One should not feel too cast down. Things could have been a great deal worse. The play had been put on. A lot of people had seen it, though how many had understood it he did not know. Not, perhaps, very many. That was inevitable. The important thing was that it ran for a while, a few weeks or a few months, so that people talked about it, about the ideas contained in it. The actors' performances were important, naturally. The warning that the play gave was more important, it was paramount. Did the audience in Shaftesbury Avenue that evening—the women bejeweled and scented, the men smart and barbered and blow-waved, some he noticed wearing discreet male makeup and yet not homosexual—did these people, any more than the workers of Wallingford, or the burghers of Brighton, know what danger they were in, in the West? Would *Queen* have opened any eyes or were they steadfastly shut, as people's eyes were shut to Hitler in the thirties?

There was no way he could know.

Josh Williams passed Vercek a pile of newspapers open at the critics' notices. Vercek read them gloomily and without surprise. The critics represented their editors and their readership (in that order) and there was no point in expecting anything else. They did at least have critics in the West. They did at least sometimes speak with their own voices. *"Strangely innocent"* . . . ? *"Picking at old sores"* . . . ? *"Take a packet of salt along with you to this play, you'll need it"* . . . ? Vercek drummed the maimed hand on the coffee table and gazed around him at the beautiful people: the glamorous Maggie, asleep (or anyway with her eyes closed), a child of the system but a talented one. He wondered if as a young man he would have found her attractive sexually. He supposed so. But he would have been totally alien to her and she to him. Obviously the director was sleeping with her, since he was not talking to her but had a negligent hand on her silken knee. It was inevitable, with her looks, that somebody would be sleeping with her. Vercek sighed. Women he had given up since his wife had finally betrayed him. He did not blame her, she had the children and the pressure had been intolerable. Still, she had told them where some of the manuscripts were and they had dug them out of the frozen earth (he had watched them do it and so had she) and finally thrown them onto the ground like pieces of pornography, laughing and excited, in their fur hats and thick overcoats. They had clapped him on the back and given him vodka before they hustled him back into the big black Mosska. His wife and the boys, expressionless, had watched him go. They had not spoken to him, or smiled, all the time the men dug in the garden, but his head was shaven and he had lost weight and possibly they did not recognize him. His wife had not waved either. She had not even cried. He had not seen her since that moment. Vercek handed the newspapers back to Josh Williams.

"Not too bad," Josh said in his understated English fashion.

"They are journalists doing their work." Vercek shrugged and dismissed the subject. He accepted another vodka. It was good to be in company. Man was a herd animal. Such feelings were natural but they were also dangerous. Personal exposure was something that might not be tolerated. How could one tell? Some official back there could put his name on an agenda with a question mark after it. That would be all it would take. No. This was foolish, and irrational, coming here. However, man was a foolish and irrational animal, and he had not quite stopped being a man. He had tried working hard to force the foolish self-pity away (the bed-sitter in Camden Town was really just another cell) but he had not succeeded and so here he was. If it had been snowing outside he would have felt the impulse to get drunk, the only pleasure left. As it was, the whole town sweated and the bed-sitter was stuffy and as hot as Nevsky Prospekt in July.

Vercek lit one of Josh Williams's cigars and inhaled deeply. Smoke was good, too, but if necessary he could do without it. In the Gulag he had not smoked for three years. He looked around the room. It was full of money. It was full of Western affluence. Chairs of soft leather, rugs of Indian design, embossed wallpaper like soft fabric, polished wood, table lighter of solid silver, cigarette box spilling with Turkish and Virginian tubes, gold flashing on the women at wrist and throat, apart from the young people, Brigid and Max, who were so sick of affluence they were trying to look poor, through sheer guilt and glut.

The room was warm, there was food and coffee and liquor in abundance. Did none of them know that you cannot keep these things unless you are prepared to defend them, you cannot flaunt them in the faces of people who eat cabbage every day and meat once a week if they are lucky and own nothing whatever in gold or even silver, and have nothing of satin or silk in their wardrobe, and are hungry, being human, for all these things? And did they expect them not to feel envious of and angry with you and wonder whether you deserved them? The next step from there being: will you hand them over without a struggle, or will you defend them, and if so, with what resolve?

Rome, Vercek thought, or Athens, must have looked, at the end, not unlike this.

JILL moved across and sat down beside Vercek. Anything was better than looking at Josh's hand resting on the knee of the sleeping Maggie.

"We are sorry we haven't seen more of you."

Verced nodded. "I have been busy. I am writing my journal."

"Not another play in the works."

Vercek shook his head. "I will write no more plays, I think."

"Why is that?"

"The audience did not fully comprehend, I feel. In Paris and Brussels and Bonn and Rome maybe they will. But in London I think not. You are behind your strip of water and you think nothing can touch you. You have not been invaded since 1066, is it?" Vercek smiled. "The others know better. In recent history they know better. So." Vercek put out Josh's excellent cigar half smoked and took out one of his awful cardboard cigarettes. The fumes from it were strong and rank, and Vercek understood Jill's amused reac-

tion. "This is the only tobacco I find satisfying since a long time."
Vercek spoke English a good deal less well than he wrote it. Jill
asked him why and he said simply, "Dictionaries. Books of gram-
mar. In prison there is plenty of time. More than you want of it. In
prison you can learn anything." Vercek tapped the ash from the
cigarette with his maimed hand. "Of course in the camps it is
different. There it is work until you die!"

Jill felt suddenly cold. She said, hastily, "I think we will get
productions for you in Europe. As you say, West Germany and
France and Belgium and so on. It depends how well it runs in
London, really. The Europeans are culture vultures. If *Queen* is
discussed seriously in the important weeklies they will see it." She
hesitated. "It is a bit plain for them. They like things difficult, they
like plays that aren't quite so direct, plays they can *discuss.*"

"Dilettantes. Would-be intellectuals," said Vercek sadly. "I
have known many of these. They will be discussing such things
when the end of the world comes. It is their education. It is too
much . . . too much . . . how to say . . . enquiry, not enough feel."

Jill said, "I've had some American interest, too. If we run for
six months here I think we'll get Broadway. If not, not, I'm afraid."

Vercek said nothing for a long moment. He did not even
smoke. He did not seem to breathe. Then he said softly, "America?"

"One or two producers were in tonight. I haven't talked to
them yet. I may tomorrow. I'm trying not to rush them."

"New York?" Vercek seemed to be talking to himself.
"America?"

"Only if we run," Jill insisted. She decided to come to the
point. "A number of radio and television people have called the
office. They would like you to appear on some programs, discussing
the play." Jill hesitated. "It might help a very great deal if
you would."

Tom Tully moved across, enormous gin in hand. "What the
lady says is absolutely right, old boy," he informed Vercek cheer-
fully. "I can get you absolutely top coverage, guaranteed, all the

major papers, plus a big spread in one of the color supplements. I think it's worth a go, dear boy."

Vercek stood up abruptly, burning cardboard cigarette in his hand. "I am an author. I have said in my play what I have said. I do not wish ignorant journalists to ask me questions about it."

"It's all publicity," said Jill, with dismay.

"Then let the actors talk about it. They will enjoy that."

Jill laughed, trying hard to save the moment. "All actors ever do is talk about themselves. You know that, Mr. Vercek."

"Vercek only, please. And why not? It is only gossip these people want. Your glamorous people can do this, not I." Vercek took a deep breath. "If there is money for me?"

"Of course. If you could call in at the office?"

"I prefer now. Cash, if you please."

Jill, startled, opened her handbag. She had forty pounds in cash. She gave it to him. "There's more due to you, a lot more."

"I will be in touch. Please to say good-night to all, for me?"

And he was out the door.

None of the cast seemed to notice that he had gone. The day was light now and they had reacted to it, and Tommi Traceham was proposing to make everybody bacon and eggs and coffee. Jill said, "All right, why not!"

She wondered where on earth Vercek lived.

VERCEK took a cruising taxi to Swiss Cottage and walked from there, stopping often in empty arcades and twice doubling back on his tracks. Nobody, except an old derelict and a policeman trying shop doors. His spirits lifted. All was well. He was becoming an old fool, paranoia was setting in. Well, why not? He had plenty to be paranoid about in his life. He was very tired indeed when he finally got to his room in Camden Town.

He took from his cupboard his bottle of vodka and drank half a cupful.

AUSTIN Ames said good-bye to Maggie at the doorstep of Jill's penthouse and took a taxi to Annabel's. It had closed, and another hot day was beginning but he did not feel like bed, alone anyway. Or even with anybody in it. He wanted Maggie in it. It was as simple as that. He felt tense, keyed up, the way he always did after a big first night. He wasn't disappointed by the reviews. He knew he had been good. He thought, I'll do better if the show should transfer to Broadway, they'll know what I'm doing there, they'll *see* what I'm doing. The president, to a Shaftesbury Avenue audience, is like the king of Siam, a creature from outer space. Okay, I can wait. He walked on the Embankment, watching the capital come to life, and finally, when he was very tired, he walked back to the Savoy, went to bed, and to his surprise, slept.

His last waking thoughts were of Maggie.

SIR Harry and Mario drove sedately back to Sir Harry's Brook Street apartment in a Corniche. "You know, Silvio," said Sir Harry, "I thought I was rather good tonight." He yawned. "Did you notice how old Piers tried to throw me by giving his big speech at the end direct to the queen? He'd never done that before, the cunning old bear. Of course, I just went upstage and left him to it. Made him look an absolute fool, delivering the speech to the wrong person, you noticed that, did you Silvio?"

"Certainly," replied Mario, who had noticed nothing except an attractive middle-aged man in the seat in front of him, accompanied, tiresomely, by his wife.

"You know," Sir Harry yawned again, "I must be getting old or something but I really am quite tired."

Mario, who had heard this before, said nothing.

Sir Harry drank a nightcap of brandy and champagne, took a shower and slept soundly, in his Harrods silk pajamas, until almost noon. When he wakened (to orange pekoe tea brought by Silvio) he felt particularly randy. "I'm most awfully sorry about last night,

Mario," he said. "You must excuse me but I'm quite an old gent and I need my sleep."

Silvio said, "That's all right. I'm Silvio."

"Oh, are you? That's what I said, isn't it?"

Mario looked around the door. "Did I hear my name?"

"Well, of course. Just talking about you, dear boy, weren't we, Mario?"

"Is this a private party? Or can anyone join in?"

"Oh," said Sir Harry fondly, "you are a naughty boy!"

SIR Piers had a late breakfast too, and was joined in bed by his quite young wife, who wore a see-through nightdress and a large dab of Chanel Number 19.

"I thought you were wonderful last night, darling," she said.

Sir Piers regarded her warmly. "Thought you weren't there. Thought you were too nervous for me."

Lady Piers kissed his cheek. "Of course I was nervous for you, darling. But I just had to be there. You were the best thing in it. The phone has never stopped ringing. These are your calls." She handed him a list of actors and agents and producers. He ran a practiced eye over it. Some were actually genuine, and not just bread-and-butter. Well, he had a following and there was no doubt surely in anybody's mind now that he had demonstrated at last that, in a fair fight, he could get the better of that crafty old thing, Hal, who had been definitely out of order in his remarks about poor dead Bobby.

"What did you think of Hal?" he asked, slyly.

Lady Piers pondered. "He was just Hal. As usual."

"You liked mine better?"

"No comparison, darling. You exuded masculinity. Hal, well, he's always just so very camp, isn't he?"

"Camp?" Sir Piers savored the word. "Yes. He is. But he has technique. Old Hal has technique. Got to give him that. Did you see how he got upstage of me in the last scene? Thought I'd turn to him, have to, since I was talking to him, wasn't I? Well, I didn't, I just gave my speech direct to the queen, to Maggie, and left him there with egg on his face, you notice that?"

"Yes, dear, very clever," said Lady Piers, who hadn't.

"D'yer know what else he said, the old thing? That I'd fancied a boy, all those years ago. In *Othello*."

His wife looked interested. "And did you?"

Sir Piers hesitated. "Not me, me dear. Nothing like that about me!"

Lady Piers looked disappointed. "Oh, I thought you were going to shock me, Piers."

"Look, once when I was in Tangier I went to this bar—I was a young fella then, married to Vicki—and I had a few drinks with this girl and we went in a sort of back room and it turned out to be a fella."

"How was it?" cried Lady Piers, in high sexuality, her fingers probing.

"Well," said Sir Piers, "it just wasn't the same!"

SHE lived in Kensington and he found her in bed. "I see your first night went well." She was reading the *Mail* he'd brought in with the milk. Max was in the kitchen making coffee. He called out, "Yeah. It won't run though. This bloody hot weather. Nobody's going to the theatre. Anyway, it's a bloody Fascist play!"

"Is it?" asked Mitzi, who like most makeup girls was beautiful but not intellectual. She made room for Max to get into the bed beside her. "Tell me about it. Can you get me tickets?"

"Get the world tickets." Max slid into bed naked, without washing or brushing his teeth, both actions he would have considered bourgeois. "It'll close." He put his arm around her and turned her so that she was kneeling, her buttocks spread. "Tell you what, let's talk later."

368

Mitzi, who liked that position (it seemed more exciting than the dreary old missionary favored by her regular boyfriend, an elderly cameraman), turned her head and smiled and said, "I thought you had a thing with that actress, Brigid whatsit?"

"Gone lez," said Max, and entered her.

Later, he told her about his play.

BRIGID Kelly was very tired when they got to Tommi's Knightsbridge apartment. Sex was not possible because Brigid was still recovering from her abortion, performed on the previous Sunday. Brigid was still sore and her pudenda was shaved and she felt, she told Tommi, like a convict, or somebody who'd just had scabies. Tommie said, "You could just as easily have got them from that turd." She made Brigid hot milk and brought biscuits and sat on the bed beside her until Brigid's eyes began to close. "I had a few things I was going to do tonight—I was going to take one or two scenes away from Maggie but I never did it. I was too tired. I was just glad to get through it. Do you suppose anybody noticed?"

"No," said Tommi. "Everybody was too busy thinking about themselves. They were all depressed before curtain-up and absolutely bloody manic afterwards." Nobody had mentioned her lovely revolve set, or the dress she had designed for the queen. Well, it was to be hoped one of the Sundays would. One lived in hopes. Bloody philistine critics, they didn't know an electric revolve from a fucking three-piece suit. "Darling, you did really well. I mean"— Tommi opened a newspaper—"the good old *Sun* says you're waiting for Mr. Right!"

They both laughed, and Brigid felt happy. "Don't lose the paper, I want to keep it."

"I'll buy you a scrapbook in Harrods tomorrow," promised Tommi.

Brigid kissed her on the lips. "You're a darling, Tommi."

"I know," said Tommi. "I know."

She sat there, holding Brigid's thin white hand until she fell asleep. Poor little cow, she thought, wondering if she meant Brigid or herself.

MAGGIE lay naked in Josh Williams's bed in Glebe Place and watched him take off the silk St. Laurent shirt she had bought him the day before. She thought what a nice man he was and how his new shirts suited him. Hadn't Jill Viner *cared* how he looked? The gold bracelet on his wrist, with her initials and his own, was further evidence of her ownership of him. Josh took off his jeans and his boots and went into the bathroom and showered. That was another thing she liked about him. He was a very clean man. So many Europeans (and that included the English) were not. They bathed when they felt like it. But this was a hot, sweaty September, and in the theatre the smell of the audience had been overpowering, nothing like a New York audience at all, who would be showered and perfumed. Of course, there was no air-conditioning in the Royal. It had been an oven. There had been times, in the heavy velvet of the queen's gown, when she had felt like swooning.

"Darling," she called. "Was I really all right?"

"What?" Josh switched off the shower.

"Was I really all right?"

"Wonderful!" he yelled and switched the shower on again.

Maggie relaxed. She had been good. She knew that. What could have been a disaster Josh Williams had turned into a triumph. So, all right, the audience had been (she had learned with shock) one-quarter paper. So, all right, some critics had complained about her very slight American accent. Still, she had triumphed. And it was all due to Josh Williams. He had held her hand, all the way. He had encouraged her, and cajoled her, and never lost his temper with her, and best of all he had loved her. He had loved her talent and he had loved her body and she had needed that, too. She had needed that very much. She had responded, as she was ready to respond now. She felt moist just thinking of him. Oh, she was lucky. He was a very talented director but not young, and the problem was going to be to get him to stay in America when the Broadway run was over. She felt they would transfer, no matter what. The play was too good not to; dark as the end of the play was, it was right. She had not argued. Maggie snuggled naked under the covers. It would all work out fine. Josh would stay on Broadway (or even off-Broadway; there was no disgrace in that) and she would do her movie parts and her stage parts as she pleased and they would buy a summer place in, say, the Vineyard or maybe Chatham and without doubt live happily ever after.

Josh came back into the room in a bath towel, and rubbing his eyes. Poor darling. He was tired, too. Maggie wished he would come to the Savoy sometime but he said he hated creeping out of women's beds at dawn. Well, so did she mind. She hated going back to the hotel alone. This time she would stay till morning. Josh got into bed and lit a cigar and smoked it quietly and she waited for him to touch her, but he just said, "Y'know, I'm absolutely bloody bushed, darling, I absolutely have to sleep," and he turned over and absolutely bloody slept. Maggie lay awake for a long time, rejected, and thought: Philip would never have done that, no he wouldn't, never. Next to her, Josh Williams snored.

JILL Viner went to bed alone, in her Bryanston Square penthouse, amid a ruin of dirty glasses and cups and plates.

She took a Mogadon.

It had been a successful first night.

There were a lot of questions.

Would it run?

Would the weather break soon?

Were the American producers really interested?

Or would their interest bomb with the news of the quarter-papered house?

Nobody could tell.

Go to sleep.

Oh, Josh Williams, you bastard, I love you.

Go to sleep.

She took another Mogadon.

HERBIE Glass was sorry.

The receipts had fallen below half and he intended to take *Queen* off in three weeks. He would be sending Jill an official letter to that effect but he was softening the blow by asking her here to supper in his South Street house and telling her personally, because he wanted to explain why he was doing it. Producers always got temperamental when you took their plays off. It was to be expected, of course. They had backers who were going to lose money and that effected them for further productions. In Jill's case he knew it was a double disaster, since it was her very first production, and a first production that closed after six weeks would be a black mark from which she might not recover. He knew all this, Herbie Glass said, sadly, sipping his Perrier and puffing on his Monte Cristo, but there it was. He was a businessman and business was bad. There was nothing else to do but cut his losses. He was personally very, very sorry.

Jill, who had been half expecting something like this, was still shocked. She marshaled the arguments she had rehearsed, coming over in the taxi, staring at the still-sweltering streets. Here they were, in October and still the temperature was in the eighties most of the day. She said, "Herbie, it's the weather that's doing it, darling. The movies are the same, nobody's going. The restaurants

372

are empty, nobody's eating out, the whole town is dead. In three weeks everything could be changed. It could be raining every day. It could even be cold."

Herbie pushed his gold-rimmed plate, with its crumbs of Stilton, away. "I know, but then it will be too late. I have an offer of a new musical, so I'm going to take it. Maybe I'll be wrong but I don't think so. I know *Queen*'s a good play, maybe a great play, but enough people aren't coming in to see it. Maybe it isn't the weather, Jill. Maybe it's the play. The subject. Jesus, you have the best cast in London. It has to be the subject." Herbie poured himself a little wine to help his Perrier. "Keith Prowse haven't improved their bookings. Nobody else has either. Face it, Jill, you relied on word-of-mouth and you haven't had it."

"My press has been terrific—" Jill protested.

"I know, I know." Herbie waved his cigar. "I'm sorry, Jill."

Jill thought hard. "I could possibly raise more money from my backers."

"I wouldn't if I were you," Herbie mused. "Could make it worse next time you go to them. If you ask for more and it still flops you're worse off than ever."

"But isn't it worth the risk?"

Herbie shrugged. "It's their money, not yours or mine."

Jill said, "I haven't taken any fat management fees. I'm still working for peanuts until we're in profit."

Herbie looked startled. "You really are?"

"Yes, I really am."

He shook his head. "Look. If this flops you can come and work for me. I could use you in my organization, Jill. You're a smart girl. Come where the bricks and mortar is. Nobody's going to knock my theatre down, unless I do. The Royal, for example, it's always there. Plays and players come and go. Managements, too. Theatres go on forever."

Jill shook her head. "Thanks for the offer. I'll have to see." She was shattered, there was no other word for it. All that *work*, for *this!*

Herbie's butler came in and Herbie nodded. "That'll be all tonight, John." The butler left and two minutes later the outside door slammed discreetly. "John thinks I'm going to score, as they say," said Herbie gently. "But of course I'm not, am I?"

"No." Jill laughed at the idea. "I like you, Herbie, you know that, but not that way and certainly not now."

"I just wondered," Herbie said, "if you would be interested, that's all. You'll pardon an old feller for asking."

"You're not old." Jill meant it. "You look so good."

"For my age?"

"No. Generally. You do."

"The truth is I'm sixty-seven."

"Never!"

"I am. I don't mention it, unless I think it helps."

Jill pressed his hand. "You're very kind and—"

"All I need is a wife, I know. I've had two and I didn't need them."

Herbie helped Jill to brandy and she sipped it slowly. At last, at the end of a long silence, looking around Herbie's huge dining room (God, he had everything—Sheraton, Wedgwood, Sèvres, you name it), she wondered why he felt he had to do this, close *Queen.* He liked her, he even seemed to half love her (the roses, the telephone calls, the intimate suppers) and now *this.* She said, "Herbie, would nothing change your mind?"

God, what was she thinking about?

She could hardly believe she had said it.

Herbie said nothing at first, looking at her with his dark almond eyes that contrasted dramatically with the thick white hair. He certainly did not look his age (all kinds of rumors were about: that he took beauty treatments, face lifts, wore makeup, went to Switzerland for the whole bit) and Jill found herself curiously sympathetic. Herbie was hanging on to life as she was hanging on to *Queen*. Herbie wanted the things that had gone. Youth, beauty, love. She had had those things (still possessed two of them; love had vanished with Josh Williams) and she wanted the things that belonged to age and success. Power, respect, admiration. Money, too, but only as their extension.

If *Queen* ran for six months, she thought, we'd get Broadway for sure. She also thought, Josh Williams does not love me and nobody else does either and my life is my own.

Into the long silence broken only by the ticking of the ormolu clock, Herbie Glass said in a measured tone, "I never mix business with pleasure, Jill."

Her cheeks stung red. "I'm sorry. That was stupid."

"No. You're desperate. I see that. More than I thought." He brooded. "Jill. I'm foolish about you. I know I am and you must know it, too. But I want you as a man wants a woman and not as payment for a debt."

Jill stared at the tablecloth. She could find no words.

Herbie got to his feet and took the glasses and bottle of wine with him into another room. Jill sat miserably on at the table, and finished her own large brandy at a gulp. She had been a fool. She had insulted a nice man. What could she say?

After a few minutes Herbie called, "Jill?"

When she went into the bedroom Herbie Glass was in bed.

He was wearing silk monogrammed pajamas and had library glasses on his nose. In his hand was what looked like a balance sheet.

"I felt tired," he said simply. "So I went to bed."

Jill looked around the bedroom. Everything was soft cream. Rugs, silk bedspreads, walls, dressing table. "I know," Herbie Glass said gloomily. "it looks like the inside of a dairy. Not my idea, my daughter had it done for me. Can't be bothered to have it changed. Don't suppose I'll outlive it."

"Nonsense." Jill sat on the bed, feeling light-headed. It must be all the wine and brandy, she thought—and the exhaustion and disappointment. Not that it has sunk in yet. "What's that you're reading?"

"The production budget of *Queen*."

"You're not supposed to have that, Herbie. You're not an investor."

"Listen, darling, I'm trying to help." He peered at the document. "You could cut salaries. Your actors are getting far too much money."

Jill shook her head. "If you cut salaries it gets around. Then everybody knows it's a failure."

"True." Herbie Glass looked at the paper again. "I see my cousin is your biggest investor apart from Prince Ahmed." Herbie polished his glasses on the silk sheet. "Hate to see him lose it all, even if he is an idiot." He sighed. "Look. I won't put the notice in for two weeks. Anything can happen in two weeks."

Jill kissed him. "Herbie, thank you, thank you."

"For what?" He rescued the glasses. "It's only two weeks. It's a reprieve, that's all. What you need, my dear, is a miracle!"

Jill stood up and dazedly began to unbutton her dress.

Herbie held up his hand. "Jill, you're a lovely girl, but no. That was a business decision and, like I say, I never mix business with pleasure. Will you close the front door when you leave? I think I'll have an early night." He held up the production statement. "Never go to bed with a book. Go with a balance sheet." He smiled wickedly. "A lot more interesting."

Jill kissed him again on the cheek and said, "I would, you know."

"Yes, I know, but you have this Josh man and I never liked sleeping with women who love other men, even when I was young." He waved the library glasses. "Good-night, my dear, and good luck, and don't forget to shut the front door."

Jill threw her stole over her shoulders and waved and was gone.

In the still-warm Mayfair street she stood for a long moment, listening to the growl of the late evening traffic moving across Hyde Park. Thank God for Herbie Glass. At least it wasn't a sentence of death. It was a reprieve, as Herbie had said. Now all she needed was the miracle.

JOSH Williams sat in the office of Queen Productions in a new pair of black leather trousers. She felt they were probably Maggie's idea.

"Two weeks, for God's sake!" He stood up and walked around the office, turning his face away so she would not see the anger and hurt. "No chance of a reprieve?"

"Seems not." Jill was cold and desperate and she had not slept very well. News like Herbie's was hard to digest. She had tossed and turned all night, had got up twice to make coffee (which had pepped her up even more), and had tried to think of ways and means. She had eaten breakfast (more coffee, and toast) feeling totally drained, and had left the Bryanston Square penthouse thinking: Well, at least the rent is paid for two more months. After that, I'll probably have to go on the streets.

I almost did, she thought, with Herbie last night.

I would have, too.

"We could ask the backers for more." Jill tried to keep her voice businesslike but she was conscious of the sympathetic eye of Molly. Molly knew how she felt about Josh. Christ, who didn't know? she wondered.

"If we did," Josh asked, "how long would we last on it?"

"Not more than another couple of weeks. And, of course, our goodwill would be gone, for anything we'd want to do in the future."

"It will be gone anyway," Josh said harshly. He sat down, then got up again. "I wonder if I did something wrong somewhere."

"No," Jill said, loyally. "The production is fine. We might

377

have done a bit better with the critics, I suppose."

"I had the *Mirror* on, asking if I hated the royal family, did I tell you?"

"No." Jill was shocked. "Did they?"

"Also, was I a member of the Nazi Bund or some such outfit?"

"Was that the *Mirror*?"

"Workers' Revolutionary Party, can't think what their rag's called. Awfully upper-class voice."

Jill said, "People seem to have been shocked by us showing the queen? I can't think why."

"We've never said it was the queen, have we?"

"No. But it is and they know it is."

"Well. We had to do it like that. Otherwise we might as well have changed everything, pretended it was a fable, and done it at the National in the first place." Josh stood up angrily. "Have you talked to Herbie, really strongly?"

"I did everything except go to bed with him." She smiled. "I'd have done that if it would have helped."

Josh did not rise to the remark, did not even seem to hear it. He sat down again, helplessly. "When do you want me to tell the cast?"

"No great hurry. Next week. Who knows, something may turn up."

"Like what?"

Jill shook her head. "I don't know. Rain maybe?"

"It wouldn't be enough."

"No, I suppose not. Oh Christ, I feel so bloody about it, after all we've done!" Jill felt tears pricking her eyes. She batted them away with her eyelashes, but one, more persistent than the rest, escaped and ran down her face. She felt more angry about that than about anything else. To cry, to behave like a bloody silly woman about a business decision like Herbie's! How did it look to Josh, who had as much at stake as herself, and was merely angry and frustrated? "I'm sorry, doing this, it's stupid." She reached for a tissue but Josh put a clean handkerchief in her hand. She glanced at it. At least it wasn't new and had not been given to him by Maggie. She coughed and wiped her eyes—the mascara had run and she had to do repairs—and Molly went very sympathetically out of the office, and Jill said, "Oh, Josh, it's terrible, we've done all this, all the work, and it's all been for nothing, it's so bloody I could die," and then she was sobbing and his arms were around her and he was saying, "There, there, Jill, no point in upsetting yourself, you know. There's always hope—"

"There isn't, there isn't!"

"No, I know. But we did our best."

"It wasn't enough. We did something wrong, Josh. I don't know what, but we did!"

"No, we didn't. Putting on a West End show is a gamble. We lost, that's all. Eight out of ten shows go down. We've joined the statistics, simple as that."

"You sound as if you don't care about . . . *Queen!*" She wanted to say about *me* and she very nearly did.

His arms were around her, after all.

"I care about *Queen* a lot more than you know."

Jill freed herself (not too far) and looked into his eyes. "Are you talking about Maggie?"

He just looked at her gravely and said nothing.

"Josh you are! You are bloody well talking about Maggie!"

He glanced down at the silk shirt and said nothing.

Jill felt only a sudden wave of gladness. She searched for his eyes but he wouldn't meet hers. He was ashamed and why not, but all she felt was the gladness.

At that moment the telephone rang.

Jill picked it up in a daze, her eyes still on Josh. The rotten bastard, she thought, to do *that*, it had all but broken her heart, didn't he know that, and yet, how had he been able to do it if he had felt nothing? She looked at him very hard and then, as if unable to bear her burning-glass stare, he got to his feet and walked over to the window, and stared down at Shaftesbury Avenue.

"Hello?" Jill said into the telephone.

"May I speak to Miss Jill Viner, the producer of . . . *The Queen of Finland?*"

"Who is this?"

"I'm the press secretary at the palace."

Jill said, slowly, "I'm Miss Viner. How can I help?"

Something in her voice caused Josh to turn around.

Two minutes later she had said good-bye and put the telephone down. White-faced, she slumped into a chair.

"What happened?" asked Josh.

"I don't know," she said slowly. "Probably a miracle."

JOSH met the press secretary at Brooks's.

He was a pleasant youngish man with a striped tie.

Ordering whitebait, he said, "Sorry it wasn't Miss Viner I had to meet but it seemed proper I should talk to you, in the end. Nice lady, Miss Viner?"

"Yes," said Josh Williams, carefully. "She is."

He had put on a plain shirt and tie and combed the wave out of his hair, which he'd had cut at Trumper's.

"The thing is," said the press secretary, lowering his voice a pitch, raising it only to say to the club servant, "the white with this stuff and then the claret, George, if you would?" He looked at the menu and said, "I suppose the hare, yes?"

Josh, who disliked jugged hare, said, "Yes. Fine." He would have said yes to anything at that moment.

"Two hare then," said the press secretary, writing it down on the order form. "Right, that's the work over. Now, where was I? Oh, yes. The thing is, Milady would like to see the play. As I told your Miss Viner." He smiled politely. "Problem. How does she do it quietly, without fuss?"

"That isn't a problem," said Josh. "There's a box at the Royal.

She could come in early and sit in the box before the house fills. Or at the last moment, when the curtain's just gone up. Either way would be pretty quiet."

"How would you suggest she enter the theatre?"

"She could come in the stage door, unless we use the pass door to the auditorium. That way everybody would see her."

"Ah. No good. What else?"

"Come in the front, but ten minutes late. We'll hold the curtain.

"Ten minutes?"

"Everybody should be in their places by then. The other way is to come in very early."

The press secretary said, "What do you think of the whitebait?"

"Fine."

"Mmm. I think a touch dry. Well now. Look here." The press secretary lowered his voice again. "Which do you think best, late or early? In the interest of Milady's privacy?"

Josh felt a sudden jolt in the solar plexus.

"You don't want any publicity at all?"

The press secretary looked slightly shocked. "Obviously not, old boy. We aren't exactly in the publicity business at Buck House, are we?"

"I would have thought," said Josh with spirit, "that you very much were."

"Not really. Not endorsing plays. If you see what I mean."

"No I don't, actually." Josh was glad his father had sent him to a Public School, anyway long enough to learn how to behave in a shitty way without actually giving offense. "I mean, it would be awfully useful to us to say she'd been *in*, you see?"

"Yes, I do see, old boy, and believe me, I appreciate it and normally, I say normally, I would say, why not?" He reflected. "I think those whitebait *are* a mite dry." And then, "It's this particular play, do y'see? It's pretty hot stuff, which is why Milady wants to see it. Personally, I think it's a damn good play and should be seen by everybody. Well, not everybody, some people would hate it, I s'pose. No, the thing is it must be incog. No point otherwise. Otherwise, I'm sorry, all bets are orf." The press secretary looked sympathetically at Josh over his glasses. "Terribly sorry about that, dear boy. Do appreciate. But there you are. You do see?"

"Yes," said Josh miserably. "Yes. I see."

"Tell me," said the press secretary, idly, "That Maggie lady? Very sexy?"

"I suppose," said Josh, sadly, "some would think so."

"Damn pretty," said the press secretary, changing tack. "Where were you at school?"

"WHAT!" yelled Jill Viner. "Jesus Christ!"

Josh slumped into a seat. Molly got up and left the room hastily.

"You don't dare to sit there and tell me you agreed to it!" Jill couldn't believe her ears. "You don't dare to tell me you didn't say no, absolutely not!"

"I tried," said Josh in a low voice. "He said, if there was any publicity, all bets were off."

"And you agreed!"

"What else could I do?"

"No. I see." Jill quieted down, as best she could. The blood was pounding in her ears. A week gone, a week in which she had felt hope that all would be well, after all a visit from the Queen *herself* . . . and now *this!* It had to be somebody's fault. It had to be Josh Williams's fault. After all, he had been there!

"Josh," she said, knowing the words were a disaster. "You absolutely ballsed it up, didn't you? Do you think it was any accident the press secretary didn't want to talk to me? Do you think it was any accident he arranged to meet you at a gentleman's club, where you could have a gentleman's agreement?"

Josh looked up dangerously. "If you want to cancel the royal visit all you have to do is pick up that telephone. I've told you what the man said to me. Now do what the bloody hell you like." He threw down a sheet of paper. "Those are the arrangements. Look after it yourself. It's your business. You're the producer. Produce!" He moved to the door. "I thought you'd changed a bit. I thought maybe you'd learned something. Plainly, I was wrong!"

He slammed the door.

Jill stared at it, heartsick and angry at the same time.

"You might have a gentleman's agreement, darling," she shouted after him. "But I sure as hell don't!"

She didn't shout it loud enough for him to hear her.

JOSH had to tell the cast the queen would be in. He left it until the evening she was expected and told them just before the performance. That was the arrangement. "Telling you as late as this is a bit tough, I know." Josh faced them all, crowded into dressing room one. "But they are absolutely strict about secrecy. She'll be in the box stage-left and probably sitting back a long way, so don't expect to see her from the stage because I don't suppose you'll be able to. And don't play to the box, I don't need to tell you that. This isn't the Royal Command Variety Performance. Just give your usual show."

"Hey, Josh," interrupted Austin. "Don't we get to meet her?"

"Not unless she wants to come backstage and I gather she won't be doing that, this time."

"Why not?" Austin looked hurt and Josh could see why. Any actor would want to meet the queen, especially after a play like this. "I mean, isn't it usual she sees actors?"

Josh said, patiently, "Like I say, not this time, Austin. Sorry."

"And like I say, why not?"

"The play itself. It's controversial. She wants to see it. But not to be known—particularly—to have seen it."

383

"You mean politics and all that shit?"

" 'Fraid so. Terribly sorry."

"Well shit, so am I terribly sorry." Austin looked mutinous.

Maggie said, "Josh, it would be really nice to meet her."

"I know. But the press secretary says it's incog, so it's incog."

"Well, thanks a whole bunch." Austin sat down at Maggie's dressing table and rolled a joint. "This year I get to meet the president. I get to play him, too. This year Maggie gets to play the queen. The queen comes to see her do it. And she won't get to meet her. Great. Terrific."

Josh said, "I'm really sorry. I tried. As a matter of fact we're not even getting any publicity. The whole idea is, she was never here."

"You mean we can't even talk about her being here?"

"That's what I mean, Austin."

"You English," said Austin, "you're incredible, you know."

"I know." Josh smiled. "It's rough. Sorry." He could see how very despondent they all were and he understood. "It seems she thinks the play is important enough to see. That's a tribute to us all."

"Not much use," said Sir Piers heavily, "if nobody knows about it." He paused. "Not, anyway, to the box office." He sighed. "Can't see how you'll keep it quiet. These things always get out."

"Not if nobody talks, it won't."

"You're asking us not to talk?"

"Yes, I'm afraid I am."

"My dear fella, it only needs one usherette to see her and it's all over London." Sir Piers shook his head sadly. "Be very useful to us. If we don't start getting better houses soon I suppose we could be in trouble." He coughed. "You heard anything, Josh?"

"Not a thing," Josh lied. "We're here for a while yet. We'll pick up. You'll see."

"It's all this shitty sun!" Brigid Kelly looked more upset than even Austin and that was saying something. "Sunshine out there now, for God's sake." She tugged at her neckline and fanned her white breasts, bringing an involuntary twitch from Sir Piers and a cold stare from Tommi Traceham, who said, "Well, that's it then. I'll never know whether she would have worn a full crown or a tiara."

"If she's surrendering, I can't see the difference," said Sir Piers.

"That only shows you know nothing about anything, especially queens." Tommi's tone held a note of jealousy. Sir Piers looked startled, glancing from her to Brigid Kelly and back again. He nodded, as if to himself. "I see, ah, yes. Of course. Well, me dear Tommi, I am an ignorant old trouper and I'm just as upset as you are, my dear. I've met the royals before, possibly too often for me own good, but to you younger people it must seem a jolt." He nodded, his Ibsen nod. "Yes, I do see that. Shame."

"Don't start him on his royal connections, dear," said Sir Harry. "He'll go on all night and it's twenty minutes to curtain-up, isn't it?" He adjusted his tie in the dressing-table mirror. As always he was made up and ready to go on before anyone else. "Curious thing about royals and theatre. Victoria never used to go. In her day, it was a den of vice. Edward VII changed all that, chasing the Gaiety Girls and such. Did a lot for the music halls and musical comedy, Edward. Hated heavy plays, wouldn't let go. Had his own chair at the Gaiety, y'know. Red plush. It's in the Savage Club now. Sat in it meself the other day, yes."

He poured himself a glass of Maggie's Soave. "Do you mind, dear? Thank you. Of course, the oddest thing ever happened between an actor and a royal was when King George V knighted Frank Benson on stage, still in his toga. He'd just done *Julius Caesar*, y'know. Covered in prop blood. Nineteen sixteen, I think. They had to send out for a prop sword for the king to dub him. Had to open a theatrical costumier's to get it." His eyes twinkled at Maggie. "Nice if you got a Dame out of it, my dear. You deserve one. But those days have passed. Everybody's respectable these days.

385

Including royalty. Everybody's gone middle-class, worrying about the neighbors, what people will think, what the public will think, what the press will think." He sighed. "Look at old Queen Mary. When she was eighty-odd, in the fifties, y'know, she wanted to see *Pick-up Girl*, hottest play in the West End. They gave her a box and she brought her own commode. Just in case. Not too good on her feet, the grand old lady. Didn't want to totter about all over the place. Now, I call that style. *And* she went backstage and talked to everybody." Sir Harry sighed again. "I tell you, the country's going to the dogs."

There didn't seem to be more to say after that, so the cast broke up (the callboy had called the quarter), looking gloomy and excited at the same time, and Maggie pressed Josh's hand and said, "I wondered why you had your suit on."

"I'm sorry. Really." He shrugged. "I'd better get out front."

Maggie started. "Are you meeting her?"

"Taking her to the box. Then whisking her away at the end."

"Lucky you."

"Yes, I know. Still." He looked at his watch. "I'd better go."

"Josh?" Maggie looked serious. "Is everything all right between us?"

"Sure, why?" Josh knew why but he wasn't going to discuss it now, of all times. But Maggie's eyes were on him, God she was beautiful, he didn't know why he didn't love her, it must be he couldn't love anybody, anymore, not in the total way she seemed to love him. Truth to tell, it scared him. "You're sure, darling?" Maggie was asking.

"Sure I'm sure." Josh kissed her on the cheek. "Don't get nervous. Just the usual performance. You'll be great."

"God, I *am* nervous," Maggie said. "Look, I'm shaking. Hold me, Josh."

He held her for a long moment, kissed her again, and released her. "Now, go slow. Take your time. You're giving a great performance. Nothing to worry about."

Maggie didn't say anything but she was still looking at him intently as he left.

Max Heston had been told to hold the curtain until he got the message from Josh that the queen was in the house. Josh could hear the audience getting restive as he stood in the foyer waiting. He heard the loud speaker announcement that reassured the patrons that the curtain would go up in "a very few minutes" and he stood, staring into the bustle of Shaftesbury Avenue, and felt more nervous than he had ever felt in his life. Then, suddenly, the press secretary was at his side, and two other men in dark suits were standing in the deserted foyer, one at each side, and then, there she was. Josh didn't know what he had expected. She seemed smaller and more pleasant and more ordinary than he had supposed, and somehow he wasn't surprised when she knew his name.

"Good evening, Mr. Williams. I'm so looking forward to seeing your play."

Josh stammered something and just stood there, and the press secretary said gently, "If you'd just lead on, old boy?" and Josh led on, to the box by the stairs and then into the box itself, and nobody at all saw them go in. Josh indicated the seats in the box and the press secretary said, "Well done, old boy, thank you," and Josh gently closed the door to the box, nodded to the man in the dark suit now stationed outside it, and went to the nearest house telephone and called backstage to Max Heston to ring up the curtain.

"About bloody time," was that worthy's retort. "What a lot of obsequious shit."

Time Out, Josh thought, or *Private Eye*, would probably be hearing from Max Heston, no friend of royalty, privilege, or anything that he thought undemocratic or unlikely to be favorably considered in East Germany. "Get the bloody curtain up, Max, and keep your mouth shut about all this. I warn you."

Max said something indistinct but plainly contemptuous of creatures like Josh, and put the telephone down, and the curtain went up. Josh watched from out front, standing at the back of the

387

stalls. The performance had never been better. Nobody looked at the royal box, not even Austin. He felt gratified. The arrangement was that the royal party would leave at curtain-down: and he was there to meet them, as Sir Harry (by arrangement) held the audience with a "special announcement." Nobody left their seats when Sir Harry said that, because Sir Harry was a great trouper and they loved him. The "special announcement" was about matinee times, but it held up the audience.

Josh and the press secretary spirited the queen down the stairs and into the foyer and into a large black car drawn up outside. "Very interesting play, Mr. Williams," said Her Majesty. "A play to think about." Then she was gone.

But not before one solitary flashbulb burst in the face of the car.

Josh stood, appalled.

Jill couldn't. She wouldn't. Surely she wouldn't.

But he knew bloody well that she *had.*

"JILL," said Tom Tully, shaking his head, "I can't do it, darling. I can't chase the story up. All right. Some free-lance got a photograph of the queen leaving the Royal." He lit a Players. "I wonder who told him she'd be there."

"I did," said Jill. She kicked off her shoes. It was good to be home, at the penthouse. It had been a long evening.

"Thanks for that anyway," said Tom Tully. "It makes it easier to say no."

"Why so?"

"Because the Palace was told you'd do your best to keep publicity down and if you give this item to the press then you're breaking that agreement." Tom Tully smiled gently. "You do see that, don't you, Jill?"

"Yes. Of course I do. I also know the story will get out anyway." Jill yawned. It was midnight and Tom had rushed over to

Bryanston Square, after a screaming telephone call from Josh Williams. "I know you'll say if it does, that won't be our fault. But frankly I'm thinking about my play and my investors. They risked their money and I'm protecting their interests." She hesitated. "What do you think will happen if this story gets full prominence in tomorrow morning's papers?"

"You'll be booked up for weeks, maybe months," said Tom Tully. "That isn't quite the point, Jill."

"Tom, it's the only point I care about."

Tom nodded. "I can see that. But it's not ethical and it's not worth it, Jill. In the long run."

" 'In the long run,' as Lincoln or somebody said, 'we're all dead.' "

Tom smoothed his black hair with a huge hand. "Darling, think a bit, please. Don't do it."

The door buzzer went. "That'll be Josh. Let him in, will you, Tom?"

Tom Tully pressed the intercom. "Josh? Come up, will you?" He poured a large gin and tonic and handed it to Jill. "I think you are going to need this. He was not happy."

"I don't know," said Jill, "what it would take to make Josh Williams happy." She took the gin and tonic just the same. She had almost finished it when Josh came into the room. He looked anything but happy. "Just what the hell," he asked, "do you think you are doing, Jill?"

"You mean the photographer?"

"I mean the photographer."

"Josh," said Tom. "Gin and tonic?"

"Nothing," said Josh. Why, oh why, Jill thought, do I always do it wrong for him? "Go on, I'm listening," said Josh.

Jill said, "I'm glad to hear that anyway. Yes, I told the photographer about the royal visit and yes, I knew exactly what I was doing, and for reasons I have just given Tom—that the story will get out anyway—I decided to let it out where it would help *Queen*."

"You haven't actually done anything yet?" asked Josh.

"No, she hasn't," said Tom Tully, quickly.

"Thank God for that!"

"Why?" asked Jill. "Were you hoping for a knighthood or something?"

"No, I wasn't, but I gave my word."

"Yes, but I didn't give mine. I didn't meet anybody."

"You're the producer. I did it on your behalf." Josh sat down. Poor darling, he looked drained, and why not, it must have been a hell of an evening for him, the tension of the visit and now this. "I'll have that gin and tonic, Tom."

"Coming up, old boy." Tom Tully busied himself at the drinks cabinet, his whole posture one of profound relief.

"Well, I'm glad you had second thoughts." Josh drank some gin and leaned his head back and closed his eyes. "I've never been so nervous in my life and that went for the cast. I thought they did splendidly, by the way."

"Yes," Jill said, hollowly. "They did."

"I think it'll get around, that she was in. We'll get some coverage. Probably in a day or two, the columnists will get it."

"Too little and too late. A para in a column's no good. You know that." Jill took a deep breath. "I gave the pic and the story—queen goes secretly to play—to every paper in town an hour ago. By motorcycle delivery service. It'll be in all tomorrow's newspapers. Front page on them all, I hope."

There was a long silence.

Tom Tully looked down at his gin. "Well, then," he said at last, "I'd better go into your bedroom and use your telephone, Jill. I'll try to get them to mix the stories a bit, no point in everybody printing the same one. Then."—he blew out his cheeks—"I'll ring the press secretary at the palace and tell him things went a little haywire, the free-lance guy got onto it and we had to blow it wide open, no choice."

"Thanks, Tom, you're a darling," said Jill.

"He may not believe me." Tom grimaced. "But as Wellington or somebody said, 'I don't care which lie we tell, so long as we all tell the same damn lie.'" Going out of the room he put his hand on Josh's shoulder, very gently, and said, "Easy does it, old boy."

He was wasting his breath.

Jill knew that. She knew Josh.

I've done it this time, she thought, but what other choice did I have?

None.

Josh finished his drink and got to his feet. He walked to the door and, once there, he turned. "I should have known. It's the nature of the beast, isn't it, Jill? You were going to do exactly this from the first moment you heard, weren't you!"

"Yes, I bloody well was! We'll run forever, Josh!"

His voice was gentle. "You shouldn't have done it, Jill. Not even for *Queen*."

"No," she shouted, unforgivably. "And you shouldn't have slept with Maggie Stride when you didn't love her, but you did that for *Queen*, didn't you? So to hell with all your talk about ethics and giving your word and all that crap. You slept with her to get a performance out of her and you didn't care whether my heart broke or I loved you or I didn't, you didn't bloody well care, did you?"

Josh looked at her for a moment, and then he just nodded, and left. She heard the lift clang in the hall and waited for him to come back, but he didn't.

Oh, why did I say that? Jill thought. Why?

Because, she thought, it's the nature of the beast.

THE morning papers were full of the story and of the picture. It was on page one of every newspaper, except *The Times*, which had it on page seven with the accurate but hardly enthralling headline, QUEEN VISITS PLAY. Otherwise the coverage was magnificent. The

Express had it top right of page one under the legend QUEEN SEES QUEEN. The *Star* said QUEENLY VISIT and the *Sun* had QUEEN POPS IN. The *Mail* gave it a full picture-spread on the inside fold of page twenty-six with a résumé of the play, and photographs of Maggie and Sir Harry, Sir Piers and Austin. Molly rang Jill at the penthouse to say that a letter for every member of the cast had arrived at the office by royal messenger, and Jill told her to send them all down to the theatre. There was one for Josh but nothing for her. Well, she was only the producer. Nobody knew what a producer did, including, it seemed, press secretaries. Unless, she thought, showering herself awake after a troubled night (and why not, for God's sake?), the press secretary suspected what had happened, in which case, what the hell?

In the office, it all started again. Lord Glass telephoned. "It's going to run, my dear, brilliant!" and Prince Ahmed was only minutes later with "My lovely Jill, you have made us all richer!" And even Miss Dobbs rang from Leeds (reversing the charges) to say she and her sister had read the *Telegraph* and they were thrilled, absolutely thrilled! The box office of the Royal rang at noon to say they were booked for three weeks and had put two more telephone lines on service. Keith Prowse rang to ask how many block bookings they could have for, naturally, a six-month period—run of the play, if possible. Jill answered everybody in a flurry of excitement (including two New York producers calling transatlantic) and all the time she waited for a call from Josh to say sorry or what the hell or anything at all.

The last call to come was from Herbie Glass.

"Well, darling. You got your miracle."

"Yes," said Jill. "But it was about all I did get."

She looked at the office window. Long streaks ran down it, through the dust of the everlasting hot summer.

It had started to rain.

QUEEN opened in New York that following March.

Jill stood in a blustery wind, outside the Trafalgar, and watched the sign go up. JILL VYNER AND HENRY JOBY PRESENT, in small letters. With the sirs both big and Maggie and Austin bigger. New York was their town. Jill had given the Broadway deal to Henry Joby after turning down three other bids, all equally good. Henry was a pro, he'd been a general manager for Merrick, he knew his business. He'd taken over the Broadway production, smoothed his way through American Equity. No problems with the sirs, who were stars and therefore acceptable, and no problems, naturally, with Maggie or Austin.

The problem was Brigid Kelly.

No way would American Equity accept her. She wasn't a star and they were digging their heels in. An American girl could play the part, why not, Maggie was playing the queen and she was American, right? Jill had wanted to fight and Josh Williams had been ferocious. "I suppose they'd like her to be American *and* black," had been his reaction. Henry Joby (a short, tubby man in a dark fur topcoat and thick glasses) had counseled acceptance.

"Darling, do the deal with the nice men. We've got ninety percent of what we want. A hundred percent I never got yet. So tell Brigid and we'll get a lotta publicity out of the new girl. It's in our favor."

Jill stood in the keen wind sweeping down the stone canyons and shivered. "It's all right for you, you don't have to tell her, Henry."

Henry Joby blinked. "I'll tell her. No problem."

"No. I'll do it. After all, I have to do something for my seven and a half percent of the box office!"

Henry Joby shook his head. "Five, I said—maybe five and a half, top. You talk me into seven, I'll lose money."

"Not you. *Queen* got the London investors nice and rich."

He looked up at the men fixing the signs. They moved slowly in the icy blast. "You got a new play for next season?"

"I have two or three new ones. One I like a lot."

"Josh gonna do it for you?"

"I don't know." She didn't. "I hope so." She did.

"Why don't you let Josh tell the girl she's out? He's the director. Actors are his job. She wouldn't be here in New York City if you'd listened to me. All those appeals, I lost a lotta goodwill an' still we lose." Henry Joby's eyes watered and he took off his glasses and dabbed at them with a handkerchief. "You see the *Post?*" There had been a long article on Maggie and Austin in the *Post.* It hinted at a close relationship between them. "Anything in that?"

"I'd like to think so," Jill said, "but I'm afraid not."

"Huh? I don't get you, Jill."

"No, I know." Jill looked around her. The New Yorkers were still wearing their winter coats and their heavy-soled boots and shoes, and they sloped forward into the icy wind. "Hey," she called to the man fixing the neon signs, "you've got Viner spelled wrong."

"Sorry, lady." He grinned down, a monkey face under a peaked gap. "No sweat. I'll change it." He did. Wrong again.

"It's V-i-n-e-r," muttered Henry Joby, a New Yorker to his boots. "You shithead."

"Hey, mister, watch your language," said the man. "Shithead yourself!"

"Come on," said Henry Joby. "Come and see the cast. See what Josh Williams is doing. And tell the girl she's out."

Jill hugged her red-fox coat around her: a very expensive closing-of *Queen* present to which she had treated herself. Hell, who else was going to buy her a present? Josh Williams? Since *Queen* had become a hit on Shaftesbury Avenue she had seen him once, when they had a closing-night party. Even then, he had only been ritually polite. He had not even acknowledged the checks she sent him and he had refused her repeated entreaties to come in and look at the books and even to read some plays. A lot of scripts had been sent in to her office once *Queen* began to play to full houses. Josh had begged off because of work (he had taken over, at short notice, a production at the Royal Shakespeare) and said, over the telephone, "Jill, you run the office. Everything you do seems to work out, so who am I to argue?" She had pleaded, trying not to. "But, Josh darling, you are a director of Queen Productions. It's in your own interests to know what is going on here."

"No, it isn't," he had replied evenly. "It's my business to look in on the production of *Queen* once a week, which I do, to see if it is running along all right, which it is. My business is directing plays and that is what I'm doing at the Shakespeare, until *Queen* goes to New York. If I'm wanted by the American producer, then I'll consider doing it over there."

"But of course you'll do it in New York. I'll make it a condition of sale!"

He had been silent a long moment. "That's nice of you, Jill."

She was silent too, and then she asked, "How are you, Josh?" She had wanted to ask, to yell, to scream, "How's *Maggie?*"

395

"I'm fine," said Josh. "As usual."

"Good. I'm glad." She tried again. "And do come by the office. I have all kinds of things you have to sign."

"Put them in the post to me, Jill, there's a darling. I must rush now. See you soon. 'Bye."

And Jill found herself listening to the dial tone.

She had sent the papers (mostly contracts and bills) and Josh had signed them and sent them back. She had not seen him, until today, for sixteen weeks—no, seventeen. Well, who was counting? Well, she was.

Jill had been to the Royal to see *Queen* often. She had taken American producers, and producers from the Civic Theatres of West Germany (the countries behind the Iron Curtain had shown no interest) and French and Scandinavian impresarios. All these men (and one or two women) had sat very quietly through the play, and gone home soberly. To them, it seemingly had a message that did not touch the Americans, who saw only the star billing and the box-office possibilities. Jill wondered how it would go in New York.

There was no knowing, Henry Joby said, no way. Broadway was a bigger gamble than ever. Only plungers like himself and Merrick and the others would still do it. They were like the professional gambler who lost big money at Vegas and couldn't stop because it was how he got his living. They were hooked. Jill didn't know the half of it. Shaftesbury Avenue was class. Broadway was the pits. Still, it was electric. Exciting. Jill felt a buzz, looking up Forty-first Street before she went into the Trafalgar. What a city. Mad, bad, and dangerous to know.

She pulled the fur collar up, framing her face.

Seventeen weeks. Was he still with Maggie?

Jill had been too proud to ask anybody in the company. There had been nothing in the London gossip columns, except the Nigel Dempster item months ago about Josh and herself splitting up over Maggie. That had hurt. Nothing else, until today in the *Post*.

396

Neither Maggie nor Josh was married to anybody else, so they weren't news any longer.

Jill took a deep breath and went into the Trafalgar.

The cast were rehearsing on stage. The Trafalgar was the newest British import to Broadway. It had become an accepted part of the Broadway scene and an excellent outlet for a successful British play. Or so they all hoped. All Queen Productions could do was gain. The investment money was American. Jill had held on to movie rights and exploitation rights worldwide. She was in business. Not rich, but in business.

Josh was standing, talking to the cast.

God, he was so attractive: her heart moved.

He'd let his hair grow long again but at least it wasn't blow-dried. He seemed to be wearing Gucci boots but they looked old and scuffed. The hated gold bracelet, she saw with sinking heart, was still on his wrist: the good news was that he greeted her with a smile, and so did the rest of the company.

Sir Piers embraced her warmly. "Jill, my love. It's going to be a smash. I feel it."

Sir Harry added, "Really, Piers, how can you tell, divine inspiration, dear? There are a few worthy fellows called critics who can make or break us with their notices. That isn't art, dear. It's a lottery." He sighed. "Did you know that when Shaw was a critic he only had one suit? Darned all over by his old mother. Shiny backside, one shirt. Short on food as well. And he wrote the best stage reviews of all time, including Hazlitt too. All that poverty and no envy of fat playwrights or rich actors. He never wrote a crit that hurt a player. Wonderful English, wonderful intellect. If he hated a play he made you laugh at it, but gently. A diet of starvation would do these New York fellows all the good in the world." He sighed again. "I expect they all live at the Plaza."

"Where are you staying?" Jill enquired.

"The Lowell." Sir Harry sniffed. "Nearest thing to an English hotel in this city."

"I'm in an apartment," said Sir Piers. "Central Park South. I have milady with me."

"Well, you have to, don't you, dear boy," said Sir Harry. "Can't have you nicked for cruising, can we?"

"Look here, you old—"

Sir Harry held up his hand. "Piers, I had an offer from Sir Tom at the National."

Sir Piers hesitated. "So did I."

"D'yer want to do it?"

"I dunno," said Sir Piers. "Do you?"

"I might," said Sir Harry cagily. "I just might. You?"

"I might too." Sir Piers hesitated. "Just might."

"What are you two talking about?" asked Jill.

"Something together again," said Sir Piers. "Play about Marx and Engels called *Manifesto*, just the play for the National. Fella called Paul Prinz has written it—or written it up, I suppose, nearer the mark. Never heard of him. Still, two meaty parts. I expect I'm Marx, the sexy one, and Hal's Engels. He was pretty sexy too, but I think Marx was sexier."

"I'm sure I don't know about that." Sir Harry closed an eye. "All this talk of sex. I'd have thought you'd have given it up by now, dear."

"Just because you're a mature male of some years," said Sir Piers frostily, "it don't mean your dingle has fallen off."

"Well," mused Sir Harry, "if we don't do it in the nude and the lighting's kept very dim we might get by."

Josh laughed, and so did everybody else, except Brigid Kelly, who was standing quite still, watching Jill intently. Jill asked, "When is this epic planned for?"

"Immediately *Queen* closes on Broadway," replied Sir Harry promptly.

"Sir Tom must expect that to be Saturday," Jill said icily.

"I rather think," said Sir Harry carefully, "that he does."

There was a sudden silence, broken by Josh. "Very encouraging, I must say." He turned to Jill. "Well, darling, how are you, you look well, just got in have you, good, I'm just giving the cast a few points, we haven't any problems. . . ."

"Yes, we do." Jill touched his arm and dropped her voice, turning away from the others. "It's Brigid."

Josh stood absolutely still. "They haven't said no. Not at this stage!"

"They have and I don't blame them. They warned us. It's our fault for bringing her over before we had it fixed."

"You mean my fault." Josh looked depressed. "I was sure they'd agree, in the end."

"They've agreed to everything else. But since Maggie's queen is American . . ."

"Yes, I know." Josh paused. "Who's going to tell her?"

"I will if you like."

He looked relieved. "Would you, Jill? I know I should but I feel . . . I've been in touch with a couple of possibilities, just in case. In fact, I gave one a script to learn."

"Where did you see them?" Jill wondered where he was living. Surely it was with Maggie.

"In my hotel room. I'm at the Pierre."

"I see." Jill's heart felt lighter, at least for a moment. Not for longer than that because Maggie came across and casually looped her arm through Josh's and then (and only then) kissed Jill on the cheek and asked if she'd had a good trip over. "The usual. I came Concorde, it's just like an afternoon nap." Jill wished everything else in her life ran as smoothly. "I'd better talk to Brigid. Josh, will you break the company for a while?"

Josh didn't exactly disengage his arm from Maggie's but he somehow eased himself free and spoke to the cast. "Take fifteen minutes for coffee, everybody."

Austin Ames loomed up. "Hi, Jill, lovely to see you." He kissed her affectionately. Jill guessed he was glad to be home. Austin was a New Yorker, wherever he was. "We're gonna really take this town Wednesday, right, Maggie?" Maggie smiled and accepted Austin's arm around her shoulder and did not seem to notice that his hand fell casually across her right breast. Jill thought, Is she just innocent or is it part of an act? She could not be sure but it took a lot more poise than she had and she hated Maggie for it. Or admired her for it. Both, probably, she decided.

"You people fixed up?" she asked Austin. "Where are you living?"

"The Plaza, where else?" said Austin. "I used to stand outside it when I was a kid, just starting out, and I used to say to myself, One day I'll walk in and own you, you big bastard." His fingers touched Maggie's nipple but she did not seem to notice. "And now I can do it, and you know what? The guy at the door didn't like my sweatshirt. A suit, in my place he would wear a suit. I said, Listen, buddy, I'm a working guy like you, I wear a shirt for work, and y'know what he said? He said, Shit."

"Austin." Maggie smiled. "You're a star now, not an unknown off-Broadway actor. Behave like a star."

"Crap," declared Austin. "That's all crap, you should get with it, Maggie. Stop going to Halston and like that for your clothes, for a start. Relax and live a little. You're too tight-assed to enjoy yourself. Look how you run around after Josh and does he care, does he—"

Jill waited agog for more but Austin must have seen the expression on her face because he shut up and then said, "Hey, where's that coffee?" and made off across the stage toward the cartons that somebody had brought in for the cast. Jill said, after a moment's silence, "And you, Maggie, how are you? I mean, Austin's nonsense apart?"

"I'm fine, Jill." Maggie smiled sweetly. Jill thought, She means it, she *is* sweet. "My nerves seem to be back to normal now. I think I'm going to be all right."

"I'm sure you'll be wonderful, darling." Jill paused. "Where are you staying?" Go on, she thought, drive the dagger home, say the Pierre, of course, with Josh, do it, do it now, why do I beg for this hurt, Jill asked herself, I must be bloody mad!

"Well, I have my own little place. The one you came to. I've always had it, you know. It used to belong to my father. He gave it to me."

He would, Jill thought: people are always giving you things. You don't even have to ask. It's the price of great beauty, the constant taking. It's a price, she thought, I wouldn't mind paying sometimes. "You're a lucky girl, Maggie," she said, at last, thinking at least if she's in his bed she has to go to the Pierre for it. A further thought drenched her delight: was Josh at the Pierre because he knew she, Jill, would be at the Plaza?

"No," Maggie was saying, quietly but quite sadly. "I'm not really lucky, Jill. Most people think I am maybe because of my looks and family, but I'm not. I loved Philip and he died and I have an idea I won't be as lucky ever again."

Jill felt elated and ashamed at the same time. "Of course you will, darling. There's Josh."

"Yes. I know."

Jill waited: but there was no more.

"I have to talk to Brigid," she said at last. "Excuse me?"

"Of course." Maggie turned away to Austin, who had brought her coffee across. "I didn't put any sugar in," Austin told her. "You shouldn't be drinking that poison."

Maggie asked, "You haven't put honey in again, Austin? I told you not to!"

Austin scowled. "Listen, honey's natural sweetness. If you have to drink coffee, which is a poison, then drink it with honey."

"It tastes horrible with honey, Austin."

"Shit, Maggie, do you want to die? Think what sugar is."

"It's sweet, Austin, which is why I like it."

They sound, Jill thought hopefully, like an old married couple.

Brigid Kelly waited in a dark corner of the stage. She had not moved since Jill came into the theatre. Now she shifted even farther into the shadows. As Jill reached her she said, in a tight, low voice, "It's no good, is it? They threw me out, didn't they?"

Jill just stared at her and nodded. She could not speak, but Brigid Kelly could. "If you thought this was going to happen why on earth did you ask me over here in the first place? It's an absolute bloody disgrace for me to hang around here not knowing whether I'm in the play or not. It's shitty, that's what it is, you didn't fight for me, did you? I got you your reviews in London and that's all you cared about! I can go and screw myself as far as Broadway's concerned, you can get more publicity finding yourself a cheap Hollywood starlet! You and your boyfriend—or is he your ex-boyfriend, Josh Williams—who is too shit-scared to come over here himself and tell me I'm out!"

It was all delivered in a scream and the company froze and looked at their feet and at one another. "Great casting, that girl, for *Maria of the Red Barn*," said Sir Harry, sotto voce.

"I disagree, Hal," rejoined Sir Piers. "Bloody bad show. The poor little gel's had a raw deal."

"If she has," said Josh icily, "it's none of *my* doing. I've tried to keep her in the show."

"Yes, but did you try hard enough?" asked Brigid, still at a scream. "If it had been for Maggie you'd have tried, oh yes, you'd have gone to see the Equity committee yourself if it had been for Maggie, but I'm not going to bed with you, am I, so I don't fucking count—"

"Not for want of trying I'm sure, dear." This, again sotto voce, from Sir Harry.

"Hold hard, Hal, the gel's some right on her side." This, loud, from Sir Piers.

Austin and Maggie and the rest simply looked on silently. Brigid had stopped screaming and was sobbing now. Josh, who had looked angry, stopped looking angry and looked ashamed and concerned. Jill said, "Somebody go out front and get a cab. I'll take her back to the hotel."

Brigid looked at her with hating, tear-filled eyes. "You'll take me no fucking place. Just have my plane tickets at my hotel for the morning flight home tomorrow and screw the whole fucking lot of you!"

With that, choking and sobbing, she ran wildly down the aisle toward the door. Jill started after her but Josh caught her arm. "No. Let her go. She'll be all right."

"Are you sure?" Jill asked. "She didn't look all right."

"She's been expecting it, fearing it. And hating herself for fearing it. Leave her alone. Let her have her dignity, let her have her big exit, let her hate us. Give her that, at least." Josh took a deep breath. "I'll have the new girl in tomorrow."

"You're cold-blooded, Josh." She looked at him. It was true—he was.

"If I wasn't, darling," he said lightly, "*Queen* would never have got on the road."

"No," she said. "I suppose not," thinking, Me too.

"You suppose right." Josh clapped his hands. "All right, everybody. Let's pick it up where we left off, shall we?"

"Places, please, everybody," called the stage manager.

The company looked at one another, sighed, and shuffled into their places on stage. Jill watched them and thought: I should go after Brigid. I should: but I won't. It wouldn't help. She felt herself hating Josh at that moment for being right and for knowing more than she did about another woman. If he knows so bloody much, she thought, why doesn't he know I still love him?

BRIGID flew back to London on the Concorde the next morning saying good-bye to a battery of photographers and journalists. She made no secret of her feelings about Jill Viner, and the *Post* ran a story that afternoon with the headline BRITISH STAR OUSTED and cited Jill Viner as the culprit, an on-the-make producer who wanted a Hollywood starlet in her place. Jill was quoted as saying, "We did what we could but American Equity would not have Miss Kelly so what more could we do?" The *Post* article implied quite a bit.

It didn't look very good. And the further note, "Miss Viner was ousted herself recently when leading lady Maggie Stride took her live-in boyfriend, Josh Williams, from her. They are still together for the sake of the play, opening at the Trafalgar Wednesday."

Jill was urged by Henry Joby to ignore it all. American libel laws were different from British ones and, besides, it was all good publicity for the play. Jill hoped Henry was right. The ticket office was reporting fairly good advance bookings but, as Henry pointed out, nothing meant anything in New York City except the first-night reviews. That was the system and a producer had to live with it, he told her, sitting in the Edwardian Room at the Plaza, and trying to look composed. Jill recalled her last meeting at that very table with Josh all those months ago.

"You've done wonders, for a new girl in this business," Henry told her, sipping his black coffee. "I tell you, all Broadway's watching us. We've done the unforgivable. We've brought in a new serious play that isn't even American. The whole country's gone isolationist, have you noticed? All we want are stories set in our own backyard. We're trying to pretend there's nothing else out there. Of course we've always been like that unless there's a war on. We're a world power and we hate the role. We want to be just folks and nobody will let us be just folks."

Henry signaled for more hot black coffee and lit a stogie. He saw nothing incongruous in it and Jill smiled, trying to picture Herbie Glass doing the same thing. That was what she liked about the States.

She said, "Henry, is what you're trying to tell me that *Queen*'s too heavy for them, perhaps they won't like it?"

Henry Joby drew on his cigar thoughtfully. "I don't think they'll fully understand it, like a European might. If they like it it'll be because it's a good drama, has great actors, and the queen of England in it." He blew out a cloud of rich smoke. "Three damn good reasons, you ask me."

"At least we have a good young actress in Brigid's place."

Josh had cast Mia Morris, a well-known, up-and-coming Broadway actress. It had been important not to cast a starlet, in view of Brigid's parting remarks to the press. Miss Morris looked like a fast study (she had to be; they opened Wednesday). She had a not-too-strong-accent, more Boston than New York ("The nearest we got to royalty," said Henry Joby), and, most important, she had never worked in Hollywood. At that moment Josh was rehearsing her all day so that she would be ready for opening night. That made a nice story too, in a slow week, and both the *Post* and the *New York Times* did a piece on her. *Time* ran a pre-opening feature, based on the London notices, under the heading BRITISH INVASION, SOVIET INVASION. It wasn't a long piece but it helped, and Jill for once was mentioned, but only because she had sacked Brigid Kelly. "Don't worry," counseled Henry Joby once more. "So long as they spell your name right, right?"

Jill hoped so. It hadn't been her idea to have Brigid over on the chance they might get permission for her to play in *Queen*. It was Josh's idea. It was another sacrifice she made for him that he knew nothing about and probably didn't care either.

"DARLING, let's just take a break, shall we?"

Mia Morris looked apprehensive. "I'm not getting it, Josh."

Josh took her hand and held it as he talked. He found directing Brigid's replacement none too easy. Mia Morris was an intelligent girl but she had never seen a princess in her life, much less played one. It was difficult to give her notes that made sense to her. It was the old difference between the two societies, and it was a basic one. "Look, darling," he said. "You have to drop the whole concept with which you have been living all your life, the absolutely rational one that all people are equal. In the States maybe they are, or anyway that's the accepted lip-service philosophy. In Europe if you are a princess you cease to be ordinary. You become better."

"Better how?" asked Mia, who was a lissome young girl of twenty, with dark serious eyes and a good pale complexion.

"Just better."

"Because I'm a princess?"

"Right! Oh, and you never say you're better. Or act as if you're better. There's no need for it."

"Why?"

"Because everybody *knows* you're better. You have nothing to prove."

Mia pouted. "How do I suggest *that?*"

Josh thought hard. "By keeping absolutely still. By never showing emotion, except in your big speech. By speaking clearly and almost sharply. You are not used to being contradicted and when the Russian speaks sharply to you . . . What's his lines, Piers?"

Sir Piers bestowed a fatherly yet lecherous smile on Mia. *"Who are you, that you presume to speak for your country? Who voted you into office? Who said to you, Go and represent me?"*

Josh cued Mia with, "And the princess replies?"

"And who voted you into office? Certainly not your workers, they haven't voted anybody into office for sixty years, they wouldn't know what to do with such a freedom!"

"Too strident, darling," said Josh, easily. "The princess doesn't raise her voice. She doesn't need to. She isn't insulting or personal either. It's just a truth, and she says it. Just like that, quite flatly."

Mia blinked, troubled, and he said, "Don't worry, darling,

406

it'll come, you're doing very nicely, stay with it, it's going to be lovely." He looked around at the rest of the cast, sitting idly by while he worked with Mia. "Take ten minutes for coffee everybody, and then we'll do a run."

The inevitable coffee arrived and Josh went out into the auditorium and slumped into an aisle seat. Maggie followed him and sat next to him. He was vaguely irritated because he wanted to think about how he could get Mia to relax and sound like a real princess. There was always, of course, the possibility that the audience wouldn't know a princess if she fell over them. That was a comfort, anyway.

Maggie sipped her coffee and said, "Josh darling, I don't seem to have seen much of you since we got to New York."

"No," Josh said. "I have been rather busy.".

Maggie looked hurt. "I know that, darling, but well, I'd hoped you'd come to the house now and then." Josh knew she meant at night. "I have to have my beauty sleep, Maggie. This is the first show I've ever put on Broadway." He coughed. "Have a word with Mia, will you, see if you can get her to understand the *quality* of the part?"

"I can try." Maggie threw back her long hair: she was so beautiful, he still couldn't think why he didn't love her as much as he should. The whole world wanted her, for God's sake. "I can try," Maggie was saying, "but Mia isn't like me. She's Boston but not quite . . . I'd let her do it her way if I were you, Josh."

"You mean she's a mistake?" Josh felt cold thinking of it.

"No, not a mistake. Just you're comparing her with Brigid Kelly and she isn't Brigid Kelly."

"No, that she ain't."

"She'll be all right. Don't expect too much, that's all." Maggie sounded casual but he'd been expecting the question. "Josh, had you thought any more about staying on in New York?"

Josh lit a cigarillo and put his feet up on the seat in front. "I don't know if I could work here, Maggie. It's a different language, different set of attitudes, it would take me a year to get my bearings. Sure, I'm all right on *Queen* but on an American subject, I don't know."

"The money's better. And you're always saying the National isn't your thing, that all that can happen is that the West End theatre will go down and down, and that only the subsidized theatres will survive to do so-called serious plays because West End costs are too high. Look at *Queen*, we only just made it with *Queen*. If you believe that, or only half believe it, why go back?"

"I could probably go back to the Shakespeare or even the National." He wondered if he could.

Maggie pressed. "Why go back when you can stay here—look for some exciting new plays—and work at what you want to work at and be well paid for doing it?"

And live with you, Josh thought, that too?

"Let's see what happens," he said. "Nobody might want me. We might bomb." He said, in a louder voice, "All right, everybody, shall we have a go?"

"Excuse me," said Maggie icily, "while I find my way backstage."

"Sure," said Josh. "No sweat."

"No, I know." Maggie looked at him. "None at all, is there, Josh, about anything or anybody."

Josh wasn't sure what she meant, but he guessed, so he said nothing—always, as his father had pointed out, the wisest thing to do, especially where women were concerned.

"Okay, let's go!" he shouted.

I'm talking in their damn language right now, he thought.

AUSTIN Ames met Manny Hiberson in the Oak Room of the Plaza for an early lunch on Wednesday. Manny wore a faint air of surprise, in addition to his inevitable white suit. "I never come to New York City. It reminds me of the bad old days. It reminds me I was once poor in these streets. These memories I can do without."

"Manny," protested Austin, drinking a tomato juice, "I've also been poor."

"Poor," said Manny scornfully, ordering a margarita. "You don't know from poor. When I say poor I mean the father's out of work, carrying his sewing machine on his back, and the son's trotting along the street behind him, crying, 'Papa, when we gonna eat?' Hear that? *That's* poor." Manny sighed at the softness of people these days. "Don't know they're born." He fixed Austin with a beady but benevolent eye. "So? When are you ready to go back to work?"

"I'm going to work," said Austin. "Tonight I have an opening, remember?"

"That I know," replied Manny. "Why else am I in New York City, which stirs up the memories I don't need?" He stabbed his cigarette at Austin. "I'll tell you for why, Austin." He lowered his voice, looking cautiously around the Oak Room, a Hollywood habit, from the Polo Lounge and Ma Maison. "Because I have the greatest little deal for you and Maggie."

"Manny," protested Austin. "We are both in this play, Manny."

Manny held up a hand. "I know that. This is for when the play closes. Which may be Saturday, am I right?"

"I hope not. It's a good play." Austin stirred. "What's this deal you're talking about? And Maggie? How does Maggie come into it?"

"Maggie comes into it because you and Maggie did *Good-bye* together, right? And it got you both Oscars, right?"

Austin nodded. "Right. So what, Manny?"

"So I have a new script by the same writer, capiche? I have a new script by the same writer called *Second Time Around.*"

"It's about the widower remarrying?" asked Austin.

"You heard about it?" asked Manny, surprised.

"No, I just guessed, Manny."

"You guessed, how did you guess, when only me, the producer, the writer, and twenty lawyers know about it?"

"Because I guessed, Manny."

"You guessed?" Manny looked put out. "So. What do you say to a million three? For you. Same for Maggie. We start to shoot as soon as you're free."

Austin sat, thinking hard. "That sweatshirt," said Manny. "It ain't right for the Plaza." He leaned forward. "So, what do you say to a million three?"

Austin rubbed his face. "I say fine, Manny. But I have to read the script and how do I know Maggie will do it, and anyway, even if she will, how do I know when? This play—"

"You're in the play for six months. The producer will wait that long. Earlier would be better but he'll wait that long." Manny sighed. He had seen times when actors fell on their knees for a tenth of the money, big actors, who had then gone and been sick to their stomachs in the can, out of excitement and maybe gratitude. Gratitude? It was a quality in short supply these days. A million three? Shit, he could have been talking peanuts. What would his own father, empty belly and sewing machine on back, have said to it all? A million three, what would his father have said to a million three? Meshugge, his father would have said and he would have been right.

"Tell me." Manny leaned forward even more. "Is there anything between you and Maggie? I read all the time in the *Examiner* there is but tell me, will you give her the script or will I?"

"There's nothing between Maggie and me," said Austin gloomily. "I wish to God there was."

"But I keep reading it all the time!" said Manny. "It has to get in the papers somehow, right?"

"Sure it does," said Austin. "I plant it there."

There was a long silence. Manny broke it. "Some other guy?"

"The director." Austin scratched his belly beneath his sweatshirt, an action Manny thought inappropriate in the Plaza. "After this, I'd do the right movie."

"Directors," said Manny, sympathetically, feeling better, feeling a deal coming on. "They pull all the broads."

"So," said Austin. "You give Maggie the script, okay?"

"Don't worry," said Manny, happy with a problem. "I'll talk to her nice, tell her what a great guy you are."

"Don't bother," said Austin. "She knows already. Love, that's something else."

"Love?" echoed Manny, looking around the Oak Room to see if there was anybody he knew. "I never went in for it." He paused. "Even with Crawford, I never went in for it."

"Manny," said Austin, "you never did that with Crawford."

"I did, too," said Manny. "You go ask her."

Austin laughed.

THE entire cast of *Queen* sat in Sardi's and waited.

Jill felt hopeful, yet her knees would not have held her had she stood up. They had got a round of applause as they went in and Henry Joby had said, "That's good, Jill, that's great. These people can sense a hit before the critics have typed their first word. I'm hopeful, Jill." He had puffed on the cigar. "Very hopeful." He got to his feet. "Now, I go and get the papers at the door. They're bringing them, they're bringing them special. Pray for me, Jill."

I'll pray for myself, Jill thought.

Josh said, across the table, "I thought everybody was great tonight. Especially Mia. Mia was terrific."

Mia nodded, white-faced. She had eaten nothing all day and been sick twice. Sir Piers and Sir Harry were drinking champagne, Manny Hiberson, who had joined them, was drinking a margarita, and so was Jill. Josh was on Scotch. Maggie had an apple juice in front of her, and so had Austin. Austin had given up alcohol

411

entirely for the run of the play, and he insisted Maggie try it, too. Maggie, who had been wonderful that evening, and was assured, Jill thought, of a great personal success, was off booze since London, and didn't seem to need it anyway. What did she need, Jill wondered, except Josh?

Jill looked around, at the signed photographs of the celebrities on the walls, and remembered that Grandfather Sardi had once had a restaurant in Hammersmith before World War I and had emigrated for better opportunities. Well, in a way, she had done the same. In New York, audiences had the money to support a success. If I have Signor Sardi's luck, she thought, crossing her fingers, I'll settle for that.

Sir Piers called across the table, "Jill, don't worry. You heard that audience, darling." He raised his glass. "To success!"

"Not yet, dear," said Sir Harry. "Wait until we have it, do."

"Yes, wait," said Manny Hiberson. "These critics, who knows with them?"

Austin responded. "Manny, everybody came tonight. You saw them."

Manny replied, "I saw a lotta actors, sure, I saw Dustin Hoffman. I saw Meryl Streep. I saw George C. Scott. This makes a success?"

"It helps, Manny."

"Lissen"—Manny surveyed his Turkish cigarette gloomily—"I never know an actor pay for his seat yet."

"You're gonna have to wait for me and Maggie, Manny," said Austin. "I'd like to bet your next year's commission, Manny."

Manny looked shocked. "Bet next year's commission? Austin, it's like I said, you've never known from poor!"

Henry Joby hurried back into the restaurant, sheaves of newspapers in his hand. He sat down heavily. His be-ringed fist rested on the pile of papers. There were tears running down his cheeks.

Jill thought: That's it. It's bombed. We've blown it.

"Dear boy," boomed Sir Piers, "don't die on us. Get your breath, there's a good fellow, please."

Henry Joby looked as if he might indeed die on them: his face was almost purple, his spectacles were fogged with his tears. He took them off and mopped them with his tie.

"So tell us, for Chrissakes!" called out Manny, a New Yorker again. "We bombed, right? We bombed. Austin, I shoulda taken your money."

Sir Harry said, "Do pray tell us, dear boy."

Henry Joby lifted his hand but he did not even look at the papers in front of him. The whole restaurant was hushed. Somewhere, somebody dropped a fork and several people called, "Quiet!"

Jill reached out blindly across the table toward Josh.

His hand did not meet hers.

She withdrew the hand, to find it grasped tightly by Mia Morris.

"Oh God, tell us, Henry!" Mia screamed.

Jill thought, Let it be, please let it be a hit, I will give anything, yes, even Josh Williams who would not take my hand a moment ago, I will give anything, my life even, *but let it be a hit.*

Henry Joby took a deep breath. "The critics . . ." he said.

Total silence now: the whole table unmoving.

Henry Joby said, "Barnes, a hit, no ifs and buts, great notices for everybody, not a single quibble. Sir Harry top billing, Maggie wonderful."

"Something to be said for these fellas, after all," said Sir Harry.

Henry Joby held up his hand.

"Rich, the *Times*, a hit, maybe a nervous hit, but a hit already! Everybody great, Sir Piers particularly."

"Who's arguing with the dear boy?" asked Sir Piers.

Henry Joby took a deep breath. "The radio and television:

413

WOR-TV, a hit; WCBS radio, a hit, a little nervous maybe; the rest I don't have yet but everywhere I hear we got a hit!"

The table erupted, the whole room erupted, as the applause began and everybody kissed everybody and cheered and laughed and yelled, and the whole room cheered and laughed with them, and tears ran down Henry Joby's smiling face and more champagne was called for and brought and toasts were given and drunk to, and everybody called to everybody else that this was the night of their lives.

Jill Viner did all these things too, and while doing them she looked at Josh sitting there and Maggie sitting next to him, her arm in his and her eyes finding his and she thought, How is it possible to have everything you want in life and yet not have it at all?

VERCEK came out of the Trafalgar on a wave of euphoria and instantly censured himself for it. No point in feeling that *Queen* had proved anything, had changed anything. It had not. All that had happened, as in London, was that a crowd of people, several hundreds but no more, had been temporarily moved by a number of cult-of-personality actors, all of them acting for themselves, as in London, indifferent to the message of the whole, everybody working, in the capitalist way, for themselves. Vercek gazed at the canyons of light, the blaze, the glare, the hustle, the noise. He was still jet-lagged, he had only reached the city that day, and he had not come by Concorde. He had come economy-class, London to Toronto, on a passport in a new name, arranged for him by his contact in Whitehall. His contact had been strangely sympathetic, respectful almost, now that Vercek's play was a success. The passport and certain other formalities had made him a Canadian citizen. He intended to fly back tomorrow to that land of snows, so reminiscent of his homeland, and disappear. He would get a job in some small town. An ordinary job. He would not be noticed because he would do nothing that would make him noticeable.

Would he, perhaps, once he had found the job, find a woman? Perhaps he would, after a year or two, if the desire came back, and with easy, peaceful living it might, for it was connected with his wife and her betrayal. Perhaps after a longish time he would marry the woman. Vercek stood bemused in the glare of lights and wondered if he should go backstage and see the cast, but he decided against it. There was no point, no more to say. It was over. He would now try to forget it, he would forget he was even a writer, he would put it all behind him. He had suffered enough, he had done his share. Let others, younger, stronger, take up the torch. He had sung his song. He had frozen and lost his fingers and almost died in the Gulag. Yes, his song was over. He would rest soon. Vercek felt very tired.

He walked up Broadway looking wonderingly at the lights and the people. They had not fully understood *Queen*, this audience, but why should they? It was something that could happen three thousand miles away, nothing that could ever happen here, in this untouchable city. Yet he had been surprised by the audience's grasp of the main theme. He had sensed their excitement. Yes, they had seen, in a way the London audience had not (perhaps because some of the London first-night audience were inevitably liberals and disapproved of royalty anyway), that it was really a play about what was, not what should be. They are a bigger danger than anybody else, sighed Vercek, with their pink spectacles and their nice liberal lives, also untouchable, or so they think. Don't they read, don't they ponder, don't they remember Jan Masaryk? Vercek sighed again. It was ever thus. Middle-class intellectuals always opened the door and once it was open, it was too late.

Vercek stopped at O'Hagan's and drank a Budweiser. Nobody took any notice of him. He had the kind of face that belonged in New York City. Graying, straggly hair brushed straight back. Squashed nose. Slavic features. Stocky and thickset. He looked around the bar. It was bright and warm and people were drinking hard, to get drunk, not politely and socially, like London. This city attracted him. It was noisy and harsh, like living in a fun-fair, but one where everybody had money to spend. Not necessarily enjoying themselves, but anyway alive. A man could melt into this city. Should he go north again? Would it be best? Vercek drank another Budweiser and smoked one of his cardboard cigarettes and debated the point. He would stick to his original plan. Go back to Canada. Find a small town. Disappear. He was tired. It was indeed over. No more to do.

Vercek took a cab to his room off Forty-ninth Street, paid the driver, and gave him a small tip. The cabbie drove away without comment, recognizing Vercek as one of the people of the world who had had it hard and did not habitually drive around in cabs. Vercek crossed the quiet street toward his room. He switched on the television set a little later, vodka in hand, and heard a drama critic declare that *The Queen of Finland* was a play worthy of the Tony award. Vercek was not sure what that was but he lit another cardboard cigarette in quiet celebration. It was possible, just possible, that there was room for hope.

MAGGIE and Josh walked into Rockefeller Plaza. It was still busy despite the hour, and probably unwise for them to linger here, but they had to talk and this was as good as anywhere. They stood and stared over the parapet, down at the rink.

"Well, we made it, Josh. We made it!"

Her hand found his and grasped it. She squeezed but he did not squeeze back. I'm losing him, she thought. He's going home. I never really had him, did I? she reasoned. He isn't a man you can own, have, share with. There will always be a part of him you can't reach, the part that will always belong to his work. Why am I so worried about that? Why do I care that he isn't emotional, like Austin, or most Americans, anyway showbiz ones? Why does his coolness worry me here, when it didn't in London? Is it because he seems so very English, with his grave good looks and his graver manner? Is there no joy in him really, or is it simply that I don't have the key to it? Am I too direct for him? Would any woman be too direct for him? Jill Viner, what success did she have? And she spoke his own very English shorthand, understood it, and yet how had she fared?

Maggie said, "We made it. Thank you, Josh."

At last he squeezed the hand. "Why the *we?* I did nothing."

"You did everything. Without you, I'd have collapsed in London."

"Not you. You're a survivor, Maggie."

"I'm not sure I can survive without you, Josh."

He stared uncomfortably at their clasped hands, as she knew he would, embarrassed by any public display of affection. Who was watching here, for God's sake, except a few wandering derelicts and two cops talking together? "Of course you can do without me. Anybody can do without anybody."

"Not without a lot of hurt."

"I didn't say that. I just said they can do it."

Maggie said, "Josh, you didn't sleep with me, cold-bloodedly and deliberately, just so I could do the part well, do it at all, did you?"

He looked shocked. That at least was something.

"Certainly not. It just worked out that way."

Maggie pressed on. "But to you I was a child. I needed help. I was like a child crying, you would give it anything, to stop it crying, was there any element of that in it, Josh?"

They walked on slowly, going nowhere, very tired in the dawn light, like sleepwalkers. If he won't say what is in his heart now, Maggie thought, he'll never say it. "Please tell me, darling. I have to know."

"Perhaps. Something of that. Perhaps. But I loved you, Maggie. That much is true."

Maggie took the blow much easier than she had expected. Well, she had been preparing herself, hadn't she? How many times had they been to bed together since they had arrived in New York: twice. And both times she had taken the lead. Even then the sexual act had been somehow forced, he had not abandoned himself to her as he had in the early days in England, when their sex had been liberating and good, sex between strangers, startling, different, but somehow, now she thought about it, really just sex, not more than that, and it should have been more, what was the use of it if it wasn't more? It was obvious: Josh was disengaging. He had made his mind up, whether he knew it or not. He was not staying on in the States. He was not going to try to make a new career for himself on Broadway. He was not content, in the last analysis, to be Mr. Maggie Stride. He was an Englishman, and he was going home.

She held out her hand bravely. "Darling. Let's not drag it out and hurt each other. No need for that. We've had a lot from each other. Let's be grateful for that."

Josh took her hand in both of his. "I couldn't stay, Maggie. You're Maggie Stride—over here you really are a queen—and I'm just another British director—"

She put her free hand on his lips. "No need to say it. No need at all. I know all that and I guess the rest. You'll be back to look at the play now and then?"

He nodded. "I'm flying back Concorde Monday. See if my Shakespeare's all right. I'll be back to have a look at *Queen*." He tried to grin. "Take out the improvements."

Then said Maggie, with an effort, "Well, we can always have lunch. Just lunch."

"Of course." He let her hand go and stood there, staring down at the rink, looking very handsome—and just a little haggard—in the soft dawn light. "Maggie, I'm sorry."

"No need for sorry. If it's not a hundred percent both ways, darling, it's no good."

"Maggie, you're an incurable romantic."

"I know it. I'm an American."

A taxi prowled by and Maggie signaled and turned away to catch it. Josh said, "I'll keep in touch."

"No," said Maggie. "Nice and clean. Like this. Good-bye, Josh."

"But, Maggie—"

The last she saw of him he was still standing in Rockefeller Plaza, quite alone, a tiny figure against the huge backdrop of the center, and she thought: He'll go back to Jill Viner, it's what he's been intending to do, surely unknowingly, all the time. He couldn't have known that, Maggie thought, he just couldn't. Her nails dug into her palm and she felt tears in her eyes.

The cabby was staring at her. "Where to, lady? Hey, your fella's waving you good-bye, over there."

Maggie did not look back.

"Thank you, Josh, just the same," she whispered.

"I'm sorry, lady, I didn't hear ya."

"Nothing," said Maggie Stride. "Nothing at all."

SIR Harry and Sir Piers took midmorning coffee together in the Park Lane. Sir Piers looked out at Central Park and said, "Y'know, Hal, I like this place. Especially when we have a hit."

"You mean a smash, dear boy."

"All right then. A smash."

Sir Piers looked inquisitive. "How d'yer get on for sex while yer here, Hal? Is it permitted?"

Sir Harry looked shocked. "Yer don't think I go to the queer bars cruising at my time of life, do yer? I'm having Mario over. Or Silvio." He mused. "Maybe both of the dear boys. Never been to the States, either of 'em. I had to wait to see if it was a hit, didn't I?"

Sir Harry graciously signed a menu for the waiter. "A pleasure, dear fella." He sipped his coffee. "Best thing in America. The coffee."

"These cruising bars?" asked Sir Piers idly. "Many of them about?"

"Best ones are in the Village," said Sir Harry.

"Really?"

"Don't look in, Piers. I shouldn't. You'll get crabs or the pox or both."

"I hadn't even considered it, you terrible old thing."

"Well then, I wouldn't, dear boy. How's milady?"

"Oh, she's fine. Spending money like water, I suppose—Saks, Bonwit Teller, all those places. Good little girl."

"Yes," said Sir Harry. "So I gather."

"Look here, Hal," said Sir Piers. "What are we going to do about this offer from the National? Would we be stupid to take it?"

"Well," said Sir Harry, eating a cookie. "It would be stupid to say anything yet. We're in a smash with *Queen*. Afterwards, who knows?"

"Shall I tell my agent a probable yes?"

"Don't see why not. We'll be a sensation, anyway. People will be coming to see if we're both still alive, if for nothing else."

"I can see why you say that," rejoined Sir Piers hotly, "being your age. Not me. Good for years yet."

"Well, then," said Sir Harry, looking out the window at the particularly good-looking boy across the street who happened to be passing. "If you do go cruising, be careful."

"Now you know I'm not that way, Hal!"

"No, dear. I don't."

Sir Piers laughed. "Don't think I could stand you and your irritations, as well as the director we're offered back at the National."

"Director? Who is he?"

"Young Max Heston. That frightful little tick who was our

stage manager on *Queen* at the Royal. Awful little prick, I thought."

"Oh, I don't know," said Sir Harry, with interest. "I thought he was rather dishy."

AUSTIN Ames rang Maggie at ten o'clock the next morning.

Maggie was still in bed but she reached over to the telephone. Few people knew her unlisted number. "Hello, yes?"

"Maggie, it's me Austin. You been thinking about what Manny Hiberson said last night?"

"Austin, all I've been thinking about is sleep. I haven't had much. Nor have you."

"I know that. I haven't been to bed." He hadn't. He'd sat up with Manny in the Plaza talking script control once *Second Time Around* got moving. Manny was leery about script control, since he also represented the producer. "He'll never give it, Austin," he had counseled. "Suggestions, maybe. A new writer, who knows?" But Manny had been happy to talk. There was nothing else to do but sleep and at his age sleep was not so important. Finally, at six o'clock, Manny had gone to bed.

Austin had not. He had sat and thought about himself and Maggie. It was going to take time, was what he decided, sitting in his Plaza suite after Manny had left. It was going to be something he had to work at. The important thing was: in six months, after *Queen* had finished its Broadway run, Maggie would be working on the Coast with him! He could wait until then. Right, so it meant no Carmen, no more visits to the little shack, no more cheap and potent sex. Could he hack that? Austin thought maybe. To shock and delight Carmen sexually had been impossible, right? To shock and delight Maggie Stride sexually, that was something he could wait for, work for, live for. He could show Maggie a whole new good time, as well as a lot of new positions, he guessed. He took sex lightly and fine, Maggie didn't. That was because of her Boston Brahmin upbringing. She hadn't been taught to enjoy life. He would teach her. He would reorganize her diet, for one thing. Also her reading. He began to make a list in his mind. Most were connected with ecology and saving the greenery of the world, and the air and water.

He had the script of *Second Time Around* and at ten o'clock, finally, he had rung Maggie. "I know I haven't been to bed," he told her, "but I've been thinking about us."

Maggie was silent for a long time. "Us?"

"Sure, us. You're going to do the movie with me, right?"

"How's the script?"

"The script is very good, Maggie. I can see a few things that could be improved, but Manny's right. There could be another Oscar in it."

"I don't think I want another Oscar, Austin."

"Sure you want another Oscar, Maggie."

"All you get after an Oscar is a lot of trash."

"I know that, but this time I'm looking after your interests, Maggie."

"All right. I'll think about it, Austin."

"Look, what are you doing now?"

"Austin, I'm trying to sleep."

Austin debated. "Well, look, Maggie. You sleep for another two hours and I'll come over for coffee at noon, okay? The press is going to be all over me if I stay here at the Plaza, *Queen* being a hit and all, so why don't we have a nice quiet afternoon at your place, and I'll tell you about the new movie?"

Maggie didn't know what she could say but yes, and Austin came on the stroke of noon. He made her decaffeinated coffee he had brought himself (she didn't like it much) and he fed her on oatmeal biscuits and English honey that he had bought in Harrods.

Maggie ate the biscuits (which were all right, she could eat anything) and then bathed and sat in her bathrobe and listened to
Austin reading the movie script, all through, playing all the characters, which took him almost two hours. They had taken the telephone off the hook and Maggie's maid had told callers she was not
at home. They talked about the movie script until almost six
o'clock, when it was time to change and go to the Trafalgar to play
in *Queen*, something they would be doing, almost certainly, for the
next six months.

"So," Austin said, as she slipped on her coat and grabbed her
bag, "you'll come and do the movie with me, out on the Coast? I'll
show you the town, Maggie. I'll show you how to live. You'll
enjoy, I guarantee. No hang-ups, no Puritan worries. Put yourself
in my hands, we'll have a ball. What do you say?"

Maggie smiled down at Austin. They were both standing up,
a thing he always avoided, if he could, when she was around. She
kissed the top of his head. "We'll see, shall we? Come on, we'll be
late for *Queen*." She paused. "Oh, and Austin, I wonder if you
could pick up a cab for us."

Austin grinned happily. There was a tone of command in
Maggie's voice. It was possible she might make a Puritan of him
before he made a hedonist of her. Well, shit, it was worth the risk.
He bounded out aggressively into the street, a fighting-cock on his
own territory, New York City. He whistled for a cab; the driver
slowed down and shouted out he was off duty. "What the fuck ya
doin' with your light on then?" he was demanding as the cab
stopped. When the driver saw Maggie he said, "Why didn't you
tell me you were lookin' for a cab for this lady? Shit, I'd drive her
up the Empire State Building!"

Maggie smiled sweetly, said, "Thank you," and got into
the cab.

"Pleasure, lady, but I don't like your hired help," said the
driver.

Austin opened his mouth, saw Maggie laughing, and said nothing.

A Puritan yet? He brooded, troubled. With a lady like Maggie anything was possible.

Shit.

JILL Viner had booked the afternoon flight on the Concorde and had made her telephone farewells to Manny Hiberson and Henry Joby and those of the cast she could reach. She rang Josh at the Pierre but there was no reply. The publicity storm, once *Queen* was a smash, had abated. The cast had been interviewed by the media, even Jill had been on television, to explain her success.

Just being a success was enough in New York. If you were a success everybody wanted to talk to you. Well, now it was over, the interview with the New York *Post* girl ("Why did you, as a woman, want success so much, Miss Viner?" . . . "Because I wanted it" . . . "Yes, but as a woman, why?" . . . "If I could tell you that I'd be very happy. I just did." . . . "Did you, as a woman, have to give up anything in your private life to get it?" . . . "Well, yes, actually, as a woman I did. . . .").

"What did you have to give up?" the *Post* girl (chic, pretty, breathless, and Bryn Mawr) had asked her.

"I don't know. I just feel I lost something."

"Speaking as a woman, like what?"

"Speaking as a woman, a man."

The *Post* girl had gone into instant orgasm. "Really? *Who?*"

Jill had smiled and said, "No names, no pack-drill."

"No pack-drill, what's that?"

"Old British Army saying. Means I'm not telling."

"Oh shit," said the *Post* girl. "It would have been so nice to have his name. I'll just have to guess."

She had guessed it in the piece. The guess had been right: "Josh Williams, once her steady live-in man, seems to be seen more often these days in the company of actress Maggie Stride, now currently having a great success with *Queen.*"

Jill sat in the Concorde, waiting for takeoff, the *Post* on her lap. Thank God not too many people knew her in New York. She tried to add up the good things. *Queen* had made her a recognized producer. It had not made her wildly rich but Queen Productions could take on a deal or two so long as they were not all misses. She was in a high-risk business, none higher, and she looked forward, with a sudden thrill, to her next play, to doing it all over again.

It was all there was to look forward to. She had to face that.

Anyway, one thing she would do. She would buy herself a Rolls.

"Hi, thought you'd be on this one."

It was Josh, traveling light as usual. He had on the jeans and a new shirt that looked unfashionable, and the first thing she noted was that he was not wearing the hated gold bracelet. Her heart leapt but she said to herself, It means nothing, don't let it mean anything to you, that way you don't get hurt.

"I thought you were staying a couple more days," she said, controlling her voice with an effort. She seemed to be having trouble, too, with her breathing. She stared out of the window. The Concorde was taking off in its long dramatic glide. "Breathtaking, isn't it?" she said. "Didn't expect to see you."

Josh nodded. "I'll go back and have a look at it in three weeks or so. My work's over, really. Like yours. *Queen*'s over for us. It belongs to the actors and the audiences now."

"How's Maggie?" She had to know.

"Maggie?" Josh's voice was casual. "She's fine. She's going to make that movie in Hollywood when *Queen*'s over in New York. Austin's going as well."

"Is he?"

"Seems so. They're quite . . . suited. They don't know it, but they are. Sometimes the penny takes a long time to drop."

Jill looked down at the city—exciting, dramatic, safe in a way

425

Europe might not be, if Vercek was right. Where was Vercek? she wondered. Where should she send his money? Nobody seemed to know. No doubt he would ring the office one day, or just walk in. She could not think about it now, she was too excited, so excited she was shaking. Oh, I'm so glad, Josh. I'm so glad you're coming home because I love you, Josh, and where will we live, in my place, yes, because it's roomier, but of course if you want to go on pigging along on your own in Glebe Place and come and see me when you want to, well, that's all right, too. . . . But she said none of this, just felt in her briefcase and put the typescript of a new play on his knee and said, "We might do that next time, if you want to, Josh. It's up to you; you're a full partner in Queen Productions, after all."

Josh looked surprised and then he said, "Fine, no hurry. We have a few things to talk about, you and I, don't we?"

She said nothing, just smiled and thought: Shall I tell him I've had his office in Shaftesbury Avenue redecorated for him? And thought, No. Shall I just tell him I love him?

No. She would say nothing.

The Concorde soared through the blue upper air.

Jill Viner closed her eyes. Always hold something back.